THE BURNING GLASS

A JEAN FAIRBAIRN/ALASDAIR CAMERON
MYSTERY

THE BURNING GLASS

LILLIAN STEWART CARL

FIVE STAR

An imprint of Thomson Gale, a part of The Thomson Corporation

Detroit • New York • San Francisco • New Haven, Conn. • Waterville, Maine • London

THOMSON

GALE

LIBRARY OF CONGRESS CATALOGING-IN-PUBLICATION DATA

Carl, Lillian Stewart.
    The Burning Glass / Lillian Stewart Carl.
    "A Jean Fairbairn/Alasdair Cameron Mystery"
        p. cm.
    ISBN-13: 978-1-59414-591-9 (alk. paper)
    ISBN-10: 1-59414-591-1 (alk. paper)
    1. Fairbairn, Jean (Fictitious character)—Fiction. 2. Americans—Scotland—Fiction. 3. Scotland—Fiction. 4. Women historians—Fiction. 5. Chapels—Fiction. I. Title.
PS3602.A77535F58 2007
813'.6—dc22   2007005480

First Edition. First Printing: September 2007.

Published in 2007 in conjunction with Tekno Books and Ed Gorman.

Printed in the United States of America on permanent paper
10 9 8 7 6 5 4 3 2 1

Dedicated to Aidan Sutton Carl,
Simran Ravi Carl,
and Maya Sutton Carl.
The next generation.

CHAPTER ONE

If two's company and three's a crowd, thought Jean Fairbairn, *then an Edinburgh sidewalk during the Festival is infinity verging upon insanity.*

Chanting "excuse me, pardon me, sorry," she fought her way through the stream of pedestrians, dodged between a blue-painted, dreadlocked youth and the tourist taking his photo, and darted into the door of her office building. There she patted herself down. Mini-backpack, check. Manila folder, check. Cool. No, she'd been losing her cool in large chunks, like icebergs falling off a glacier, for quite some time now.

She stepped carefully up the spiral turnpike stair. The elongated triangles of the stone treads had been worn by centuries of feet into shapes resembling melted Brie, and injuring herself by falling up a staircase was just the sort of thing she was likely to do. Ditto for injuring herself right before running away with her lover . . . She wasn't running away, she told herself. And she and Alasdair weren't lovers. Not yet, anyway. Not in the full-body-cavity-search meaning of the word. Although the meeting of true minds counted as an intimate connection.

The *Great Scot* offices might be several stories up, but still the clamor of voices, amplified music, and tooting horns drifted through the windows along with the August heat and the perennial scents of diesel and cooking food. As Jean shut the door, the fresh-faced youth behind the reception desk looked up. "Ah, it's yourself, is it?"

"It is, Gavin, a rat leaving the sinking ship. Not that Edinburgh's sinking. Teeming ship, maybe. Leaping off the ark. Are lemmings rodents, do you know? I may be a rat, but I haven't got an ounce of lemming blood."

He stared, petrified in the act of lifting a mug to his lips. For seven months now they'd worked together, and still he occasionally looked at her as though she were speaking in tongues. Not that it was her American tongue that baffled him. Gavin was a smart kid, but when it came to following her mental arabesques, he was no Alasdair.

Although even Alasdair might be nonplussed at the lemming remark. "Never mind," Jean said. "Is Miranda here? Or is she off on the cocktail and show-opening circuit?"

The cup completed its journey to Gavin's lips, and he swallowed a fortifying swig. "Oh aye, she's here just now. Had me buying tickets for the Puppetry of the Peni . . . Well, mind, the lads that use their, well . . ." His cheeks colored, not, probably, at the raunchiness of either title or concept but at mentioning them to a woman of his mother's generation. Jean wished she'd seen his face when Miranda asked him to order the tickets.

The competition for audiences at the Festival Fringe meant that each show was more outrageous than the last. World-wise and world-easy Miranda would be entertained by a program straining at an envelope that was just fine in its original shape, thank you. Jean, though, was likely to turn scarlet, wince, or guffaw. Or all three. Especially since her thoughts were already playing delicately with aspects of male anatomy. One male. One anatomy. Connected to a psyche that could never be contained in an envelope.

Partly taking pity on Gavin, partly to conceal her own blush, she turned to inspect the stack of mail by the door. A letter with her name handwritten on a cream-colored envelope sat atop several press kits and beside the current issue of *The Scotsman.*

A notice on the newspaper's front page read: "Stanelaw councillor goes missing. See page 4." *Stanelaw?* Great. Just the village Jean wanted to see in the news yet again, when she was booked to spend two weeks there. First a famous antiquity had been stolen from the local museum, and now some function-ary . . . She hadn't even read the article yet, and already she was drawing dire conclusions. It would all turn out to be either a tempest in a Brown Betty teapot or something that was beyond her ken—if not beyond her brief as a journalist.

She collected the newspaper and the letter, left the press releases for Miranda to winnow, and pitched the manila folder onto Gavin's desk as she headed for her office. "My expense ac-count."

If he hadn't quite regained his composure, he was at least no longer decomposing. "It's not been two months since you were running up bills at Loch Ness. Now she's sending you to the Borders, is she?"

"Miranda and I," Jean said, reminding him that she was a full partner in the history-and-travel magazine, "decided to kill several stories with the same stone. And I use the word 'kill' advisedly," she added, with paranoia aforethought.

"No surprise you'd go turning up the murder mysteries. They're stories, aren't they now?" Gavin added the folder to one of the piles leaning against his desk like flying buttresses. The lad had learned his filing techniques from Miranda—and both of them could find what they were looking for as quickly as Jean could with her tidily labeled files. It wasn't fair that the neatness of one's records was in inverse proportion to the neat-ness of one's life.

Gavin had also learned to repeat Miranda's justifications of Jean's unintended but still perilous adventures. "Right," she said, and realized she was imitating Alasdair's noncommittal coolth.

The editorial offices of *Great Scot* magazine occupied one story of a stone-built tenement, a medieval building that, like its neighbors, was tall, thin, and stern as a Calvinist elder. The scuffed pitch-pine floor of the hall creaked even without the pressure of footsteps, and furtive drafts rustled among the papers, so that every now and then Jean would find herself watching a page in a book turn by itself. But her allergy to the paranormal had never sniffled there, let alone exploded in a full apparitional sneeze. The rooms that had housed generations of people living, loving, dying, now held no resonances of them at all. That was just as well. Encountering a few souls who were not resting in peace was enough to make Jean grateful that so many were.

Miranda was sitting at her desk, holding the telephone receiver with her left hand and typing on her computer keyboard with her right. Jean waved, but there was no reason to stop and say, "Speak now or hold your peace until I get back." With cell phones, e-mail, and several good highways between Edinburgh and Stanelaw, she was hardly going to be out of touch.

Miranda waggled her keyboard hand toward the door, rings glinting, and said into the telephone, "Oh aye, we're after adding a Tours and Travels page to the website."

And *Great Scot* territory expanded, Jean told herself. Soon there would be Miranda Capaldi action figures, complete with miniature computer, cup of café latte, and social register.

Her own office was a room that had been called a closet by the eighteenth-century household, and by twenty-first century standards was no more than a cupboard with a window. The trapped air was so hot and humid she could have raised orchids on her desk. Her books, manuscripts, magazines, and prints were limp and musty. This time of year, in her old office at the university in Texas, she'd have shivered beneath the vent of an air-conditioning system set to give frostbite to a penguin. Not that frigidity had defined all her former life as an academic, just too much of it. When she'd broken free, she'd done so with a vengeance, reporting a student for plagiarism and thereby initiating an academic scandal that had ended in court.

Jean threw open the casement window to be rewarded by a gust of noise like a slap in the face. *The Borders,* she thought with a sigh. Ferniebank Castle was half a mile from Stanelaw, which in turn was three miles from Kelso. Neither community was a metropolitan hub. No one except a tourist or two would disturb the peace and quiet. Ferniebank wasn't yet a prime attraction on the theme-park-Scotland route, although with the new development, it would be.

Stanelaw. The theft. The councillor. Before she could open the newspaper, a brisk tap of boot heels announced Miranda's entrance. Today her hair was stroked upwards and frosted at the tips, and she was wearing a denim jacket studded with crystals over flared jeans. Despite her own plain-vanilla twill pants, cotton blouse, and tapestry vest, Jean did not descend to making cracks about rhinestone cowgirls.

"You're away, then?" her friend and partner asked.

"My bags are packed and ready to go, but by the time I stocked up for two entire weeks, I had to go ahead and hire the car yesterday. Now it'll take me forever to get out of town."

"Not a bit of it. The traffic's coming into the town. You'll be missing all the fun. I've got extra tickets for the Tattoo this weekend. Massed pipe bands. Loads of men wearing kilts."

"Gavin tells me that's not all you have tickets for."

Miranda grinned. "Where's your sense of adventure?"

"Yeah, I know. Party pooper. Wet blanket. Going off with Alasdair is a pretty big step for me."

"Your first dirty weekend together, eh? A dirty two weeks,

come to that." The arches of Miranda's beautifully plucked eyebrows made question marks, inviting confidences. But the days were long gone—twenty years gone—when they had sat giggling in their dorm room, comparing the mating rituals of British and American boys.

"Just because you connected him up with the job at Protect and Survive," retorted Jean, "doesn't mean I owe you the gory details of our love, er, like-life."

"No gore on this assignment." Miranda handed down her decree. "In any event, if you'd not been involved in two criminal cases you'd not have met Alasdair, would you now? And don't go saying that's a mixed blessing. You've got roses in your cheeks you've not had for years."

No use rationalizing that the roses in her cheeks owed more to the heat or the excesses of the Fringe Festival than to her new relationship. Jean reached for a letter opener and slit open the thick, beige envelope, revealing a thick, beige note card. Like the address on the envelope, the note was handwritten in a careless scrawl that implied the writer was too successful to bother with mundane issues like legibility.

"Mrs. Councillor Angus Rutherford is inviting me to tea," Jean said, deciphering the missive. "Glebe House, Stanelaw, three p.m. on Saturday, 23 August. RSVP . . . Whoa." Frowning, she grabbed the newspaper and flipped quickly to page four.

Stanelaw councillor goes missing.

Angus Rutherford was last seen on Thursday, 21 August, leaving the Parapluie Noire Hotel in Brussels for a flight to Edinburgh. He had attended a European Union workshop on "Countryside Resources and the Tourism Dilemma." It was from the Stanelaw Museum that the famous Fernie-

bank Clarsach, a medieval folk harp, was stolen on Sunday
17 August. Then, Rutherford said . . .

Miranda plucked the invitation from her hand. "Ah, Minty
Rutherford's afternoon tea. Cucumber sandwiches, lemon curd,
and Montrose cakes to die for."

Jean turned the newspaper toward her.

"Oh my. Well, that's easy enough to explain. The good gray
Angus, embarrassed at losing the one notable artifact to the
town tourist board's name, decided to stay on and drown his
sorrows in the fleshpots of the Continent. Stanelaw, even Kelso
—as you Yanks say, they're podunk. The boondocks. Never mind
Minty and her cooking school."

Cooking school? Jean envisioned boxes of Haggis Helper.
"The letter's postmarked day before yesterday. The same day
Angus disappeared. Minty—Mrs. Councillor Rutherford must
be worried about her husband. Maybe Alasdair can . . . No.
He's not a policeman, not any more."

"The Rutherfords' marriage might not be any more, either.
Angus has been getting a bit restive, I'm hearing, though I'm
hardly a close friend. You can ask Minty, if you like."

"Or even if I don't like?"

Miranda handed over the note and turned a mock severe
look on Jean.

"Yes, yes, I know. Let my conscience, my curiosity, and my
courtesy be my guide." Jean tucked the card into the envelope.
"I'll see what Mrs. Councillor Rutherford volunteers to tell me.
If I meet her. With Stanelaw having a mini crime wave, she may
cancel the tea. I wonder how she knew I was coming? Oh.
Elementary, my dear. Because I've got an interview with the
woman who just bought Ferniebank. Karen, Kara—something
like that—Macquarrie."

"Ciara Macquarrie. She's made a good fist of her Mystic
Scotland tour company. We'll be linking to her site from our

own, like as not, though I'm after vetting her spiel beforehand. When you have your interview—"

"See if she's telling her clients that Cairnpapple Neolithic Site is a landing pad for flying saucers. Alasdair's and my ghosts being all the woo-woo you've got the patience for."

"You're not writing about Scotland if you're not writing about ghosts," Miranda returned. "Stanelaw Council, with or without Angus, is sure to have given Macquarrie public funds or tax breaks in addition to planning permission for renovating Ferniebank, and they'd not be doing that if she had no head for business."

"Speaking of 'countryside resources and the tourism dilemma,' " murmured Jean.

"Dilemma it is. Macquarrie's planning a conference center in the castle and New Age spa on the site of the chapel and holy well. I reckon she's the excuse for the tea, not to rain on your own parade."

"Rain away. I'm only a mild-mannered travel-and-history writer, after all."

"That you are." Miranda didn't descend to making any cracks about rhinestone detectives. She picked up a Ferniebank leaflet from Jean's desk and held it to the light, so that the pen-and-ink drawings seemed particularly dark and dour.

The drawings probably catch the spirit of the place, Jean thought. As castles went, Ferniebank was nondescript. Not massive and imposing like Edinburgh or Stirling, not winsomely personable like Cawdor or Craigievar, not elegant like Floors or Culzean, it was a slab-sided, bare-bones Borders tower house. Few famous people had ever visited, and none of them had done anything noteworthy there. Supposedly Mary, Queen of Scots, had dropped by, but then, supposedly George Washington had slept in half the beds of colonial America. No, Ferniebank's claim to fame was its chapel and healing well.

Miranda, as usual, was on the scent. "When you're writing about Ferniebank Chapel and all, play up the connection with Rosslyn Chapel. That's become quite the tourist attraction after the book and that film, what are they, *The Michelangelo Cipher*?"

"They're a load of baloney, if you ask me, although, oddly enough, no one ever does, fiction being much more appealing than fact. It always has been. Some of the legends popularized by that book have been around for centuries, not that a legend is necessarily fiction."

"There's your job description in a nutshell."

"Exploring the debatable shore where fantasy and reality intersect?"

"An area," Miranda said, "that could do with being a demilitarized zone. As though it's not bad enough censoring the novel, some folk have rioted over the film."

"Too many myth-mongers have big chips on their shoulders," agreed Jean, "especially when it comes to selling a product. And a belief system can be a heck of a product."

"There you are, then." Miranda cast the leaflet onto the desk like bread upon water. "I'm expecting a multi-part article on the facts, fictions, and fancies of Ferniebank, as well as anything else you'd care to add in: The Rutherford connection. The quest for the clarsach. The castle ghost. A white lady, is it?"

"A gray lady. There's always a white lady or a gray lady or a green lady. Me, I'm holding out for a purple polka-dotted gentleman."

Miranda laughed. "Obliging of Alasdair to caretake the place himself the fortnight, instead of assigning it to someone else. But that's his privilege as chief of security for P and S, I reckon."

"He trolled through the properties they manage until he found one that was private but fodder for *Great Scot*. Plus, Michael and Rebecca Campbell-Reid are spending the month in Stanelaw. Alasdair couldn't have known Ferniebank was going

15

to interest his crime-solving side, but then, not only can the man see ghosts. I swear he's got ESP."

"No one's needing ESP to see that Ferniebank's privacy is gone for good," said Miranda. "Well then. Duncan's arriving at six for an early dinner and the show. Best get cracking."

"Cracking your whip over me, you mean? Yep, I need to get going. And get something to eat. I'll need more than butterflies in my stomach."

"One can't live on love, no."

"Love? It's way too early to go there, Miranda." Jean raised her hands, in a gesture partly "I surrender" and partly "back off, unexploded ordnance."

With one of her patented wise smiles, Miranda backed off. She had never been married, let alone divorced, while both Jean and Alasdair had been there, done that, and bore the scars. Her long-time relationship with silverback lawyer Duncan Kerr had a lot to say for it—their parallel lives regularly intersected and then parted again, as though in the ordered steps of a minuet. What Jean was dancing with Alasdair was a traditional country reel, with lots of stamping, hand-offs, ducks, and twirls, all leading up to some seriously heavy breathing. As for leading up to love-cum-commitment, well, the best-laid plans of mice and men gang aft agley . . . Time to get off the rodent kick.

She swept the newspaper, the invitation, and several printouts referencing Ferniebank's long history into a folder and thrust the leaflet in after them. A glossy booklet with four-color photos was in the works, she was sure of that.

A siren sounded outside the window. Gavin's telephone bleated and he answered. A moment later the phone in Miranda's office beeped. She took a step toward the door, then back, her smile widening into a grin like a salute. *Damn the torpedos! Full speed ahead!* But all she said was, "I'll RSVP to Minty on your behalf. Give my regards to the Campbell-Reids, and thank

Michael for the article on the amen glass. Kiss Alasdair for me. And don't go borrowing trouble, not about him, not about your articles, not about"—the glistening pink nail on her forefinger tapped the folder in Jean's hands—"the castle, the clarsach, or either of the Rutherfords. Cheerio." She clicked off down the hall and into her office.

Jean shut her window, hoisted her bag, squared her shoulders, and headed for the front door. Trouble had recently been finding her. She didn't need to beg, borrow, or steal it.

Just as she set her hand on the knob of the outer door, Gavin's phone emitted another double bleat. "*Great Scot* Magazine," he answered. "Oh aye, she's just away, one sec. Jean?"

CHAPTER TWO

Thwarted in her getaway, Jean mouthed, "Who is it?"

"Chap named Keith Bell," Gavin returned with a shrug.

Jean hadn't the foggiest idea who Keith Bell was—and couldn't exactly ask if the man's middle name was "trouble"—but talking to strangers was part of her job description. She stepped back across the reception area and took the telephone from Gavin's hand. "Jean Fairbairn."

"Hello," said a deep but soft male voice. "This is Keith Bell."

"Hello," Jean returned, and when nothing more was forthcoming, "Is there something I can do for you, Mr. Bell?"

"Er, ah, well, you don't know me."

"I don't believe so, no."

"I'm an architect. With Cruickshank and Associates, Glasgow." Full stop.

"Yes?" Jean prompted. He might work in Glasgow, but his accent was flat as a hamburger bun, his vowels pointing listlessly toward his origins on the western side of the Atlantic.

"I'm, ah, um, I'm designing the conference center conversion and new healing center at Ferniebank."

Ah! "You're working with Ms. Macquarrie, then?"

"Yes, I am." A clock chimed on his end of the line, counting out twelve strokes.

It was midnight that was the witching hour, Jean thought, not noon. Bell can't have turned into a frog. She'd have heard him croaking. She prodded him again. "How can I help?"

"You're scheduled for an interview with Ciara tomorrow afternoon."

"Yes."

"Today's Friday."

"So it is." Jean's foot started tapping the floor, and not from any innate sense of rhythm.

Gavin leaned over his keyboard, but his ears flicked back toward her like a cat's.

"I hear you're staying at the caretaker's cottage at the site."

"At Ferniebank, yes."

"I'm gonna be there this afternoon," said Bell, "if you'd like to ask me some questions, too."

"I'd like to do that, yes," Jean said, noting that he wasn't promising to actually answer those questions. "I won't be there until five or so, though."

"That's okay. I've got to take some pictures and measurements and stuff. But I wanted to check with you first, you know, since you're the temporary caretaker."

"I'm not the caretaker, I'm visiting. The actual caretaker should be arriving there just about now. Opening time. He's, er, he's . . ." This time she piled up against that full stop. *He's what? Friend? Companion? Significant other?* "Security chief for Protect and Survive. Just filling in for the rest of the month."

"The boss himself? No kidding. I bet he's having fits finding another caretaker for Ferniebank after what happened to the last one."

Jean didn't like the sound of that, although if anything sinister had happened there—recently, not historically, something sinister was always happening historically—then Alasdair would have told her. Wouldn't he? "What happened to the last caretaker?"

"Oh wow, you haven't heard? It was on the eleventh, Monday before last. The local cop noticed that the place was still open past closing time, so went to check. And there was the old guy, the caretaker, stone cold dead in the dungeon."

"Oh," Jean said faintly. "Any suspicion of foul play?"

Gavin turned around, leaning his chin on his fist and his elbow on his desk.

"Naw. The inquest ruled he died of a heart attack."

"In the dungeon?"

Bell was speaking quite fluently now, with volume and intonation. All he needed was an echo chamber for effect. "Ciara thinks he was checking the place out before he locked up. He felt the pangs while he was in the dungeon and was too weak to climb the ladder."

"So he died there, all alone." Jean's imagination could be a bit too vivid, especially with a story that had two phobias for the price of one, her dread of enclosed spaces and her dread of the dark. Alasdair hadn't told her about the man's death because it didn't concern her. Or because he knew it would spook her. He couldn't help being protective, he was trained to protect. What she had to train herself to do was to stop, well, borrowing trouble.

"And then there was the old lady the week before that," Bell was saying. "Well, elderly people have a tendency to keel over, don't they? Gotta go. See ya. Bye-bye."

"Bye." Jean held the telephone at arm's length, looking at it as though it had piddled on the rug.

Gavin took it from her hands and replaced it in the cradle. "What was he on about?"

"Working at Ferniebank. Telling me that the old caretaker died of a heart attack. No foul play. Nothing suspect."

"But you're suspicious even so."

"It's only my free-floating paranoia. Ferniebank and Stanelaw have three strikes against them—four, if you're counting something about an old lady—and I'm not even there yet."

Again Jean shrugged her bag up onto her shoulder.

Gavin handed over her folder, which had found its way onto his desk. "You'll have your fine braw policeman keeping an eye on things. And on you."

"Yeah," Jean said, with a rueful laugh. "I'll have my fine braw policeman. Let me try this again. I'll see you via e-mail for the next couple of weeks."

"Aye then, have yourself a grand time," Gavin returned with a broad smile, every tooth gleaming so innocently Jean knew just what he was envisioning. But when it came to privacy and discretion, she was in the wrong profession to get up on her high horse. Or even a short pony.

She descended the staircase as carefully as she'd climbed, the echo of her steps in the cylindrical stairwell sounding like a distant drum. In the street she heard a drum that was a lot closer, a jazz quartet noodling tunelessly away across the narrow channel of the High Street. Or, in tourist-speak, the Royal Mile.

The heat, exhaust, and aromas of fried fat trapped between the tall buildings made Jean feel that she could chew the air. Thinking nostalgic thoughts of the cold, quiet—if dark—days of January, the month she'd arrived in Edinburgh with her goods intact and her illusions shattered, she played human pinball up the street. It tapered before her, squeezing a view of the Castle Esplanade blocked with bleachers between the last two buildings as though through the sights of a rifle.

In front of her walked a shaggy person of indeterminate gender wearing a functioning television screen in a backpack. "Tonight!" proclaimed the sound and color advertisement. "Puppetry of the . . ."

Jean took a swift right at Ramsay Lane and skimmed downhill and around the corner into Ramsay Garden. Home sweet home was one of a collection of flats in a sprawling building that gave new meaning to the words "apartment complex," its Scots baronial turrets and balconies and its English cottage half-timbered gables perched on a cliff top beside the Esplanade.

For someone intending to keep a low profile, Jean lived in the most conspicuous dwelling in Edinburgh. But as the realtor who sold her and her ex-husband's McMansion back in Dallas had said, in real estate what mattered was location, location, location. Jean couldn't have found a better one, and not just because it was so near her office that its not-inconsiderable expense would eventually be offset by her savings on transportation. That the whimsical assortment of facades was tucked defiantly between the glowering medieval castle and the glum Victorian university suited her goal of living larger, of pushing her own plain brown-paper envelope, of breaking free.

Be careful what you ask for, Jean reminded herself as she unlocked her front door. In breaking free of her old life, she'd broken the shell of a certain police detective. Now she was hostage to the vulnerable creature inside. And vice versa. No surprise they were building a relationship with all the bravado of wounded soldiers facing renewed fire.

From her living room, she gazed out over the human tide that surged through the gardens below and broke in waves on Princes Street. Beyond the rooftops of the city shone the water of the Firth of Forth. The blue line on the horizon was the coast of Fife. Here, she no longer felt as claustrophobic as she had in the university history department, to say nothing of in her marriage. But here, she was a little too close to the Tattoo. Massed bands would be performing the musical spectacle only yards away.

Two weeks ago, she and Alasdair had treated themselves to dinner in the red velvet gothic excess of the Witchery Restaurant. He had worn his kilt, knowing full well its energizing effect on her hormonal system. What was worn under the kilt? asked the old joke. Nothing is worn, went the answer. It's all in fine working order.

That night they'd forged ahead to "the talk," about precautionary measures and previous partners—of whom Jean had only the one, but then, they weren't competing. And Alasdair's finely honed sensibilities meant he'd never been Caledonia's answer to Casanova. They'd strolled home through the August dusk, leaning together, actually holding hands in public. Tonight was to be The Night.

And then, just as they'd walked in her door, pandemonium erupted on the Esplanade. Pipes and drums would only have heightened the heat of the moment, as would the sounds of Hugh Munro practicing his fiddle or guitar next door. But this was a drill team competition, with brass bands playing brassy show tunes that made the light fixtures and drawer pulls vibrate, and colored lights flashing like demented fireflies in the bedroom window.

In a sitcom featuring youthful go-for-broke characters, the moment would have been funny. In real life, featuring two not-so-youthful terminally cautious characters, it was no go. Wryly, Alasdair had gone on his way back to Inverness to continue uncoupling himself from the Northern Constabulary, leaving their relationship unconsummated.

At least, Jean thought, turning away from the window with a wry smile of her own, the occasion had made a good test case. Alasdair Cameron, ex-cop, sensitive New Age guy. Not that she'd intended to test him. Testing the—significant other, partner, inamorata—was an adolescent trick.

She paused for one last wash and brush-up, polishing her glasses, renewing the pink lip gloss she'd chewed away, running a comb through her short brown hair that, as usual, stood up in ungovernable waves. There was no way she was going to lose five pounds in the next few hours, not that Alasdair was expecting his perfectly presentable, er, intended, to turn into a glamor girl. Or a girl, period.

Her other significant other was asleep on the couch with his ball of yarn caught in a proprietary claw. Good. Maybe she could get the little guy into the cat carrier without waking him up. Jean collected the pet taxi from behind the bed, tiptoed back into the living room, and pounced. Before he knew what was happening, Dougie found himself behind bars. She could read his expression through the air holes. *Good grief. Not again.*

"You're coming with me this time," she told him. "Although not as a chaperone, mind you."

Dougie assumed the shape of a gray pincushion, whiskers bristling. She was just setting his cage by the front door when Beethoven's "Ode to Joy" trilled from the living room. Racing back down the hall, she excavated her cell phone from the depths of her bag and checked the screen. Ah, the object of her affections! "Hi, Alasdair."

"Hello, yourself," said his brushed-velvet voice. "I've arrived at Ferniebank, had me a look at the premises, and opened for business. How has the mighty Detective Chief Inspector fallen, to be doling out admission tickets and selling sweeties like a spotty lad in a cinema."

"You are joking, right? You're not regretting your retirement?"

"I'm joking," he returned with an indulgent chuckle. "I haven't caught you driving, have I?"

"No, I'm packing the car. Is Keith Bell there yet?"

"Who?"

"I guess not, then. He's the architect working for the woman who bought Ferniebank, Ciara Macquarrie. He called a little while ago and said he'd be out there this afternoon."

Silence. Abyssal silence. Silence deeper than that of the grave.

Jean looked again at the screen. She was still connected. "Alasdair? Hello?"

"Oh aye, I'm here." His voice had gone so cold and hard Jean thought of one of those Siberian mammoths, flash-frozen by an avalanche.

"What's wrong? Something about the caretaker dying in the dungeon?"

"Oh. That. The inquest returned a verdict of natural causes, though I'm not so sure." A pause so long Jean felt frost prickling in her ear. Finally Alasdair concluded, "Nothing's wrong. I'll be seeing you in a few hours. Safe journey."

The ether rang hollowly. That time he had disconnected. She switched off her phone, asking herself, What the heck? Was this another test case? If they were going to make the running, he couldn't just dismiss her like that. Something about the caretaker's death had him worried. He'd been investigating criminal cases for so long, his reflexes were set to hair-trigger sensitivity. . . . She hadn't mentioned the caretaker until after he'd frozen her out.

She needed to get down to the Borders and get him unplugged, unbuttoned, loosened up. Like she wasn't wired into a 220-volt socket, buttoned to the chin, and nervous as a long-tailed cat in a room full of rocking chairs?

Frowning, Jean strode into the kitchen, where she forced some crackers and peanut butter through her dry mouth. Then she filled a cooler with the perishables she'd accumulated after a painful bout with a cookbook and notepad. Meal-planning was a skill she'd let lapse ages ago.

Alasdair claimed he could cook. . . . She reminded herself that it was reverse sexism to expect a man to be domestically incompetent. Between them, they wouldn't starve. And they didn't have to spend the entire week isolated at Ferniebank. The Stanelaw pub was not only notoriously music-friendly, it was near the B&B that Michael and Rebecca Campbell-Reid were minding for the month.

She packed the car with food, clothes, her bag of knitting—it behooved her to have something to do on her own—and her laptop. She strapped Dougie's pet carrier into the back seat to the accompaniment of a not-so-distant trumpet playing "When the Saints Go Marching In." Everything was accounted for except her wits, and she devoutly hoped they'd turn up along the way.

Just as Jean was locking her front door, the next one opened and emitted a stocky man armed with a guitar case in one hand and a fiddle case in the other. "Away to the south, are you now?" Hugh Munro called.

"I'm away. I was just going to bring you the key." Jean met his grin with one of her own.

Never one to skip a neighborly blether, Hugh joined her beside her car and set the instrument cases down at his feet. His T-shirt was the size of a pup tent, the printed logo of June's Midsummer Monster Madness Festival barely contained by the suspenders that held up his canvas pants. The top of his head gleamed pink and smooth as a baby's bottom, as did his cheeks, making the white hair and white beard seem incongruous. His blue eyes were as adult as any Jean had ever seen, flashing with a wisdom and a humor that indicated his preference as much for the milk of human kindness as for the whiskey of human perception.

"Good job I've caught you, then," Hugh said. "I'm off to rehearsal. The band's playing tonight at the Assembly Rooms. You're making your getaway in the nick of time. Not to worry, I'll keep an eye on the actors renting your place, mind that they carry away the rubbish and water the plants."

"For what they're paying, they can redecorate it. Just as long as they put everything back before they leave."

"Are you quite certain wee Dougie'll get on at Ferniebank? He can stop with me, if you like." Leaning into the car, Hugh offered his forefinger to one of the air holes in the pet carrier. Dougie honored it with a delicate sniff. He had much better taste than to bite the fingertip that played such fine music. After all, he was named for piper extraordinary Dougie Pincock.

"Thanks, but he'll be okay in the caretaker's cottage," Jean said, and, thinking of music, "Have you ever played at the pub in Stanelaw? The Granite Cross, isn't it? Odd name for a pub. Unless it used to be the Engrailed Cross, the coat of arms of the Sinclairs of Rosslyn."

"Like as not the original owner got shot of the local gentry —Sinclair, Douglas, Kerr, petty tyrants the lot of them—and then turned about and named his establishment after them. Sucking in to the high and mighty in return for their patronage. We're never free of it, are we? The little guys always get the short end."

Jean smiled. Hugh had once been a little guy himself—he had been bequeathed the Ramsay Garden apartment by an admirer with an exquisite sense of irony.

"Aye," Hugh went on. "I've played there. Fine place for a Saturday night session, come one, come all. The local councillor had me in to the local museum in April to play the Ferniebank Clarsach as well, though I'm not so dab a hand at the harp as some. Still, a musical instrument unplayed is like a woman unloved, or so I'm thinking."

That brought new innuendo to the expression "let's make beautiful music together." "Was that when the harp—the clarsach—was put on display?"

"Oh aye. And a bonny thing it is, carved from stem to stern, with hollows for jewelry—that's long gone, no surprise there. Unusual to see an artifact so valuable on display in its own home. Small museums the length and breadth of the UK have no more than photos of their own heirlooms. The big museums take the most expensive items, all the better to attract the punters."

"Michael and Rebecca Campbell-Reid would say the artifacts are better protected in the big national museums. And they made their point with the clarsach. I was going to write about it, too. You know, all things Ferniebank."

Hugh mimed the curves of the harp, no more than three feet tall, then played invisible strings. "A pity, that. A seven-hundred-year-old clarsach's not the sort of thing most thieves would want, even if one of the Sinclairs played it for Robert the Bruce, King of Scots, and another for Mary Stuart, Queen of Scots, two centuries on. Even if those stories are nothing more than legend."

"Ah, but you know how I feel about legends." Like tonguing a sore tooth, she asked, "Was the councillor who asked you to play the clarsach named Angus Rutherford?"

"That he was. Long, lanky chap with a face like the Queen of Faerie's milk-white steed and a wife holding the whip-hand. But you'll be meeting up with the pair of them this weekend, I expect."

"I doubt it. *The Scotsman* says Angus went missing in Brussels. Funny how Stanelaw becomes a hotbed of intrigue just as the developers move in." She let "just as Alasdair and I move in" twist gently in the breeze.

Hugh's smile was annotated by a firm nod. He patted his T-shirt, evoking the events at Loch Ness in June. "No problem, Jean. You've got D.C.I. Cameron on the premises."

"Except he officially retired from the police last week." Gavin and Hugh both meant well, but neither of them seemed to think she could fend for herself. "Now Alasdair's making security arrangements for properties managed by Protect and Survive. Castles, abbeys, stately homes. Conservation areas. Local museums, too, I bet, but apparently not the one in Stanelaw."

"You've barely seen the man since June. You've earned yourself a bit of peace and quiet."

"*He* has." She'd sensed when she first met Alasdair that he was burned out, and therefore pushing himself harder and harder. When she discovered he'd turned in his own partner for corruption and the man subsequently committed suicide, she realized he'd been burning for a long time. All she could do for him was suggest, at first gently, then with the offer of a new job, that he move on. Now she sent up a prayer to whatever hard-bitten being passed for Alasdair's guardian angel that this career would not be fraught with life-and-death matters, the unfortunate caretaker and the old lady notwithstanding.

Judging by the sympathetic gleam in Hugh's eye, she was looking like a human version of Dougie's pincushion effect. But he picked up his guitar and his fiddle without further comment. "I'm away then. Have a good honeym . . . er, holiday. I'll be looking out for you and Alasdair both soon."

"Well, yeah." Alasdair had sold his house in Inverness and put his belongings into storage, and was going to stay at Fernie-bank until he found a new caretaker. Which might take longer than he'd intended, now. And then . . . Well, she could almost see P and S headquarters on George Street from her living room. Her flat wasn't too small for two if they were on good terms.

Even that McMansion in Dallas hadn't been large enough, at the end. She and Brad had staked out their individual territories, occasionally meeting in the kitchen like strangers at Starbucks. Jean had no idea where Alasdair had lived his married life. He only ever mentioned his marriage in the same way a cancer survivor mentioned his excised tumor. Jean didn't even know his ex-wife's name.

Her flat was small. Stanelaw was small. Scotland was a small country. One where you had to make your peace with the past, because that past was never really gone.

Hugh was already several paces away, laughing back over his shoulder.

"Can I drop you off anywhere?" Jean called.

"I'll get there faster on Shanks's pony. Cheers." He made it across the courtyard in time to join the conga line of costumed dancers snaking its way up Ramsay Lane.

With her own laugh, Jean turned to her car. *Once more unto the breach,* she told herself, and then remembered that line ended with something about filling a wall with dead bodies. Never mind. Wishing she had eyes in the back of her head, she inched out onto the narrow medieval street and into what was less the flow of traffic than the curdle.

CHAPTER THREE

By the time Jean pulled into the small, shady parking lot beside the Granite Cross, she'd caught her breath, soothed her nerves, and committed herself to her fate. Which had more than once proved to be a jokester, but then, she and Alasdair had more than once proved to be fighters.

In the back seat, Dougie was sound asleep, his tail wrapped around his paws. The contents of the ice chest beside him were presumably still chilled. As Jean had hoped, the air here was cooler and fresher than that in the city—if scented faintly with aroma of cow. She'd leave the windows cracked and make her visit a quick one, she assured herself, and climbed out of the car.

Stanelaw was an attractive town. Its main street was lined with one- and two-story buildings, some covered in white-painted stucco, others revealing walls of local gray stone. A shop, a tea room, a hardware store, and other commercial establishments proclaimed the viability of the community. Down the occasional side street, Jean glimpsed modern houses. Beyond them, the countryside was tamed into farm plots of green and gold, bunched around the steep-sided hill, or law, that had probably given the place its name. Above, the vault of the sky shone clear and blue as Alasdair's eyes.

This was a much gentler land geologically than the crag, moor, and loch of the Highlands. But the Borders were no gentler historically. For centuries the region had been macer-

31

ated between the jaws of Scotland and England, debatable lands supporting debatable folk, hardy souls who lived as much by plundering as by farming and herding. The myth of the miserly Scotsman had begun here, where no possession and no person was free of threat. Jean took a second look at the house across the street from the pub, obviously one of the oldest in town, its thick walls and small windows proclaiming it as much fortress as home.

Several steps led up to its front door and a sign reading, "Stanelaw Museum, Home of the Ferniebank Clarsach." On the door itself, a notice added, "Closed. Please Call Again." Was it coincidence that a police car was parked half on the sidewalk in front of the building, or was the local plod dusting for fingerprints? Again, Jean assumed, since the theft was old news by now.

She turned toward the pub. Hanging baskets of flowers softened its stern stone facade. A signboard read "The Granite Cross," the words arching above a painted knight bearing a black shield with, sure enough, the white engrailed, or scallop-edged, cross of the Sinclairs. That family had ridden the storm of centuries of Scottish history, but were popularly known today for building Rosslyn Chapel just outside Edinburgh in Roslin village, confusingly enough.

A burst of pipe music diverted Jean to a side entrance, a gate in a stone wall. A woman was just leaving. She was even shorter than Jean was, with short, almost crew-cut blond hair and a sleeveless blouse that revealed a Celtic-interlace tattoo on her bony shoulder. The long red fingernails of her right hand pressed a cell phone to her ear and those of the other hand held a lit cigarette. "Derek," she was saying, every crow's foot in her face clenched, "Derek, you're not listening. I'm your mum, Derek, listen to me." She strode off up the street.

Derek must be a teenager, Jean thought, with a sympathetic

glance at the woman's retreating back, and entered the gate to discover a beer garden. An open doorway in the back of the pub overlooked an assortment of tables, some shaded by an arbor covered with leafy vines, some in the sun. A dozen people sat around drinking and snacking, getting a head start on happy hour. If they'd planned on having a quiet conversation, though, they were out of luck. Michael Campbell-Reid was playing his bagpipes in the far corner, the sun glinting auburn off the waving locks of his rock-star haircut, the musical tidal wave crashing against the surrounding walls.

Jean grinned. Nothing like a set of well-tempered pipes, played by a loving hand, to stir the heart and rile the soul of the Scot. A few more minutes and the pub's clientele would take up their butter knives and rush the English border.

She hadn't lived in Scotland long enough, accumulating an ultraviolet deficiency, to bake herself in the sun. Neither, manifestly, had Rebecca Campbell-Reid. She was seated in the flickering shadow of the arbor, a tea tray on the table and a baby carriage close by. Her honey-brown hair was held back from her face with a plastic clip, an accessory Michael could perhaps have used. Her features were as genial as his, if, like his, sculpted by an intelligence so quick as to be impatient.

Rebecca called over the music, "There you are, Jean."

"Here I am," Jean shouted back. She sat down in a plastic chair and peered into the pram. Two-month-old Linda was asleep, her little pink rose-petal face utterly at peace. Add a halo and wings and she would make your average Renaissance cherub look like a gremlin. Jean sat back with a smile that was fond but hardly wistful. She had learned long ago, after one very brief pregnancy, to take out her maternal impulses on other people's children. "So she's already used to the sound of the pipes?"

"Passed along with the tartan DNA. If you'll sit here with

her, I'll run inside and get you a cuppa. Or do you have time?"

"Thanks, but no, I don't. I need to get on out to Ferniebank."

"Oh, you'll love Ferniebank." Rebecca's tone said, "Oh, you'll love having a root-canal."

"Let me guess. The Gray Lady is based on a real ghost."

"So say the locals. Mind you, with the place closed and all, we've only peeked in through the gate, but there's something properly uncanny about it."

Jean had trouble seeing uncanniness being at all proper, but then, Rebecca's slight paranormal sensitivity picked up resonances more than actual ghosts. Jean filched a morsel of shortbread from the tea tray. "Thanks. I think. So where's the B&B you're minding?"

"Just around the corner. The Reiver's Rest. Named for the reivers who were bloody-minded power-hungry thieves taking advantage of unrest along the border. The Highlands have no monopoly on romanticization."

"You remember the old story about the beggar in the Border village? No one would give him the time of day, let alone a penny or a crust of bread. Finally he asked, 'Are there no Christians here?' And someone answered, 'No, we're all Armstrongs and Elliots hereabouts.' "

"The Fairbairns are Armstrongs, aren't they?" asked Rebecca with a grin.

"Yep. One branch of my family goes straight back to this area. There's a comment on determinism versus free will." Jean finished her cookie. "The Reiver's Rest. Okay."

"There's a comment on the heritage business."

"If it weren't for the heritage biz, I'm not sure Scotland would have a viable economy. I know Miranda and I wouldn't. Ironic, how Alasdair's now working for the exact industry he's made so many snide remarks about."

"You need a little pragmatism in amongst the flights of fancy."

"That's exactly what he'd say."

At the far side of the garden, Michael segued into a hornpipe, his long fingers springing on the chanter like the legs of a ballerina. Several people clapped in time. Rebecca's sharp brown eyes focused over Jean's shoulder, and Jean turned to follow her gaze through the gateway.

A policeman was leaving the museum. His blunt, heavy features and stubbled jowls would have looked at home beneath a reiver's steel bonnet. What he placed on his head, though, was a black cap with a checkerboard band. He opened the passenger side door of his car.

From the museum stepped a woman with the face of a Roman matron, from her upswept dark hair stroked with silver to her deep-set eyes with their heavy lids to her jaw as smooth and hard as marble. Her turtleneck, tweed jacket, trousers, and boots fit her svelte body like kid gloves would have fit her hands. Locking the door behind her, she tucked the key and something else—a small box—into her large leather handbag. Miranda would have recognized the make and model of the bag, to say nothing of the clothes, but even fashion-impaired Jean with her canvas mini-backpack got the message: countryside chic. The woman needed only a riding crop to complete the effect.

She seated herself in the police car as though the officer's uniform was that of a chauffeur. Without cracking an expression, he slammed her door, paced around to the driver's side, and drove away.

"Araminta Rutherford." Rebecca's American accent, migrating further east all the time, gave a quick tickle to every "r." "Maiden name Maitland, from Thirlestane Castle just up the way."

Jean wasn't going to swoon in astonishment at that identification, although the thought of such a cool customer laboring over a hot stove did take her aback. "She has a cooking school?"

35

"Oh, yes. Half the people who stay at the B&B are signed up for courses. She's the director of the museum as well, has done a great job of keeping the local antiquities out of Edinburgh's clutches, not that I don't see Edinburgh's point. You have heard about the clarsach?"

"I'm afraid so. Did you and Michael get a chance to look at it?"

"No. We got here Saturday and it vanished on Sunday. P.C. Logan—the Richard Nixon lookalike with Minty—answered an alarm at the museum in the wee hours of the morning. He found a window pried open and the clarsach gone, but everything else, including the Roman and medieval coins, accounted for. Michael and I flashed our credentials as museum curators and asked to look around, but Mr. Councillor Rutherford, Angus, wasn't best pleased with our trying to push our way in and sent us packing."

"Two Edinburgh know-it-alls, right?" Jean asked, at the exact instant Michael stopped playing. Her statement came out more loudly than she'd intended, hanging in the still-vibrating air like a fart after a dinner party. Wincing, she lowered her voice. "And now Angus is missing."

Michael strolled across the garden, graciously accepting the plaudits of his audience, and laid his pipes across the table. They deflated with a sound between a groan of weariness and a sigh of repletion. "Hullo, Jean. Come to look out the local mysterious events, eh?"

"Stanelaw seems to be teeming with mysterious events," she answered, without pointing out she was hardly looking for them.

"Development," said Rebecca. "Tourism. Money makes things happen, good or bad."

Michael leaned into the pram and smoothed the Black Watch tartan blanket over Linda. Then he sat down beside Rebecca. "There's a resort, a golf course, and a water park across the river, and St. Cuthbert's Way just beyond, and the cooking school here in Stanelaw. Now Ciara Macquarrie's turned up with her New Age conference center and spa—excuse me, healing center—at Ferniebank."

"Who'd she buy the property from, anyway?" Jean asked.

"Themselves, Councillor and Mrs. Rutherford. Angus and Minty. No surprise that Stanelaw Council granted planning permission for the renovation of the castle and a new building down by the chapel."

"Ah," said Jean. "No surprise at all."

"The—ahem—Royal Commission for the Ancient and Historical Monuments of Scotland funded a dig and a bit of stabilization work in the nineties, and the Rutherfords opened the place to trippers through a management agreement with Protect and Survive. Pity the chapel was already a ruin."

"Pity about it all becoming just another product," Rebecca said.

"Without folk like the Rutherfords and Ciara Macquarrie," said Michael, "secondary sites like Ferniebank would be piles of rubbish plowed under for car parks. Your Alasdair's arriving just in time to organize the transition from scheduled site and listed building to money-making facility."

Everyone was noting that Alasdair was, in however awkward a fashion, hers. Maybe she'd come to terms with that concept herself some day—and with its corollary, that she was his. Jean had only recently come to terms with the concept of selling history like a commodity. But then, if it came to a choice between marketing and oblivion, she'd have to choose marketing. "Too many of these places are no more than white elephants. I can't fault Macquarrie for hoping Ferniebank will be a money-making facility, even if it means exploiting all the publicity about Rosslyn Chapel—that bestseller claiming that Mary Magdalen was buried there, for a while, at least."

"Ferniebank Chapel was built by the Sinclairs as well," said Rebecca, "and dedicated to Saint Mary—the virgin, not the Magdalen, I bet—near the same time and in the same style as Rosslyn, which was dedicated to Saint Matthew, not that anyone remembers that."

"Except for Rosslyn being bigger and in better shape," Michael said.

"And for Ferniebank having a perfectly genuine fourteenth-century clarsach instead of a collection of hare-brained, half-baked, off-the-wall legends. Just the sort of legends," Jean added with a shameless grin, "that are my stock in trade."

"Just the sort of legends that give historians and curators like us the cold shivers," said Michael, "but they go down well with the consumer."

A man wearing a green apron high as a cummerbund came strolling across the garden. If Michael had been standing up, the publican would have been a head shorter and twice as wide. His genial face had nothing in common with Logan's saturnine features and Minty Rutherford's stony elegance. An interesting cast of characters, Jean thought, here in Stanelaw.

He handed Michael a pint glass brimming with a foam-flecked dark liquid that wasn't Coca-Cola. "There you are. Well done."

"Cheers." Michael took a deep drink. "Aah. My compliments to the brewer."

"Jean," said Rebecca, "this is Noel Brimberry. Noel, Jean Fairbairn. She'll be staying at Ferniebank for the next couple of weeks."

"Good to meet you," Jean said, secretly delighted. The man not only looked like a hobbit, he had a hobbit name. She was surprised the pub wasn't named the Green Dragon or the Prancing Pony after one of Tolkien's fictional inns, but then, Brimberry had probably bought it as a going concern, Sinclair attribution and all. The expected influx of tourists would be gratified either way.

"You'll be Mr. Cameron's wife, then," said Brimberry, his plump cheeks puffing up in a smile so broad his eyes disappeared.

"Ah, no, we're not . . ." Jean saw Michael's blue eyes dancing, and Rebecca's pink lips crinkled with a suppressed grin. *To heck with it.* She finished, "I'm sure we'll be in for a meal and music."

"And right welcome you'll be. Good job we've got Protect and Survive's top man here. A former police detective with a grand reputation, is he? With all that's on, both good and bad, he'll be finding work enough. A shame about the clarsach going missing, as well as . . ." Several people walked in the gateway and headed for the back door, probably following the seductive odor of garlic and baking bread—pizza, perhaps. "No rest for the weary. Leastways, none for those tugging our forelocks for a living." Brimberry scuttled toward the newcomers.

Beside the cast of characters in Jean's program book, she jotted down the hint of social friction. "What was he going to say, a shame about Angus's disappearance?"

"Everyone seems to think that Angus will find his way back to the stable," said Rebecca. "At least, no one's assuming there's foul play involved."

"Yet," Michael added ominously. "Although I'm hearing that he goes walkabout every now and then. It wasn't Minty reported him missing, but his council colleagues." He drank again, and wiped his mouth. "I reckon Noel was saying a shame about the Ferniebank caretaker."

Ah. Yes. With a shudder that bracketed horror and sympathy, Jean said, "I heard about that, too. Gave me one of your shivers. Was he a local man?"

"Oh aye. Wallace Rutherford, Angus's uncle."

"And no indication of foul play there, either?" Except for Alasdair's *I'm not so sure,* Jean added to herself.

Rebecca shook her head. "People were shocked about him dropping dead the week after Helen Elliot dropped dead—she was Noel's mother-in-law, lived at Ferniebank Farm across from the castle. Neither death's suspicious, no."

"These things come in threes," cautioned Michael.

"Not necessarily," Rebecca told him.

Amen to that, Jean thought.

"Wallace died," Michael summarized. "The castle closed down, then the sale and the consent for alteration went through, and Alasdair arrived. And that's where we're standing now."

CHAPTER FOUR

Jean glanced at her watch. "Except I'm sitting here instead of standing there. It's already past five."

"We're expecting tonight's guests at the B&B." Rebecca piled her crockery on the tea tray. With one last swallow, Michael added his glass to the collection.

A faint gurgling came from the pram. Jean smiled again on the wriggling baby, who was now as bright-eyed as her parents, then wrinkled her nose. Linda was leaving a bit of a vapor trail. But then, that's what the gurgling signified, a request for nutritional and hygienic assistance.

Their chairs scraped on the concrete. Rebecca gathered up a bag patterned with Kelly green Loch Ness monsters, a baby gift from Jean. "Michael's parents put us on to the Reiver's Rest. The owner went off to Canada for a family wedding."

"Which was not scheduled for the convenience of people in the hospitality trade," said Jean.

"Good job all round," Michael added, collecting his bagpipes. "We're outwith Auld Reekie during the Festival and turning a few bob from renting our own place. I'm driving into the National Museum twice a week and the rest of the time we're working via internet, phone, and fax."

"And Noel's daughter Zoe helps with the cooking and cleaning at the B&B." Rebecca stowed the bag beneath the pram and wheeled toward the gate.

When Jean opened her car, Dougie let out an inquisitive

mew, the feline equivalent of, "Are we there yet? Are we there yet?"

"Bring Alasdair round for a meal," Michael instructed Jean. "It's well past time we were making the man's acquaintance."

"I warned him about y'all, but he still says he's looking forward to meeting you." Jean slid in behind the wheel and called through the open window, "See you soon!"

She squeezed her vehicle between cars parked haphazardly at the sides of the road and picked up speed at the edge of town, where the road curved up a hill. Then she tapped the brakes. Behind a lichen-encrusted stone wall rose a similarly lichen-encrusted church, its slate roof sagging with age. The square, stumpy tower and slits of windows testified to the way this building had served as a physical sanctuary as well as a spiritual one. But then, neither Scot nor Sassenach had hesitated to burn down a church with the congregation inside, an act that surely merited a special place in Hell. Depending on how you defined Hell. Much of the conflict in the Borders stemmed from religious conflict, Catholic against Protestant, Protestant against other Protestants.

The road lay empty in the afternoon sunshine, a gray-black ribbon between the fields on her right and the trees concealing the river on her left. Jean stopped the car.

The church seemed deserted, doors shut, windows blank. But a notice board out front was freshly painted, reading: "The Church of Scotland. Rev Janet Wilkins, present incumbent. Church open by appointment—contact Mrs. Rutherford at Glebe House. Services every Sunday at 12 noon." So there was some divine life left in the old shell yet.

From the cemetery in front of the church rose polished granite headstones inlaid with gilded letters, very recent burials, if not as recent as the one closest to the road, a long pile of wilted flowers extending from the vertical of wooden plank.

Jean couldn't make out the name painted on the temporary marker, but she could guess. This was the grave of the luckless caretaker. Not far away lay a second grave with a temporary marker, a few days older—the flowers were well on their way to mulch. Mrs. Elliot, no doubt.

Shaking her head at these intimations of mortality, Jean accelerated past a grove of trees, then braked again in front of a handsome stone mansion. Since its dormers and gables didn't rise to the full excess of Scots Baronial, the place had likely been built when Victoria was a slip of a lass. A small sign on the front gate read: "Glebe House." Casa Rutherford, in other words. Jean wondered whether she'd get points at Minty's tea for knowing that a glebe was land that paid rent to a church. Assuming Minty carried on with the tea.

Jean coasted on by, noting the police car parked in the driveway next to a no-nonsense Range Rover. A movement in the bay window fronting the house might be a woman in tweed and leather, or it might not . . . Jean wrenched at the steering wheel to keep from driving into the weed-filled ditch between the road and the wall enclosing the lawn. When she looked back, every little pane of the mullioned window met her gaze blandly.

Behind the house, in the place that might once have been taken by a barn, stood a contemporary timber and glass Euro-insipid building. A large but still tasteful signboard, reading "Cookery at the Glebe" rose beside a second drive. The Rutherfords had not been strapped for the money to invest in their cooking school, then, even before de-accessioning a property.

Onwards, then, over the last half-mile to Ferniebank. Which wasn't going to be as peaceful as Jean had intended. As for Alasdair's intentions, professional or personal, she probably didn't need to fill him in on the question of the missing councillor or the case of the stolen clarsach. And the unfortunate incident of the caretaker was already on his mind. Forewarned was forearmed, she told herself, a concept that applied to relationships as well as to crimes, ghosts, and Borders warfare.

A farmstead appeared on her right, complete with hillside pasture dotted with black and white cows. Here the sign was a simple painted shingle wired to the fence: "Ferniebank Farm."

The trees on her left opened ranks and shed some of their thick undergrowth. Ash, rowan, alder, oak, birch, willow, hazel —she knew them by reputation, if not personally. Their long shadows reached down to a sparkle that was the River Teviot, then suddenly were enclosed by another stone wall of such antiquity that the one around the church might just as well have been made of Legos. This one stood eight feet in height and was topped by jagged stones, here and there clumsily cemented into place. Above the stone teeth rose the dark gray walls, parapets, and chimneys of Ferniebank Castle, even on this sunny August afternoon exuding the grim chill of long winters and longer warfare.

Jean took the left turn through the narrow gateway with care. Alasdair's Renault and a mini-bus sat in the gravel-paved courtyard defined by the perimeter wall, the castle's sheer facade, and a low structure roofed with corrugated metal. It sported the plate-glass window and door of the ticket office and shop, while a second door was marked "Toilet," and a third was blank. Park benches and some potted plants proclaimed a welcome that dashed itself futilely against the forbidding face of the castle.

Jean saw the archway of the main door gaping atop a flight of wooden steps, and the glass in the irregularly spaced and unevenly sized windows shimmering with distorted reflections. What she didn't see was the cozy caretaker's cottage she'd been anticipating. Maybe it lay farther down the slope leading to the river, along a path that disappeared into the trees. Through dappled shadow, Jean could just make out more gray walls.

She pulled in beside the bus. Its side was painted with the words "Mystic Scotland" written in lavish imitation-Celtic script. Was Ciara Macquarrie here as well as Keith Bell? Fine. The more the merrier, she told herself briskly as she climbed out of the car. She'd put on her reporter's fedora and get in some work before the castle closed at seven-thirty. Before she and Alasdair were left alone together.

First she had to get everything stowed in . . . The cottage. There it was, not a free-standing building at all but a flat tucked into the lower left corner of the castle. Its modern wooden door, gleaming with white paint, and its two modern windows, hung with lace curtains, seemed to huddle together, compressed by the bulk of the keep looming beside and above.

Now that, she had not anticipated. That, Alasdair hadn't bothered to mention to her either. Eating, talking, sleeping with darkness gathered just on the other side of the wall, ghosts eavesdropping on intimacies as though envious of warm flesh.

Get a grip. The castle was, and had always been, a place of refuge. She and Alasdair had dealt with ghosts before. Ghosts were emotional videos, without awareness or even the will toward awareness. Alasdair was treating her with respect by not thinking this was something she should be warned about. What accessories did she need to set the scene, anyway? A Jacuzzi shaped like a champagne glass, like in the tacky honeymoon hotels by Niagara Falls? Give her—give them both—historical truth as the strongest foundation for stories personal or public.

Jean opened the back door of the car and reached for the cooler. A breeze made the leafy branches above her plunge and rustle and brushed cool kisses across her cheekbones. Crows, the corbies of many a grim Scottish tale, called from the stained black slate of the castle roof.

Alasdair stepped out of the shop.

His solid, compact body stood to attention, head thrown back, as though he was a scout listening for voices and watching for movements in a building under siege. How odd he looked wearing not his detective's uniform of suit and tie but canvas pants and a light sweater over an open-collared shirt. How odd that he'd stand there turned away from her. The man had eyes in the back of his head and could hear a needle falling into a haystack. He had to know she was there.

He turned around. *Oh yes,* Jean thought, her heart dropping like a cannonball. He knew she was there. He'd been steeling himself to face her. His eyebrows were drawn so tightly together a vertical crease ran between them. His blue eyes were glints of sea-ice. His mouth was tightly closed, crushing the elegant curve of his lips. She'd tasted those lips, and knew them to be supple and sure.

Jean straightened, bracing herself. Maybe she should ask for a cigarette and a blindfold.

Alasdair raised his hand toward her, palm open, and then closed it into a fist that fell heavy as a battle-axe back to his side. "Jean," he said.

"Alasdair," she replied.

Behind his back, in the main doorway of the castle, appeared two people. The cadaverous young man with the long dishwater brown hair, the stooped shoulders, and the somber, sallow face was dressed in a polo shirt and khakis. The camera bag he carried over his shoulder made him list to one side.

The woman with the dazzling smile had that gorgeous British complexion, all soft fair skin and rosy cheeks. She might have been plump, but it was hard to tell—her flowing skirt and top of many colors made her look like a piñata, an effect enhanced by the scarf holding back her mop of red curls. Keith Bell and Ciara Macquarrie, no doubt. Quite the odd couple.

Jean tentatively returned Ciara's jolly wave and looked again at Alasdair. *What?*

His body jerked as though a steel-tipped arrow had just pierced the armor between his shoulder blades. His voice was rough. "I didn't know it was her buying the place. I didn't know she'd be coming here. Not 'til you said her name on the phone."

"Who? Ciara Macquarrie? Why . . ."

His gaze was steady, uncompromising, sparing nothing. "Oh aye. Ciara Macquarrie. My ex-wife."

CHAPTER FIVE

Jean didn't feel as though she'd been punched in the stomach. She didn't feel as though the rug had been pulled out from under her. She didn't feel anything at all. From some remote place, Death Valley probably, she watched herself watching Ciara stroll across the courtyard. Keith Bell slouched along behind, appearing more like her shadow than her companion.

A farm tractor rumbled down the road outside the gate, startling the crows on the battlements into harsh complaints. An ache in Jean's chest nagged her into breathing. Shuddering, she inhaled. And her thoughts plummeted downward and shattered against the jagged stone of fact.

Alasdair was in full lead-shielded, locked-down mode, his face less expressive than the stark facade of Ferniebank. But she could read the set of his broad shoulders all too well. She herself had pared away his defenses, bit by bit, leaving him vulnerable to this surprise attack. Once she had gotten the vapors at the thought of Brad perhaps talking to Alasdair on the phone. Now here was Alasdair having to introduce woman past to woman present. He and Ciara made such an odd couple that Keith and Ciara looked like Tweedle-dum and Tweedle-dee.

The dratted woman was grinning as though this unfortunately not-likely-to-be-brief encounter was the best joke she'd heard in years. She'd known Alasdair was here. She was enjoying the heck out of surprising him. . . .

No. She wasn't gloating. What she was doing was extending

her hand toward Jean. "Jean Fairbairn, I presume. Ciara Mac-quarrie. I'm your predecessor with this po-faced specimen here" —she nodded toward Alasdair, who took a short step backwards —"or so I'm hearing from my local contacts. No worries, though. I come in peace."

Jean managed to lift a paw, allow Ciara to clasp it, and drop it back down to her side. The woman's hand was soft and rather damp. Around her hung the thankfully faint aroma of one of those perfumes—lotus, patchouli, gardenia—that was a molecule shy of bug spray.

"Hi." Keith had a surprisingly deep voice considering the circumference of his neck. "We talked on the phone."

Jean opened her mouth but nothing came out. She could see herself reflected in his aviator-style glasses like in twin mirrors, her eyes and her mouth both wide, dark blotches.

"Poor lamb, she's had a bit of a shock," Ciara said to Keith. With a toss of her head that set her dangling earrings to tinkling as gaily as wind chimes, she shooed him toward the path that ran from the parking area to the river. The lilt of her voice drifted back into the courtyard. "If we come back after nightfall we'll see the ghost walking from the castle down to the chapel, trailing her shroud behind her like the wedding gown she refused to wear. Could you not feel the disturbance on the up-per floor, where she died?"

"Nope," said Keith.

"She's there, right enough. The vibrations were rattling my teeth. How sad that she's lingering so near a place of power like the chapel, and yet cannot let go. Wallace now, he's gone on to the next plane." The motley pair disappeared into the shade of the trees.

Oh, Jean thought. Those gray walls down that way, they were the chapel's. Those shadows that lay long across the courtyard, they indicated that the day was dying. That man standing beside her, face shielded, eyes impenetrable, that was Alasdair. Her Alasdair. He had expressionlessness down pat, oh yes, but "po-faced" implied arrogance as well. Jean had thought him arrogant, once. What? Had Ciara never broken his shell? Or had she reinforced its thickness?

He wasn't a po-faced specimen, Jean thought, any more than she was a poor lamb. Mutton, maybe, but then, Ciara wasn't daubed with any mint jelly herself.

Ciara, that was a pretty name. Not plain-jane, like Jean. The woman was pretty, taller than Jean—which wasn't saying much, most people were taller than Jean—and pleasingly plump beneath her layers of fabric. She was the sort of woman who lived large, speaking her mind, laughing loudly, enjoying rich food and drink without fearing the sort of dyspepsia Jean felt stirring in the depths of her stomach at that very moment.

No need to do a compare-and-contrast. No need to torture herself with jealousy. Manifestly, Alasdair had moved on. A long way on, to end up with Jean. But speaking of letting go . . . The words came in a rush. "*She's* your ex-wife? She's not what I—I mean I wasn't expecting anything, the way you've avoided talking about her. Why didn't you tell me?"

The rumble of the tractor stopped and the soundless void was filled by Alasdair's slightly hoarse voice. "Why should I have told you?"

"Well, it would have made this moment a hell of a lot less awkward!"

He didn't blink, let alone flinch. He turned his head so that he was facing her. Still his gaze was steady and uncompromising. Even the short-cropped strands of his hair were clenched, like his jaw when he at last squeezed words out between his teeth. "Oh no, lass, there's nothing could be making this moment less awkward."

From the road came a whistle, followed by a gruff male voice shouting, "Hector! Jackie! Come down by me."

Sheep dogs, Jean assumed. Or cattle dogs. Whatever. A whiff of peat smoke tickled her nostrils.

"I knew she'd started up a tour company," Alasdair went on. "I didn't know it was her buying the property. Not 'til you said her name. Then I had a look at the small print on P and S's papers and there it was, several pages in. I'm thinking she meant to surprise me, here."

"As an attack?"

"As a joke. She's never vindictive. That would mean taking notice of others." He turned away. Any other man would have cursed until the air was blue, or thrown his fist through the stone wall, or made it all Jean's fault. Alasdair said, "Let's be getting your things into the flat."

It's only a flesh wound.

She wanted to reassure him with a hug or a soft word. But to try and scale his defenses right now would make things worse. She turned toward her car. Groceries. Suitcase. Cat. Flat. The cat in the flat. Alasdair pulled the pet taxi from the back seat and returned Dougie's suspicious gaze through the bars, two males, each sizing up the other.

Ciara's merry laugh echoed from the woods. Quickly, efficiently, Alasdair strode off toward the apartment inserted into the lower corner of the castle. Jean followed, lugging the cooler.

When he opened the door it glided on oiled hinges, with no horror-movie groans. He placed Dougie's carrier inside and turned back toward the car, leaving Jean to inspect her temporary home.

Breathing in the odor of cleanser with nuances of frying food, she eyed a kitchen separated by a table and chairs from a living area provided with the usual furnishings. A television sat next to a medieval stone fireplace fitted with an electric fire, across from, Jean was pleased to see, a shelf of books and magazines. A desk held an aging telephone/answering machine combo and an analog clock but was otherwise bare except for a thick padded envelope, addressed to Alasdair from Protect and Survive. His marching orders, no doubt.

Only the fireplace, an original feature, and the two-foot-deep sills of the large and in no way original windows on either side, revealed that the flat was nestled inside the stony exoskeleton of a medieval keep. Judging by the florid wallpaper and fabrics and the air of benign shabbiness, the flat dated to the nineties, when the triple attraction of castle, chapel, and well had been stabilized and opened to sightseers.

Jean set the cooler on the dining table, wondering whether the reading material or anything else in the place had belonged to Wallace Rutherford.

From the far end of the living room, a short hallway led past a bathroom almost large enough to swing a cat in—not that Jean had any intention of doing so—to a bedroom. A double bed, wardrobe, and chest of drawers almost filled the room, but then, togetherness was the point of the exercise, wasn't it?

The tall bedposts were set against the whitewashed stone wall separating the flat from the main building . . . Don't start that again, she told herself. There was already a ghost haunting the bedroom, its earrings tinkling.

A large window pierced the wall opposite the bed. Just as from the two big windows in the living room, Jean saw a hillside sloping down to the river, textured with stones, saplings, shrubbery, and bracken resembling giant Boston ferns. Here was the original fernie brae or bank of the castle's name. Jean remembered the words of Thomas the Rhymer:

> And see ye not that bonny road,
> That winds about the fernie brae?

That is the road to fair Elfland,
Where thou and I this night maun gae.

Although just because you took the road to Faerie didn't mean you weren't as likely to end up in Podunk . . . . She was lowering her expectations about Alasdair. Hoping he didn't expect too much of her. It wasn't that she didn't trust him. It was, as they'd been reminded a few moments ago, that they had only so much emotional capital to spend trying to assemble a relationship out of two reclamation projects. But then, hoarding their emotional capital meant nothing but bitter loneliness, like Scrooge before that visit from his own ghosts.

Across the stone-punctured and foam-frilled surface of the Teviot stood a belt of trees, the green of their leaves lightly brushed with gold. Beyond them rose a hillside streaked with the purplish-pink of a few late foxgloves. The misshapen shadow of the castle stretched toward the east, where it lay across the water of the river damping its sparkle.

Jean opened the window and leaned out. To her left, beyond the gray flank of the castle and the back of the outbuilding, stood St. Mary's chapel. Its roofless walls were pierced with arched windows and carved with the weathered shapes of fruits, foliage, human and demonic figures. It rested upon a small rocky prominence that might be either a natural outcrop or a manmade terrace, one that blended into a low-walled courtyard that disappeared in turn into the forested hillside. There a grotto of the same time-stained gray stone marked the site of the ancient holy well. It might have originally been dedicated to the goddesses Kerridwen or Coventina, making the attribution to Mary a simple matter of policy change.

The chapel rose phoenix-like, not from flame but from the stony bones of the earth and the eternal rush of water. No, there was a fire. Or a rippling glint of light behind the broken tracery of a window. Something was reflecting a low sunbeam through the leaves.

Ciara and Keith ambled around the side of the chapel to the terrace. She was burdened by no more than her woven shoulder bag, but he was holding an electronic gadget, probably a camera. He aimed it at the grotto, trying various angles, and fired away.

Ciara considered several plants, collected a flower or two, and gazed over the railing protecting the tumbled slope where one end of the terrace had subsided into the river. Her attitude was that of Juliet on her balcony, gracefully baying at the moon. But Jean doubted if she was declaiming, "Wherefore art thou Cameron?" Maybe she was pondering bottling the well-water, labeling it with a Celtic-interlace logo, and endorsing it with Mary or some other saint's name. That would bring a fine old medieval custom into the modern marketplace.

Even as Jean looked, the sun sank below the western hills and the shadow of Ferniebank melted away into the dusk. Exhaling through pursed lips, she headed back into the living room.

Her suitcase was sitting beside Dougie's cage, and bags of groceries lined the kitchen counter. Alasdair's footsteps crunched across the gravel, coming back with another load. This time when he stepped inside, he closed the door behind him, with a solid thunk that evoked bolts thrown and draw-bridges raised. At least now, Jean thought, I'm hunkered down inside the castle with him instead of standing on the other side of the moat, watching him run his standard up and his guns out. Aren't I?

Alasdair deposited her knitting bag and laptop case beside the desk. "That's the lot. Your car needs locking, but I've not got the keys."

"You think Stanelaw's mini crime wave will get to us out here?" she asked, not entirely joking.

"Hard to say," he said, with a quick frown that conveyed

nothing humorous at all. He bent over Dougie's cage and released the latch. "There you are, laddie. Make yourself to home."

The little gray cat poured himself out through the opening and sat down to wash his face, signaling his utter boredom with his new surroundings. Alasdair can be every bit as cool, Jean thought, although he isn't as given to posturing.

"The hall cupboard's large enough for his litter box." Alasdair gestured toward a narrow door opposite the bathroom. "You're not thinking of putting him out the night, are you now?"

"No way. Hector and Jackie from across the road might decide to welcome him to the neighborhood. The Elliots live over there, right?"

"Just Roddy Elliot. Cantankerous old chap. Lost his wife, Helen, at the beginning of the month, I'm hearing. His daughter Polly's married to Noel Brimberry at the Granite Cross."

"I met Noel earlier this afternoon. His daughter Zoe is helping Michael and Rebecca with the B&B. They told me about Helen Elliot. Small town, Stanelaw. Everyone's interconnected."

"Oh aye. Everyone's interconnected, bugger it all anyway." The faintest of wry crinkles turned up one corner of Alasdair's mouth.

There it was, a quick spark like a candle lit behind a frost-covered window. He was trying, wasn't he? In both meanings of the word.

Jean wrapped her arms around his chest. For a moment he stood unyielding in her embrace, too too solid flesh. Then with a subtle but perceptible shift he softened, just a bit, and returned her embrace. "Ah, don't mind me," he said. "We'll manage well enough."

She liked hearing that *we*, even though she had to wonder at his choice of words. He'd been lowering his expectations, too. Fair enough. She rested her head against his shoulder—he was of less than imposing stature himself, and they fit nicely. Standing up, anyway.

Dougie made a figure eight around their legs, then trotted off toward the closest windowsill. Alasdair vented a dust-dry chuckle which ruffled the hair above Jean's ear, and said, "We've things to put away. And a dinner to cook, I reckon."

Reluctantly, Jean subtracted herself from the embrace. She'd never expected him to indulge in gratuitous fits of billing and cooing, and in that she hadn't been disappointed. Doing him the courtesy of remaining silent, she went to work sorting things into the refrigerator and various cupboards, discovering a good supply of food and drink already there, including some aging spices and condiments that must have been Wallace's.

As in any good holiday home, there were plenty of dishes and cooking implements. Not that this is a holiday home, Jean thought as she shoved aside a stack of plastic foodkeepers. The odd vase or print suggested attempts at interior decorating, but the bric-a-brac was neutral, detached, and the place looked a bit bare. Wallace's personal effects had been cleared away.

Especially from the bedroom, where Jean found Alasdair's clothing folded in the dresser drawers or hanging to attention in the wardrobe, including his kilt and its appurtenances swaddled in a garment bag. The clothes were arranged on one side, just as his toiletries occupied only one shelf of three in the bathroom, leaving room for her things. She hoped Alasdair wasn't as meticulous in his personal habits as he was in his intellectual ones. It would be like living with a drill sergeant and his white gloves.

But then, he'd seen her fidgeting around her apartment, card-cataloguing her books and washing his coffee cup almost before it left his hands, and was probably worrying that she'd climb into bed beside him and whip out a clipboard with a pre-flight checklist.

If both of them found it necessary to have command over their environments, did that hint at underlying and possibly troublesome control issues . . . Good grief, Jean told herself as she started back to the front room, you're focusing so tightly on all of this you're magnifying gnats into dinosaurs. You sure weren't indulging in this sort of analysis before your wedding.

And herself murmured in reply, this time you know what you're getting into.

In the hallway, Alasdair was emptying a bag of cat litter into Dougie's box. Just as he'd estimated, it fit into one end of a misshapen closet, two feet deep and probably six feet long, that must have originally been a chamber or even a chimney in the original castle wall but now contained a water heater and cleaning supplies.

Dougie himself was stretched out on the windowsill like a miniature sphinx. Jean draped the blanket from his basket across the hollowed seat of an old easy chair, one that wasn't going to bring any second looks on *Antiques Roadshow.* "So," she said, and her voice seemed like a shout in the silence. She reminded herself that it only seemed silent because she was used to living in the city.

Alasdair left the door of the cupboard ajar. "So?"

"How long did Wallace Rutherford live here? Was all this stuff his? There aren't any personal effects lying around—no reading glasses, no toothbrushes, no monogrammed mugs."

"He moved house here when the castle was opened, so aye, I'm supposing the furnishings were his."

"Did you ever meet him?"

"I spoke to him on the phone the day before he died is all. He said he was just after having a look at the roof. He knew the place inside and out, I reckon."

"Did climbing up to the roof—what is it, five flights up?—bring on his heart attack?"

"There's four flights from the ground floor to the cap house and a ladder down to the dungeon."

"Where Wallace was found."

"Oh aye. Where he was found." There was that quick frown again, not a full-fledged scowl of suspicion, just a pucker of skepticism along the top of Alasdair's brows. Policemen were skeptical. It came with the territory. And Alasdair had probably been a skeptic before he'd ever been a cop. Still . . .

A sudden series of sharp raps made them both jump, then each look around to see if the other had noticed. No, the sound wasn't a message from the next life, but from a former one.

In one stride, Alasdair reached the door and threw it open. Ciara stood on the front porch, her curls and flounces outlined against the darkening courtyard. "Cheers, Alasdair. We're away. I'll be talking with you, Jean. Have a good night. Ferniebank's bogle is a harmless one, I'm promising you that." With a good-natured megawatt smile, she turned to go.

Instead of slamming the door, Alasdair watched Ciara stroll across the courtyard. Jean craned past his shoulder, trying not to heave an aggravated sigh in his ear.

Keith Bell stood beside the van. He said, as though continuing a conversation, "The surveyors need to outline the foundations of the medieval hospice so we won't damage them. We can leave transparent panels in the floor over the old footings." He climbed into the passenger side and slammed the door.

"No need for surveyors," replied Ciara as she wafted into the driver's seat. "I've got a friend who dowses a treat. He'll trace the foundations and the line leading to Rosslyn as well. A shame Wallace will not be here to see the final designs, but then, it's all built on his foundation, isn't it?"

The engine started. The red of the taillights gleamed. The van backed and filled and rolled sedately through the gate and out onto the road, leaving Jean's and Alasdair's cars alone. A lamp attached to the front of the shop buzzed and came on, shedding an eerie blue-tinted light across the courtyard.

"From ghoulies and ghosties and long-leggit beasties and things that go bump in the night, Mystic Scotland turns a profit, eh?" Alasdair's tone was flat, emotionless. He wasn't being sarcastic. He was simply stating a fact. "The woman would not recognize a bogle, a ghost, a spirit, or a specter if it pinched her on the bum."

"Really?" Jean shoved aside the vision of Alasdair pinching Ciara's ripe, round behind. "She has no ESP? She got all that about the ghost walking down to the chapel and feeling a chill and everything from the Ferniebank leaflet?"

"You and I, lass, have got more of a ghost allergy in our fingernail parings than she's got in her entire body."

"Well, telling stories is a respectable profession. Probably about the third-oldest one."

"The problem is, she's not recognizing that they're stories. Not a bit of it."

"Ah. I see." Not that Jean was seeing the entire vista, far from it, but at least she was peeking through the keyhole at why the Alasdair and Ciara project had ever gotten started, let alone why it had gone so sour.

Alasdair checked his watch and plucked an industrial-strength flashlight from its bracket next to the door. "It's time to be closing the place down. Fancy a private tour of the keep?" His lips were clamped in a straight line, not just his upper one but his lower one stiff as well, and his jaw was set. And yet his eye sparked again, if not with humor then at least with resignation.

Well it only took a few sparks to set tinder alight, if the tinder was susceptible to flame. "So there really is a ghost."

"Decide for yourself," Alasdair answered, and escorted her into the dusk.

CHAPTER SIX

Modern wooden steps led up to the entrance of Ferniebank Castle. Jean levered herself over the stone threshold into a small room so dark she could make out only the rectangular shapes of three more doorways, two opaque with shadow, one dimly lighted. Chill oozed from the gritty floor through her shoes and up her legs. A musty odor, like that of a wet dog, hung so thick in the air it felt like a pillow pressed to her face.

No, Ferniebank was not making a good first impression. To heck with her feminist principles—she inched closer to Alasdair's steady, sturdy body.

He was either oblivious to her discomfort or too polite to comment. "This entrance might not have been the original. Hard to say. These places are like mazes in three dimensions."

"Your average Virginia plantation looks simple by comparison," Jean managed to reply.

He leaned past her. A switch snapped and a light came on, a bare bulb dangling from the vaulted ceiling like a spider's prey from its web. "The electricity supply's a bit dodgy in these airts," Alasdair said, brandishing the flashlight the way he might once have brandished a truncheon. "The electric flex dates back to the last spasm of restoration round and about 1900, before the place was abandoned. I'd not go in here after dark without this torch."

She could say something about not going into the place after dark at all, but she was inflicting enough of her phobias on the man as it was.

"Say the word 'castle,' " Alasdair went on, "and most trippers from your part of world think of something like Floors, outwith Kelso."

"Well, yeah. Too many Hollywood set designers." Floors was a vast Georgian country house, remodeled and romanticized by the dictates of Victorian fashion into a fairytale castle, its roof bristling with turrets, pinnacles, and cupolas. Jean visualized carriages manned by white-wigged footmen decanting bejeweled guests into Floors's marble halls. Here, at Ferniebank, she imagined reivers in steel bonnets riding down out of the mist like avenging—not angels. Demons.

Setting one of his large, comforting hands in the small of her back, Alasdair guided her through the lighter doorway into a square vaulted room. Each of its three windows contained a gleaming slice of the twilight. This room, now, had a sort of derelict charm.

If her sense of direction wasn't too badly skewed, the wall that was covered on this side with paneling so old it looked moth-eaten was the one that on the other side was neatly whitewashed stone, the line of demarcation between castle and flat. The paneling was interrupted by a probably eighteenth-century Georgian door, its frame lopsided. In the narrow slices of space between door and frame Jean saw nothing but charcoal-gray stone. On the apartment side, then, the doorway had been filled in and painted over. There was something—not necessarily eerie, but definitely evocative, perhaps even symbolic—about a blocked doorway.

But then, in this part of the world home renovation didn't mean a garage conversion. It meant generation after generation remodeling for convenience, safety, and fashion. She started breathing through her nose again and discovered that she was getting used to the smell. "This is the Laigh Hall, right? The lower hall, where the flunkeys and the petitioners awaited the lord's pleasure. I bet the flat used to be the kitchens, although that fireplace in the living room is too small to have been the main one."

"Right you are. The High Hall's just this way." Alasdair waved her on toward a spiral staircase leading upwards. She placed each foot with care on the misshapen treads. If she slipped he would break her fall, but breaking him wasn't what she had in mind.

"Ferniebank's a right ordinary border keep," Alasdair said to her back, "built of whinstone rubble with sandstone dressings and an unusually tenacious lime mortar. The place might once have been related to the royal stronghold at Roxburgh."

"Which went into a decline after James III's favorite cannon blew up and took him with it," said Jean. "Sort of the story of Scotland in microcosm, hoist with its own petard."

Behind her Alasdair made a sound between a snort and a chuckle. "We've got a second-, perhaps third-rank castle here. The action was always somewhere else, 'til now, at the least."

They emerged into a large, tall room, this one with a wooden floor that made each footstep resound like a drumbeat. In the sudden light of another bare bulb, Jean saw stained plaster ceilings, windows gleaming from deep embrasures, paneling revealing the ghosts of old paintings, and the empty maw of a fireplace big enough to set up an office for Keith Bell, complete with drafting table and water cooler. The place was growing on her, she decided, and not like mold.

A rustling noise, almost like whispering, seemed to emanate from the stone itself. But her sixth sense, the ghost detector, didn't react. "Bats? Birds? Rats?"

"All of the above." Alasdair shot a glance upwards, but even he didn't have x-ray vision. His spook sensor must not be sounding an alarm, either. "The well might date to Roman times or before, the original chapel to the ninth century, perhaps. The castle's right modern, dates to the fourteenth century, built by Robert the Bruce's henchman, William Saint Clair of Rosslyn and Orkney. The William Saint Clair who built Rosslyn Chapel in the fifteenth century built a new chapel here as well, obliged to maintain his status with the neighbors."

"And the hospice? Does that go back to Robert the Bruce looking for a cure for his leprosy or syphilis or whatever it was he had?"

"So it seems. Though the most famous patient was Mary Stuart, Queen of Scots, in 1566. I cannot tell you a thing, can I?" he added, not in the acid tone he might once have used, but like a teacher indulging a bright pupil.

She'd loosened up enough that she was able to curtsey, spreading imaginary crinolines around her bent knees. A good thing she wasn't actually wearing a skirt, though. There were sneaky little drafts in this place, teasing her ankles like invisible cats. "You've done your homework, too."

"Of course." He acknowledged her curtsey with a regal inclination of his head. "Soon after Mary's son James succeeded Elizabeth, becoming king of England as well as king of Scots, Ferniebank fell into the hands of the Kerrs, who were widely considered to be ruffians."

"And who now own Floors. Miranda's Duncan owes a lot more to that branch of the family, the, er, smoothians."

That time Alasdair actually laughed. "At some point the place was handed off, voluntarily or otherwise, to the Douglases. One of them updated it in the 1680s or so. Good job he wasn't wealthy, or he'd have torn it down and built himself a mansion."

"Plus he probably wanted to hang on to some of the defensive elements. Peace hadn't exactly broken out yet in Scotland."

"Who's to say if it ever will do?" Alasdair's outstretched

flashlight guided Jean into another stairwell. "The last Douglas was a wastrel who mortgaged the place to the Rutherfords. They foreclosed in the mid-eighteen-hundreds, but only Gerald, Wallace's grandfather, ever lived here. He was an artist and poet—a ruin suited his fancies, I reckon."

"They'd have fueled mine, too, but in a different way," Jean said.

"After Gerald died in the flu epidemic just after World War One, the place fell further into disrepair, until Angus Rutherford, white knight, rode to the rescue. And there you have the potted history of Ferniebank. Mind your head, that lintel's a bit low."

It was really low if Jean had to duck. She maneuvered out of the stairwell and followed Alasdair's guiding light through the two upper stories. He paused only once to get his bearings—his inner compass was directional as well as moral, it seemed—and spoke again when they'd achieved the cap house, a tiny, gabled room perched atop the castle like the pilot house atop a steamboat. Indicating the door leading out to the roofs, he said, "Fancy a dander round the parapet?"

"I'll pass, thanks. When they were handing out the phobias —phobii?—I missed out on the fear of heights. Still, the roof of a crumbling old building isn't a good place for a moonlight stroll."

"Or a sunlight one." Alasdair led the way back down the narrow, twisting steps to the top floor, where he directed her to one of the rooms beneath the eaves. The nineteenth-century door in its sagging frame was held open by a piece of twine running between the rusted knob and a hook embedded in the wall.

This time when he clicked the switch there was no burst of harsh, yellow light. "Well, then," he muttered, and switched on the flashlight to guide them to a dormer window filled with twelve panes of dusty antique glass. Then he cast the light around the empty room. Behind the splintered paneling the stones were black, almost as sooty as the stone in the empty fireplace.

Jean felt as though a drapery settled over her, cold, heavy, and sad. Trying to evade her unease, she turned to look out at the dark countryside. Its constellations of lights were distorted by the old glass, so that they seemed distant in time as well as in space. If she made her way to one of those lights, would she find herself in, say, an elegant eighteenth-century drawing room whose inhabitants were speculating on Charles Edward Stuart's claim to the throne . . . A car passed on the road below, headlights feeling their way, the engine noise blending with the rush of wind in the trees.

With a shiver, Jean looked back into the room. Forlorn antiquity got her every time, and with its peeling paint, chipped mantelpieces, collapsing plaster, cracked paneling, and cob-webbed cupboards, Ferniebank was certainly forlorn. To say nothing of fascinating, layered with the debris of lives beyond counting.

As Michael had said, if it weren't for people like Ciara, these old buildings would fall to ruins. If she and Keith could be trusted not to throw the historical baby out with the trendy bath water, her conference and healing center would mean new life in the old vessel. Jean gritted her teeth and sent a feeler of appreciation toward the Mystic Scotland van, which would be past Kelso by now. But then, why should it even be past Stanelaw? Ciara and her minion were probably staying in the village, now that Ferniebank was at last the scene of the action.

"What are you thinking?" Alasdair stood so close beside her she could feel the prickle of his energy field. His grave profile was pale against the gloom outside the beam of light. He wasn't asking what she thought, but what she felt.

She focused, pulling her thoughts around her like a cloak.

Warily, so nothing would leap out at her, she eased a psychic toe into her sixth sense. *Heavy. Sad. Cold. Uneasy.* The chill teased the back of her neck, crushing her shoulders with the inert weight of earth or clay. *"The prime of our land are cauld in the clay,"* went the old lament, "The Flowers of the Forest."

"This is the room that's haunted," she whispered, stating, not asking.

"Oh aye."

"Quiet as the grave, still as death . . . I can't see or hear a thing."

"Nor can I. But I can feel it, a dirty great stone in the pit of my stomach. An icicle in my gut."

The gelid pressure seemed to lift, and the fine hair on the nape of her neck settled back into place. Jean swung around to face Alasdair. In the backspatter of light from the flashlight, his regular, even ordinary, features looked as though they'd been hacked out of whinstone and assembled with an unusually tenacious intellect. "Is that how it feels to you?" she asked.

"It's different for you, is it?"

"It's like a wet blanket, a literal one. And a sensation on the back of my neck like invisible cobwebs." She glanced over her shoulder, but nothing was there that hadn't been there a moment earlier. Ghosts weren't dangerous. They were only recordings of emotions long past. It was the emotions themselves that hurt.

"Reality can be slippy at best," murmured Alasdair. "But losing it entirely can be a bit . . ."

"Disconcerting," Jean finished, opting for a milder word than *horrifying.* "I was wondering back in June if the two of us together made a sort of critical mass when it comes to ghost-spotting."

"Aye, I was thinking that as well. No joy this night, though—the ghost's not walking."

"Or no sorrow, depending. Somebody has to have seen this ghost to know it's a her. Did Wallace sense her, do you think? Or did he pick up the story from the leaflet, too?"

"It was Wallace who wrote the leaflet, as well as illustrating it. Like as not he heard the tale locally. It's the sort of tale you're always hearing locally, fancies made up after the fact."

"If he did hear it locally, he didn't fancy it up any. The account in the leaflet's pretty bald—Isabel Sinclair died trying to elope. Do you know the details?"

"A longer version's in the P and S files, written in full nineteenth-century verbiage by Gerald Rutherford." Alasdair lowered the flashlight, creating a bright puddle at their feet like a spotlight on a stage, the actors waiting in the wings for their cues. "Isabel was the daughter of the Sinclair who was laird of Ferniebank during the time of Mary Stuart. A time of grand confusion and conflict, with religious issues fanning the flames and Mary in it to the starched ruff at her neck, but then, Scotland's always having times of grand confusion and conflict."

"Let me guess. Isabel loved one man, but her father wanted her to make a marriage of convenience. A guy twice her age but filthy rich." Jean gazed again around the room. No, whatever was here earlier was gone. The room still seemed sad, but it was the prosaic sorrow of dereliction.

"Got it in one. What makes this tale a bit different is that Isabel's lover—figurative or literal, who knows—was one of the monks serving at the hospice."

"So the relationship was doubly doomed."

"That it was. The laird, her father, locked her away here, in her room, 'til the wedding day. And she pined, playing sad songs on her clarsach."

"The Ferniebank Clarsach, the one dating back to Robert the Bruce?"

"Oh aye. The one Isabel herself played for Mary during her

visit to the hospice, landing herself a position as lady-in-waiting. The one stolen from the village museum. Next time," added Alasdair, "they'd jolly well better be asking P and S for assistance."

"No kidding. Have you heard anything more about that? Is there a suspect? A trail? Clues?"

"No clues. Or none for me, at the least. It's not my business." His tone had an edge that made Jean glance around sharply, but he was already going on with the story. "The monk —he must have had a name, but that's dropped out of the telling—he and Isabel worked out a plan."

"They probably found a sympathetic servant to exchange messages. Or he'd signal to her from the chapel—not as many trees then, I bet."

"I'm not seeing them waving semaphores," said Alasdair. "However they managed, they agreed that on the day of the wedding, midsummer's morn, she'd set the keep afire. Everyone would go running outside, bringing her along, and she'd make her escape with the monk."

"Except, like so many best-laid plans, this one went agley."

"Isabel used a burning-glass, a lens, to focus the sunlight onto a bit of kindling . . ."

"Well, this window faces east of north, sort of." Jean felt again the weight of time and grief oozing from her neck down her back, and she stepped closer to Alasdair's warmth, bracing herself for the denouement of the story.

He put his free arm around her. "Although using the embers of her own fire seems much more likely, considering the chance of cloud. In any event, the flames got away, blocked her escape, and she died. Suffocated by the smoke before she could burn, I'm thinking, if that's any comfort to you. And the monk died soon after of some foul disease he caught tending to the sick."

"There's not much comfort in that story, Alasdair, typical or not. True or not." Shuddering, Jean imagined the suffocating pall of smoke, the door locked, the only window high above the unforgiving ground. The shrieks, if not of Isabel herself, then her family. The monk seeing the dark smoke spread like a storm cloud before Death's pale horse . . . The stones behind the paneling were sooty not with age but with fire. She coughed, her lungs turning themselves inside out, ridding themselves of something that was no more than blistering memory.

Alasdair embraced her shoulders, holding her close, head bowed as though he was feeling that weight in his own gut. Then with a sharp intake of breath, he looked up.

Jean listened. She heard again that faint whispering or rustling, this time with what sounded like distant, light steps. "That noise, that's not a ghost."

"Not a bit of it. Someone's in the building. Come along, quick smart!"

CHAPTER SEVEN

Alasdair seized Jean's hand and pulled her out of the room. Deliberate as a hunting cat, he paced down a flight of stairs and along a corridor, then down another flight, sweeping every room, every corner, with his light.

She'd meant that the noise was caused by a draft or a branch tapping a window. But Alasdair had leaped nimbly to the conclusion that the source was human, someone who was hiding from them. He had a point. Stray pedestrian visitors would have made themselves known by now, wouldn't they?

She held onto his hand and concentrated on keeping her feet, glad he knew where he was going. All the ravaged cavities of rooms looked alike . . . Alasdair stopped dead in the middle of the High Hall, beneath the glare of the light bulb, and Jean caromed off his side.

His ears almost curled forward as he listened. She retrieved her hand and held her breath. Silence. No. Not silence. Subtle creakings from the building and the moan of the wind outside. And a not-so-subtle thunk from one of the tall windows.

Alasdair leaped forward into the largest window embrasure and pivoted, turning his flashlight toward the pitch-black slit of a cupboard cut into the thickness of the wall. For a moment Jean, at his heels, thought she was seeing two giant crows huddled in the narrow chamber. Then she realized she was looking at two teenagers, their slight bodies layered in snug black pants and shapeless jackets adorned with multiple pewter buckles, their white faces screwed into grimaces at the sudden light.

"Right," said Alasdair, slipping instantly into police mode. "Come out of there. Move."

The first one to respond was a boy, Jean decided, judging by the prominence of his Adam's apple, the thickness of his eyebrows, and the six or so dark hairs on his upper lip. The second was a girl wearing three earrings in each ear, a slash of red lipstick, and so much black eyeliner and purple shadow she resembled a punk raccoon. Both of them had hair blacker than nature intended for their gene pools, his rising in startled spikes, hers back-combed into a rat's nest and dusted with what Jean at first thought were bits of plaster but then realized were little butterfly clips.

Gallantly the boy extended his hand to help the girl step up from what must have been an earlier flooring level. She ignored him, her hands thrust deep into the oversized pockets of her jacket, even when she almost stumbled.

"How do you do," Alasdair said. "I'm Detec—Mr. Cameron. This is Miss Fairbairn. You are . . ."

The teenagers slouched carelessly, but their eyes darted right and left, up and down, as though seeking escape routes. "Derek," said the boy at last.

Jean remembered the woman leaving the pub, talking on the cell phone to her recalcitrant son. Here was the boy himself.

"Surname?" demanded Alasdair.

"Trotter," Derek said, trying to deepen his voice.

Another hobbit name, Jean thought, if coming from a goblin-child. The poor kid probably suffered for that. Teenagers could make taunts out of names a lot less tempting than "Trotter."

"Stanelaw lad, are you?" Alasdair asked.

"I am now, sod it all. Me mum and me, we've just moved house to be near her relations. Coulda had relations in London,

71

but no, they're either here or in Middles-bleedin'-brough."

Middlesbrough? No wonder Jean detected an accent originating in the rust belt of the English Midlands. "Has your father moved here, too?"

"He's done a runner, hasn't he? Walked out."

"I'm sorry to hear that," Jean said.

"Rotter like him? Past time to see the back of him, mum says."

Ouch, Jean thought. No wonder the boy's tone was so bitter. With a grim nod, Alasdair turned to the girl. "And you?"

"Zoe Brimberry," she replied, her crimson lips pouting.

"You're Noel's daughter. You work at the Reiver's Rest," said Jean. The girl no doubt cleaned up nicely and didn't leave black fingerprints on the linen and tea cups.

"A couple hours a day, aye," Zoe said.

"Well then," said Alasdair, "as a local lass you're knowing the castle's closed just now."

"We was having us a look at where that old bloke bought it —" Derek began.

Zoe jabbed him with her elbow, still without removing her hands from her jacket pockets.

"Where Mr. Wallace Rutherford died? The place has been locked up, hasn't it? No one giving tours 'til muggins here arrived." Alasdair wasn't any taller than the couple, but he had mastered the feline ploy of making himself look bigger, and the kids bowed in front of him like miscreants before the bench. After a long pause for effect, he turned toward the door. "Come along now. Hop it."

Derek and Zoe started off across the floor at a fast clip, their boots thudding, then caught themselves and slowed to a devil-may-care saunter behind Alasdair's marching pace. Smiling with something between amusement and sympathy—she'd been that young, once, and that desperate for a persona—Jean brought up the rear and even remembered to turn out the light.

But when she walked into the Laigh Hall she frowned, confused. The front door should have been on her right, not on her left. Maybe the rooms and passages had shifted around after they passed and even now waited, just outside the corners of her eyes, poised to slip sideways . . . No. Alasdair had merely led Jean and the teenagers down a second staircase.

Now Zoe and Derek were craning eagerly as Alasdair bent over a patch of stone flags in the deeply shadowed corner of the room next to the entrance. He grasped a metal ring the circumference of a dinner plate and pulled.

The wooden planks of a trap door swung upwards with a tooth-scouring screech. Alasdair laid it down gently. "There you are. The death chamber. It's closed to the public. But you know all about it, don't you now, Zoe?"

"Aye," the girl admitted, while Derek leaned precariously over to peer into the depths.

Alasdair reached out, plucked the boy back from the brink, and set him down a pace or two away. His gaze never left Zoe's face. "Mr. Rutherford showed you round the place, did he?"

"Every year the school has a day out here. Not the water park, no. This old place. And there's Wally, handing out leaflets, selling sweeties, telling the same old, same old stories. The healing well. The lairds buried in their armor. The Gray Lady, Isabel's ghost."

"Lies, the lot of them," Derek muttered.

"Lies?" repeated Jean. "Stories aren't necessarily lies. Of course, they're not necessarily the truth, either."

Rolling his eyes, the boy assumed a pose obviously meant to be nonchalant but that ended up simply sloppy.

"Mr. Rutherford," Alasdair enunciated. "Your folk knew him, didn't they, Zoe?"

The black fabric covering Zoe's pockets writhed. She must

be clenching and unclenching her hands. "He'd come drinking at the pub. And my granny and my mum, they'd bring him hot meals and stay for a blether, with him living on his own and all."

"He wasn't so much on his own. Your grandparents, the Elliots, live just across the road."

"What of it? My grandad, he said Wally was a nutter and spying on him. Said he expected Granny to look after him as well as doing her own work. And then he said he killed her."

Derek had apparently heard all this before—he didn't react. Jean, though, repeated, "Killed her?"

"Your grandfather said Wallace killed your granny?" Alasdair established. "What happened?"

"They found her lying in the road, dead, not three weeks since."

"Was she hit by a car?"

"Not a mark on her. Heart gave out. My grandad's saying she was always rushing to and fro, dancing attendance on Wally. So down she went, all alone, with no one to help her, and she died."

Alasdair glanced at Jean, who could only cock her eyebrows back at him. No, Ferniebank didn't seem to be a particularly healthy place for the elderly. *These things come in threes.* "That's stretching it a bit, then," he told Zoe, "to be saying Wallace killed her."

The girl shrugged. Derek gazed raptly at his boots.

"What's this about Wallace spying?" Alasdair prodded.

"He kept a telescope atop the tower. Star-gazing and train-spotting and naff goings-on, such like."

"Astronomy has to be a frustrating hobby in this climate," commented Jean.

"Was Wallace spying, then?" Alasdair asked.

Zoe shrugged again. "Might have been, though there's nothing worth spying on in a dump such as Stanelaw, let alone Ferniebank Farm."

"The arsehole of creation," added Derek.

"It's dead boring, but it's all we've got, save the pub," Zoe told him tartly.

"No accounting for tastes." Jean strolled over to the trap door and looked down. She saw nothing but a modern metal ladder, its upper rails bolted to the sides of the hole, plunging into subterranean darkness. Again she coughed. But this time the tickle in her chest was quite literal. The musty miasma was emanating from the dungeon. Or, more properly, from the pit prison. A luckless offender—and offense was easy, in the Middle Ages—would be dumped into the underground chamber and left to reflect on his sins and/or rot while the business of daily life went on above him. He or she would have been able to hear voices and music, and smell the food cooking in the kitchen. Now there was highly refined torture.

Alasdair's hand holding the flashlight appeared in Jean's peripheral vision. "Thanks." She took the heavy metal cylinder and flicked the switch.

The tiny chamber below her leaped into definition. She saw no ineradicable bloodstain, like that supposedly marking a sixteenth-century murder in Mary Stuart's apartments in Holyrood Palace. No, the dungeon floor consisted of prosaic gray dirt, broken by humps of living rock and imprinted with the ribbed bootprints of the team that had rescued not Wallace, but his body. The walls were the foundations of the keep, stones of all shapes and subtle gradations of gray piled one upon the other. Two rough steps led up to the rim of a small pit within the larger one—the prisoner's privy. In the opposite corner something glinted in the light, a glass disk, it looked like, and beside that winked an almost microscopic gold dot. Neither had been there long enough to gather much dust.

From her height, Jean couldn't estimate size. Was she seeing the lens and nosepiece from a pair of old-fashioned round eyeglasses? Or was the glass the pane protecting the bulb of a flashlight? Although, manifestly, not the flashlight she was holding, which was a shiny new one. As for the gold, small as a punctuation mark, well, it was probably part of a candy wrapper. She sure wasn't going to climb down and investigate.

Imagining an electric torch dropping from Wallace Rutherford's ill, shaking hand, she stepped back from the edge and switched off the light. Alasdair didn't need any more lamps for his third-degree.

He was still gazing, po-faced on purpose, at Zoe. "Why were you sneaking about the place in the dark? It's been open all day. I'd have let you in without paying."

Through his guise of utter boredom, Derek insisted, "We was after seeing where the old bloke died is all. No harm in that."

"Just having ourselves a giggle." Zoe's body language conveyed nervousness, not boredom.

Alasdair pounced. "Turn out your pockets, Zoe."

Her hands stopped moving beneath the fabric. She stared. Derek's not terribly square jaw dropped. "How did you know . . . ?"

"Derek," Zoe hissed, a remarkable feat when his name had no sibilants in it. She yanked her hands from her jacket pockets and displayed an MP3 player, a penlight, some change, and a lipstick.

"And?" Alasdair asked, extending his hand.

Jerkily, resentfully, she pulled out what might have been a jumbo-sized flint flake and dropped it into Alasdair's outstretched palm.

Jean stretched her neck to better see the piece of weathered stone roughly the size of a paperback book, carved with the letters "IC" and "J." Years of freezing and heating could have caused the flake to slough off of a larger piece. Or it could have been hacked off. "Where did you find this?" she asked.

"Upstairs. On a windowsill. On show, like." Jean could see something of Zoe's father in the curves of her face, but her gaze through the thorns of her eyelashes, first at Jean, then back to Alasdair, held nothing of Noel's affability.

"Give that answer another go," said Alasdair, his voice whetted and drawn a handsbreadth from its scabbard. "Where did you find this?"

In other words, Jean told herself, that stone had not been part of any windowsill displays when Alasdair did his tour of inspection this afternoon.

Zoe's crimson lower lip extended even further, making a shelf. "In Isabel's room. The Gray Lady's chamber. Lying on the floor. Derek trod on it."

"Eh? What?" blurted Derek.

Zoe, obviously the brains of the operation, elbowed him again.

"And just when did you find it?" Alasdair asked.

A silence so long Jean could have counted each of the quartet of breaths, Alasdair's the slowest, Zoe's the fastest. Then Zoe said with a sigh, "Ten days since. The day Wally died."

"Were you here with a school group that day?"

"No. I was here on my own."

"You was with me," Derek snorted.

Zoe's dagger-like glance indicated that with him around, she might just as well be alone.

"And now you're bringing the stone back," Alasdair said.

"It's bad luck, isn't it?" exclaimed Zoe. "The oven at the pub packed up, and my mum sliced open her hand working for Flinty Minty, and my sister Shan's failed her exams. And Old Wally, Soor Ploom Logan found him dead there, in the dungeon. The exact same day."

"I see." Alasdair's tone indicated that he did indeed see

something, if not the aptness of Zoe referring to Constable Logan as a sour plum or Minty Rutherford as flinty.

"None of that happened because you took the stone," Jean told the girl. "It was right to bring it back, but not because it's bad luck."

Zoe didn't react. Neither did Alasdair. Since at the moment he was the brains of their operation, Jean said nothing more.

Derek abandoned nonchalance for impatient little jiggles. He probably felt he should intervene to protect the girl, but didn't dare. Status emergency in progress. As soon as Alasdair let them go, Derek would find someone younger or smaller to start a fight with, maybe even Zoe herself.

"What made you decide that this was bad luck, then?" asked Alasdair.

Again the girl looked around for an escape, but saw none. "It was the Macquarrie woman, wasn't it? Poncing in here, everyone bowing and scraping like she was the Queen herself, and her going on about ghosts and fairies and secret codes. She's not half loony."

Alasdair did not disagree.

"She says it's a bit of gravestone, it should be put back where it came from."

"In the castle? Not in the chapel?" Alasdair, by now encased in his full professional suit of armor, stared down at the miscreant and her guilty-by-association confederate. If it were anyone else, Jean thought, she'd swear he was enjoying making them squirm.

"I found it in the castle," Zoe stated.

"And you nicked it the day P.C. Logan found Mr. Rutherford dead? What time, exactly?"

"How should I know that? Before tea-time." By now Zoe had shrunk so far down into her jacket she looked like a turtle.

Tea-time being a flexible concept, Jean assumed that the

stone had left the building mid- to late afternoon. But Wallace wasn't found until after closing time, seven-thirty this time of year.

"Were there many visitors that day?" Alasdair asked.

"I wasn't keeping count, was I? You'd best be checking your own records for that."

Touché, Jean thought.

Alasdair registered no amusement. "Did you see anyone else here?"

"A bus tour. The Mystic Scotland woman, Macquarrie. She was hanging about the chapel whilst Wally lectured her group here."

"Yeh," added Derek. "And one gent was right upset with Wally, ticking him off good and proper, and Wally giving as good as he got."

Zoe rolled her eyes. "They were just having a bit of a chin-wag, is all."

"I know an argy-bargy when I hear one," Derek retorted. "Heard enough of them when we was living with my dad, didn't I?"

"You heard a man arguing with Wallace," established Alasdair.

"Yeh," said Derek. "After the day trippers moved on."

"No," Zoe said at the same time, loudly.

"Do you know who it was? Was it Roddy?"

Derek looked even blanker. Zoe's red lips thinned. "It was never my grandad, no."

Upstairs something tapped and then stopped. Now *that* was a branch against a window, Jean told herself. Wasn't it?

Alasdair waited, but both the ashen faces in front of him had closed down, locked up, and put out Do Not Disturb signs. At last he drew the hearing to a close, handing Zoe back her things but keeping the bit of carved stone. "Very well, then. Away with you, the pair of you. And mind your manners in the future." He was smart enough not to add, "And don't let me catch you here again." That would have been throwing down the gauntlet.

Liberated, the kids jogged briskly across the Laigh Hall and out the entrance into the cool, fresh air. Alasdair and Jean less herded than followed them, and stood on the steps watching as they crunched off across the courtyard. Their shadows made amorphous blobs in the light of the yard lamp and an oval moon, rising luridly in the east.

It was dangerous for them to walk along the narrow road in such dark clothes, Jean thought. "Do you need a ride back into Stanelaw, Zoe? Derek?"

Zoe said, "No, I'm stopping with my grandad across the road."

"We've got a house just up the way. Nice and quiet, Mum says. Dead dull." Derek's left hand fluttered toward the south, past Ferniebank's entrance gate.

After a few more steps, Zoe called back, incongruously, "Ta, madam." And the two figures diminished and disappeared out the gate and into the night.

CHAPTER EIGHT

A dog started barking, Roddy's gruff voice bellowed, and a door slammed. Jean hoped Derek wasn't going on his way with Jackie or Hector clamped onto his coattail.

She looked around to see Alasdair standing so still and silent frost might just as well have gathered on his jaw and cheekbones. "Well?" she asked. "What do you think about Zoe's story?"

"What were you after doing there?" he demanded, so unexpectedly she flinched. "Playing good cop to my bad cop, were you?"

"What? You're not a bad cop." *Oh,* she thought. *Damn.* "Did you think I was butting in?"

"If I did do, it'd be too late to say so now."

"What it's too late for is another *who's in charge here* territorial skirmish. There's no territory to skirmish over."

"No, there's not. Just the property to protect." His tone was cool and distant as a snow-tipped mountain on the edge of sight, but a flash in his eyes hinted at possible avalanches, the sort that could be triggered by a loud noise. Or the wrong noise.

Jean opened her mouth for a snappy retort, but found she had nothing. She reminded herself that she was inside his battlements now. Sapping his foundations would bring down her castle, too. Just the property to protect. Just a relationship to survive.

Jean waited until she sensed the set of his shoulders slowly loosening, armor thinning, ice melting. Still, his earlier pucker of skepticism had pleated into outright suspicion—at Zoe and her inscribed rock, she hoped, not at her. She tried, "I didn't have any ulterior motives for wading in. If you can call a couple of sentences wading in. You know what they say, though, about catching more flies with honey than with vinegar."

"Oh aye. And there's a fly that needs catching. Young Miss Brimberry knows more than she's letting on, I reckon."

"About Wallace? You'd be better off questioning Derek. He's the soft underbelly . . . I know, I know, there's no case, there's no mandate to question either of them." She waited, but the figure beside her said nothing. "What is it about Wallace's death that's got your antennae twitching, anyway?"

"What had them twitching before Zoe's testimony, not to mention her exhibit?" He held up the carved stone. "I phoned Wallace the day before he died. He was going on about being chuffed with the sale and the renovations, how it was time for him to retire. Again. The stairs kept him fit, with his dicky heart and all, but his knees were too dodgy for the ladder to the pit prison. All he'd ever do was shine the light of the torch about. The rubbish that collected there, he'd have someone from the town clear it away."

Jean felt her own antennae sitting up and taking notice. "But Logan found him in the dungeon. Did he fall in? Or was he pushed?"

"There was not a mark on his body. The postmortem found that his heart gave out."

"Heart gave out. Not a mark on his body. Same with Helen Elliot. There's an echo here, and not a pleasant one."

"That there is."

"Maybe Wallace had some compelling reason to get himself down into the pit prison, and it was too much for him. Although if he was used to doing the stairs, that doesn't seem likely." Jean looked accusingly at the blank, even secretive face of the castle.

"Did you see what looked like the glass from his flashlight down there, as though he dropped it?"

"I'll be fetching that up. No reason, I suppose, but still . . ." Alasdair stopped.

"But still?"

"The answerphone on the desk. I was setting it up with my own particulars, and found the last part of a conversation saved. I'm thinking Wallace set the machine to record, to preserve the evidence."

Jean's antennae became positively stiff with interest. "Evidence?"

"A man's hushed voice telling him that meddling with things that didn't concern him might be dangerous. To remember he was an old man, and on his own. To remember what happened to Helen. Wallace replied with a version of 'do your worst' and the other party rang off."

"Whew. I don't blame you for being suspicious. Was that a friendly warning? A hostile threat? Or a bad joke? What 'things' were they talking about? And what about Helen, anyway? Just that she died alone, if not mysteriously?" Jean shook her head. "If Wallace was anything like us, a call like that would be the equivalent of waving a red flag in front of a bull."

"Oh aye," Alasdair agreed. "According to the date and time stamp—and that's set accurately—the recording was made the morning of the day he died. Of natural causes."

"There are ways of killing people that don't leave a mark, or much of one, anyway, but if the medical examiner thinks everything is routine, he's not going to look for those, is he?"

"Got it in one."

"Or are we just sensitized to murder cases, and building one, maybe two, out of nothing here? I mean, we'd have to have a killer with a motive, and means, and opportunity."

"Motive, that's the sticking point," Alasdair replied, without gagging on her repeated "we." He tilted his head to look up at the battlements, blunted teeth against the pale sky.

Jean followed his gaze. That high window, that would be Isabel's. "So Zoe sneaked that inscription out past Wallace the day he died. I'd have second thoughts about keeping it, too, after that. What I wonder is why she took it to begin with."

"A good question. We've got too many good questions."

"So what else is new?" She took the bit of stone from Alasdair's hand and held it up to the collision of light and shadow. At first it seemed warm from his clasp, then chilled. She thought of Ciara Macquarrie strolling around as though— well, she did own the place, from leaky roof to shattered inscriptions. Was she independently wealthy? The one thing Alasdair had ever said about her was that he was not paying her alimony, not that any alimony a policeman could provide would buy more than a doll's house.

"Ciara's right," Jean said. "This is a piece from a gravestone. *Hic jacet* is Latin for 'here lies,' as in 'here is buried,' not 'here someone isn't telling the truth.' *Hic jacet* someone. Not Wallace."

That elicited a fissure of a smile. "It's from Isabel's grave. A second bit of that inscription was found in Wallace's pocket, the *ac*, fittingly enough."

"In his pocket?"

Alasdair made a tight gesture that from anyone else would have been a flail of frustration. "Gary Delaney at Lothian and Borders Police sent me the report of the inquest, it being a matter of public record and all. The ruling was that Wallace was elderly, he had a heart condition, he died. Slam the file. Close the case. I'm guessing the inquest on Helen Elliot ruled the same."

"But the answering machine tape is evidence that Wallace's case shouldn't be closed. And there's a connection between the two deaths, sort of."

"I left a message on Delaney's voice mail soon as I found the recording, but he didn't ring me back. Why should he have done?"

That was a rhetorical question, but Jean answered anyway. "Because it's not your case. Any more than the theft of the clarsach is your case."

"And because I'm a civilian now."

A glimmer of light rose above Jean's eastern horizon. That was it. Despite protesting he had no regrets, Alasdair was feeling left out, unwanted. His status emergency was a lot more complex than Derek's. So was his reaction. "Alasdair, you didn't quit your job for me. You didn't even quit it because of me, not really. I'm just the catalyst."

He looked at her incredulously, his eyes glinting doubly blue and doubly chill in the lamplight. "Eh? What are you on about?"

He thought she'd changed the subject, and for once couldn't keep up with her. Or refused to try. No need to pick at scabs, after all. Jean called a truce by gesturing toward the castle. "You were going to lock up, weren't you? It's past dinner time, and when I get hungry I get irritable."

Despite that opening, all he said was, "Aye. Time to be locking the doors," and marched back up the steps. The harsh yellow light framed by the arched entrance winked out, leaving only the queasy blue-tinted light caught by the ancient walls, and a wash of silver on the sky above—clouds were moving in, seeing off the last rosy gleam of sunset and veiling the stars and moon. The delectable odor of peat smoke was coming from the farm across the road. Jean imagined Roddy offering Zoe tea and bannocks, and she rejecting them for a Coke and a bag of crisps.

With a reverberating thud the thick, wooden, iron-ribbed door slammed shut. A jingle, like ice cubes in a bucket, must be

Alasdair wielding a ring of keys.

Skeleton keys? Jean imagined particles of bone, chalky fingertips, turned in the keyholes of walled-up doors. The facade of the castle looked even darker and more dour, with only the two dim squares of light in the lower corner, the front windows of the flat, to indicate that the place was not a natural cliff face. She thought of all the shadowed rooms behind those thick walls, and wondered to what sort of step the floorboards creaked.

Walking rather than marching, Alasdair locked the door of the shop, too, then returned to her side.

"The kids were going to find their way up and down those staircases with no more than a penlight?" Jean asked. "And let themselves be locked in?"

"They were playing at goths and vampires, I reckon, the way Ciara plays at auras and ley lines. Might explain the fossilized condom I cleared away from an upper room."

"Gross! That's hardly the sort of place I'd choose for a romantic encounter." She could sense Alasdair's wry gaze on the side of her face. "You know what I mean. Cold stones, old wooden floors, splinters, whatever."

"I'm not thinking romance had anything to do with it."

"Please tell me it wasn't those kids. They're so young. Sixteen, do you think? I was a lot younger than that when I was sixteen."

"As was I."

She could imagine all sorts of creepy-crawlies, but not Alasdair as a child. "Were they eavesdropping on us? I'm not even sure what I said."

"Nothing incriminating," he returned. He didn't go so far as to stretch, but his carapace had obviously cracked a bit. A good thing he didn't realize what the thickness of that shell revealed about the vulnerable creature inside.

Jean said, "I guess the kids could have let themselves down from a window."

"After they replaced the inscribed stone. Assuming Zoe was not lying about bringing it back. I should have had Derek turn his pockets out as well."

"What does he have in his pockets, precious?" Jean murmured, evoking Tolkien to drive back the dark.

Alasdair emitted a dusty chuckle. From the heights of the castle came not the harsh calls of crows but the cooing of pigeons, liquid warbles blending with the sough of the wind.

Jean decided to take the switch in ornithological commentary as a good omen. "You can show me the chapel tomorrow. Now it's time to get, er, cooking."

He rose to the bait with a thin smile. "The gate needs closing. Then I'll cook our dinner."

"No need, I've actually worked out some recipes."

Headlights raked the side of the keep like flares bursting over a battlefield. A car turned in through the gateway, a tall boxy car that was probably a Range Rover. Where, Jean asked herself, had she just seen a Range Rover? And as its lights silhouetted her and Alasdair like soon-to-be highway hamburger, she remembered. In the driveway at Glebe House.

CHAPTER NINE

In the moment before the car stopped, Jean envisioned their faces screwed into grimaces at the sudden light, caught in the act. Then the headlights went out and she blinked.

When she could see again, she saw Minty Rutherford stepping out onto the gravel, graceful as a mink in the dim illumination of the car's dome lamp. Now her tweed jacket was draped over her shoulders, revealing a string of pearls looped down the front of her sweater. She pushed the door to, extinguishing the light, and turned toward Jean and Alasdair with her hand extended. "Good evening, Mr. Cameron, Miss Fairbairn. Araminta Rutherford. Minty, to be as casual as most folk feel they have a right to be these days. Welcome to Stanelaw."

"Thank you," said Alasdair, and shook her hand.

Jean always found Miranda's designer clothes to be entertaining. Minty's impeccable tailoring, though, made her feel like a peasant clinging to the back of the turnip truck. Even the woman's neutral shades—clothing, skin, hair, all in tints of brown and cream—held their own in the unflattering fluorescent glow of the yard light, while Jean knew her own complexion was glowing like fungus.

Fashion inadequacy was her problem, not Minty's. "Good to be here," Jean said, baring her teeth in what she hoped was a pleasant smile. Changing the stone flake to her left hand, she grasped the paragon's smooth, dry fingers, which only perfunctorily returned her grasp and then wafted away.

"What have you got there?" Minty asked.

"A bit of inscribed rock," answered Jean.

"We found it in the castle just a few moments ago," Alasdair added, his words signaling Jean not to spill the entire story.

Minty reached for the stone. "Could it be part of the inscription on Isabel Sinclair's grave? That's been vandalized repeatedly over the years."

Having no rational excuse not to, Jean handed over the stone.

"The style of the letters is sixteenth century," said Minty, holding the artifact at pearl level.

"You're well informed," Alasdair told her.

"Thank you. My husband, Angus, and I are antiquarians. He's responsible for setting up the town museum, as you probably already know, Mr. Cameron."

Whether he knew that or not, Alasdair nodded sagely.

"Angus was hoping the excavations some years ago would turn up the missing bit of the inscription, a carving of the clarsach, but, sadly, no." Minty handed the stone back.

Jean glanced suspiciously at it, but if Minty had anything up her sleeve, it was more likely to be an extra ace or two than a counterfeit shard of gravestone. She stuffed the stone flake into the pocket of her jacket, where its weight pulled her off-balance. "You've seen pictures of the original inscription?"

"Yes, there are drawings in the museum made by Angus's great-grandfather Gerald. Along with, I'm sorry to say, a copy of Gerald's epic poem on the subject of Isabel and Ferniebank, written in the style of James Hogg's 'The Queen's Wake.' " Minty slipped her jacket off her shoulders and put it on. The scent of what had to be Chanel No. 5 tickled Jean's nostrils and was gone. "Your colleague Miss Capaldi tells me you'll be joining us for luncheon tomorrow."

"Lunch?" Jean knew that small black holes infested her brain, but she didn't think the time of the invitation had fallen into one.

"Then Miss Capaldi hasn't informed you yet. I've taken the liberty of planning a small luncheon instead of tea, hoping you and the other guests will be kind enough to taste some of my new creations that are bringing traditional recipes into the present day."

"Oh. No problem." Jean glanced at Alasdair, who shrugged slightly in response. The castle opened at noon, but unless a three-ring circus arrived on the doorstep, he could handle it alone.

"Dr. Campbell-Reid will be coming as well."

Rebecca and Michael were both PhDs of long-enough standing that neither of them bothered answering to the honorific any more, but Jean assumed that in the ladies-luncheon context, Minty meant Rebecca. "I'm looking forward to, er, hearing about the new development in the area."

"All of which has brought negative developments as well, I'm afraid." Minty's deprecating smile was just a bit fixed, but her voice, low and mellow as a cello, didn't waver. Neither did her dark eyes beneath their heavy lids.

Alasdair said, "We're very sorry to hear of Mr. Wallace Rutherford's death."

"And the theft of the Ferniebank Clarsach," added Jean.

"These unfortunate happenstances do seem to come in waves."

Happenstance? Jean asked herself. *Or even coincidence?*

Alasdair leaped boldly onto another item on the Stanelaw blotter, one that might imply criminal action. "Have you had any news of your husband?"

"He'll be returning straightaway," Minty replied, her lashes dropping over those cavernous eyes.

Jean darted a glance toward Alasdair, meeting his glance at

her in mid-air. Did that mean Minty had heard from Angus? If not, why was she giving an estimated time of reappearance? There might be something to Miranda's rumor about the marriage being in trouble.

After a long pause, Jean did the right thing and said, "Please come in." She didn't actually gesture toward the flat—Minty might see her crossed fingers.

"Thank you, no, I shan't intrude upon your evening. I wanted merely to bring you a light supper." Opening the back of the Rover, Minty produced a wicker picnic hamper the size of an ottoman. She handed off the basket like Queen Victoria sitting down, not bothering to look behind her for a receiver.

Jean and Alasdair both lunged. Jean came up with the handles of the basket. It was heavier than she'd expected, and she almost fumbled it. From inside came the clatter of crockery, hopefully still intact.

"Very kind of you." Alasdair relieved Jean of her burden and set it down at his feet.

"Thanks," Jean added, to him as much as to Minty. She shook out her right arm, wondering whether it was now an inch longer.

Minty shut the back of the car and looked around. "It's getting on for nine o'clock, isn't it? I'd expected the gates to be closed by now."

"We were delayed," Alasdair told her, and when she waited for further explanation, went on, "Two local youths hadn't yet left the premises."

"Zoe Brimberry, I expect. Only yesterday she was wearing hair ribbons and pinafores, and now she looks to be the worst sort of guttersnipe. No respect for her elders at all, and telling the most outlandish tales. And Derek Trotter—he's a bad influence on her. No surprise there, his mother Valerie, well, we all wished her and her child well when she left the area. Pity that she saw fit to return after all these years. As the twig is bent,

91

I'm afraid, as the twig is bent."

Jean thought of Valerie Trotter attempting twig-bending by cell phone outside the pub, and decided that for all her demands, little Linda Campbell-Reid was a parenting pushover.

"Zoe's sister Shannon, now, is less intent on playing the toerag, but still . . . Well, poor Noel and Polly, they're doing their best."

Minty was fishing for the identity of the youths, wasn't she? Alasdair parried. "Good job the gate wasn't closed or you'd not have gotten in."

"I've got a key."

Jean's gaze moved from Minty's serene face to Alasdair's lack of expression. *Wait for it . . .*

"That's right good to hear," he said. "Protect and Survive's after accounting for all the keys. I'll be collecting them in good time to turn over to Ms. Macquarrie."

Minty's peach-colored lips curved up at the ends. "Ciara Macquarrie's your former wife, I believe, Mr. Cameron?"

"Aye, that she is."

Minty's aloof gaze turned toward Jean. "Changing partners is quite the thing these days. Even without benefit of matrimony."

"You've been married for a long time?" Jean tried her own parry.

"Thirty years last spring."

"Do you and Ang—er, Mr. Rutherford have children?"

"We have not been so fortunate, no."

Jean would have guessed that from Minty's criticism of the Brimberrys and Trotters. "It's very kind of you to take an interest in Zoe, then."

"Her grandmother Helen was my assistant for many years. After she unfortunately became ill, Zoe's mother Polly did her best to take her place. And her grandfather Roddy"—Minty gestured toward the farm—"he provides milk, butter, and cream to the community, although it's not always of the quality that I require."

"I'm hearing that Helen Elliot died recently," said Alasdair.

"Such a sad event, but then, the traditional Scottish diet contributes to coronary disease."

"Roddy must have been gutted at losing Wallace as well, so soon after."

"That's hard to say. Roddy and Wallace went on at each other like stags in rut. At their ages! Helen always said they were harmless enough, but then Helen was often the issue. Well, it's all in the past now."

"Wallace must have been very fit for his age," Alasdair persisted.

"Once he was spry as a mountain goat. But, sadly, our Wallace's eighty years were catching him up. Another unfortunate example of our national epidemic of heart disease."

"He'd worked for P and S since the castle was opened up."

"It was very good of Protect and Survive to keep him on here, even though he should have been retired some years ago. But he did so enjoy his job. That was one reason we opened Ferniebank to visitors, to give him useful work after the death of his wife and his retirement as headmaster of Kelso High School. The site was becoming a bit of a danger as well, to say nothing of an eyesore. Much better to tidy it up and allow it generate income for the community."

Jean compressed her lips. Alasdair, having guided the conversation to where he wanted it, said nothing. The old policeman's trick, the old reporter's trick, letting the subject ramble on. Assuming so collected an individual as Minty would let herself ramble.

She at least strolled on a few more paces. "Our Wallace's mind was failing, too, had been for quite a while, sadly, but he tried to keep up with his interests. One moment he'd be on the roof with his telescope, the next he'd be poking about in the pit prison—he feared there would be no further excavation with the new owner. Tragic, that he should go down at last, like an ancient oak."

Where he had gone down was into the pit prison. Jean didn't look at Alasdair. She could sense him not looking at her.

"Well then. I must be off. Tomorrow at noon, Miss Fairbairn. And Mr. Cameron, if there's anything I can do to assist Protect and Survive . . ."

"I'll not hesitate to ask," Alasdair finished for her.

Minty had already opened the door of the car and levitated into the seat. "Have a good night, then." The engine roared, and the headlights flashed—this time Jean shielded her eyes—and the car maneuvered out the gateway and disappeared.

So far, Ferniebank Castle hadn't turned out to be nearly as private as they had anticipated, had it? "Last year this time," she said ruefully, "you probably could have set up a table on the main road and eaten a four-course dinner without anyone driving by."

"Ciara's caused some changes here," was all Alasdair said, and started for the gate.

Jean told herself that maybe Ciara was just taking advantage of changes that were already under way—the heritage industry, New Age trends, the aging of the local population. She crossed her arms over her chest, warding off the increasing chill, and retreated to the front steps of the flat.

With a mighty heave and a squeal of hinges Alasdair swung the gate shut. Again the rattle of keys, and he came back across the courtyard, scooping up the hamper on the way. The noisy gravel, Jean realized, made a dandy early-warning system. She opened the door and he followed her inside.

For a moment she stood with her hand on the doorknob, disoriented. This ordinary, even pedestrian, room occupied a parallel universe from the hollow chambers next door. It was a warm nest of sanity at its most dull and most comforting, like a tuna casserole. And here she and Alasdair were alone at last, with everything that implied.

CHAPTER TEN

Peeling off her jacket, Jean pried the inscribed stone from her pocket and set it on an unoccupied lace doily atop the bookshelf. Alasdair snapped the flashlight back into its holder, shot a hard look at the answering machine on the desk, and thumped the basket down on the kitchen counter.

"Don't you trust Minty," Jean asked, "or have you played your cards close to your chest for so long you're still doing it?"

Alasdair opened the lid of the basket. "I'm no gambler, Jean."

"Sure you are. You simply calculate the odds to the last decimal point. Or maybe you're a scientist, suggesting a hypothesis and then testing for reproducible results."

"I've got no hypothesis now. Not as yet. Still—you heard, did you, what Minty said about Wallace digging in the pit prison?"

"Maybe that was before his knees gave out. He was here for a long time."

"Or maybe, like Zoe, Minty knows more than she's telling."

"Does she know Wallace had a chunk of that inscription in his pocket when he was found?"

"As next of kin, she and Angus claimed all his belongings," Alasdair said. "I reckon it was them cleared this place of personal items."

"Understandably leaving the tape in the answering machine. You took it out, right?"

"Oh aye, it's tucked well away in a sock. But then, odds are whoever phoned has no idea Wallace was recording them."

"Was it Roddy who called? Maybe he was trying to get Wallace to leave the neighborhood."

"I'm thinking it was Roddy arguing with Wallace the day he died, never mind Zoe."

"She sure clammed up once she realized she might have said too much." Jean looked again at the inert bit of stone. Then her eye moved upwards to a print of the nineteenth-century painting of the murder of Mary Stuart's secretary Riccio at Holyrood, stabbed repeatedly by disaffected nobles including a Kerr and a Douglas—and perhaps witnessed by Isabel Sinclair. The characters were lavishly costumed and the scene expansively acted to suit romantic-era tastes, not that it hadn't been genuine high drama to begin with. No wonder she'd thought of just that event as she looked down into the dungeon. "Minty says Zoe tells tales, but then, so do I, bimonthly in *Great Scot.*"

"There are stories, and then there are lies."

Jean conceded his point with a shrug. "And there's missing Angus."

"We've got no concrete evidence that anything here's wrong, save the clarsach pinched from the museum and an answerphone message that might mean nothing at all. Like as not I'm . . ."

"Tilting at windmills? Straining at a gnat? Borrowing trouble? Those are my specialties."

"Oh aye, those and bouncing off walls and jumping to conclusions. You're having a bad influence on me, lass." Focusing on the interior of the hamper, Alasdair started producing not rabbits but a glittering array of cutlery and dishes, each item wrapped in tissue paper.

"Yeah, right." Jean inspected the bookcase, noting that the bottom shelf was bare except for a garish "Glasgow's Miles Better" souvenir ashtray. The middle two shelves held astronomy, botany, geology, and geography texts as well as history and archaeology books and lots of thin bright-colored paperbacks of legends and ghost stories. The Ancient Monuments Commission logo, a lion and crown, was printed on the plainly bound spine of the tallest book on the shelf. She pulled it out. With it came a folded piece of drawing paper.

On the book's cover was printed: *Ferniebank Castle and St. Mary's Chapel. Excavation and Renovation Report.* Cool! She set that on the coffee table for later, then opened the paper to reveal a sketch of archaeologists digging next to the chapel, in the same rough-and-ready style as the drawings in the leaflet. Still, each face was clearly defined with only a few pencil strokes, the youthful diggers, male and female, and an older man crouched beside the excavation holding what looked like a small chest. This drawing had a tiny, tidy signature: *W.B. Rutherford.* The man had been a one-man band, it seemed. She laid the sketch on top of the bookcase, next to the decorative doily.

The door to the hall closet opened and Dougie emerged, whiskers as erect as his tail. He performed a silky swirl around Jean's ankles, then padded purposefully into the kitchen and sat down beside his bowls, one filled with water, one still empty. "Yes," Jean told him, "it's dinnertime."

"Long past dinnertime," added Alasdair, perhaps with double meaning aforethought.

Jean found the box of kitty kibble, measured brown lumps redolent of rancid fish into Dougie's dish, and left him scrunching away contentedly. The only appetite he had to satisfy tonight was one for food. Whether that made him lucky or otherwise was not a good question, period.

Alasdair was twisting two tall candles into their holders. His appetites were as complex as the rest of his personality, but she'd never know it by looking at him. Even though his face was no longer stony or icy, neither was it an open book. He was far too good at expressionlessness—something Ciara had taken pains to point out. Had he been applying intellectual rigor to dangerous emotional situations all his life? Which came first, his rational chicken or his emotional egg?

She really needed another hobby than psychoanalyzing Alasdair. Counting the number of angels that could dance on the head of a pin, maybe.

He tapped a champagne flute against a translucent plate, evoking a chime. "Mrs. Rutherford does nothing by halves. If that's not sterling silver, bone china, and crystal, I'll eat the lot."

"No need for that. Wow." Jean pulled a chilled bottle of champagne, wrapped in its own little fitted quilt, out of the seemingly bottomless basket.

"Moses' entire family has staterooms in there," Alasdair said, and met her laugh with a smile.

He had an appealing smile, if stiff from lack of use. He was making a calculated effort to lighten the proceedings, wasn't he, maybe even to apologize for his spasm of bad temper. *Hey,* she beamed at him, *that's all right, I needed to know there was a burr beneath your saddle.* Speaking of which . . . "So what's the latest in the Northern Constabulary soap opera? Did Sergeant Sawyer, a.k.a. the Troll of Inverness, finally get his just desserts?"

"Depends on how you're defining justice. The Chief Constable suggested he work a bit harder at being a team player, so Sawyer asked for a transfer and now's with the Strathclyde Police, a thorn in some other D.C.I's hide."

"And D.C. Gunn?"

"He's swotting for the exams for promotion to sergeant. A bit prematurely, I reckon, but he'll do well in the long run."

"He's got your example before him."

Alasdair shook his head, but said nothing else.

Okay, Jean told herself, they'd covered all the important topics except one, and this was emphatically the wrong time to open the Pandora's box of Ciara. She pulled a thick beige envelope from beneath the lid of the basket.

The stationery was the same as her invitation to Minty's culinary function—oh, it wasn't just that the handwriting was idiosyncratic, Jean was holding the card upside down. She flipped it over and read: " 'Quail's eggs in a Parma ham nest. Salmon in sorrel beurre blanc with roasted vegetable couscous. Gooseberry and elderflower fool with shortbread biscuit.' I hope the fool is a dish, not an editorial comment."

"It's mushy fruit with cream, I'm thinking." Alasdair lit the candles—Minty had even included a book of matches—while Jean sorted the aromatic contents of several insulated plastic containers onto the dishes. Similar containers were stacked in the cupboard, weren't they? Wallace had probably been happy to play beta tester for Minty's preparations, conveyed to his doorstep via Helen and Polly.

Despite her dig at their unmarried status, Stanelaw's Martha Stewart had provided the compleat honeymoon repast, lacking only a gypsy violinist tuning up in the courtyard. That couldn't be a coincidence, either. Minty had put one and one together from comments made by Ciara or the Campbell-Reids, or Alasdair himself.

Judging by the wry curl developing in his brows, he was thinking the same thing. He reached for the bottle, saying, "I'm surprised Minty didn't send oysters as well."

The man could actually do comedy if he set his mind to it. "Heavens no," Jean replied. "August doesn't have an 'r' in it."

He popped the cork from the champagne bottle, the small explosion making Dougie's ears twitch, and filled each flute with sparkling liquid the color of straw spun into gold.

She took one from his hand and held it up. A couple of high-flying droplets landed on her glasses, making little prismatic UFOs. "To, er, Ferniebank."

"To us, Jean." He tapped her flute with his and set it to his lips. His look over its rim, the tiny reflection of the candle flames thawing the blue depths of his eyes, made her face flush even before she drank. If she'd ever doubted that the man was versatile enough to do romance, too—however cynically she might define that word—they evaporated like the champagne. And that was so dry it was more effervescence than liquid, teasing her tongue and throat with the subtle flavor of grape.

Ignoring his blanket, Dougie retired to the couch to apply his pink tongue to his anatomy until his gray fur was even sleeker. Outside, the sound of the wind in the trees reminded Jean of the rhythm of waves on the shore, advancing, retreating, advancing a bit farther. She sat down beside Alasdair and tried a bite of her glorified ham-and-egg appetizer. The mix of firm and soft textures filled her mouth. Suddenly she was starving.

There was no need to make idle chitchat, not now. Silently, companionably, they ate. Salt and sweet, brine and earth, sharp and mellow, the flavors warmed first Jean's mouth, then her stomach, then radiated outward until her fingertips and toes tingled. She had always suspected Alasdair had a sensual side, if deeply buried beneath layers of police canteen bangers and mash, and sure enough, he tasted and sipped as though assessing each savory molecule for its full potential. Maybe his toes were tingling, too.

He lifted the bottle of champagne to refill their glasses. But she was already balanced on that knife's edge between sober and tipsy, tingling but not yet numb. "No thank you," she murmured, and Alasdair put the bottle down without topping off his own glass.

There was a protocol to this kind of event, after all. Not just the food, not just the champagne, but the lingering looks and the fingertips barely touching between the rims of the plates and then slowly, entwining. Jean wasn't only picking up on the prickle of his energy field, she was getting the snap, crackle, and pop as well. Funny, she'd thought she knew what foreplay was, but even their meal at the Witchery had not melted her down this effectively.

The dessert might or might not be just, let alone foolish, but it was delicious, a fruit puree whipped with cream, delicate and rich at once, and buttery shortbread dissolving on her tongue. The set of Alasdair's jaw eased at last, and his lips relaxed into their graceful and yet masculine curve, like gothic tracery. When an almost microscopic bit of the food clung to the corner of his mouth, Jean wiped it off not with the corner of her linen napkin but with her fingertip, and then pressed the sweet morsel against her own lips.

His velvet voice was brushed against the nap. "There's a packet of coffee in the basket. Shall I put on the pot?"

"No thanks. Caffeine after dinner keeps me awake."

He waited, his mouth widening in a slow, supple smile.

This time her face didn't just flush. She felt herself go red as a beet. A traffic light. A fire engine. Positively scarlet. No scarlet letters here, though. No scarlet women. She dared a quick tickle of his ribs, like a row of iron bars through his sweater, and he laughed. The sound was a bit rusty, but it was a laugh.

Jean leaned toward him, leading with her lips—and from the corner of her eye saw her backpack lying on the desk, her car keys beside it. The cold water of obligation dashed her face and she halted. "Dang it, I never locked my car. Keep up the momentum. I'll be right back."

Alasdair was behind her as she stood up. "I'll do it."

"No, no problem." Seizing the keys, she stepped out of the front door and stopped, grasping the railing beside the steps. Why did alcohol always go to her knees? Placing each foot carefully on the vociferous gravel, right, left, right, left, she walked across the courtyard, punched the button on her remote, and heard the car doors clunk in reply. There, already!

The cold light and the colder wind pressed in around her warm glow like besiegers around a castle. Like the night around the courtyard, growing darker by the minute as the clouds crept forward, devouring stars and moon. Was that a movement among the trees? Jean froze like a dog at point. No, it was just the wind in the underbrush. Was that a light winking in and out of the leaves or a will-o'-the-wisp hovering above the ancient well? No. She saw nothing in the shadow-rippled darkness, not even the ghostly shapes of the chapel walls.

Turning toward the keep, she detected a gleam in an upper window, Isabel's window, a warm gleam not at all like the thin, off-color luminescence of the yard light. Nothing was there, either, just a sheen on the uneven window glass. Jean's gaze rose to the serrated roof line and beyond, to the overcast sky that faintly reflected the glow of the great cities to the north and west.

Maybe her paranormal allergy was playing tricks, or her nerves were overreacting to Wallace's dubious death, or her imagination was responding to the setting, the air stirring with time-drowned memory and desire burned to ash, nothing left behind but ravaged stone. What she'd seen at the chapel, as-suming she'd seen anything at all, was the glint of headlights from the main road across the river. She hadn't seen that much at Isabel's window. *Never mind.* With something between a sigh and shrug she started back toward the sanctuary of the flat.

Alasdair stepped into the doorway, his body silhouetted against the light. His solid, concentrated body, contents under pressure. She stepped inside and he locked the door behind her. "Let's be getting ourselves to bed, lass. No splinters. You get on, I'll clear away."

She brushed his lips with her own, needing to make no other reply, and headed down the hall. By the time she stepped out of the shower her nerve endings were doing the wave around the stadium of her psyche. She'd only known the man for three months. They were mature people, they knew what they were getting into. But she hadn't shared a bed in years. Heck, she hadn't had sex in years. Alasdair had admitted that he'd last had sex a couple of years ago but hadn't made love in a very long time. Sex was a basic biological urge. There was a lot more to it than biology, however.

She fussed around with dental floss, tweezers, and emery board—this was no time for a hangnail—then considered her flushed face in the mirror. He'd never seen her without makeup, meager though that was. Maybe she should reinstall her eyeshadow, mascara, and lip gloss, just for the occasion. But then, he wouldn't want to leave the lights on, would he? Maybe she could get the candles from the dining table and . . . No. Falling asleep with candles burning was stacking the odds against a long relationship. Especially here at Ferniebank, with Isabel's cautionary tale.

Jean settled her new nightgown over her curves, sucking in her stomach and throwing out her chest. The gown was simple cotton, if with some darting and shirring to keep it from hanging like a potato sack. Appearing before Alasdair in a black lace spider's web with a push-up bra would have been, well, fake. If they couldn't be real now, when could they be?

You know, she told herself, *you're going to spend a lot more time worrying about it than actually doing it.* She stepped out into the hall. *Alasdair?*

The dishes were stacked in the drainer beside the kitchen sink. Alasdair sat on the living room couch, feet propped on the coffee table. His left hand stroked Dougie and the right held open the large, flat book of the Ancient Monuments report. His sturdy forefinger tapped one of the pages as though considering testimony in a case. But at her step he looked up, then sat up, pulling off his reading glasses.

She hadn't seen those for a while. He was just a bit vain, wasn't he? "The bathroom's all yours," she said. "I'll turn out the lights."

Again that quick touch of lip to lip, a lick and a promise. The bathroom door shut. Jean eyed the inscribed stone lying in state on its doily and turned off the ceiling light. The front windows were pale rectangles, the pale glow of the yard light cheered by yellowed lace of the curtains.

Dougie gazed at her over the back of the couch, his eyes twin dots of phosphorescence. "Sleep tight," she told him, and retreated to the bedroom. There she found a small nightlight beside the wardrobe. Ah good. It emitted a rosy shine, making the shadows soft and suggestible and yet providing enough light to keep the proceedings from turning into a farcical scramble.

Jean glanced out the window toward the river, no more than a skein of shimmer, and toward the chapel, invisible in the darkness. No lights flickered through the trees. The wind rattled something loose in the outbuilding.

She pulled the curtains and turned back the duvet. The sheets beneath were lightly scented with smoke—they'd been dried outdoors, downwind of Roddy's peat fire. Inhaling, she sat down on the edge of the bed. No, that made her look as though she was waiting for a bus. She lay down, flat, like an effigy on a tomb. No. She tried rolling onto her side, but wasn't sure where to put her limbs so that they appeared seductive and not awkward. She sat up again.

Alasdair walked in, wearing striped pajama bottoms and a fresh white T-shirt. Without taking an extra step, he came straight to the bed, sat down, and drew her back against the breadth of his chest. His exhalation across her ear sent a frisson of delight down her spine. "You're sure about this, are you?"

Every single one of her nerve endings turned toward his true north and hung there, quivering. "Yes. Are you?"

His answer was a caress, his large, capable hands making the serendipitous discovery that, cupped, they were just the size of her breasts. *Wow,* she thought again, and as his fingertips put the discovery to investigation, *oh yes.*

Time stretched, slowed, stopped. Space contracted. The nightgown and the T-shirt and pajamas discorporated. Curious and shy at once, he touched her as though she was made of crystal, and she touched him as though he was made of the finest bone china, until the inspirational tour of the erogenous zones intensified each caress. His skin beneath her lips was salt-sweet, blending with the scent of smoke in her throat to make him taste like a fine Islay whiskey—they'd sat beside Loch Ness sipping Islay whiskey the night she'd realized it was all going to come to this.

Making love was like riding a bicycle. The body memory was still there. The mechanics were ordinary, murmured that ineradicable lump of intellect, like a stone in her shoe, that held down one corner of her senses. It was the partner who was not.

She hoped she was skilled enough to please him. If Alasdair could hold himself and everyone he dealt with to high standards in other areas, then he might do so when it came to sex, too . . . She was pleasing him. The smooth banks and braes of his body sang to her hands, her lips, her tongue, verse and response, and singed them as well.

She glimpsed his face in the shadows, intense, set, eyes slitted. His body was heavy, but not too heavy—it was comforting, solid . . . She suppressed a quick *ow,* and when he stopped, whispered, "Go on, go—oh."

Yes, that was what she wanted, what she needed—bodies interlocked, limbs entwined, forehead pressed to forehead—yes. The bedposts beat muted time against the stone wall, stopped, started again as they shifted around, playing variations on a theme. His breath came in syncopated gasps, in counterpoint to hers, and that cool observer in her senses murmured that still he was holding something back, assessing and evaluating even as he enjoyed. *Contents under pressure,* not just for him, for her as well—let go, let go, it's all right. *Not yet.*

Her unfocused eyes saw something beyond his shoulder, a glow moving against the window curtains—more headlights, certainly, headlights across the river, fluttering through the trees. . . . If she was seeing fireworks, they were inside her own mind. Her eyes shut as her body arched back against the pillows, *ah, yesssss.*

When she opened her eyes again, Alasdair was looking down at her, sweat glistening on his forehead and pooling between their bodies. And suddenly she felt the chill of the room that a moment ago she could have sworn was hot as a conservatory growing tropical plants.

His lips were rosy, almost bruised. They parted. She pressed her fingertips against them before he could speak—*don't say anything, above all don't ask if it was all right for me—it's good, it's good.* But still a faint arctic gleam lurked deep in his eyes, and she thought of Yellowstone Park in the winter, the hot springs steaming up through drifts of snow, rimmed with ice bright as gemstones. *Not yet. Soon.*

One more time the bedposts thumped the wall, as though knocking at the blocked door in the Laigh Hall, and he was beside her, pulling the cool duvet over them both. She lay back into his arms and cast a wary glance at the window, but if any light shone through the curtains at all it was simply the ambient light of a starless, moonless night.

And then footsteps walked across the ceiling. Jean turned her head so quickly to look upwards that she missed Alasdair's nose by a millimeter. Her body seemed to sink into the mattress, that cold spectral sensation heavier than Alasdair's full weight could ever be. She didn't need to ask if he heard the steps. His body grew so hard and brittle, she felt as though she was lying in the embrace of a fully-armored knight.

The light steps moved slowly from one side of the room to the other, paused, then came back again. After what seemed like two hours, but which was probably only a few minutes, they faded away into the profound silence. But no sooner had Jean taken a deep breath and swum up from the depth of her sixth sense, and Alasdair had shaken off his petrifaction and with a similar deep breath relaxed against her, then the harp music filled the night.

The strains rose and fell, slow, then fast, then slow again, lovemaking in melody. The strings vibrated in the same frequency as Jean's nerves. Alasdair's fingertips stroked her flank in the same rhythm, as though she were the musical instrument. The music came from another dimension, the prickle on the nape of her neck told her that. And yet it wasn't at all fearsome, just melancholy.

Alasdair's hand stopped moving, his body went inert, and his breath slowed. He was asleep. Jean drew his arm further around her and clasped his hand between her own. She lay there, her thoughts drifting like thistledown, listening to the otherworldly music, until at last, it, too, faded into silence and time, and she slept at last.

Chapter Eleven

Jean woke suddenly, a ray of sun shining in her eyes and birds singing arias outside. Whatever she had been dreaming sifted through the fingers of her memory and disappeared, leaving only a vague, unsettled, melancholy.

Alasdair was no dream. He was lying beside her, the duvet not quite pulled up to his naked shoulders. His hair was a bit longer than the severe style he'd worn when they first met, and was actually tousled. Once he'd been blond, she supposed, but now those amber waves of grain were touched by frost. She'd never known him without the gray in his hair and the creases beside his mouth and eyes, now partly erased in sleep. His unshaven cheeks and jaw made him look not hard-bitten but tender, taken unawares.

She had only known him for three months. For one of those they'd ignored each other, giving their mutual attraction every chance to wither and die. And yet here they were, coupled, flesh of each other's flesh—more or less. For all the dithering and all the doubts, sex was the easy part.

The sunbeam faded. Jean wallowed, drowsily replaying the sensations of the night before, and the footsteps, and the music of the clarsach. . . . The clock beside the bed read nine a.m. Where was Dougie? Usually he wanted his breakfast by now. The little cat must be sulking somewhere, his role as the man of Jean's house usurped by another male.

She climbed out of bed into the cold air, her feet landing on the nightclothes puddled on the floor. The long muscles of her thighs twinged. Wincing, she huddled on her robe and headed to the bathroom, only to discover that muscles weren't the only part of her anatomy signaling how long it had been since she'd practiced the amatory arts. She and Alasdair would have to work hard to alleviate her condition.

She was still not wearing any makeup, in the full light of day, even. She shrugged. As for her hair, she would probably win a Medusa lookalike contest. There. A wet comb helped.

Back in the hallway she looked around. Still no Dougie. You've never been properly snubbed, Jean thought, until you've been snubbed by a cat. She walked gingerly into the bedroom and threw open the curtains so that the light fell on Alasdair's face. He twitched and groaned, and then, with a ghost of a smile, muttered, "Bonny Jean."

She kissed the top of his head, then found her glasses on the dresser and put them on. A look through the window showed her patches of blue sky between white billows of cloud, the distant green hillside, the gilded trees, the river glittering to another ray of sun. Just because she couldn't see the main road from here didn't mean that headlights wouldn't reflect this way.

Alasdair sat up and gazed at the bedside clock as though trying to remember how to tell time.

"Coffee?" asked Jean. "Tea?"

"Please."

Smiling, she tottered off to the kitchen and found the packet of coffee inside Minty's basket—it was like Dr. Who's Tardis, bigger inside than out. Within moments she had the pot dripping away. The delectable scent alone helped to jump-start her brain. Dutifully she ascertained that both cars were still occupying the otherwise empty courtyard and the piece of inscription was still sitting on the bookshelf. But Dougie was nowhere to be found, not under the couch, not under the bed, not behind the television.

Her smile curdling, Jean rattled the box of kibble and called his name. That produced Alasdair, back in pajamas and T-shirt. "Misplaced the moggie, have you?"

"Where could he have gotten off to? The windows are shut, he couldn't have slipped out. I mean, y'all don't have window screens here—I'm always worried about him back in Ramsay Garden. Dougie?"

Alasdair opened the door of the broom closet and flipped on the light. "He's used his loo."

"Dougie! Breakfast time!"

Alasdair switched the light off, then with almost a double-take, peered into the shadows. "Well, now, that's right interesting."

"What?" Jean tried to peer past him.

"See that bit of light just there?"

She shoved him half a step aside and looked. The far end of the closet was illuminated by a thin strip of, well, not light exactly. Not-darkness. Which wavered suddenly as a small body leaped through it and into the closet.

Both Jean and Alasdair jerked back, then laughed as Dougie came strutting past the brooms and piping, whiskers at full smirk. Brushing by his attentive audience, he headed straight for the kitchen. "Fetch the torch," said Alasdair, squeezing back into the closet.

Jean got the flashlight and placed it in his outstretched hand, then pressed herself into the closet behind him. The beam of light revealed an opening cut through the thickness of the stone wall, perhaps a foot tall and eight inches wide. At the far end it was partially covered by a broken piece of wood—the paneling in the Laigh Hall. It moved aside when Alasdair pushed at it, opening onto shadow.

"He's found himself a secret passage. Is that an arrow slit

that was once on an outside wall? Or a serving hatch from the old kitchen?"

Jean eased herself back out into the flat. "It's too small for a hatch, and that was never an outside wall. I bet it's a squint, a spyhole. The Laird's Lug."

"I'll tack a bit of plywood over it, keep the moggie within bounds." Alasdair emerged from the closet and switched off the flashlight.

Dougie was sitting next to his bowl, his head cocked to the side, obviously thinking, *first they run about looking for me, then they neglect me. Humans!*

With a low bow, Jean made him an offering of kibble. Then she poured out two cups of steaming black elixir, handed Alasdair a cup, added milk to her own, and drank. Another brain cell stirred to life. "The Laird's Lug, or 'ear.' The laird would eavesdrop on his guests or petitioners or workers—the people waiting around to see him. The hole was probably covered by a tapestry or something, the equivalent of a secret microphone today."

"He'd learn a thing or two to his advantage, if not to theirs." Disdaining the proffered milk carton, Alasdair took a swig of coffee, straight up. "That's likely listed in the old P and S survey. I'll have a wee keek after breakfast."

"Speaking of which . . ." Jean gathered the supplies she'd brought and assembled muffins and eggs. They ate off the ordinary pottery from the cabinet, leaving Minty's crystal and china gleaming in the drainer. "I'll take her things back when I go to lunch, er, luncheon. I hope her new creations are as good as last night's food, and she hasn't gotten carried away with something weird like anchovy ice cream."

"The food was good, but then, we had a bit of an appetite." Alasdair only kept his deadpan lack-of-expression for a few seconds. His grin broke through like sunshine through storm clouds, exposing slightly uneven teeth that just added to the charm. Alasdair. Charm. Who knew?

Jean knew. She grinned back at him. "You did hear the footsteps, right? And the harp music?"

"Obliging of Isabel to play accompaniment—if that's what we were hearing."

"I don't think we were hearing the wind, or anything like that, but no, it might not have been the ghost playing the Ferniebank Clarsach."

"Usually these things are explained away with, it's music from a radio, or, it's someone playing a CD or the like. Though if it's someone playing silly beggars, I'd like to know how they managed it."

"And why they bothered." Jean grinned again. "But what if it was Isabel? We might have been hearing the same music played on the same instrument that Robert the Bruce heard. By the same hands that Mary Stuart heard playing. No matter how you try to un-romanticize them, they're still important historical figures. Suddenly I'm not so dubious about that dratted paranormal allergy."

"Even though it was when we found we had the same allergy . . ." He let the sentence trail away into a rueful smile.

He understood. Jean reached over and took his hand. Outside, the gate clanged open. Feet clumped across the gravel. With a quick squeeze, Alasdair released her hand and leaped to the window. "Well now. Roddy Elliot's got a key as well." He reached for the doorknob, then spun around and strode back to the bedroom.

No, Jean thought, the P and S caretaker wasn't going to impress anyone wearing pajamas. Especially not a farmer who'd probably been up since dawn. She peered out from behind the curtain to see a raw-boned man lumbering across the courtyard. His wellie boots were splashed and his pants stained, and his sweater, an intricate Fair Isle knit, trailed broken ends of yarn.

Crows called from the top of the keep. Roddy stopped and looked up, shading his eyes with a knobbly hand. Jean thought he was going to start cawing back.

Then Alasdair brushed by her and through the front door, fully dressed, although, she assumed, still unshaven. Since he wasn't as dark-complected as P.C. Logan, though, he didn't appear disreputable, just casual. "Mr. Elliot," he called.

Roddy looked around, his hooked nose leading, like an accusatory finger.

"Good morning. May I be of assistance?"

"My fishing tackle needs seeing to." His voice was deep, his words slow, as though he was pulling each one from a bog.

Alasdair waited.

"It's in the wee shed here."

"You have yourself a key, then," said Alasdair.

Lifting his hand, Roddy displayed two keys dangling from a ring looped over his middle finger. In the U.S., that would almost have been a rude gesture.

"There's fishing tackle in the lumber room, aye, but it's listed on my inventory as belonging to Wallace Rutherford."

"He's left it to me, hasn't he?" Roddy was almost a head taller than Alasdair. His face was leathery, weatherbeaten, although Jean suspected that the bloodshot ruddiness of his cheeks and nose, as much as she could see of them above his scraggly gray beard, also signaled a taste for the water of life. He might look nothing whatsoever like Zoe, but the coiled, head-forward stances of grandfather and granddaughter were not dissimilar.

Alasdair drew himself up. "And why's he done that? You were mates, were you now?"

From somewhere behind her, Jean heard the warble of "Ode to Joy." Her cell phone. She'd never turned it off last night. She lunged for her backpack, pulled out the phone, and peered at the screen. *Miranda Capaldi.* "Hey, Miranda."

"I'm not waking you, am I?" her partner's dulcet voice asked.

"Heavens no. We're up and about and Alasdair's outside having words with the farmer from across the road." She sidled back to the window. The two men had moved toward the far end of the outbuilding. Even as she watched, Roddy applied his key to a lock and pushed open a door. Both men stepped inside, out of her sight.

"Well then," said Miranda, and paused delicately.

"No gory details," Jean reminded her. "No gore. Not in this century, anyway."

Miranda laughed.

"If you're calling to tell me that Minty changed the time of her function to noon, you're too late. The woman herself dropped by yesterday, with the sort of picnic hamper you'd expect to find at Balmoral."

"Oh aye, that's one reason I'm phoning. Sorry. The Puppetry show last night was a bit—distracting."

Jean thought of several double entendres but restrained herself, not wanting to direct Miranda's attention back to her own night's activities.

"Also, I've got a bit of catnip for you. I met John Balfour—John-the-ledger-book, our accountant—for breakfast and tax strategies this morning. When I told him where you've gone, he said he's strategizing for Ciara Macquarrie as well, helped organize Mystic Scotland some years since."

Hm, Jean thought. If Alasdair had been married to Ciara before Mystic Scotland . . .

"Mind you," Miranda went on, "he's not at liberty to reveal all. Nor should he do."

"You don't want him talking about us to anyone else."

"Quite right. Even so, when I was working on the series about the financial aspects of the tourist economy, he handed me several examples of councils giving tax relief and permissions to create tourist destinations, one of them being Stanelaw and Mystic Scotland."

"Plus, I hear Ciara bought Ferniebank from Angus Rutherford to begin with."

"So John was saying. Clever Angus, eh?" Miranda said. "There's more. John hemmed and hawed, but I finally drew him out. A very large sum indeed went into Ciara's account this last month, at least a hundred thousand pounds, I reckon."

Jean whistled. "Did it come from Angus? Or from somewhere else?"

"Not from Angus. He and Minty went into debt to build the cooking school, I'm hearing—though not from John, mind. What I am hearing from him is that Ciara already had the backers for her health center and all before she went to Stanelaw Council, though I suppose the money could have been a late investment."

"No reason to think something underhanded is going on here. Well, other than the usual conflict of interest or pork barreling or whatever." Jean strolled into the kitchen and back again. "The Rutherfords got a grant from the Ancient Monuments Commission for the dig and stabilization. Protect and Survive was paying Wallace his salary. Angus and Minty probably never got much income from Ferniebank—these places cost more to maintain than they bring in. No surprise they'd finally sell up."

"Ah, but John was telling me they're getting a percentage of future income."

"That's a good move, taking profits but not liability. Assuming there are profits, although with Ciara peddling the whole occult thing along with massages and aromatherapy, there will be. Ciara and Minty are stranger bedfellows than . . ." *Ciara and Alasdair,* Jean finished silently.

Miranda's throaty laugh tickled Jean's ear. "Now I'd best be sharpening my blue pencil. One of the free-lancers has handed in an article twice as long as we've got space for. No rest for the weary, Saturday or no."

Jean's phone beeped. "No rest for the rested. I'm getting another call. Just a minute."

"No problem. I've said my piece. As for you, I'm expecting a report on Minty's newest concoctions. Cheerio."

"Will do. Bye." Saved by the beep. Eventually Jean would have to thrill Miranda with Ciara's not-so-secret identity as the former Mrs. Cameron, but until then . . . She pressed buttons. "Hello?"

"Good morning, Jean." Hugh sounded chipper, as usual. Well, it was past ten o'clock now. He was probably making good progress on his first mug of milky tea.

"Hi, Hugh. How are things back at Ramsay Garden?"

"Ah, the music, the singing, the drinking. A proper Festival ceilidh, it is."

"Just remember to throw out the empties, please. The bottles, although there will probably be people you'll need to throw out, too."

"Not to worry," Hugh said with a chuckle. "I've got some eye-opening news for you, although I'm thinking your eyes must already be open."

Jean had just redirected her eyes to the window. Roddy was exiting the outbuilding empty-handed, while Alasdair locked the door. The farmer stomped through the gateway, hands clenched at his sides, upper body so stiff Jean could almost detect the bolts driven through his neck. Alasdair tossed Roddy's keys up in the air, caught them, then strolled across to shut and lock the gate once again. *Very good,* Jean thought. *My hero.* To Hugh she said, "Sorry. What news is that?"

"The Ferniebank Clarsach. It's been recovered."

"Really? Cool! We were just talking about that. Where? When? Who took it? Why?" The door opened and Alasdair stepped inside. Jean waved frantically, stopping him in his tracks. He shut the door slowly, as though wondering whether he should take cover behind it instead.

Hugh was saying, "It's turned up at an auction house in London. My pal Dominic works for them, evaluating and repairing musical instruments and the like. They knocked him up early this morning, told him to be getting himself to the office quick smart. The clarsach was left on the doorstep in a pasteboard box, like a clutch of kittens."

"He recognized it immediately, then."

"Oh aye. The description and photos and all, they've been posted on the stolen art and artifact network for days now. Dominic rang me straightaway."

"Wow. It sounds like the person who stole it had an attack of conscience. Or decided it was too hot to handle."

"Thanks to modern communications for that," said Hugh. "Almost makes me feel better about illegal file-sharing and muzak."

"The clarsach?" Alasdair asked, stepping closer.

Jean gave him a thumbs-up, then turned her thumb warily sideways. "It's all right, isn't it?"

"Well," Hugh answered, dragging out the word, "Dominic's saying it's been disassembled. Just as well it wasn't carved from a single block of wood like many—it could be dismembered without ruining it. Dominic reckons all the parts are accounted for and it can be restored."

"It was taken apart? Why?"

Alasdair's brows drew together in a frown.

"I haven't got a clue. Neither did the villains that vandalized it, apparently," Hugh stated.

"Thanks for letting me know. I'll tell . . . Well, no, I bet Minty Rutherford was on top of the 'need to know' list, being director of the museum."

"No question of that. Take care, Jean. Oh, and I hope you're enjoying yourselves."

"No question of that," she replied, hit the "end" button, and turned to Alasdair.

CHAPTER TWELVE

"The clarsach's turned up? Where?" Alasdair demanded.

Swiftly Jean filled him in. However, his frown not only didn't yield, it became deeper, so that his eyebrows almost shook hands over his nose.

"Are you thinking what I'm thinking?" she went on. "If an APB for the clarsach was broadcast all over Europe, then so was one for Angus Rutherford, with photos and everything. So why hasn't he turned up? In one piece, I hope, not disassembled."

"Plenty of places to hide a body. Or he could be hiding himself. Like as not he has turned up, and we've not yet heard. Good of your friends to be phoning and telling you—us—about the clarsach."

Oh. This time she didn't bother adding *damn.* "I'm sure P and S would have let you know."

"Eventually, aye. But the Stanelaw Museum's not on my patch, is it?" Jingling Roddy's keys, Alasdair paced over to the bookshelf and gazed mutely at the inscribed stone, although whether he was seeing it or the intelligence loop he was no longer a part of, Jean couldn't say.

"Miranda was telling me that Ciara got an awful lot of money from somewhere last spring, though it might not have anything to do with Ferniebank."

"You'd not expect a woman with bats flying in and out of her ears to be quite so canny with her money, would you now?"

That was a rhetorical question if Jean had ever heard one. Without beating any more dead horses—or bats—she walked back into the kitchen and pitched the breakfast dishes into the sink. Then she wrapped up Minty's elegant dinner service and packed it back in the basket. By the time she'd wrung out the dishrag and draped it over the faucet, Alasdair's stance had eased and he was turning the inscribed stone over and over in his hand.

Jean was able to stroll rather than totter—the strained muscles were calming down—into the living room and stroke Dougie's smooth head. Having accomplished his night's work, he was now reposing on his blanket, paws tucked up and tail tucked in. Alasdair had accomplished his night's work to an even higher standard, but the day's work loomed ahead, with no catnaps on the schedule. "So did you learn anything from Roddy?" she asked, indicating the keys he was inserting into his pocket.

"He's claiming he and Wallace were the best of friends, and Wallace wanted him to have his fishing tackle." Alasdair's brow was still furrowed, if now at a different angle. "There's tackle in the lumber room, right enough, and tools, and Wallace's telescope. And a stack of boxes all taped up."

Jean didn't suggest a box-cutting expedition, not just yet. "People can argue a lot and still be friends. My aunt and uncle are like that, always wrangling—I said this, no you said that, well I meant this. It drives me nuts, but it doesn't mean they're enemies."

"Or Roddy could be lying. He does have a wee bittie chip on his shoulder."

"Sure, it's the whole status protection thing . . ." Jean let that sentence evaporate. "What are you going to do with that bit of inscription?"

Alasdair set it back on the doily, saw Wallace's drawing, unfolded it, and nodded appreciatively. "I'll be consulting with headquarters, to begin. And I'd like to know whether Angus and Minty have that piece from Wallace's pocket."

"I can ask her. She saw us with this bit last night."

"Aye, she was right interested in that. Look here." He picked up the Ancient Monuments book from the coffee table.

"That was on the shelf," said Jean. "You were looking at it last night."

He showed her Wallace's name written on the flyleaf in the same neat hand as the signature on the sketch, then opened the book. "Here are two drawings of the inscription made last century. Note the credit lines—they were drawn by Gerald Rutherford and owned by Angus."

"And managed by Minty, I bet. Those must be the drawings she was talking about, the old family ones in the museum." Jean took the heavy book, carried it to the window to the right of the fireplace, and set it down on the sill. The photographs of the drawings were murky—the original paper had yellowed and the ink faded—but the facing page held a simplified black and white sketch.

The small, vertical letters of the inscription were crammed together, making them look as much like a stylized picket fence as words. Jean squinted at them, then defaulted to the legend beneath the main sketch: *Hic jacet isbel sinncler que abiit anno dni MDLXIX orate p aia eius requiescat in pace.* " 'Here lies Isabel Sinclair,' " she translated, " 'who died in the year of Our Lord 1569. Pray for her soul. Rest in peace.' Assuming that 'p aia' is 'pro anima,' but I guess that's a standard contraction like 'dni' for 'domini.' The sculptor must have run out of room, the 'peace' is crammed up against the 'in'—but then, he broke 'requiescat' into two parts. And the 'er' on 'Sinncler' is twisted up at an angle, even though there's plenty of room. Is that a squiggle or a crack or what right after the 'r'?"

"Take note of the harp at the top—the Ferniebank Clarsach,

nicely-detailed—and the cross at the bottom." Alasdair stepped up beside her and his hand tapped the page.

"Not the engrailed cross of the Sinclairs, but a flatter one. Sort of an X marks the spot with splayed arms. Didn't Minty say the piece with the clarsach is missing? How many other pieces are gone?"

Alasdair turned to another page in the book, to a picture of the gravestone itself, with the legend, "Photograph by Gerald Rutherford, 1912."

Jean shifted so that the light wasn't reflecting off the page, the movement bringing her shoulder companionably up against Alasdair's. "This shows the inscription complete except for the harp. Which is appropriate, I guess. It's hard to think of poor Isabel being played by flights of angels to her rest."

"Perhaps that's why she's still playing herself." Alasdair pulled a piece of paper from the book. "I found this tucked between the pages. Wallace's hand, again, I'd say."

"I see." What she saw was a copy of the complete inscription, perhaps traced from the book, perhaps free-handed. Dotted lines ran through this version, like roads across a landscape, marking out half a dozen cross-hatched segments. Jean's forefinger tapped the paper exactly as Alasdair's had done last night. "These pieces that are shaded in are the ones no longer on the gravestone, right? So most of the inscription's still there. But there are six pieces missing now. Five disappeared on Wallace's watch. The *icj* is here and Wallace's *ac* should be accounted for. Maybe the other three pieces are in the museum. It might be only the harp that's actually gone AWOL."

"Well done, Jean. That's the way I calculated it as well."

"I ace the test?" She looked up at him with a grin. "Here we are, an academic and a cop, evaluating the secondary sources when we could just walk down to the chapel and look at the inscription."

"Then we'd better be getting on with it." Alasdair set the drawing of the inscription on the bookcase along with the one of the dig, and pointed toward the desk clock.

Whoa—the morning was on a collision course with noon. Opening time. Minty's hen party. Muttering something about time flying and having fun, Jean fast-forwarded through her usual rituals of clothing, cosmetics, and bedmaking, pausing only to check the wall behind the bedposts for damage. But the whitewashed surface was unscathed. Funny how it had never occurred to her that they were beating time on a medieval wall. Those far from subtle rhythms might have roused the ghost.

Eavesdropping seems to be quite the thing around here, Jean thought as she hurried back into the living room, although presumably the laird with his secret lug had been more interested in gossip and schemes than in intimacies of the flesh.

Alasdair was waiting by the door, the picnic basket in hand. With a glance at Dougie—yes, he was asleep, as apparently boneless as only a cat could get—Jean stepped out into the cool, fresh breeze. Alasdair stowed the basket in the car while she admired the play of cloud and sunlight, then led the way toward the chapel.

The path was a ribbon of gravel undulating between humps of fern and mossy rocks and the age-gnarled trunks of trees that were, still, younger than the building they helped conceal. Beneath the leafy canopy the air was more than cool, it was chill, and heavy with the rich scent of damp earth. "I wonder how old Isabel was?" Jean asked.

"Seventeen." Alasdair extended his hand to help her step past a muddy patch.

"Is her body still buried in the chapel, beneath the grave-stone?"

"I'm supposing so, though I did no more than leaf through the book—it's not light reading."

"What about Ferniebank lairds buried like the ones at Rosslyn, in full armor but without coffins? Even Zoe's heard that tale."

"And it's no more than a tale, either here or there."

"Well, Rosslyn's still an operating place of worship, no one's going to let the archaeologists, or worse, the conspiracy theorists, have their way with the place. In spite of—or especially with—the recent publicity about the Templars and the Holy Grail, not that any of that's got so much as a toehold in—" Jean stopped dead.

Alasdair walked on a few more steps, until his back-of-the-head sensors realized she was no longer behind him. He spun around. "A toehold in reality, you're saying?"

"Well, yeah. But the cross on Isabel's gravestone. It's a cross patte, a Templar cross."

"Oh aye, Ciara was going on about that."

"Of course." Jean hurried on down the path. "It's a great story. When the pope and the king of France discredited and murdered the Templars, a bunch of them packed up their treasures and came here to Scotland, where Robert the Bruce was glad to have them—he was on the outs with the pope right then anyway. Supposedly, those Templars turned the tide for Scotland at the battle of Bannockburn in 1314. And there might be some sort of connection between the Templars and Scottish freemasonry."

"That's as may be, but the rest of the tales, the underground societies and religious conspiracies persisting through history, when most people cannot keep a secret for five minutes . . ."

"Yeah, I know. One thing, though." Jean followed Alasdair onto the terrace just as a ray of sun shot down between the clouds, making her feel she'd stepped into a spotlight. *Perfect timing.* "Why would Isabel be buried beneath a cross patte? I mean, her ancestors were up to their armored necks in Templar business, but Isabel died in 1569, two hundred and fifty years after the Templar order was disbanded."

"How many ways are there of forming a cross?" Alasdair retorted. "The Nazi's Iron Cross is the same design. Does that mean the Sinclairs were Nazis?"

"And a swastika figure is a good-luck symbol in Buddhism. Yeah, I know that, too. It's just that it's highly entertaining to watch the storyteller waltz with the historian."

Alasdair snorted something under his breath, words which Jean could fill in for herself. Now that she'd met Ciara, she understood all the better why he'd decided to sit this one out, thank you, and leave the floor to the less inhibited. Or the more ignorant, as the case might be.

There was the grotto, a stone cavity with an arched roof backed into the hillside. Jean bent over to look inside. The holy water was contained less in a well than a pool, fed by a stone trough clogged with an entire civilization of moss and lichen. A trickle of water still dripped disconsolately into a basin with the square footage of a bathtub. No doubt the afflicted would have immersed themselves in it, with all appropriate supplications, of course. Now the water was dark and turgid, dead leaves floating on top and a few modern coins glimmering faintly about twelve inches down. She was not moved to insert any body parts into it—especially not the ones that happened to be sore right now. Whatever sanctity the well had once had was now gone, replaced with the less fraught concept of "good luck," although Jean suspected it was the believers who brought both sanctity and luck to begin with.

Wondering just what Ciara and Keith planned to do with it —turn it into a hot tub?—she backed out of the grotto and looked over the far edge of the terrace, to a relatively flat field overgrown with nettles, thistles, loosestrife, willowherb, foxglove, and other leafy unnamables. Butterflies wafted about. A path or two meandered between barely visible tumbles of worked stone —the remains of the hospice, no doubt. Usually monastery buildings were south of the church, to catch the sun, but there were exceptions. Ferniebank was obviously one of them, the plan of the structure dictated by the site of the ancient well and the lay of the land along the river.

Like the castle, the derelict chapel grounds were romantic, in the Shelley-Keats-Byron sense of the word. Picturesque. Something to spark a bittersweet sigh just before tea time, so the cuppa and the scone would go down all the better.

As for the chapel itself . . . Jean looked around. Wordlessly, Alasdair gestured toward the roughly truncated walls. These pinnacled buttresses were less assertive than Rosslyn's, but were still lavishly sculpted with dragons and other less fantastic animals. Jean headed toward the round-headed doorway but was diverted by a freestanding informational plaque the size of her office desktop and helpfully tilted at a forty-five-degree angle.

Like the flat, the plaque was not new. Its plastic cover was warped, the message beneath faded by the sun and stained by leaking rain. But a quick and dirty history of Ferniebank was legible enough, names and dates and Isabel's story illustrated by a drawing of the keep with smoke flowing from an upper window while appropriately garbed people gesticulated below. Other drawings—both more skilled and more generic than Wallace's—showed the chapel under reconstruction and hooded monks offering medicinal brews to reclining and no doubt declining patients.

Another ray of sun glanced through the clouds, reflecting off the surface of the plastic so brightly that Jean winced. Ah, this was the rippling glint of light she'd seen from the bedroom window yesterday afternoon, thinking at first it was a fire. From her angle it had seemed to come from inside the chapel. She'd seen the plaque reflecting headlights last night, too.

Jean stepped through the doorway. The interior of the chapel wasn't much larger than the castle's High Hall and was paved with lichen-mortared flagstones. A double line of pillars, four to a side, led toward the empty chancel. They were wrapped with stone tendrils that looked as though they had grown up out of the earth and then petrified. The broken bits of vaulting at their tops were frenzies of ornament: fruit, leaves, flowers, human figures and faces—some with skin attached and some as bones —stars, musical instruments including several harps, and multitudes of protruding geometrical shapes like stony vertebrae. More botanical garlands encrusted the window frames.

Her breath escaped in a whistle. No photo she'd seen, and certainly not her distant inspection from the window, had fully revealed the glories of Ferniebank Chapel. Oh yes, the carvings were in the same style, perhaps from the same hands, as those at the much better known Rosslyn. How sad that these were worn and stained by dripping water and splotched with yellow, white, and black fungus.

"Supposedly," said Alasdair at her side, "you've got the Seven Deadly Sins, the signs of the zodiac, an entire family of green men, who knows what all. Interpretation's at your own risk."

Jean looked up at the sky, or what she could see of it between clouds. "I'd sure like to have seen the ceiling. Arches, vaults, pendant bosses—the works, right?"

"There are drawings in the book, Gerald's and earlier ones as well."

"The roof didn't collapse until the 1890s, right? Never mind religion, reform, depopulation, whatever—if it hadn't lasted that long, most of these sculptures would have wasted away long since." Jean imagined the interior of the chapel as it had once been, in the light of candles, the dark gray stone gleaming, the carvings such intricate patterns of light and shadow that they would have seemed to move. They would have seemed to worship. "You have to wonder what was going on in William Saint Clair's mind. Or the minds of his masons, more accurately. This sort of over-the-top decoration was unique in Scotland even before the Reformation, let alone after. And neither Ferniebank nor Rosslyn was destroyed by the Protestants."

"Giving ammunition to the conspiracy mongers," Alasdair said.

"Yeah." Jean looked back over her shoulder. The severe top of the castle rose above the trees, a typical border keep, matter-of-fact, dour, and doughty at once. Masculine to the chapel's femininity.

Alasdair was walking toward the chancel, where the building narrowed into a square extension, the holy of holies. Jean picked her way respectfully among the various commemorative stones that marked the graves of the movers and shakers of their times, and paused beside one set into the wall beside the sumptuously carved but harshly decapitated arch separating the two parts of the building. The inscription was almost illegible. *"Henricus Sinncler,"* she read aloud. "Chip, smudge, *naut,* chip, *adie,* another chip, and *MCD.* That's 1400. But that was before this chapel was rebuilt, wasn't it? Was this particular Henry left over from the earlier building? A relative deserving a memorial stone?"

Silence, except for the wind in the trees and the murmur of flowing water. Jean walked on through the archway. Alasdair was standing straight and still as a prehistoric monolith. "Alasdair?"

"It's gone," he said, each word a hailstone shattering on the pavement below.

"What?" She looked down at the tips of his shoes, pointing toward a rectangular slab of a different color and texture than the surrounding flagstones, its edges hinting at a rosy blush despite its age. But the central part of its surface was a raw red the color of dried blood, scored with parallel ridges, sharp and unweathered. Jean felt the certainty fall through her chest and into her stomach like a rock into a well. "This is Isabel's gravestone?"

"It was. The inscription's been chiseled clean away, and all the bits gathered up. It's not been vandalized, it's been stolen."

CHAPTER THIRTEEN

Erupting with an emphatic "Damn and blast!" Alasdair lunged for the door.

No! Jean stumbled, found her feet, and sprinted behind him as he double-timed it out of the chapel, over the terrace, up the path. *No!* The antiquity violated, and Alasdair too—he'd barely been here for twenty-four hours—it wasn't fair!

Someone could have taken the inscription at any time during the ten days when Ferniebank had no caretaker, but no, the thieves came last night. Was that coincidence, too? There were too damn many coincidences.

And she stumbled again, the second certainty punching her in the gut. She thought she'd seen lights last night, and she hadn't told him.

He catapulted into the courtyard, headed for the flat—P.C. Logan and yet another APB, you get the clarsach back and you lose the inscription—a harp was one thing, a stone jigsaw puzzle was another . . . Jean ran out of the trees and stopped dead beside her car.

The Mystic Scotland van was idling outside the gate. The courtesy gate—now it was Ciara who was turning a key in its lock and pushing it open. Jean looked around at Alasdair. He had halted so abruptly the gravel banked up around his feet. *Not fair, they're piling on!*

Ciara climbed back into the van, drove it into the courtyard, stopped. The doors opened and half a dozen tourists decanted themselves and raised their cameras. What, Jean asked herself, had she been thinking about a three-ring circus?

Ciara was still sitting in the van, talking to a man wearing a cloth cap, its small bill low over brushy eyebrows. As if sensing Jean's gaze on him, he glanced around. Through the reflections of light and shadow on the window, like glints from a disco ball, she saw muddy eyes set close together in a long, almost convex face that flared outward along the jaw. His skin was such a pasty white that his emergent moustache, little more than fuzz gone to seed, looked like a smear of dirt between lengthy nose and lipless mouth.

Dismissing Jean, he leaned toward Ciara as though making some plea. After a long, frozen moment, Ciara laughed in his face. If that wasn't an up-yours rejection of his statement, albeit delivered in Ciara's own unique way, Jean had never seen one.

The woman leaped from the van. The man exited the vehicle much more slowly, almost tripping himself up on the doorframe and landing on the gravel with a thud. "The castle's not yet open for business," Alasdair called, his stance that of a fighter poised to break from his corner.

Ciara aimed a flounce at him, a gesture made more effective by her billowing skirt and pink fun-fur jacket. Her matching pink lips turned up in something that was neither a smile nor a snarl. "Give it a rest, Alasdair. Even you cannot say I'm bending the rules."

"Away with you then, and good luck to you if you're expecting to see Isabel's gravestone." Alasdair pivoted and strode on toward the flat.

Ciara brushed by Jean, her face puckered with puzzlement, not resentment. Jean knew her own poker face fell woefully short of Alasdair's professional version, but she gave it her best.

The erstwhile Mrs. Cameron—or did she ever take his name?—herded her flock onto the path. Her tall, lanky companion shambled along behind, his tweed country-squire suit and tie standing out from the casual windbreakers and jeans of the others. Jean would have found the contrast amusing, if she'd had an amused bone in her body just then.

". . . chapel sculptures are pagan, occult, and alchemical, marking the azimuths of sacred sites throughout Europe which were erected atop ancient Druidic holy places," Ciara was telling her acolytes. "Ferniebank's playing as significant a role in the underground stream of knowledge as Rosslyn, well-known for its ancient secrets—Grail legends and Templar mysteries. Remember now, Marie of Guise, Mary Queen of Scots' mother, wrote to Lord William Saint Clair vowing eternal gratitude for his showing her the great secret at Rosslyn. And Isabel Sinclair here at Ferniebank played the ancient clarsach for Queen Mary, therefore . . ." Ciara's voice faded away.

Therefore two and two make seventeen, Jean finished for her. Although Ciara's mathematical abilities were not the issue, not when she was successfully running a business, whether it was founded on moonshine or not. No, the issue was standing on the front porch of the flat, one hand grasping the railing so hard his knuckles were stark white.

As Jean mounted the steps beside him, she sensed his laser-like gaze skimming her shoulder, aimed at the now-empty path. His flash of anger was buried so deeply under that polar ice-cap he could don at will, she couldn't believe he'd actually grinned, even laughed, such a short time ago, let alone . . . Well, what could she expect? Of course he'd default to the same Alasdair she'd first met.

What she did expect was for him to say again that Ciara had caused some changes here, but he didn't. He didn't say anything. He opened the door and stood aside while Jean stepped into the flat. Then he shut the door behind them both and headed for his official P and S envelope. He was going to have to tell them about the theft, that it happened on his watch, that he hadn't heard or seen a thing. Some caretaker *he* was. Some chief of security.

Jean slumped against the kitchen cabinet, feeling every bit as boneless as Dougie, who was still in his chair, sleeping the sleep of the virtuous.

If she didn't tell Alasdair, if she just kept her mouth shut, would that be the equivalent of lying to him? He needed all the evidence he could get that, yes, something was wrong here, badly wrong, whether anyone had died because of it or not. And yet she didn't have any evidence to offer, not really.

Get it over with. "Alasdair, I thought I saw something near the chapel last night. I thought I saw lights, maybe. But when I took a good look, I didn't see a thing. So I decided I was wrong. And the lights I saw later on, I'm sure they were headlights from the road across the river."

He put the envelope back down. He turned toward her. "You saw something? Lights? When?"

"When I went outside to lock my car. And later on, in the bedroom window, from the corner of my eye, just for a second."

"You didn't tell me." His voice was flat as road kill.

"But I didn't actually see anything. If I had, I'd have told you, and you'd have gone out and searched up and down and . . ." She was just making it worse by sounding possessive.

"Why didn't you tell me?"

"It never occurred to me. You said yourself we had a bit of an appetite last night."

"That's no excuse."

"I didn't think I saw anything!"

"That's for me to decide, isn't it?"

Oh yes, the same cold, crisp, take-charge, arrogant Alasdair she'd first met. "Don't talk to me like I'm some wet-behind-the-ears detective constable."

"Even the rawest recruit would have known to make a report. And I'd have told you that you cannot see headlamps from the road across the river, because it runs behind the hill."

Shit. She'd thought she'd seen an ice sheet covering his expression. She was wrong. His face was cold as an alien moon cut by frigid crevasses opening onto . . . Not onto nothingness. It was only because she knew him so well, after all, that she could see the disappointment flickering in those depths, disappointment and anger and even, horribly, fear.

Instead of saying, *You were right, now that I've broken your shell, I don't like everything that's inside,* she turned away.

"It's going on for noon," he said. "The castle needs opening. You've got an appointment."

"Right." She didn't trust her voice to say anything more. She grabbed her backpack and sprinted out to her car, the gravel cracking beneath her feet. By rote she snapped the catch on her seat belt, turned the key in the ignition, drove across the courtyard, and turned onto the road.

A blast from a horn slapped her back to her surroundings. She hadn't looked one way, let alone both, and the driver of a mud-splashed blue car behind her had had to brake. Fortunately —*she,* Jean saw, recognizing the abbreviated blond hair of Valerie Trotter—had been driving as slowly as the narrow, winding road demanded. Jean pulled into a layby just beyond the end of the perimeter wall and waved contritely as Valerie accelerated around her. She returned the wave with a gesture that might have been dismissive but was not, at least, obscene.

Assuming neither Hector nor Jackie was flattened on her grille, Jean pulled out onto the road again. In her viscera she felt the cold vacuum of space, so strong she expected to see the perimeter wall break up and its component stones spiral toward her. She expected to see the outbuildings at Ferniebank Farm collapse and fall, and Roddy himself—there he was, oblivious to her distress, taking long strides across the yard—sucked into her black hole. She expected trees to shatter into kindling and the river itself rise from its bed in great globules of water.

Alasdair Cameron asked no quarter, and he offered none. His anger and disappointment were justified. Not the way he chose to express it, slamming his drawbridge in her face like that—especially after last night. But it was justified. Her instincts had nagged her about those lights, but no, in one moment of cavalier dismissal, she'd betrayed his confidence in her. In the cases they'd worked together, she had never had the power to make him fail. And now she did. In the end, though, in whatever end, he wouldn't blame her. He'd blame himself.

That choking sound was her own breath. Another minute and she'd start crying. . . . She had just driven past Glebe House. Jean hit the brakes, backed up, and dived into the driveway leading to the cookery building. She was barely off the road before a police car rolled out of the driveway in front of the house and accelerated toward Ferniebank, Logan crouched grimly over the steering wheel like Charon looking for passengers to taxi across the Styx. What? Was the police station here at Glebe House, too?

Jean stopped more or less in a parking spot and climbed out of the car. Then she got back in and stared into the rearview mirror. Yes, her face was a disaster area. There was nothing she could do about the lines at the corners of her mouth, stress fractures from her clenched jaw, no doubt, or her color, which was closer to fish-belly than blooming rose. She dug lipstick and a comb from her purse and made what repairs she could.

She slammed the car door, headed for the house, did an about-face, and hauled the picnic hamper out of the trunk. One more time. She wended her way across the immaculate lawn—she imagined Minty down on her hands and knees with nail scissors—and past the housebroken flowers and shrubs to the front door. Which opened before she raised her hand to knock.

There was Minty herself, today clothed in a neat skirt and blouse accented with a cream and coral paisley scarf. Instead of speaking, she took a step backward, no doubt quailing from Jean's glittering eyes. But Minty was made of stern stuff, and summoned a smile. "You Americans are an eager lot, aren't you? Please, come through."

Oh. She was early. Attempting a similar smile, Jean held out the basket. "Thank . . ." There was a frog in her throat. Or a toad, most likely, one of those South American creatures with poison glands. She tried again. "Thank you very much for the dinner. It was delicious."

"My pleasure." Minty whisked away the basket and set it down beside a grandfather clock. Her extended arm guided Jean into a sitting room furnished with all the subdued colors, rich fabrics, and old-money bric-a-brac as that of a good hotel. The bay window looked out over the front garden and the road, while a fireplace dominated a back wall. The marble fireplace surround seemed out of place, although Jean's benumbed brain couldn't think why.

Rebecca was already ensconced on a soft couch. That explained the "you Americans." She was looking fresh, if not exactly rested, in a flowery frock. Her infant appendage must be back at the B&B with Michael, since she wasn't old enough to hold a tea cup, let alone quirk her little finger while doing so.

At Minty's approach, Rebecca pretended she wasn't trying to stuff throw pillows behind her back. One good look at Jean's face and her grin faltered into a dubious smile.

"P.C. Logan was just here, sharing a bit of good news," Minty said.

"The clar . . ." Jean croaked again. "The clarsach has been found."

"It was left on a doorstep in Knightsbridge," Minty affirmed.

"Disgraceful. I understand that it's been damaged. I've arranged for it to be airlifted to the National Museum in Edinburgh. They'll deal with it much more expertly than any London auction house."

Jean's curiosity rose up like a zombie and staggered forward. "Has the instrument been in Stanelaw all these years? Ever since Isabel died?"

"In my husband's family, yes. The tales about these things make them all the more valuable, don't they? May I offer you a fruit juice? Malvern water? Rebecca?"

"Water," said Jean, barely remembering to add, "please." She sat down beside Rebecca, leaned back, and leaned, and leaned, and finally came to rest at a drunken angle.

"I'd like some juice, please," Rebecca said, and when Minty disappeared into the dining room across the hall, leaned closer to Jean. "Are you all right? You look as though you've seen a ghost, if you'll excuse my saying so. Did everything go all right last night?"

Jean closed her eyes. Her and Alasdair's intimate moment had turned into a Middle Eastern wedding night, with friends and relatives gathered beneath the window of the nuptial chamber waiting to be informed of the successful completion of the contract. Well, the contract had been signed, and sealed, and now . . . Like so many things, getting there was only a battle. Staying there was the campaign.

She looked around at Rebecca's worried face and cut to the catalyst. "We just found the inscription on Isabel's gravestone chiseled away. Stolen."

"Stolen? Oh no! That explains why Logan took a call on his mobile phone and then went rushing out of here as though he'd been goosed with a cattle prod."

"Minty knows, too, then."

"Minty knows all, sees all."

"Does Logan live upstairs or something?"

Rebecca lowered her voice. "He's got a vine-covered cottage, and pretty much a vine-covered wife, in town. But he's thick as thieves with the Rutherfords, you've got that right. He was here when Michael dropped me off, spreading comfort and joy about the clarsach."

"Right," Jean said with a sigh. "Speaking of ghosts, guess what? Ciara Macquarrie is Alasdair's ex-wife."

Rebecca's eyes bulged. The only reason her jaw didn't drop into her lap, Jean guessed, was because she needed it to exclaim, "What? No way!"

"I wish there was no way, but it's true."

"Well now, that's awkward. I remember when one of Michael's old girlfriends turned up at the Rudesburn dig . . ."

Minty walked back into the room. A teenage girl carrying a tray tiptoed behind her. Jean had to look twice. Zoe was stripped of her goth accessories and cosmetics and clothed in a demure skirt and blouse. Only the stiff black pouf of her hair still insisted on personality. She offered the tray and the glasses it held to Jean and Rebecca.

"How are you, Zoe?" Jean managed to close her hand around her glass.

"Very well, madam, thankyoukindly," the girl returned in a rush. As soon as Rebecca had her drink, Zoe bobbed up and down and fled. Judging by her wary glance at Minty as she passed, her employer had imposed such old-fashioned courtesies via a program of intimidation.

"A quick tour of the cookery school, then, before Ciara arrives?" Without waiting for a reply, Minty strolled to the front hall and opened the door.

Rebecca stood. Jean hauled her body up from the couch. Just as they walked outside, the grandfather clock struck noon. There was something about those reverberating chimes that rung a smaller chime in Jean's mind, but with her diminished mental capacity she couldn't grasp it.

Minty shooed her guests along a flagstone path toward the Euro-barn, her royal estate. "Ciara rang to say she had to deal with a tour group. Her new assistant didn't appear for work this morning, the more shame to her."

"Her new assistant?" Rebecca asked at Minty's side while Jean lagged behind. "So she hired Shannon Brimberry after all?"

Another Brim . . . That's right, Jean told herself. Zoe's older sister who had failed her exams due to the bad luck exhaled by the bit of inscription.

"Quite so," Minty replied. "Shannon was sent down from university. She's an intelligent girl, more than one would expect from her background, but she'll not apply herself—well, poor Noel and Polly have done the best they could with those girls. Shannon's set to be the tour guide here in Roxburghshire while Ciara deals with her other tours and the renovations at Fernie-bank, trying to help Shannon's family, over and beyond her helping us all by bringing so much new business to Stanelaw. One is quite willing to forgive certain eccentricities, consider-ing."

Considering the money involved, Jean concluded, and shared a bemused glance with Rebecca while Minty unlocked a glass door and walked them through a vestibule.

The interior of the classroom was cool, the air layered with subtle traces of garlic and onion, cinnamon, bread, roasting meat. Jean realized she was still holding her glass, one ice cube joggling around in the water. Ice. Alasdair, the Ice Prince. The Snow King. She drank deeply.

Minty's mouthful-of-marbles accent, all posh girl's school and none of Scotland, rose and fell in Jean's ears like the muzak Hugh decried. She was supposed to be writing about this. She tried to focus. Granite countertops. Cooking implements ranging from gleaming knives and pots to machines so arcane they might just as well be torture devices. Bright Italian pottery. Wreaths of dried herbs, peppers, garlic. Bottles of powders and liquids of all shapes, hues, and national origins.

Rebecca held up the side by responding to Minty's mission statement, something about teaching the local schoolchildren domestic skills, then making a business of it—refusing to descend to the lowest common denominator, don't you know —exclusiveness are us. Jean trudged blearily along behind. It wasn't her glasses that were smeared, but her brain. Reality can be slippy, Alasdair had said. He would agree that reality could be slippery without the least paranormal overtone. Like her, he might get pretty damn impatient with reality.

They walked through a greenhouse lush with variegated leaves and the sharp sweet scent of herbs—Jean recognized parsley, rosemary, basil, as Minty carried on about fresh quality ingredients and evading the cheapening effect of EU regulations —and then outside past the brick-walled garden with its bird netting and tomato props and flowers in vast array. Rebecca said, "This is all very interesting, Minty. Ciara will be sorry she missed out."

One of Jean's ears perked up. Oh yeah. She was scheduled to interview Ciara this afternoon. Right now, hiking back to Edinburgh held more appeal. Maybe she could explain that she didn't have her laptop, so would have to postpone the moment of truth, although all she ever did for these things was take notes in her paper notebook anyway.

"Ciara's taken more than one of my courses. And she's been stopping in our guest cottage since the first of the month, whilst my husband and I deal with the paperwork generated by the Ferniebank sale." Minty indicated a newish one-story addition beside the main house, which was more of a guest wing than a cottage proper, not that it mattered.

Jean shared another meaningful look with Rebecca. Did Minty mean that the damned elusive Angus had reappeared? Now *that* mattered. Since she was in no mood for beating around bushes, not even Minty's Princess Diana roses, she asked, "So Angus is back?"

"I'm expecting him directly." Minty turned not one hair of her tidily coiffed head. Rebecca shrugged—Angus was an easy-come, easy-go proposition, it seemed.

The driveway and the path passed beneath Jean's shoes and they were back at the front door, Minty opening it before them. The interior of the house seemed still and stuffy and surreptitiously Jean flapped her cotton coattails.

Zoe was setting the table in the dining room. "Tell your mother just a few more minutes," Minty instructed, and the girl vanished through a swinging door.

"Polly's here today?" Rebecca asked, leading the way into the sitting room.

"Yes," said Minty. "Polly does her best to be of help."

"Zoe was saying she cut herself."

"I insist upon properly sharpened knives, they're much safer than ones allowed to go . . ." Minty stopped, arms crossed, gazing out the multiple panes of the bay window, then murmured, "Well then. Jean, Rebecca, if you'll excuse me." She glided into the dining room.

Jean looked out of the window expecting to see the Mystic Scotland van. Instead she saw a small brown car in the driveway, Ciara emerging from the passenger side and Keith Bell the driver's. Aha. Minty hadn't invited Keith, had she? But here he was, stowing his camera bag in the trunk while Ciara eyed the landscape like Caesar inspecting Gaul. Her body language was not as tense as Jean expected, with the inscription and all, but it was less easygoing than it had been yesterday afternoon.

The same muddy blue car Jean had almost collided with stopped at the end of the driveway. Valerie leaned out of the window, Ciara stepped forward, Valerie made a comment and drove on, back toward home and, presumably, Derek.

Turning away, Jean was confronted again by the marble fireplace with its classical fluted columns. A Georgian-style fireplace was out of keeping with this Victorian house, but it would be of the same time period as the blocked door in Ferniebank's Laigh Hall. Like the clarsach, had the fireplace, too, been—taken, borrowed, rescued—and passed down through generations of Rutherfords? What had the Rutherfords been to the Sinclairs, the Douglases, the Kerrs? Squires? Opportunistic tenants? Thorns in various metal-plated or silk-clothed sides?

Jean walked over to inspect the photos arranged along the mantel, each silver frame polished to a fare-thee-well. Most photos were of Minty, hanging onto a long-faced man's arm as though hanging onto a dog's leash, standing in front of Buckingham Palace, the Great Pyramid, the Taj Mahal, the Grand Canyon. The odd photo out was of an elderly man—the late Wallace?—smiling on the steps of the flat at Ferniebank. Where Alasdair had stood this morning, grasping the railing.

Wait a minute. Jean focused on Minty's companion. Hugh had described Angus as a long, lanky chap with a face like the Queen of Faerie's milk-white steed. That fit the man in these photos, all right. That also fit the man from the Mystic Scotland van, the only difference being the provisional moustache.

What the . . . ? Jean spun around. "These photos are of Angus, right?"

"That they are," Rebecca replied.

"I swear to God," said Jean, suiting action to word by casting her gaze upwards, "I saw him arguing with Ciara at Ferniebank not an hour and a half ago."

CHAPTER FOURTEEN

The doorbell rang. Jean sprang for the couch and sat down on its edge just as Minty sailed past the sitting room door.

"Are you sure it was Angus?" Rebecca hissed.

"If it wasn't him, it was his identical twin." She was going to have to tell Alasdair about this. Although she would have told him even without that crack about "making a report."

From the entry hall came the sound of the door opening and Minty's voice, exuding if not warmth, then at least neutrality. "Ciara. So glad you could join us. And Keith. What a lovely surprise. Zoe, take Miss Macquarrie's coat."

Again the crash of cutlery. Zoe hurried into the hall as Keith ambled into the sitting room and saw the two women sitting on the couch. "Oh. Hi."

"Keith Bell," said Jean, "Rebecca Campbell-Reid from Holyrood Palace in Edinburgh."

"We've met," Rebecca said. "Keith's staying at the Reiver's Rest."

"Oh. Hi." Keith pretzeled himself into an armchair and held a paper folder out to Jean. "Here. Have a press kit. I didn't get to talk to you yesterday."

No kidding. Saying, "Perhaps I can talk to you and Ciara after lunch," she took the folder. The cover was printed with "Ferniebank Conference and Healing Centre. Getting in Touch with the Secret Wisdom of the Past." Inside were elevations, floor plans, maps, testimonials, all of which spun across the surface of Jean's mind like snowflakes across a blacktop and vanished. She tucked the folder next to her backpack in the space between the couch and the legs of an end table.

"Naw, after lunch won't work," Keith said. "We've got to go into Hawick, you know, regional police headquarters, to make a report about the inscription. Some detective inspector's coming all the way from Edinburgh, big whoop."

For a split second, Jean was actually grateful to the thief with his nasty little chisel. But then, if not for him, she and Alasdair wouldn't have lashed out at each other.

Minty led Ciara through the doorway while in the background Zoe retreated, clutching Ciara's Abominable Barbie fake-fur jacket. ". . . all right between you, then," Minty was saying.

"We had a bit of a miscommunication is all," answered Ciara. "No harm done. Shannon's with our clientele now, showing them round Floors and Kelso, with high tea at the Abbey Close."

"The Abbey Close does a—nice—tea," stated Minty. "Drinks?"

"Pink Zinfandel, please." Ciara sat down on another armchair, the ruffles on her blouse palpitating gently. "Hello, Jean. Hello—Rebecca, isn't it? We met at the Granite Cross a few nights since. Your husband was piping."

Rebecca nodded, smiled, and said nothing about Ciara's past affiliations.

"Keith?" asked Minty. "Juice? Malvern water? Ah, wine?"

"I'm fine with water." Keith's colorless eyes followed her as she once again trekked across to the dining room. In a bigger house, Jean thought, Minty would have had buttons and bells to summon the servants. But then, this way she could keep a close eye on the peons at their work.

The clock clunked, whirred, and played the melody of the Westminster chimes, followed by one emphatic *dong*. Now that Jean wasn't trying to dredge it up, the memory appeared. She'd heard that same clock strike yesterday, in the background when Keith called her at the office. That was no mystery, with Ciara staying with the Rutherfords. She'd probably urged him to set up his own interview, so that her project would get even more column inches.

Ciara's blue eyes were fixed on her. Something moved in their—shallows, Jean thought waspishly. Condemnation, perhaps. Or simple curiosity. She returned the stare. *Yes? No? Maybe?*

Ciara tossed her head, and again her earrings, cascades of tiny gold stars, tinkled behind the red curls. "Dreadful, isn't it? The inscription and all. And there's me, rewriting my lecture in mid-stream. Alasdair . . . Well, Alasdair's dealing with it, I'm sure."

"He's dealing with it," Jean said, even as the echo of his "Damn and blast!" ran through her body like an aftershock.

Minty returned, Zoe at her heels with the tray. Zoe served while Minty pulled forward a smaller chair and seated herself, her hands with their plain gold wedding band folded tightly in her lap. "Bad news indeed about the inscription. Good job we have the bits that we do. The one with the *ic* and *j*, the one with the *ac*, and three others from the left edge, all in the museum."

Zoe flinched, almost throwing Ciara's wineglass into her lap. Deftly, Ciara fielded it.

"That will be all, Zoe," instructed Minty. "Tell your mother luncheon in ten minutes."

Again plowing straight through the underbrush, Jean asked, "So y'all have the stone inscribed *ac*, then, the one that was in Wallace's pocket when he died?"

"Why yes, I do," Minty replied, ignoring Jean's second-person plural. "Ciara, if you'd like to donate the *icj* to the Stanelaw Museum, the two pieces could be fitted together. The entire inscription should have been removed to the museum long since. But that was P and S's decision, to risk damage and even theft by leaving it *in situ.*"

"The museum's welcome to keep the pieces for the time being," said Ciara graciously. "A shame the villains struck just now, but it was all to a higher purpose."

Right, Jean thought. Funny how the air seemed to be leaching from the room.

Rebecca looked from face to face. Ciara eyed the row of photos on the mantelpiece, her auburn brows tightening. Keith inspected either his fingerprints or Ciara through his glass of water. Minty said, "Publicity. The more the fairy-tales about Ferniebank are publicized, the more likely it is to attract hooligans like that Derek Trotter. I told P.C. Logan that boy needs questioning."

Wondering if Minty meant "publicity" as a dig at Ciara, Jean repeated, "Fairy tales?"

"Isabel Sinclair," conceded Minty, "was a lady-in-waiting to Mary, Queen of Scots. She died in a fire at the castle in 1569, soon after Mary stopped there on her flight to England."

"A Catholic queen, fleeing to a Protestant land at a time of religious ferment," said Ciara. "No wonder she was done to death in 1587."

"Her messy relationships lost her Scotland as much as her religion did do," Minty said.

Rebecca smiled, not mentioning that her PhD dissertation considered Mary's role in sixteenth-century politics, including her supposed plots to overthrow her cousin Elizabeth of England—a distinct possibility, with Mary's son James being next in line to childless Elizabeth's throne.

"And Isabel's ghost has walked at Ferniebank ever since," concluded Ciara, her smile at Minty more cheery than cheeky. "But then, there's more to Isabel's story than Wallace printed in the brochure. His grandfather Gerald, typical Victorian gentleman that he was, plastered sentimentality over bothersome historical truths."

Minty reclaimed the floor by raising her voice the merest fraction of a decibel. "In any event, our museum has a burning-glass that is said to be the one with which Isabel ignited the fatal fire."

"It survived the fire?" Jean asked.

Minty smiled. "I've brought it here until I can consult with Alasdair about security issues at the museum. I'm sure he'll recover from the embarrassing theft of the inscription quite quickly."

Jean pressed her lips together, not that she had any effective retorts, and caught Rebecca's lifted eyebrow. They'd seen Minty, outside the museum, putting a small box into her handbag. That must have been the burning-glass. Some nerve, to regard the museum as her own private treasury.

"I've got a friend who's a dab hand at psychometry," said Ciara. "If he's holding an artifact, he's sensing what happened all round it. I'll be bringing him along in time, so's he can have himself a go at the burning-glass. And the bits of inscription as well."

Minty's alabaster complexion grew just a bit ashen at that. Rebecca's mouth turned down in a frown, probably because she was trying not to smile. Keith chewed pensively on a fingernail.

Feeling more breathless by the minute, Jean went on, "Thank goodness Gerald Rutherford made sketches of the complete inscription. And Wallace had some skill with a pen, didn't he? Last night I found a drawing he did of the dig at Ferniebank. Is Angus an artist, too?"

Again Ciara's eyes focused on the mantelpiece, then darted in Jean's direction. Jean met her gaze evenly. *Yes, I saw you with him. Is something going on behind Minty's back? Or does Minty really know and see all?*

Ciara looked away. If Alasdair was right about Ciara's abilities—and he was rarely wrong, even when he was infuriating—she hadn't caught a hint of Jean's telepathic transmission.

"As an artist," Minty was saying, "my husband has a tendency to dot his t's and cross his i's. But then, there are very few people whose abilities live up to their self-images. Much better to bear their shortcomings without complaint. Luncheon is served. If you'll excuse me for a moment, Zoe will show you to your places."

Jean and Ciara bounded to their feet. Jean's thigh muscles twinged and she lurched into Ciara. They spun away from each other, two magnets touching negative poles. "Sorry," said Ciara, and headed onwards, Keith in tow.

Jean was left with an impression of softness, soft fabrics, soft pillowy flesh. A man could get lost in a body like that. It's a jungle in there. For a moment she felt dizzy.

Rebecca took her arm. "You're sure you're all right?"

"Yes, I'm fine, thanks, I just got up too fast." Jean plowed on toward the dining room. The table gleamed with what might have been Minty's third-best service, painted pottery and stainless steel ranged around a vase of flowers so fresh dew clung to the petals. Rebecca sat down across from Ciara, Keith rather crammed in next to her. Jean found herself seated at the foot of the table, while Ciara had the guest of honor slot on the right hand of Minty. *Inhale*, Jean told herself. *Exhale*.

Zoe stood bracing the door open and balancing a tray. Beyond her, Jean saw a heavyset woman, swathed in an apron reading "Cookery at the Glebe," scowling with the effort of daubing morsels of food onto myriad small plates. As though that wasn't enough to identify Polly, the bandaged left hand did so. Her drab hair, encased in a net, looked like mouse sausage.

Minty reappeared, seated herself, and announced, "I'm organizing the catering for the new conference and healing center. Today we have a tasting menu of dishes. Zoe."

Zoe started distributing the plates as though she was bowling and trying to make the spare, then hurried back for more.

Jean considered the array. Right now she would have done just fine with bread and water, although the mingled aromas were quite appealing. Despite its acid coating, her mouth began to water. When she saw Minty lift her fork, she followed suit. *Inhale. Exhale. Prepare to swallow.*

"We have haggis wonton and plum sauce," said Minty, "haggis tortellini with a spiked salsa verde, haggis beignets with diable sauce, haggis pakora, and haggis dumplings."

What Jean swallowed at first was her incredulity. Rebecca was making little hiccups, trying not to laugh. Minty wasn't joking. Piled in artistic mounds on the plates, decorated with sauces, enclosed in pastry, was haggis in all its liverish glory.

"And we have," Minty went on, "a clapshot of diced root vegetables—potato, turnip, parsnip—*al dente,* with a sprinkling of parsley, as well as salad lettuces fresh from my garden. The water is the new select brand from the springs near Balmoral. Enjoy."

Considering her mood, Jean expected the food to taste like ashes. Or at least like it sounded, an unholy combination of ethnic foibles. But no. It was good. It was delicious, even. Minty had chosen well—the salad and vegetables cleared her palate between bites of richness.

Propping himself on his forearm, Keith put his head down and ate, apparently having lived in Scotland long enough to overcome squeamishness about the national dish. Unless his body shape indicated that he simply never got a decent meal.

Minty nibbled. Rebecca tasted and nodded. Ciara made appreciative foodie rumbles, interspersed with soliloquies about hiring therapists for massages, hypnotherapy, color readings, and the like—why, she was already getting applications—

understandable, as Ferniebank had long been associated with natural healing energy.

Jean hoped so. After centuries of feuds, raids, blackmail, kidnappings, arson, protection rackets, and outright terrorism, healing was necessary. Healing all around.

From the kitchen came Zoe's voice. ". . . putting it about that she and Shan had 'a bit of a miscommunication.' The neck! Ciara phoned to say Shan could have the morning out, didn't she? I knew that woman was bad news when Grandad's Nero died the day she moved here. Poisoned, he said."

"That dog was near as old as you," Polly returned, "and like to die any moment. You know your grandad, nothing ever just happens, there's always folk plotting against him. Going on about Wallace killing Mum. The idea."

"It's Ferniebank, isn't it? Val's saying that Isabel left a curse, and I believe her." Zoe's voice rose. A frantic hiss was either a teakettle or Polly warning her daughter that the walls had ears.

Interesting, Jean thought, with another look at Ciara that this time was more of a glare. Did she tell Shannon to take the morning off because she knew she'd have Angus with her? But then, they were hardly jovial companions. And the mention of poison . . . Filing those nuggets, too, in her "something's rotten in the state of Ferniebank" in-basket, Jean pitched Val Trotter's curse in on top.

Ciara's voice rose and lightened as she careered among her enthusiasms, not muzak to Jean's ear, but experimental music, clunking one minute, soaring the next. She spoke about the archaeology of standing buildings and conservation versus restoration. She considered aspects of cultural resource management. She expressed concern about environmental impact studies at Ferniebank—the hospice drains, for one thing, might still be teeming with every bacterium known to man, including little numbers like the Black Death.

"You're very quiet, Jean," said Minty.

"A journalist has to listen," Jean returned with a bland smile.

"Tell us about your work," Rebecca asked Keith.

He mumbled about how the wiring in the castle had probably been done by Edison himself, and how the plumbing wasn't much better than the original latrines, then warming to his subject, said, "You know what's cool? There's a garderobe in one of those mural chambers off the Laigh Hall, and it's still got a slate lid. Man, can you imagine plopping yourself down there on a cold night, a stone seat and a draft whistling up your butt from beneath. Constipation would have been a real problem, but then, the hospital was right there, and medicine back then meant bleeding you or giving you a purgative. That garden wasn't just to look pretty, they had herbal remedies and tonics and stuff to put hair on the seigneur's chest so he could help himself to the peasant brides."

Minty's brows went ever so slightly lopsided, and with an audible gulp, Keith slumped back down. "Zoe," instructed the lady of the house. "Dessert."

Zoe cleared away the dishes, then doled out not haggis with chocolate sauce, thank goodness, but a simple mousse garnished with berries, everyone's reward for good behavior during the culinary infomercial. Jean passed on coffee. The meal had filled some of the void in her stomach, reassuring her that she was not going to lose structural integrity. No need to upset the delicate equilibrium with caffeine.

Piling her napkin on the table, Ciara said, "Thank you, Minty. That was delicious. I'm sure our clients will relish every bite. Now I'm obliged to get on to Hawick and some po-faced detective inspector named Delaney. It being my fate. That sort of man keeps recurring in my life." She looked at Jean.

Jean deployed her bland smile once again, her teeth clamped together, even as she thought *Delaney*. That was the detective who had dismissed Alasdair's concerns about Wallace's death. Good. If he was coming down from Edinburgh, the theft of the inscription had raised Ferniebank above his event horizon.

Chairs scraped. Voices muttered. Jean managed to stand up. Minty, her arms spread in a "we are the world" sweep, said, "Jean, Ciara, how good that the two of you can be so civilized."

Jean shared a quick glance with Ciara. They had, she estimated, a second thing in common—irritation with Minty's noblesse oblige. But Ciara needed Minty more than Jean did, which made her sneaking around with Minty's husband even more puzzling.

Jean needed fresh air. She needed to move around. She needed Alasdair, on so many different levels. Right now she wasn't going to ask herself what he needed, over and beyond to salvage his self-respect—and perhaps his reputation—by solving at least one of the accumulating Ferniebank mysteries.

CHAPTER FIFTEEN

The group straggled toward the door, murmuring compliments and thanks. Zoe appeared bearing Ciara's pink pelt. Keith said to Jean, "We'll do the interview tomorrow afternoon, okay?"

"Oh aye," Ciara added. "Two p.m. at the Granite Cross— most everyone's there of a Sunday afternoon. Will your husband be playing again, Rebecca?"

"That can be arranged," Rebecca returned.

"Super," said Ciara.

"I'll write up what I've learned today and we can take it from there." Jean retrieved her bag and the folder and made a break for the door. "Thank you, Minty, wonderful food—Rebecca, I'll drive you back to town—Ciara, Keith." She was on the path, across the lawn, and in the car before she stopped to breathe.

Rebecca climbed in beside her. "So then, what did you learn today?"

"Ciara's not a total airhead. She's got a good grasp of what it's going to take to restore Ferniebank. As for playing 'what if,' well, I do that, too, although as Alasdair was saying, there's a difference between stories and lies. Who was it who said you're entitled to your own opinion, but not to your own facts?" Jean exited the school driveway and turned toward town just as Keith's car exited the house driveway and turned the other way. Jean veered, he veered, and each car steadied as it went.

Jean watched the other car dwindle in the rearview mirror, then concentrated on the road. Within moments she was pulling up in front of the Reiver's Rest, a white-painted modern house that looked more efficiently comfortable than stylish.

"Speaking of Alasdair," said Rebecca, so casually Jean knew the jig was up, "would you like to do just that? Come in for tea and sympathy. You know, girl-talk. We'll send Michael to his room, although his opinion would be worthwhile."

"What happened when his old girlfriend turned up at Rudesburn?" Jean countered.

"Ah. Well. She was murdered."

Jean winced. "Ow. I knew y'all had been involved in a couple of murder cases—it's like the plague, it's going around—but . . . I'm sorry I asked."

"It all brought us closer together. Eventually."

Eventually. "Do you think being involved in murder cases has made you, well, a lot quicker to suspect crimes?"

"You mean are we wondering about losing both Helen and Wallace in the same way, in the same place, at almost the same time? Yeah, we've speculated about that, but coincidences happen, and there's no evidence anything's wrong. Or is there?"

Jean reminded herself that Alasdair the gambler, the scientist, liked to keep his cards face down and his formulas private. "I need to get back to Ferniebank and tell Alasdair about Angus and Ciara. Plus I overheard Zoe say that Ciara told Shannon to take the morning off, and that Derek's mother has been telling people Isabel left a curse on the place."

"The thot plickens, then." Rebecca clambered out of the car. "Keep us posted on the inscription and everything. The 'everything' being at your discretion, of course."

"Thanks," Jean returned, with the first genuine smile that had broken her face since sometime that morning. And it was now, she noted as she drove away, almost three p.m., four and a half hours until closing time. Until she had any hope—or fear—of getting Alasdair's undivided attention.

The road to Ferniebank unfurled ahead. " 'O see ye not yon narrow road,' " she declaimed to the windshield, " 'so thick beset with thorns and briers? That is the path of righteousness, though after it but few enquires.' Should be enquire, singular, but that doesn't rhyme."

The distant hillsides were brushed with a faint tint of pinkish-purple heather. Autumn was just over the horizon. Even now, the occasional ray of sun was still warm, but a coolness in the breeze and an opacity to the lengthening shadows hinted of chill, dark days to come, hopefully not soon.

There was the farm, with Roddy now leaning on the fence contemplating a herdlet of fat cows on the hill above. The two black and white lumps at his feet were the dogs Hector and Jackie, minus the patriarch Nero. Maybe the deaths of the elderly had come in threes. All of them since Ciara made her deal and moved to Glebe House, although a more unlikely angel of death Jean couldn't imagine.

There was the gateway in the ancient wall, and the glowering castle parapets. Jean guided the car into the courtyard much more sedately than she had guided it out, and was surprised to find the parking area almost full, with people standing around holding leaflets and candy bars. She squeezed her car in next to Alasdair's.

She'd barely slammed the door when he stepped out of the shop. They looked at each other, separated by five or six yards of gravel and several fathoms of outer space. His expression was pared to the minimum, stern but no longer icy. Jean hoped her own expression was a better containment field than it had been earlier. "Business is good today," she ventured.

"We're picking up Rosslyn's overflow," Alasdair replied, "just as Ciara intends."

From inside the shop came a strain of harp music. The hair twitched on Jean's neck. Then she realized she was hearing a

CD, setting the scene for the visitors, and her nape slumped back down.

"I've covered up the spyhole," he went on. "I've reported the, ah, loss of the inscription."

"I saw Logan heading this way." Jean didn't think either of them had blinked so far. That much she would concede—she closed her burning eyes and opened them. "The tall tweedy guy who was with Ciara this morning. It was Angus. There are photos of him at Glebe House."

"Eh?" Alasdair's forehead pleated into its police-inspector frown. "He came peching back up the path and hid himself in the van just as Logan arrived. What game is Ciara after playing now?"

"Right now she and Keith are off to Hawick to talk to D.I. Delaney about the inscription. He's come down from Edinburgh. Maybe he'll listen to you this time."

"Chance would be a fine thing," Alasdair said sarcastically. "Logan, now, he's gone haring off after Derek, looking to interview him about the inscription."

"I doubt if Derek would have chiseled it out so carefully and picked up all the pieces."

"He might have done if he had a buyer waiting."

"I can't see a sixteen-year-old kid working the international antiquities trade. And a grave inscription isn't going to get buyers as excited as, say, the Mona Lisa."

The harp music stopped, to be followed by a soulful tenor singing about buttoning up, and being cheery, and taking a dram before going. Alasdair was just plugging in the CDs that were already there, wasn't he? She'd have to give him the ones she had in the car, Hugh Munro, Runrig, Wolfstone, Gallowglass, Seven Nations. Sentiment wore thin pretty fast. Didn't Ciara say something to that effect, about Gerald Rutherford's tales of Ferniebank?

A bubble of garlic burst in her throat. Music and food could be ends in themselves, but they were also sublimation for embraces. Not necessarily sexual embraces. Just the pressing of flesh to flesh, to close out the chill . . . She was still looking at Alasdair. He was still looking at her. Apology seemed to be a possibility, which was more than she would have thought three hours ago, but who was going to bend his or her stiff neck by going first?

A family came out of the castle, parents herding children toward the shop and its booklets and souvenirs, not to mention its snacks. "We'll have us a blether," Alasdair said, just as Jean said the same thing, "We'll talk," and turned toward the flat.

The avian day shift, several crows, began squabbling among the appropriately named crow-stepped gables. The haggis and its sauces and pastries shifted in Jean's stomach like an insomniac irritably punching his pillow. If she had to eat crow later on, fine, she could choke it down, but Alasdair was darn well going to have to share the meal.

Inside the flat, she discovered Dougie dozing on the window-sill, paws and tail tucked so tightly beneath his body he resembled a tea cozy. She changed into jeans and a sweatshirt, smoothed the covers on the bed—not that they were at all untidy—and returned to the living room humming about taking drams and long remembering this night.

What she couldn't remember was the rest of the song. She didn't really want to, since it was a song of parting, but looking it up on the internet was something to do. Casting a sharp look at the answering machine, she set her laptop on the desk and hijacked the telephone line.

Ah, yes. The song was written by a Sinclair from Caithness, the lowlands beyond the Highlands, the rolling green county at the northeastern peak of Britain with its steep sea-girt cliffs overlooking Orkney. One branch of the Sinclairs was connected with the Borders and Rosslyn, the other with Caithness and Orkney, although it was hard to tell the players without a program. A Henry from Rosslyn had fought with Bruce at Bannockburn. One from Orkney and Rosslyn both had supposedly sailed to America, with the evidence being stylized ears of corn —or as they called it here, maize—carved around a window frame at Rosslyn. Jean, who had grown up picking corn kernels out of her teeth, thought the carvings looked as much like maize as she looked like Marilyn Monroe.

But there was definitely a stone in the chapel wall here at Ferniebank inscribed *Henricus*, Henry. The *adie* could be *Orcadie*, Latin for Orkney, and the *naut* probably was *nauta*, navigator. Maybe that was a memorial to the sailor Henry, who had died about 1400, perhaps even in America. The William who built Rosslyn and rebuilt Ferniebank was that Henry's grandson, after all. *Cool!*

While she had the connection, she checked her e-mail, then surfed to her favorite discussion group at The One Ring.Net, which had, as its banner phrased it, served Middle-Earth since the First Age and was the haunt of Tolkien geeks of the darkest dye. For a while she was lost in the erudite essays and clever jokes. Then she realized she was tying up the phone line and disconnected. Constable Logan or Inspector Delaney might try to get through to this number rather than to Alasdair's cell phone.

Speaking of her partner, sparring or otherwise, maybe she should make a cup of tea and take it out to him, as a, well, a detente offering. Jean stood up and looked out of the window just as Alasdair emerged from the shop, sipping a canned drink. Okay, he was self-sufficient, she got the idea. She was self-sufficient, too, darn it. With her own interests and her own work. She picked up the Ancient Monuments book from the windowsill and leafed through it. *Great Scot* readers enjoyed archaeology articles. She could use the story of Isabel, the Gray Lady, as a hook.

The book opened with a note of appreciation to Angus and Araminta Rutherford and Wallace Rutherford, and mentioned Gerald Rutherford's amateur excavations of 1912. No surprise there. Gentleman—and sometimes lady—archaeologists had left their fingerprints all over British antiquity, for better and for worse.

The next page listed the participants in the chapel dig, among them Valerie Trotter, in her student, prematernal days, no doubt. The head of the dig had been one Donald McSporran, an elderly, more tolerated than respected, faculty member at the University of St. Andrews—or so Jean remembered from writing his obituary soon after she arrived in Scotland. She turned to the body of the book.

As usual, Alasdair was right. The text was heavy going, consisting of blocks of fine print cut with tables of arcana such as pollen analysis and the chemical composition of plaster and paint. The drawings, while exquisitely detailed, were of pottery shards and masonry details, not the sort of thing that would wow a mass audience. . . . Aha—a photo of the chapel stripped of its flooring to reveal the honeycomb of crypts beneath was titillatingly macabre, with chalky bits of bone peeking out from collapsed coffins. Jean saw no armored skeletons, although there was a close-up of one that had been hacked and sliced by various bladed weapons. That, she thought with a shudder, was what Mary's secretary Riccio looked like. The illustration was helpfully labeled "Plate 5."

She was squinting at the diminutive columns of the index when the electronic notes of "Ode to Joy" made her jump.

Closing the book and leaving it on the coffee table, she pulled her phone out of her bag. *Hugh Munro.* All right! A dose of sanity! "Hi Hugh," she said.

"Hullo, Jean," Hugh replied, his voice underlaid by snatches of melody played on a keyboard and the wail and squawk of inflating bagpipes. "We're on stage in half a sec, but I knew you'd want to hear the latest turn-up in the adventure of the clarsach, as conveyed by my pal Dominic."

"He's the musical instrument expert, right? Oh yes, please. Minty said she was having it, well, conveyed to Edinburgh."

"She did that, a first-class seat for Dominic and one for the harp. He went along to the conservator's lab, and you'll never guess what they found."

"My capacity for wild guesses is a little strained right now."

With a sympathetic chuckle, Hugh said, "Many clarsachs had cavities in the post at the back—traveling minstrels kept a change of clothes tucked away inside. But this one has a small hole inside the front brace, hidden beneath a bittie carving. Inside's a scrap of paper that looks to be sixteenth century, with an ink mark or two. But it's stuck fast. They'll need all their dental picks and whatnot to remove and read what's on it."

"Sixteenth century? A time of grand confusion and conflict, with the Reformation drawing blood, and Mary Stuart escaping to England, and Isabel's family supporting her, and the Borders a war zone—just the sort of setting for secret messages, right?"

"Folk were always carrying musical instruments to and fro, a smuggler's delight . . . Coming! Must run, Jean, sorry."

"Thanks for letting me know. Break a fing—er—good luck with the show."

Whoa, she thought. Had the harp-thief dismantled it looking for the message? Did he find it? Had he pulled out most of it and left a scrap behind? How did he know to look for it? And who was *he*—or *she*—anyway? Plopping herself down in the desk chair, Jean punched the Campbell-Reid's cell phone number.

Michael answered, "Reiver's Rest, Villain's Villa, Thieve's, erm, ah . . . Never mind. You have news for us about the inscription, Jean?"

"Not the inscription, the clarsach, which is in Edinburgh already." Her words falling over each other, Jean explained the situation and concluded, "Could you call up the museum and find out what's going on with the paper scrap?"

"Try and stop me. The documents boffins will be dancing a springle-ring!" As the connection evaporated, Jean heard Michael calling, "Eh! Rebecca! You'll never . . ."

Jean put her phone down and stared blankly at the clock on the desk. The harp could be—would be—repaired, but the fingers that had played it, that had tucked a secret message inside it, were forever lost.

At least when it came to writing articles about Ferniebank she was spoiled for choice. She opened both her word-processing program and the folder labeled, "Ferniebank Conference and Healing Centre. Getting in Touch with the Secret Wisdom of the Past."

As she'd dimly noted earlier, Keith and Ciara had resisted the temptation to indulge in stunt architecture. The white-painted and slate-roofed building designed to sit above the river both evoked and simplified traditional style. The ruins of the chapel would be the centerpiece of a sort of cloister garden. The new structure didn't even carve out much landscape, since the landscape itself was marketable. The castle, though, would retain only enough of its structural members and architectural features to allude to that quality beloved of advertisers, authenticity. Would that deprive the ghost of her haunt, or would she still walk, for those who had eyes to see and hearts to know?

Jean pulled out a brochure advertising Cookery at the Glebe, including sample menus and recipes. Another piece of paper was folded in quarters—ah, a map of the Borders, with an arrow pointing to Ferniebank and . . . *Oh good grief.* Ciara wasn't just waltzing with history, she was break-dancing with it.

Lines were superimposed on the map the way lines were superimposed on Wallace's drawing of the gravestone. Except here the lines joined dots indicating towns and other sites into triangles, spears, and crescents, with cryptic notations such as "The Rose Line" and "The Harp." In other words, Ciara was trading on the—theory, notion, illusion—of sacred geometry, the exceedingly creative concept that human-built locations were arranged in patterns of occult significance. The fact that in an area as densely and lengthily populated as Western Europe you could find enough sites to draw Mickey Mouse mattered not to the true believer. Secret wisdom was very much in the eye of the beholder.

Jean started to fold the map but was stopped by the words at the bottom: "Courtesy of W.B. Rutherford." Again Wallace . . . That's what he was doing on the roof with the telescope, plotting sites as well as stargazing. Had he breathed in so much mold and mildew at Ferniebank he'd completely lost track of the dividing line between fact and fiction?

No. That wasn't fair. The Orkney-Rosslyn-Ferniebank nexus had some perfectly genuine plot points. Or points to be plotted, as the case might be. As for the Templars and harps carrying secret messages, well, it was all highly entertaining, the same way making constellations out of the random distribution of stars was entertaining. Wallace and Ciara's great minds thought alike, it seemed. What had Ciara said about her confederate? A shame Wallace will not be here to see the final designs? *Or the final profits,* Jean amended. Angus and Minty would see them, though.

Miranda would get a kick out of all this. And it was time to check in with her anyway, before events got completely out of hand. Although, with the return of not only the clarsach but also Angus, officially or otherwise, the inscription was the only identifiable crime. Everything else was innuendo at best. Or at worst. Jean picked up her phone.

And reached Miranda's voice mail. It was either tea time or happy hour in Edinburgh. Jean dutifully left a message. "Hi, it's me, reporting in. Minty's luncheon was something else again, lots of dishes made from, wait for it, haggis. Pretty good, though. And in more serious news, an important grave inscription's been stolen from the chapel. Yes, an inscription, chiseled out and carried away. No, Alasdair's not happy. You've heard that the Ferniebank Clarsach's been recovered, I bet, with more news to come. And . . ." She grimaced. No help for it. "Brace yourself for this one. It turns out that Ciara Macquarrie is Alasdair's ex-wife. But everything's okay. Enjoy the Tattoo or wherever you are tonight, and I'll talk to you tomorrow."

Wondering if her tone had been much too cheerful, even careless—not that tone necessarily came across on the telephone—Jean pushed "end." But in neither public nor personal matters should she be spilling her guts. *Figuratively,* she told her gurgling stomach.

The small clock on the desk read 5:45. She made a cup of ginger tea, and drank it while looking out of the front window. The day was darkening, she saw, as the clouds swelled and thickened. Cars came and went. People roamed around. Alasdair walked a group to the castle doorway and another to the chapel path, no doubt explaining about the unfortunate incident of the inscription, and let that be a lesson to us on the protection of historical and cultural resources. Most of the time he was out of sight in the shop.

Jean pressed her nose to the glass. That scrawny, blond, crew-cut woman heading down to the chapel had to be Valerie Trotter, braving whatever she meant by Isabel's curse. What? Had Logan given her and Derek such a hard time she wanted to check out the scene of the crime for herself? Again—she'd been on the excavation team.

The phone on the desk blurted a double beep. By the time Jean had her hand on the receiver, she realized it wasn't going to ring again. Alasdair must have picked up the extension in the shop. She hoped it was good news, something that would cool the anger and fear she'd seen bubbling up from his underground magma pools . . . Time had already done that. And guilt as well, probably, about snapping at her as much as about losing the inscription.

A small plate dusted with crumbs indicated that he had had lunch. She could go ahead and cook something for dinner, then, something that did not involve beaks and black feathers but did involve fowl. Chicken soup. That was supposed to be good for what ailed you.

Jean found her painfully assembled recipes and starting slicing and dicing vegetables, very carefully, for the knife was dull. Minty would have been horrified—not that Polly hadn't proved that you could slice yourself just fine with a sharp knife. A tickle at her ankle was Dougie, roused from his nap by the smell of cooking chicken. *Yeah, to a dog you're part of the family. To a cat, you're staff.* Jean forked over a shred or two.

By the time she started the pot simmering, it was past six-thirty. The clouds were now thick gray roils like bales of wool, blocking the sunlight and sucking the color out of the landscape. Turning on the lights in the living room, she added a row of stitches to the sweater she was knitting for Alasdair while the raucous laugh track of an American sitcom tried to bludgeon her into believing that a couple insulting each other was funny.

At last it was seven-thirty. Jean hiked up the burner beneath the pot of soup and set the table. Then, taking a deep breath, she stepped out into the premature dusk.

CHAPTER SIXTEEN

Outside, Jean watched the taillights of the last car flicker past the gate and disappear. The castle door thudded shut. Alasdair walked briskly down the steps and continued on to the gate, where he stopped.

The cool air was growing more chill and more still by the moment. The leaves were no longer rippling, but were making only the most subtle of motions, as though invisible hands eased them aside so invisible faces could look between them. Jean crossed her arms over her chest and moved in a measured stroll toward Alasdair. He glanced around at the sound of her steps.

"Who was that on the phone?" she asked.

"D.I. Gary Delaney, in person. In a filthy mood as well. Not so keen on apologizing for ignoring my message about the answerphone tape, I'm thinking."

"But still he apologized. That should make you feel better." The time for tiptoeing through the thistles of Alasdair's feelings was past. And he had feelings. He was not austere in emotion, just in expression.

"If I'm apologizing," he said, "for speaking to you so harshly, will you be feeling better as well?"

Naturally he'd find a way to both apologize and save face. "Of course I will. How about if I apologize for—well, darn it, I'm still not sure what I saw last night, if anything, but I could have said something. I've caused you enough trouble already."

He pulled her against his side. "No, lass, I reckon the

trouble's on both sides."

She sagged against him, wrapping her arm around his waist. He was still exuding a slight force field that pushed her away, if only by millimeters. *We'll manage well enough.* But wasn't that what she and Brad had ended up doing, managing?

The green of the precipitous pasture on the other side of the road faded. A light shone in Roddy's farmhouse. A dog barked, an eerie echo in the silence. And the cows at the top of the field started for home, lurching down the slope as fast as they could run. Their bloated bellies swung from side to side above their spindly legs, like water balloons balanced on toothpicks. Jean gasped, expecting a twenty-Holstein pileup at the fence, but no, the cows skidded to a halt, milled around a moment, and then filed off toward the barn.

Jean laughed. Even better, so did Alasdair. For one glorious minute they stood laughing together. Then Alasdair shut and locked the gate. Side by side they headed back toward the lights and warmth of the flat, pausing only for him to retrieve a small cardboard box from the shop and lock that door, too. He locked the door of the flat and tested it twice. So it's not just me with nerves, Jean thought.

The flat was filled with the homey fragrance of chicken soup. Alasdair sniffed the air.

"I fixed dinner," Jean explained.

"You fixed it? It was broken, then?" He set the box on the desk and pulled off the lid, revealing a smudged glass disc and a gold blot resting on a bed of tissue paper.

"Those are the things from the dungeon floor. You climbed down there? All alone?"

"You'd not be fitting a backup team into that small a space," he replied, and, as she picked up the disc to look at it more closely, "I'd have collected this lot in any event, but now, with everything falling apart in my hands . . ."

"Things were falling apart before you got here," Jean told him, not that anything she could say would convince him. She raised the glass and peered through it at the clock, only to recoil at the distorted smear. "I thought this was the lens from a flashlight, but it's not."

"It's the magnifying lens from Wallace's telescope," said Alasdair. "It fits the one in the lumber room a treat. He was using it as a magnifying glass, I reckon."

"Looking at what? What attracted him down that ladder, knees and all? Something more than general curiosity, surely."

"One more fine, mystifying question. What do you make of this?" He pressed his forefinger onto the bit of gold and held it up.

Jean took his cool, dry hand and steadied it before her face so she could focus on the dot. Except it wasn't a dot. It was a lilliputian gold star. Something very small, but packing quite a punch, exploded in the pit of her stomach. "Good God. That's from Ciara's earrings. You remember, she was wearing them yesterday. They sounded like Santa Claus and his eight tiny reindeer. I got a good look at them this afternoon—they're cascades of little gold stars."

His hand went icy. He pulled it away, replaced the star on its tissue bed, and covered the box.

"Alasdair, she owns the place, she's been living in Minty's guest cottage all month, she's in and out all the time—heck, she and Wallace were working together, he drew the map in her press kit." She was babbling. She didn't need to defend Ciara, even though they were, in a way, sisters in arms. Sisters in Alasdair's arms.

He shook his head, whether rejecting her words or his reaction to them she wasn't going to try and guess. "Ciara came here and things began happening. Starting with one of Roddy's dogs, likely poisoned, he was saying. Then Helen, Wallace, the clarsach, the inscription."

"Speaking of the clarsach, Hugh called this afternoon. Thanks to Minty, his friend Dominic got it to the museum in Edinburgh, where it's under repair. Turns out it's got a hidden compartment with a scrap of paper inside that looks like a message from the sixteenth century. They'll need some techie hocus pocus to get it unstuck and out of the hole, though."

"Sixteenth-century cloak-and-dagger, eh? Isabel as a secret agent? Not the first time a lady-in-waiting's been used in a royal plot."

"Hugh jokes about arming people with musical instruments, but I never thought he meant it literally. I've got Michael on the case."

"The case," Alasdair repeated. "Delaney had a report on Angus Rutherford as well. The man was seen at a pawn shop in Peterborough on the Thursday. I told Gary we'd seen him here, but Angus is still on his missing-persons list. If it was him with Ciara this morning, he's not yet found his way home."

"He hasn't yet found his way back to Minty, at least. It sounds like he stays gone until his money runs out and he has to pawn something. It's an odd relationship, but . . . Well, here, take a look at this while I get the food on the table. I think I've figured out what Wallace was using his telescope for—plotting occult sites. Maybe he was doing something with the arrangement of the Border abbeys or prehistoric henges, but God only knows what, and He's not telling." She handed Alasdair the folder and headed for the kitchen. She might not have much appetite, but he had the lean and hungry look of someone who'd been thinking too much.

Jean made sure Dougie had kibble and water, then opened a box of crackers and dished out the soup. "By the way, I bet that stone in the chapel with the name *Henricus* is a memorial to Prince Henry Sinclair the Navigator. The one who might have sailed to America a century before Columbus. It's possible. The Vikings sailed back and forth and Henry lived in Denmark for a while and actually held Orkney from Norway, not Scotland."

Alasdair's gaze rolled from the map to the ceiling. "Oh well now, that explains everything."

"All the fringe history, legends, stories, might explain *something*. One shape on that map is labeled 'The Harp.' Like the Ferniebank Clarsach, nudge nudge, wink wink? The one piece of Isabel's inscription that disappeared before the dig and renovation was the harp."

"How long's this madness been going on, then?" He jammed the papers back into the folder and pitched it onto the desk, where it landed on Jean's laptop.

"Since Gerald Rutherford? Since Isabel? Since William Sinclair and the Templars?" When he didn't answer she said, "Soup's on. Come and get it."

He sat down and gazed as somberly into his bowl as though he were an oracle looking for omens among the celery slices and noodles.

Jean tried a simple yes-or-no question. "Have you heard from Logan about Derek?"

"No."

She could almost hear him thinking, *No one's reporting to me any more.* She couldn't offer him any comfort, so she offered him crackers. Food. Sublimation.

He said, "Come the morn, I'm looking about for a postern gate."

"A way of getting in that doesn't involve the gate and the gravel? I'll help, if I can."

"You can do, aye." He spooned up a bite of the soup.

It was okay. Not up to Minty's standards, presumably, but okay. Jean toyed with her portion and recapped the luncheon—Shan, Valerie, Ciara, Minty's recipes—as much for its amusement value as for any possible clues, while Alasdair ate with what even for him was less than good appetite.

"Valerie Trotter," he repeated. "Hackit woman with a head of short, bleached hair?"

"Worn-looking, you mean? That's her. Did you talk to her? What did she want?"

"She was asking me whether P and S would be working security for Ciara, whether we were planning any more digging before the handover, whether we were closing off the dungeon, considering what happened to Wallace. No, no, and no was all I could answer."

"She's listed in the book as a member of the dig team back in the nineties. I guess she's still interested. Although she could have asked Ciara herself—she stopped and said a couple of words to her outside Minty's house, before our haggis extravaganza lunch."

Alasdair placed his spoon in his bowl and touched his napkin to his lips. "Haggis."

"The food wasn't as bad as it sounds. Neither was Ciara, to be honest."

"Sounds like she was rabbiting on as usual. Worse than usual, if that folder's to be believed."

"She isn't letting the lack of facts stand in the way of a good story, but who ever does? So she's leaped onto the secret-history bandwagon. She's still got a feel for the heritage business."

An oscillation of his brows conceded that, if reluctantly.

They stood side by side, washing and drying the dishes. By the time Jean spread the dishtowel on its rack, the night had fallen so silent she fancied she could hear Roddy's cows chewing their cuds. . . . No. All she heard was the *tick tock* of the clock, an almost subliminal noise compared to the resonant *clink chonk* of Minty's grandfather clock, like stones thrown down a well.

And then footsteps walked overhead. Jean bowed over the kitchen cabinet, gelid unease oozing down her spine. Alasdair stood stock-still in the center of the living room, grimacing in something that wasn't quite dyspepsia. Even Dougie sat up and sniffed the air, as though he could smell something the humans could not, and the fur on his back rose into a serrated edge.

"So does the ghost walk down from the castle to the chapel? That's in the brochure, but . . ." Jean didn't have to describe what she was feeling to Alasdair.

Stiffly, he pulled the massive flashlight from its holder. "Let's have a look."

She got a sweater from the bedroom, then stepped out onto the porch at Alasdair's side. Beyond the eerie luminescence of the yard light, the night was dark and thick. Wisps of mist curled up from the river and gathered among the trees. The castle facade was a featureless cliff, sepia-toned, like an old photograph —no, there again was that hint of a warm gleam in Isabel's window. But tonight the clouds were too low and dark to reflect the glow of city lights.

Alasdair switched on the flashlight and swung its beam around the courtyard, casting the old stones of the wall into harsh relief, and then focused it on the path into the trees. Several gnarled trunks sprang into definition. The shadows between them were all the darker . . . No, there was a movement—Jean tensed—it was the light glistening on a tendril of mist.

The uncanny was here, not there. That all-too-familiar paranormal burden pressed down on Jean's shoulders. Ice prickled along her neck. Alasdair set his hand in the small of her back, fingers spread, the one warm spot on her body. She set her hand on his arm, hard as steel. He switched off the flashlight.

A dim shape was forming near the path, a slanting blur of luminescence, faint and pale, but with a human figure inside it . . . There. The body solidified. Jean either saw or sensed—or both—not a shroud but long skirts held in clenched hands, a stiff bodice, a starched ruff, a feathered cap, a small face looking back, grimacing so intently with—fear? determination?—that the teeth flashed between stretched lips and the eyes, nodes of darkness, focused far, far beyond the surrounding walls.

The ghost crossed the courtyard swiftly but in utter silence, trailing skirts fluttering, slippers rising and falling several inches above the gravel, making a mad, headlong dash for the entrance of the castle. Distantly, echoing through the deeps of time, a door slammed, and all was still.

Just as Jean started to exhale, she saw another light spring up, at the chapel, leaping and glinting like fire—reflecting off that plastic plaque—and her exhalation reversed into a gasp. "Do you see . . . ?"

Taking her hand, Alasdair switched on the flashlight and pulled her forward onto the gravel.

She staggered, shaking off the fourth-dimensional pressure field, and her feet crashed and crushed. Then she was with him, moving quickly if not quietly toward the path. Walter Scott's words whirled through her mind, nebulous and fragmented as clouds before a storm: *Seem'd all on fire that chapel proud, where Roslin's chiefs uncoffin'd lie, blazed battlement and pinnet high, so still they blaze, when fate is nigh, the lordly line of high St. Clair . . . What fate,* she wondered, *whose fate, here, now?* Clasping Alasdair's large, steadfast hand, she ran into the shadows beneath the trees and the mist trailed clammy kisses over her face.

The light at the chapel dimmed and steadied. The light of Alasdair's electric torch counted coup along the tree trunks, leaped triumphantly onto the terrace, and flashed among the stone-carved pinnacles, making the gargoyles dance.

The holy well was glowing with a pale golden light. *Inhale,*

Jean told herself. *Exhale.* And she whispered, "It's not paranormal, it's . . ."

"A torch in the water," Alasdair replied.

They stepped forward over the uneven paving stones. Yes, a flashlight was shining up through the murky water of the well, casting a spectral glow on the human form sprawled along its brink, head and one arm and hand hanging into the water.

Alasdair thrust his flashlight at Jean. She seized it with both hands, trying to hold it motionless, but the beam of light wobbled back and forth. Cold chills ran down her back and off her limbs. "Please tell me that's not Ciara."

"It's never Ciara," said Alasdair. He crouched over the body, heaved it from the water, and rolled it over on the terrace.

Big feet clad in heavy shoes. Long legs, a tweed jacket, a matching vest buttoned over the unmoving chest. A cloth cap lying crushed on the damp stone. A face turned upwards, glistening wet, mouth open beneath the shadow of a moustache, eyes flat, seeing nothing. A bloated face like the Queen of Faerie's milk-white steed. A bleached face like Death's pale horse.

Alasdair's voice was a whisper at the rim of hearing. "Angus Rutherford."

CHAPTER SEVENTEEN

Jean heard what he said. She saw Angus's hollow face, drained of humanity. Her mind didn't comprehend, but shriveled in denial. *No no no.*

Gently Alasdair touched the blanched wet throat and tested the waggle of a limp hand. "He's been dead for an hour."

No.

Standing up, Alasdair reached into his pocket to produce both the keys and his cell phone. He held the former out to Jean and flipped open the latter. In the glow of its screen his complexion seemed almost green. "Unlock the gate."

Jean's feet and legs responded even though her thoughts were caught in a loop, *not here, not now, not again, no . . .* She stumbled in slow motion up the path, the flashlight sending a bright beam leaping madly before her—tree, shrub, boulder, mist, pale and stark and then gone. Alasdair's peremptory voice spoke behind her, small in the dark silence of the night, fading away by the time she reached the courtyard.

Jean thudded across to the gate, tucked the flashlight beneath her arm and jabbed the key into the lock. Her fingers were so cold she could hardly turn it. The mechanism clanked. Grasping the icy iron bars, she threw her weight backwards to drag the gate open. The scream of the hinges rasped the enamel of her teeth. The grumble of a dove sounded from the battlements and then stilled.

Now what? What could she do? Screaming wouldn't help.

175

Neither would banging her head against the harsh walls of Ferniebank.

Illuminated by the lamp on the outbuilding, the courtyard looked surreal, severe as a moonscape. The splash of light from her electric torch was diffused and swallowed by the bulk of the castle. And yet that rosy gleam still lingered in Isabel's window, rising, shifting, fading.

She hadn't walked with stately tread from the castle to the chapel. She'd run from the gate to the castle as though the hounds of hell were on her heels.

The nape of Jean's neck puckered and she pulled the sweater closer around her body. *Inhale,* she reminded herself, and tasted smoke. Roddy's fire, not Isabel's. A cozy fireplace at Ferniebank Farm, in the flat, at Glebe House, and empty chairs before them all.

She and Alasdair had seen a light moving around the chapel. But Angus—Angus's body—was cold. Cold as the grave. Someone else had been there. Someone must have seen his body sprawled half in and half out of the well. The healing well.

Once again Jean imagined a flashlight dropping from a shaking hand, this one not ill but frightened. Or even culpable. Perhaps those hands had dragged Angus into the well to begin with, perhaps held him down in it until he drowned.

She could barely see the watery glow, the ripple of submerged light, at the end of the tree-lined path. A will o' the wisp, like she thought she'd seen there the night before. But her sixth sense had never been able to foresee the future.

The light winked out and then shone again as Alasdair paced back and forth, keeping vigil over the crime scene. That was Alasdair's body cutting off the glow, wasn't it? It wasn't the . . . witness, the person who'd dropped the flashlight . . . lurking in the trees, waiting to pounce. . . . Jean lunged toward the path, then twirled at the sound of a car, the roar of its engine loud as a jet plane's. With a squeal of brakes, headlights burst suddenly through the gateway and gravel spattered.

The lights went out, a blob in a yellow reflective coat hurtled from the car, the slam of the door ricocheted across the yard. Logan's face seemed gray and sagging as dirty laundry.

"He, they, they're on the terrace by the chapel . . ." Jean began.

"Into the flat with you. Lock your doors." Logan swung his own massive flashlight toward the building in an arc so broad that Jean dodged. By the time she'd found her feet again he was pounding down the path, his light licking the trees, the mist tattered behind him.

Why should anyone bother to say please? Or tolerate her presence? Switching off her flashlight, Jean plodded up the steps and into the flat, shut the door, and locked it.

The room looked the same, furniture, dishes, the book on the coffee table, the inscribed stone on the shelf, Alasdair's cardboard box and Ciara's folder . . . *How long's this madness been going on, then?*

And Angus made three.

Now, with events pushed from puzzle to chaos, something should have appeared different . . . Something did. Wallace's drawing of the dig was no longer lying beside the stone. Had it been there this afternoon? She hadn't noticed.

They'd run down to the chapel without locking the door. How long had the place been open? Five minutes? Ten? What if that rattle she'd heard last night hadn't been the wind catching at something loose. What if it had been someone trying the doorknob? Only if that someone had levitated over the gravel. Although someone apparently had, getting down to the chapel.

For all she knew, all of Ferniebank was honeycombed with secret passages. Clutching her flashlight like a truncheon, Jean searched the apartment and found no one. Not even Dougie.

But the panel over the spyhole was in place. She gave it a rap and then tensed, waiting for something to rap back from the other side. Nothing did.

She kneeled down to look beneath the couch. A tip-tilted pair of amber eyes looked accusingly back at her. "If you had any room," she told Dougie, "I'd be under there with you."

For an eon or two she sat on the floor beside the couch, her brain feeling like an amoeba, oozing from side to side of her skull. Then, slowly, she gathered her will. Time to put the kettle on. No matter what the crisis was, in this part of the world the remedy was as much the mundane act of brewing up as the resulting cup of tannic acid moderated by generous dollops of milk and sugar.

She made tea, and stood at the window letting the mildly scented steam soothe the tight tendons in her face. Then she sipped. Each droplet of liquid caramel fell like lead shot into the pit of her stomach. She flexed and loosed her fingers on the cup. She was alive. Angus was not. Wallace was not. Helen was not.

Isabel Sinclair was not.

A second set of headlights splashed the courtyard. Two policemen scrambled out and disappeared down the path into the thickening mist. They were from Kelso or even Hawick, probably. It would take a while longer for the full official cascade from Edinburgh HQ to wash over Ferniebank.

She couldn't see the lights in the chapel. She could lean out one of the larger windows. She could step outside. Or she could stay put, as ordered . . . There. A dark blur in the glistening gray tunnel beneath the trees resolved itself into Alasdair's compressed form. Jean unlocked the door and let him in.

He stood hunched as though waiting for a blow to the solar plexus, downcast face scoured with grief, anger, knowledge that this, too, had happened on his watch. Wordlessly she gathered

Alasdair, her lover, her significant other, her other half, into an embrace.

This time he did not resist. His arms came up and wrapped her waist, and pulled her so tightly into the chill aura gathered in his clothing that she had to suppress a squeak. His sweater warmed beneath her breast and hands, and his cheek, prickly with whiskers and frost, warmed against her forehead, but the sinews of his body remained taut as bowstrings.

At last his grip loosened and a deep breath shuddered down into his chest. "Tea?"

"Tea." Releasing him, she filled a cup, doctored it, and pressed it into his hands.

He managed to force the rim of the cup between his stiff upper lip and his rigid lower lip and downed the restorative in one thirsty gulp. The fault lines in his face eased, microscopically.

Hating herself for opening yet another one, Jean asked, "Did you move the drawing that was lying on top of the bookcase? The one of the dig?"

Alasdair swivelled toward the shelves. "No. It's gone, is it?"

"Yes." Jean couldn't stop herself from glancing over her shoulder toward the door. "I didn't notice whether it was there this afternoon. Sorry. We left the door unlocked when we ran down to the chapel, but it could only have been for a few minutes."

"I sent Logan in to view the drawing of the inscription and the remaining chipping, and the drawing of the dig was there as well. . . . Bloody hell!" Handing the cup in Jean's general direction, he darted toward the bookcase and frisked it. "Aye, the inscription drawing's gone as well."

"But Logan's one of the good guys!"

"Muggins here assumed he was, and so turned his back."

"Alasdair . . ."

The phone bleeped. Alasdair grabbed the receiver off the

desk. "Ferniebank." He cleared his throat. "Aye, Mr. Elliot, we're having a spot of bother here—no, no need for you to—a car driving away at speed?" He cast a sharp blue glance at Jean. "I'll have a constable stop by. Thank you kindly."

"Someone driving away? From where? When?"

"We'll find out soon enough. Ah." Alasdair threw the door open.

Jean watched between the curtains while he intercepted a Hawick constable returning to his car. The man's sharp features working impatiently, he jotted down a note and then pointed toward the flat. Alasdair straightened, indignation written in the angle of his chin, but obviously chose discretion over presenting his resume. He stalked back inside and shut the door very quietly, a sign Jean recognized all too well. "He said thanks and now go away, huh?"

"Oh aye. Just as he said down by the chapel. Officious young pup!" Another car entered the courtyard. Alasdair leaped for the window again. "Hm. A suit, not a uniform, this time round. Hawick's resident D.C., I reckon."

Lothian and Borders would handle the situation as competently as the Northern Constabulary, Alasdair or no Alasdair. Leaving him braced against the windowsill, Jean retreated into the bedroom with her bag. It was past ten-thirty, too late to call Michael and Rebecca. Let them have a night's rest before it all hit the fan. But Miranda, now . . . Again she punched in Miranda's number.

"Good job, Jean," said her partner's smoky voice. "You've caught me between acts, catching a whiff of oxygen in the great outdoors."

"Here we go again, Miranda."

"Please tell me you're not telling me what I'm thinking you're telling me."

"I'm telling you that there's been a murder. Another one.

We've suspected all along that two deaths here earlier this month were, well, assisted in some way—and even now I suppose the man could've keeled over on his own, except someone was there with him when he did . . ."

"Jean, you're breaking up. And I don't mean your mobile."

"Sorry." She sat down on the bed and bounced gently, making the bedposts pat the wall. "We saw Angus Rutherford with Ciara earlier today. He's not missing anymore. What he is, is dead. We just found his body lying half in the well at the chapel."

"Ah," said Miranda, her voice trailing away. "And here's me, thinking that Ciara's previous engagement, as per your message, was hair-raising news."

"So was someone stealing the inscription. And . . ." Jean carried on about Wallace and sacred geometry and secret messages smuggled in harps, Helen and sheep dogs and Flinty Minty now bereaved, Zoe, Polly, Derek, Valerie, and the ghost, while Miranda made understanding murmurs. Finally she reached a full stop.

"How's Alasdair getting on?" Miranda asked.

"How do you think?"

"Well then."

"I know." Neither of them had to spell it out. It might not just be Alasdair's job and Jean's assignment that collapsed under the press of circumstances. Making love with twenty drill teams whooping it up outside the window seemed like a piece of cake in comparison.

"So why then," said Miranda, "are you talking to me and not to him?"

Because I'm afraid. Of what, Jean wasn't sure. Whether he would reject her? Or whether he wouldn't? He might interpret her caring as smothering. She might interpret his self-sufficiency as callousness. In many ways, just managing was a lot easier. . . . The relationship was not the priority.

"Jean? Duncan's telling me the second act's begun. Are you all right?"

"Yeah, I'm all right."

"Then ring me the morn. We're having a wee dram with one of Ciara's investors after the show."

Right now Jean didn't give a rat's ass about Ciara and her financial accomplishments. But she would tomorrow. "Thanks."

"You and Alasdair, have a care."

"We're not in dang—" Who had just been searching the apartment for an intruder? "Thanks," Jean said again, and switched off the phone.

For what seemed an hour she sat, curved like the clarsach, feeling as though a cold, lead-lined shawl was draped around her shoulders. Alasdair's voice echoed from the living room, rough and low, reporting the situation to P and S. Confessing his sins, with no hope of absolution, not yet.

She was also hearing ghostly steps from above. *What do you have to do with this, Isabel Sinclair? Did you put something into motion all those years ago? Is that why you're still running away in terror? And what about you, Wallace? Did you stir something up? Or is Alasdair right, and it's Ciara's fault?*

The unearthly steps became fainter and fainter and died away. Alasdair's voice stopped but his footsteps continued. Those steps did not leave Jean heavy, chilled, and dull. She sat up, hearing her own limbs creaking, then stood up and stretched.

He'd returned her embrace without hesitation. He'd asked her for tea. They'd agreed to try a relationship, and while no one had actually uttered the words "for better or for worse," surely they were implicit. Hiding under the couch with Dougie was cheating.

Jean walked into the living room. Alasdair looked around. His expression wavered, like bedrock seen through running water, then solidified again. "Giving Miranda the scoop, were you?"

"*Great Scot* isn't a tabloid, I wasn't . . . Oh. Sorry."

He turned back to the window. "Never mind."

If he'd wanted to talk, to speculate, she'd have talked. He didn't. If he had, she'd have thought the apocalypse was near.

She sat at the kitchen table and tried to read the tea leaves in the bottom of her cold cup, but unless her future involved wet mulch, she had no clue. Alasdair prowled from the window to the right of the door to the window to the left of the door and back again. Outside, the mist thickened, so that moisture dripped from the eaves onto the courtyard, the repetitive plink-plink echoing the tick of the clock as it inched past midnight. Water torture. Time dilation. Relativity in action.

The room grew colder as Jean's adrenaline ebbed into chill. She was about to switch on the electric fire when another car arrived, and a second behind it, and then a third. Like flashbulbs, the headlights bleached Alasdair's stern face, then were gone. "At long bloody last!" he exclaimed. Outside, doors slammed. Voices spoke in curt phrases. The gravel fractured beneath multiple feet.

"It takes a lot longer from this side of the crime scene," Jean said.

"So it seems," replied Alasdair.

Jean claimed a place at the other window and watched human figures in their reflective coats vanish into and appear out of the mist while lights danced on the dim strands that were the tree branches and on the density that was the perimeter wall.

Alasdair provided technical commentary—the scene of crimes officer, the medical examiner, all the omnium gatherum of officialdom. "Ah, that's Gary Delaney. He's been down to view the body."

"You know Delaney already?"

"We've met." The acid tone of his voice did not bode well, as though anything here did. Valerie might have a point about the place being cursed. Once again Jean cast her gaze upwards, but the shadows on the other side of the wall did not speak.

CHAPTER EIGHTEEN

Alasdair wrenched the door open, admitting a chill, gasoline-tinged breath into the flat. He catapulted himself down the steps, only to be intercepted by the Hawick constable, who was unaware he was risking dismemberment. This time Alasdair batted the man aside as he would bat away a midge and strode over to two men in conversation by the path. Their bodies were silhouetted against a nebulous glow rising from behind the trees. Jean knew that was the luminescence of floodlights set up at the chapel, but she couldn't help but feel aliens had landed.

Jean watched Alasdair shake hands with a heavyset figure, then with a slender one taller than them both. Strain as she might, she couldn't hear what they were saying. Their body language, rigidly formal, told her nothing, although she found it encouraging when Delaney gave the Hawick constable, who had tailed Alasdair across the yard, a down-boy signal.

And here they came, shedding their fluorescent jackets. Jean stepped back from the doorway. Alasdair ushered the two men inside and shut the door. "Inspector Delaney and Sergeant Kallinikos, my—ah—er, Jean Fairbairn."

"Hello," Jean said.

"Good evening. Morning. Whatever in hell it is." Delaney briefly grasped her cold fingertips in his damp hand. With his tie loose and askew and his glasses riding down his protuberance of a nose, he looked more like a rumpled and rotund academic than a police detective. But while Delaney's gaze might be half-obscured by eyebrows like wooly caterpillars, ones that had crawled out of a sagging shock of dark hair streaked with gray, it was a gaze as shrewd as any she'd ever encountered. Alasdair's "ah-er" hadn't fooled him one bit, but then, why should it? Here she was and here he was, shacked up together.

The sergeant, now. Oh my. The tea leaves should have foretold meeting a tall, dark, handsome stranger. With a sprinkling of stone dust, the man could have walked into the British Museum and assumed a pose among the Elgin Marbles. Neither his plain dark suit nor the severe trim of his black hair could conceal the classical perfection of his face and body, marred only—to Jean's hypersensitive eye—by soft, rounded lips.

"How do you do," Kallinikos said. The gaze of his dark eyes glanced off Jean's rather than meeting it, and darted around the room. His handshake was a quick catch and release. In one long graceful step he was standing by the desk, a notebook and pen in his hand.

"Well then," said Alasdair to Delaney. "P.C. Logan's identi-fied the victim, and—"

"You're telling me Rutherford was here this morning? Recognized him, did you?"

"No. We'd never met. Jean here recognized him from his photos."

"Got that good a look at him, did you?" Delaney asked Jean.

"Well, yes."

"You've got a good eye to link the man with his photo."

"He had a distinctive appearance," Jean said, although she knew as well as any cop the unreliability of eyewitnesses.

Kallinikos used the end of his pen to flip the top off the cardboard box.

"Who else saw him, then?" asked Delaney.

"Everyone on the mini-bus. He was having, well, words, with Ciara Macquarrie, the tour director."

Delaney targeted Alasdair again. "This Macquarrie, she's your ex-wife, is she?"

"Aye, that she is," Alasdair answered without elaboration.

So Delaney already knew about Ciara, Jean thought, either from Logan or from his previous—meeting? professional relationship?—with Alasdair.

Soundlessly, Kallinikos opened Ciara's folder and paged through the papers.

"And now you're working for Protect and Survive?"

"That I am. Chief of security."

"And here's me thinking you were on the fast track, superintendent before the age of fifty, eh? But no. The laurels, they got too heavy, I reckon."

Thumbscrews would not have gotten an expression out of Alasdair now. Jean swayed toward him, but he didn't need her to step protectively closer.

He'd introduced Delaney as "inspector," not "chief inspector," his own former rank. The rank he'd held for less than two years, after he'd been promoted for honesty and courage up to, if not beyond, the call of duty. For arresting his own partner for corruption. Another reward like that and he'd have gnawed off his own foot to escape.

Alasdair's reputation had indeed preceded him, as Noel Brimberry pointed out. But Alasdair wasn't the issue. Jean redirected the agenda. "How did Angus die?"

"Not a mark on him, is there?" Alasdair added quickly.

"Not a one. He was not forcibly drowned, or so it seems just now. The M.E.'s muttering in his beard about heart attacks. That might have killed him. He might have fallen unconscious into the water and then drowned. If so, the postmortem will find water in his lungs."

"Someone was there with him," stated Alasdair.

"Because you saw the light of the torch moving about, you're saying?"

Jean caught the emphasis on "you're saying." And Delaney had hinted it wasn't Angus she'd seen this morning at all. *Crap.*

Alasdair squared both his shoulders and his jaw, catching the same implication. Guilty until proved innocent, if not of criminal behavior, then of slipshod testimony. Been there, done that, Jean thought wearily. Except this time Alasdair was in the dock beside her.

Kallinikos, head tilted to the side, used his pen to probe inside Alasdair's P and S envelope. She and Alasdair were getting a similar probe. Maybe if she tried to act more like a gracious hostess than a frazzled witness, let alone a suspect . . . "Please, sit down."

"Thank you kindly. A cup of tea would be lovely," said Delaney.

Okay. Jean started toward the kitchen.

Delaney went on, "Sit yourself on the sofa, Cameron," stumped over to Dougie's chair, and dropped down onto the furry blanket before Jean could warn him away. Not that his suit wasn't already dusted with lint and crumbs.

She looked at Kallinikos. He could speak. He'd said four whole words earlier. But now he strolled to the bookshelf and inspected the inscribed stone chip without comment, leaving Jean to deduce he'd like a cup of tea, too. Sending the woman to make tea was a way to divide and conquer the witnesses, although if Delaney had really felt the need to interview her and Alasdair separately, he'd have taken one of them outside. Suspecting them was a necessary formality. Fair enough. As she'd learned when Alasdair was facing her rather than standing beside her, the more you cooperated, the faster the ordeal was over, like getting that root canal.

Mouth crimped into a tight line—so this was how the other

half lived—Alasdair sat down on the sofa. Dougie squirted out the far end and made for the bedroom, paws pattering.

"What was that, a giant rat?" Delaney demanded.

Kallinikos said without looking around, "Cat. Domestic short hair. Gray with yellow eyes."

Jean put the kettle on. Food might lower the nervous tension meter. She found a package of crumpets in the bread box, and split and buttered them as quietly as she could, her ears rotated backwards.

Delaney asked, "What's all this about other suspicious deaths?"

"Helen Elliot, who lived at Ferniebank Farm across the road, was found dead without a mark on her," Alasdair replied. "The inquest ruled heart disease. Then Wallace Rutherford, the caretaker here at the castle, was found dead without a mark on him. The inquest ruled heart disease. And now Angus Rutherford. Three similar deaths in three weeks. It's getting a bit repetitive, isn't it now?"

"Were any of these people suffering from heart disease?" Kallinikos sat down in the desk chair and applied pen to notebook.

"So I'm hearing, for Helen and Wallace, at the least," Alasdair answered.

"Their hearts stopped and they died," said Delaney. "Seems simple enough."

"Everyone dies when their heart stops. It's why the heart stops, that's the question."

"What are you suggesting, Cameron?"

Jean looked around. *Wait for it . . .*

"Poison," Alasdair said. "Drug overdose. Something of that nature. Murder, in other words. If the death seems ordinary, so that the M.E.'s not extending the postmortem to toxicology tests, the murderer gets clean away. Until he does it again. And again."

Delaney shoved his glasses up the bridge of his nose. "This Wallace chap, and the woman. Had they any enemies?"

"I never met Mrs. Elliot at all, and only ever spoke with Wallace on the phone. But he was telling me then that his knees were too dodgy for him to be climbing down the ladder into the pit prison, yet that's where Logan found him. And there's the answerphone tape."

"Ah, that. Where's that now?"

"Inside a sock in the dresser." Alasdair started to stand.

Delaney waved him down and his sergeant up. Kallinikos paced down the hall. The bedroom light came on. Drawers opened and shut. Jean tried not to think about a stranger's hands, no matter how nicely sculpted, going through her things. The flat as sanctuary. Right.

Like a siren, the kettle began to whine and then shriek. She poured steaming water into the pot, popped the crumpets into the toaster oven, and assembled crockery and condiments.

The light in the bedroom went off and Kallinikos returned with the tape, which he inserted into the answering machine. He handed the entire unit to Delaney, holding the cord out of the way like a waiter standing ready with a napkin. Delaney pressed buttons. An electronically fuzzed voice, speaking over a sound like a brief peal of deep-throated wind chimes or like large bottles knocking together, filled the room: ". . . can be right dangerous, meddling in matters that are of no concern to you. Mind, you're an old man and on your own. Mind what happened to Helen."

A second voice, speaking with the bellow of the hard of hearing, said, "Get on with it, then." The speaker hummed, a computerized voice said, "Thurs Day. August Thir Teenth. Twelve Past Ten," and with a click the tape stopped.

"Blessed little to go on, that. The second voice, that's your Wallace, is it?" Delaney returned the machine to Kallinikos, who placed it back on the desk, if not in the exact spot it had occupied, then no more than a centimeter away. Producing a plastic evidence bag from inside his jacket, he inserted the tape, labeled it, and tucked it away. Rather like a dog owner, Jean thought, would go around with a pocketful of plastic bags to act as pooper scoopers.

"It's Wallace's voice, right enough," Alasdair said. "And the date's the day he died."

"And the first voice?"

"Sounds to be a man, but it's a bad connection, likely from a mobile."

"What of that noise in the background?"

Jean, loitering beside the kitchen table, repeated his question to herself. What was that noise in the background. . . . *Oh!* "That's a clock."

"Eh?" Delaney looked around as though he'd forgotten she was there. "What's that?"

"The noise in the background of the tape, it sounds like a clock chiming the first four notes of the Westminster chimes. For ten-fifteen, quarter past ten, probably." She had to say it, even with Angus now no more than an exhibit in a crime scene. "There's a grandfather clock, a longcase clock, inside Angus and Minty Rutherford's house. It plays the Westminster chimes. I heard it strike in the background when Keith Bell called me yesterday. Friday. Whenever it was. Of course, a lot of clocks play the Westminster chimes, including Big Ben. The sound on the tape could even have been from a television or radio."

"Keith Bell?" asked Kallinikos.

"The architect working with Ciara Macquarrie. She's staying in the Rutherfords' guest suite, so it's not surprising he called me from their house. That's not his voice on the answerphone tape, though. He's American, for one thing." An acrid odor alerted Jean that the crumpets were burning. She jerked out the baking sheet and dumped them onto a plate. Tea. Milk and sugar. Marmalade. Spoons. Napkins. She hoisted the tray, only to have Kallinikos glide like Baryshnikov to her side, take it from her hands, and set it on the coffee table.

They couldn't make her stay in the kitchen now. Jean sat down beside Alasdair, who glanced at her sidelong. She caught a glint through the narrow slits of his eyes that had to be approval. So he didn't mind her butting in when it was him on the hot seat, did he?

She poured and passed, and for a few moments the only sounds were those of spoons rattling in cups, doors slamming outside, and the everlasting crunch of gravel underfoot, like a large animal gnawing dry bones. "Someone," Jean said at last, a bite of crumpet catching in her throat, "has to tell Minty about Angus."

"P.C. Logan's volunteered himself." Kallinikos returned his cup to the tray.

"Logan," Jean repeated. Sour plum. One of the good guys. Thick as thieves. Again she caught Alasdair's sideways glance, not approval this time so much as agreement.

Depositing his cup on the corner of the desk, Delaney smacked his lips and folded his hands over his waistcoat-covered stomach. "The message on the tape. Some do-gooder might have been warning Wallace he needed help."

"By telling him that he was meddling and that meddling was dangerous?" Alasdair replied. "May be, but where's the danger coming from, then? I'm thinking it was a threat."

"Speaking of repetition, Cameron, did Mrs. Elliot or either of the Rutherfords have enemies?"

Alasdair put down his cup and saucer. "I'm hearing that Roddy Elliot, Helen's husband, was not over fond of Wallace.

That he blamed Wallace for Helen's death."

"Helen was cooking for Wallace, generally paying too much attention to him," added Jean.

"The eternal triangle?" asked Kallinikos.

Delaney snickered. "They were quite elderly, weren't they?"

"Age has nothing to do with romance. Relationships. Emotional attractions." Jean did not look at Alasdair.

"Wallace was a married man?" Delaney asked.

"A widower," replied Alasdair.

"Minty said something about Wallace's wife," Jean went on. "She died and Wallace retired from Kelso High School and came here. Minty implied that opening the castle and chapel to visitors was her and Angus's way of keeping Wallace busy. She's one of the people who said that Roddy and Wallace didn't get along. Roddy and Helen's granddaughter, Zoe Brimberry, said the same thing."

Delaney opened his mouth. Alasdair put words in it. "Mind you, that's all hearsay. Roddy himself is saying he and Wallace were mates."

Kallinikos checked another page in his notebook. "Roddy Elliot. Ferniebank Farm. He heard a car starting up and driving away around the time you were finding the body."

"You'll be questioning Roddy, then," said Alasdair.

The chair creaked as Delaney leaned forward. "I believe you've retired, Alasdair?"

Alasdair's eyes narrowed. "Get off it, Gary. I'm not threatening your patch, I'm offering my expertise. Only a fool'd reject help from another professional, but you're never a fool."

The two men eyed each other. Kallinikos eyed them. Jean waited for one or the other to throw down a gauntlet . . . No. The armored glove of a gauntlet was already lying there, warm and fuzzy as a child's mitten compared to the cold steel in Alasdair's eyes.

"Who's protecting whose patch, here?" Delaney asked at last.

Alasdair didn't blink, but one corner of his mouth tucked itself in. "Point taken. So am I helping you with this case, now that you're owning it is a case, or are you cutting me out?"

"Now that I'm owning it is a case," Delaney said, with his own pucker conceding another point striking home, "I'll not be rejecting any help."

"Well then." Alasdair sat back on the couch.

Jean wasn't sure if any tension ebbed from his body, but a few motes did from hers. She'd almost expected a duel at dawn on the field of honor, the courtyard at ten paces, with her and Kallinikos as seconds. She glanced over at the sergeant just as he looked down at his notebook, eyes concealed behind lowered lashes.

Alasdair followed her gaze toward the desk. "The items in that pasteboard box. I brought them up from the pit prison where Wallace was found dead."

Interesting distinction, between "where Wallace died" and "where Wallace was found dead."

Kallinikos picked up the box and tilted it toward Delaney.

"The lens," Alasdair said, "is from his telescope. Not the sort of thing commonly used in a dungeon. The wee gold star was lying beside it."

"I've seen similar stars in Ciara's, Ms. Macquarrie's, earrings," Jean finished.

Delaney's glance toward the box became a stare. "Well, well, well. Label that, Nik."

No sooner said than done. Restoring the lid to the box, Kallinikos bagged and labeled it and then retrieved his pen, ready for his next task.

Jean was beginning to wonder if the sergeant had any siblings who could be persuaded to work for *Great Scot*, as a contrast to Gavin's slapdashery behind the reception desk.

"We've got a chain of evidence," Alasdair stated, his quiet voice putting a slight but unmistakable emphasis on the first-person plural. "A chain of incident, you could be saying."

With exaggerated patience, Delaney waited for the pronouncement.

"Mrs. Elliot's death. Wallace Rutherford's death. The theft of the clarsach. Angus Rutherford's disappearance. The theft of the grave inscription. And the disappearance of two drawings from here, this flat, some time today."

"Both the clarsach and Angus have turned up, if neither in good condition," said Delaney.

"Drawings?" Kallinikos asked.

"Two of Wallace's. One of the archaeological dig—I found that on the bookshelf—and the other of the complete grave inscription, which we found in this book." Jean pulled the Ancient Monuments book out from beneath the tea tray and handed it over. "Both drawings were on top of the shelf the last time I saw them."

Kallinikos leafed through it, then gave it to Delaney, who weighed the tome in his hands. "Heavy reading, that, heh."

"Two drawings," said Kallinikos, making a note. "Who visited here the day?"

Alasdair got up, retrieved the book, and held it before him like a breastplate. "It was P.C. Logan who most likely took the drawings, though I didn't think to ask him about them just now."

"The local bobby?" Delaney asked. "Come now, Cameron, just because you're thinking yourself too good for the police force doesn't entitle you to go slandering those still in it. You were watching the door all afternoon, were you?"

Alasdair's jaw shifted and his lips clamped—Jean could almost hear his teeth grinding. "No, I didn't have my eye on the door the entire time. The place was locked up, though, and Jean was here since—when, Jean?"

"I got back about three."

Delaney cocked his hedgerows of brows. "Who has keys?"

"Everyone, including the sheepdogs across the way." Alasdair paced over to the window.

"Those keys need collecting."

"Feel free," said Alasdair, a marginally more polite response than "No kidding."

"Is there anything else?" Kallinikos asked.

Jean could think of any number of things—speculations on sacred geometry, comments on architecture and fine cooking—but not now. Not tonight. Maybe not ever, depending on what Delaney considered evidence. Alasdair now, Alasdair never counted anything out.

He said, "Not at present, no. Here's one of your chaps just coming up the steps."

The door reverberated to a knock. Delaney heaved himself up from the chair. Stowing his pen and notebook, Kallinikos stood and collected the cardboard box. Alasdair set the book on the desk and opened the door.

Another be-suited and yellow-jacketed man stood in the opening. Locks of sandy hair were plastered to his forehead by what was now a misty drizzle and his cheeks were pink. "You're needed at the scene, Inspector Delaney. They'll be removing the body directly."

"I'm just coming." Delaney ambled toward the door, stopping short to confront Alasdair. "Here's your chance to go telling me my business. Toxicology tests? Oh aye, on all three bodies as soon as may be. Incident room? Where should we set ourselves up to suit you? The dungeon?"

"There's a lumber room just beyond the shop." Alasdair's inscrutable, humorless smile rose above Delaney's bait. "Clear away the boxes and all into the castle and it's yours."

"And the castle itself?"

"Closed 'til further notice."

Delaney glanced over at Jean. "Have a look round, make sure nothing else has gone missing. I'll have my lot give the place a quick check the morn."

Nodding, Jean did not point out that she and Alasdair weren't hiding clues in their dirty linen. For all she knew, their linen had already been carried away by criminals unknown.

"We'll take your formal statements the morn as well. By then the media will be after us like a pack of wolves." Muttering to himself, Delaney left the building.

Kallinikos paused in the doorway. "You're the Jean Fairbairn writing for *Great Scot*? Grand stories, one and all." Leaving Jean gaping—the sergeant had unexpected depths, not to mention good taste—he stepped out into the mizzle and was gone.

Alasdair closed the door, locked it, and stood with his back against it, eyes closed, less expressive than the granite gravestones beside the church.

Jean thought of the murder of King James I, how a noblewoman had tried to block the door against the assassins by thrusting her own arm through the slots intended for a bar. To no avail, in the end. Keith Bell would enjoy that story. The king had hidden in the catchment area for a privy, so that his last breath had been one of slime and stink.

Inhaling a deep breath flavored with nothing nastier than charred crumpet and cold night air, Jean added Delaney's cup to the tray and picked it up. Her bones turned to spaghetti. Not even *al dente* spaghetti at that, but the flabby kind poured out of the can. With a clash of crockery, she plunked the tray down on the coffee table and herself down on the couch.

Roused by the noise, Alasdair plodded to her side, pressed her shoulder briefly, then carried the tray into the kitchen and began washing the dishes—his way of reassuring her, or encouraging her, or perhaps simply distracting himself.

Jean managed to stand herself up, not without a groan that was as much mental as physical. Her brain hurt as though it had been pummeled by large mailed fists. "Dougie?" she called down the hallway. "You can come out now."

Unimpressed by her reassurances, Dougie did not appear.

Jean fluffed the throw pillows and straightened the bookshelf, tidying the room as much as checking it over. Nothing else seemed to be gone, but then, she'd hardly inventoried the place.

Water ran and cups clinked in the kitchen. She thought of joking about what Minty had said, Wallace and Roddy going on at each other like stags in rut, and how it was Alasdair and Delaney who'd left the floor strewn with bits of antler. But not only was that a weak joke, it brought her back around to Minty, who had been so sure her husband was coming home any moment, and yet he had come back to Ciara instead. Jean asked Alasdair, "How did you meet Delaney?"

"I was obliged to ask for Lothian and Borders' assistance in a case three or four years since. He made it plain I was on his patch and on his sufferance. We got on well enough, though. I didn't outrank him then. I don't outrank him now, come to that."

"He doesn't seem to be very, well, quick on the uptake."

"Gary can see through a brick wall in time. Or a stone wall." Drying his hands, Alasdair returned to the window. "I've made a proper dog's dinner of my new job."

"You're not responsible for Angus dying on the property."

"I'm responsible for the inscription. And for the two drawings as well."

"Yeah, but . . ." What could she say? They won't fire you? So what? He might be thinking he'd compromised his responsibilities by designating Ferniebank as a honeymoon cottage. He might be thinking of resigning. How long before the stress fractures in his face—in his psyche—widened and crumbled and he collapsed into rubble, crushing Jean as he fell. She'd already been winged by a falling gargoyle, when she told him about the lights in the chapel.

She tried telling herself she wasn't responsible for him, for his psyche, for any part of his anatomy physical, emotional, or symbolic. But the set of his shoulders as he stood at the window, the angle of his head, the resonance of his voice lingering in her ears—each minor aspect of his presence had combined into more than the sum of his parts.

Maybe she wasn't collateral damage just yet. She tried, "And here we thought we'd be far from the madding crowd."

"The madding crowd's away for the rest of the night," he replied, to the accompaniment of doors slamming and engines revving. "What's the time?"

"Too late for owl set and too early for lark rise."

That drew a scorched chuckle.

Jean picked up her laptop and the Ancient Monuments book. "I'm taking these back to the bedroom. Oh, and that bit of inscription, too."

"I'll bring that along presently." He was still staring out the window, she could only assume at the constables who'd been left to watch the crime scene.

"Aren't you coming to bed, Alasdair?"

"You're not expecting me to sleep, are you?" he said over his shoulder.

"I never said anything about sleeping." Her smile was about as suggestive as the teapot, and was downright wobbly at the corners, but surely he'd pick up on the message. The pressing of flesh to flesh, to close out the chill, because they still had warm, living flesh to press. Because otherwise they'd both lie awake during the bitter watches of the night. Because they were a couple now.

He turned the rest of the way around. One of his eyebrows creaked upwards. "Ah. Well then."

"I'll be waiting." Jean headed down the hall, telling herself to worry about tomorrow when tomorrow arrived. Knowing that tomorrow was already breaking down the door.

CHAPTER NINETEEN

Jean floundered upwards from the deep dark pool of her dreams, a place where monsters glided, their silent tentacles brushing her ankles. Where did that outboard motor come from? She pried open an eye to see Dougie crouched at her shoulder, directing his purrs into her ear. Beyond him the window curtains glowed faintly. Either it was very early or it was very cloudy.

She rolled over, noting dispassionately that she ached in every muscle, and peered past the mound of Alasdair's shoulder at the clock. Seven a.m., less than an hour past dawn. They'd only slept for . . . No. Refusing to recognize how short the night had been would keep it from taking its toll.

Alasdair was asleep, lips parted on a slow breath that was almost a snore. His face in repose was so smooth, as though air-brushed of its creases and knots, that she wanted only one thing more than to kiss its every angle, and that was for him to rest. She eased herself from the warm nest of the bed, tiptoed first to the bathroom, and then to the kitchen.

Dougie was waiting. Automatically, Jean fed him, then turned back toward the bed just as first one vehicle and then another drove into the courtyard. Doors slammed and gravel crunched in time with Dougie's kibble-chomping. From the bedroom came the sound of bare feet hitting the floor.

So much for a good lie-in, then. Tying the sash of her robe, Jean checked out the caffeine situation. There was Minty's coffee, but Alasdair's Scottish taste buds would prefer tea for

201

breakfast. She filled the kettle, set it on the stove, and leaned blearily on the cabinet.

The inscription. Minty. Ciara. Angus. Alasdair, morning and evening, fire and ice, austere in public and in private—well, there hadn't been any candlelight and roses in last night's encounter, just a desperate urgency to seize the moment and each other, no preliminaries, no elaborations, and no supernatural harp music, either, despite the clump of the bedposts against the wall. Jean stretched, wincing. But physical healing was easy.

The unwatched kettle began to boil with a shriek that made her jerk to attention. She was staring at the remaining eggs—soft-boiling required split-second timing, frying required a delicate touch, poaching was messy, scrambling, she could handle scrambling—when Alasdair appeared from the hallway, walked straight to the window, and swept the curtain aside.

"Good morning," Jean said.

He looked around. His face seemed out of focus. Wrinkling her nose established that she really was wearing her glasses—it was him, not her. Even as she looked, though, his features firmed and steadied. It wasn't seeing each other in the nude that was revealing. It was seeing each other at moments like this.

"Good morning." He raised an arm, giving her just enough room to tuck herself against his side, and held her close.

She looked out the window into a hazy, smeary, colorless morning. A constable was drooping at the top of the path, a second one rendering aid and comfort in the shape of a thermos flask and a package wrapped in waxed paper. Past them walked a couple of coveralled technicians, hauling boxes and bags down to the chapel.

"They're starting in again now that it's daylight," said Alasdair.

"Yeah." Jean turned her head so she had a view of his

unshaven cheek. Some whiskers were golden-red, some were silver.

"I'd better get to clearing away the lumber room," he said.

"Then I'd better get some food on the table."

Easing away from his arm—maybe they would learn how to fit together, after all—Jean poured two mugs of tea and set a skillet on the stove. Simultaneously they put together a breakfast, its shortcomings concealed by marmalade and butter, and outlined the situation, from the apparition of Isabel hot-footing it for the castle—relevant, Jean thought, but Alasdair abstained—to the curious incident of the car speeding away in the nighttime.

By the time they scooted back from the table, another vehicle was arriving in the courtyard. Alasdair ascertained that it did not contain either Inspector Delaney or Sergeant Kallinikos. Still, he left Jean to wash the dishes while he washed himself and dressed in his caretaker's uniform, khakis and sweater. He was out the door, keys in hand, before she'd dried the last plate.

Now it was her turn to stand and look out the window. Alasdair dragooned a constable and started him removing things from the lumber room while he unlocked the front door of the castle. Either Delaney had left instructions that Alasdair was to be obeyed, or Alasdair's habit of command swept the young man along. Not that that particular constable was the officious one from Hawick who'd given Alasdair such a hard time the night before.

Jean showered, then returned to the bedroom, where she arranged the covers around Dougie's peacefully sleeping form—must be nice—and dressed, gingerly, in jeans and a sweatshirt, the better to carry boxes, search for secret passages, or do whatever else sprang from Alasdair's agile mind before it was time to head into Stanelaw.

She had every intention of dragging him to the Granite Cross with her this afternoon, interview with Ciara or no interview with Ciara. Not only were beer and music good restoratives, he could do some interviewing of his own, depending on how many of the cast of characters showed up. As for making statements, presumably at Logan's office, well, she and Alasdair would await Delaney's pleasure—although interviewing Logan himself was definitely on the agenda.

Jean pulled back the curtains from the east-facing windows, admitting daylight but no sunshine. Opening the one to the left of the fireplace, she leaned out and looked toward the chapel. A human figure swathed in a protective bunny suit was inspecting the terrace, now wrapped in blue and white police tape. Would they pick up any traces of the criminal who chipped out the inscription? Or were they even looking for clues for that crime, eclipsed as it had been by a worse one?

She closed the window against the chill and proceeded to search the bedroom. No, nothing else was missing, not even the dirty laundry. The bit of inscription, her laptop, and the heavy tome of the Ancient Monuments report all lay in the bottom of the wardrobe beneath an extra pillow. It was probably overkill hiding the book—there had to be other copies of that, even though, with its academic slant, not many. Still, Jean told herself, she should sit down and read it from cover to cover. What if Wallace had picked out a coded message with pinpricks or invisible ink?

Right. Wallace had a lot to answer for, certainly, but there was no need to get carried away.

Now that sunlight, however thin, was shining in the eastern window, Jean saw a pattern on the stones between the two bed-posts, a shadow-rectangle with a dot close to the upper edge. Kneeling on the bed, she ran her fingertips across the dot. There was a tiny, well-defined hole in the mortar between the stones, big enough for the nail of a picture hanger. And the whitewash was lightly scratched just where the corners of a picture would have bumped.

So what had hung there? One of Wallace's drawings? Why else would it have been taken down? All the other pictures in the flat were copies of "heritage" paintings like the Mary, Queen of Scots, murder scenario in the living room. Just as well that one wasn't hanging over the bed.

Jean stepped back onto the floor. Dougie opened an eye, looked at her with an expression that would have made the queen's *we are not amused* warm and inviting, and went back to sleep with a soft sigh. "Sorry," Jean told him.

She plugged her cell phone into its charger and took advantage of cleaning out the litter box in the closet to listen at the Laird's Lug. The aperture channeled the sounds from the Laigh Hall with startling clarity—the thumps and bumps of objects landing on the wooden floor, Alasdair's calm voice directing, the constable interjecting "Aye, sir" every so often. Both the task and the subordinate, Jean thought, should make Alasdair feel a little more in control of the situation.

She herself had lost control thirty-six hours before, when she pulled up in the courtyard to see Ciara emerging from the castle. Now all she could do was hang on.

White-knuckled, figuratively speaking, Jean stepped out of the front door to see the haziness starting to lift, the mist resolving itself into lowering clouds that were neither black nor white, just shades of gray. The leaves of the trees shivered as though fingertips ran down their spines. The air was as cool and moist against her skin as an earth-scented lotion.

Why was that constable pulling the gate shut? Talk about locking the barn door after the horses had swum the Channel and been served up with *pommes frites* . . . Oh. A media van was parked on the road. There were probably two or three others on the far side of the wall—they ran in packs, as Delaney had pointed out. Yep, there was a transmission antenna, appearing like a periscope over the jagged topping stones. If she hadn't taken up with Alasdair, she'd be waiting on the far side of the wall with all the other reporters. . . . No. Recent crime wasn't her vocation. She'd never intended it to be her hobby, but here she was.

Dogs barked from the farm, only to be quieted by Roddy's gruff bellow. A couple of reporters equipped with cameras and microphones jogged past the gate, scenting blood, no doubt. Well, Roddy could defend himself.

Jean stepped through the doorway of the lumber room. It looked as she'd expected, with a concrete floor, a barred window high on one cement-block wall, and a light bulb protruding from the ceiling. Hints of paint and machine oil hung on the still air. Plant-trimming and tidying equipment sat in one corner, building-repair tools in another, fishing rods and related equipment in a third. Wallace's telescope, shrouded in plastic, stood beside the door, along with two cardboard boxes surrounded by scuffed dust. It would make a rough and ready incident room at best, but Stanelaw's miniature police station was just up the road, and full facilities at Kelso not much further.

As for those boxes . . . Jean deciphered the words written almost illegibly on the top one: "Miscellaneous clothing. Oxfam." Was that Minty's writing, designating Wallace's clothes for charity?

"Begging your pardon," said a male voice at her back, and Jean jerked aside. It was the young constable, his freckled face open and affable beneath his cap. Returning his smile in kind, Jean stood by innocently while he picked up the clothing box and carried it away.

Aha. The one on the bottom was labeled "Drawing materials and papers." Her palms itching, Jean reached forward and tugged at the taped-down flap.

"Caught in the act," said Alasdair behind her.

"It's a fair cop, guv'nor." She looked around. "Don't tell me you're not wondering what's in these boxes. Maybe there are some more drawings."

"Maybe so, but I cannot open them up without permission of the owner. Or failing that, a warrant."

"I guess the clothes and the telescope and the fishing gear actually belong to Minty now, through Angus, but what about the drawings that were taken from the flat? Are they Minty's, too, or do they belong to P and S?"

"There's a fine point for you. I wonder if she'd bother arguing it, now. Why?"

"The thief didn't take those drawings because of their artistry. He took them because they were Wallace's. They must reveal something."

"You'll sprain yourself, jumping to conclusions like that."

"Come on, Alasdair. Wallace's antiquarian interests and the inscription and the occult stuff has to have some role in all this. Why was Angus's body found at the chapel, huh?"

"That's where he was standing when he fell over. Same reason Wallace's body was found in the dungeon, like as not."

"Wallace had to have climbed down to the dungeon, for whatever reason, but maybe Angus was dragged to the chapel."

"Have you ever tried dragging a body? A bittie woman like you'd be right heavy to pull along, and Angus was a big man. Almost broke my back just rolling him over."

"So he got himself there, and someone either watched him die, or came along and found him dead, and panicked and dropped the flashlight. Someone who got in and out without passing go and collecting two hundred dollars."

He smiled at that. "Without passing through the courtyard. Oh aye, it's a fine iron gate, but it's only stopping law-abiding folk." Alasdair picked up the last box.

"So as law-abiding folk, you're going to get permission to search that box."

"I'll have a word with Delaney. Until then, we've got enough to be going on with." He turned toward the castle.

"Kind of depends on where we're going, doesn't it?" Grabbing a fishing rod, Jean followed him out into the courtyard. "The door of the flat's not locked. You've got the keys."

He stopped, letting her catch up with him. "They're in my front trouser pocket."

She reached into his pocket and groped for the keys. From the corner of her eye she saw the constable tug the gate open again and a car entering. There were the keys on their ring, warm from their proximity to Alasdair's body. Straightening, she looked around to see Inspector Delaney and Sergeant Kallinikos climbing out of the car. Delaney's grin indicated that Jean and Alasdair's pose was the funniest thing he'd seen since the last Benny Hill comedy. Kallinikos gazed upwards, trading dark stare for dark stare with the crows.

Jean turned her back on them and counted through the keys until Alasdair said, voice bland as pudding, "That one. Good morning, Delaney. Sergeant."

Still toting the fishing rod, she locked the door of the flat and considered writing an article on the varieties and uses of British locking mechanisms, a topic she was getting more experience with than she could ever have anticipated.

Behind her, Delaney's soft Edinburgh accent, less mouth-filling than Alasdair's West Highland diction, replied, "What's good about it? By the time we'd knocked up an innkeeper in Kelso and got rooms, it was time to turn round and come back out here. God, I hate these small towns. Like desert islands, they are, with the natives making fire from flint and tinder."

"Or from burning-glasses," said Jean under her breath. Yeah, you set a fire and it gets away from you—story of the human

208

race . . . That's right, Minty had the burning-glass from the museum.

"I'm native to Fort William, myself," Alasdair was saying. "Grand place, if never so small as Stanelaw. Unless you're thinking it's Kelso that's the wee peasant village and Stanelaw's no more than something to scrape off the bottom of your shoe."

Snorting with either amusement or a hairball, Delaney crunched toward the lumber room.

Jean tucked the keys into her own pocket and fell into step beside Alasdair. "And where are you from, Sergeant?" she asked Kallinikos as she passed.

"Glesga," he returned, giving "Glasgow" the local pronunciation so emphatically it had to be deliberate. He added, probably because he was used to adding, "My grandparents left a small shipyard in Greece for a big one along the Clyde."

"Me, I only got here a few months ago," Jean called back to him, and followed Alasdair into the castle.

Either the place smelled a bit better today, or her nose knew what to expect. The small room just inside the door seemed less dark and gloomy, if hardly cheerful with its stark walls and gaping doorways, one into a closet-sized guard chamber and the other into Keith's garderobe. In the Laigh Hall, the constable peered out one of the windows. "A lad's scrambling down the brae behind the building."

Alasdair dumped his box next to five other boxes. "Come along then, Freeman, let's have him in." The two men hurried back out the entrance.

Jean laid the fishing rod across the boxes, then walked over to the blocked-off door. She eyed first the small pawprints in the dust at its base, then the expanse of broken paneling beside it —that patch there, that must be covering the spyhole. The hair stirred on the back of her neck and her shoulders puckered.

Never mind. She sprinted off behind the men, wondering

whether she'd ever stay alone in the flat, and if that would bother her. Wallace had slept there, year after year, behind a door that led nowhere, and Gerald had lived in the castle itself. . . . She popped out of the entrance to see Alasdair leading the charge with not just Constable Freeman at his heels, but Kallinikos as well.

The three men double-timed it through the gap between the flat and the shop and around the corner of the building. A fraction later, Delaney stepped out of the lumber room, mouth open to give orders. It hung open as he looked around for his vanished minion.

Jean trotted past and into the gap, rejecting her impulse to say something about heading them off at the pass. She contented herself with a tally-ho gesture and a terse, "Trespasser."

She hung a right onto a water-pitted path that snaked through the bracken and around tumbled stones, close beside the moss-plastered foundation blocks of the castle and beneath the windows of the flat. She slackened her pace—to her left, the slope fell steeply away toward the river. If she tripped over a root or slipped in the mud and fell, she'd have to be rescued, not a good use of police resources.

Kallinikos, running like an antelope, disappeared around the far corner. By the time Jean got there herself, running more like a tortoise, the chase scene had ended close beneath the steep stone escarpment of the castle. P.C. Freeman stood upslope from Derek, blocking his retreat along the muddy path. Alasdair was doing his looming routine again, helped by his position also higher up the incline. Kallinikos had his notebook out and pen primed.

Jean caught her breath. Behind her, Delaney stumbled around the corner and stood puffing, barely managing to pant, "What the hell's all this, Cameron!"

Alasdair indicated the teenager. "I've warned him off once

already. But he keeps turning up, like a bad penny."

In his oversized black garb, Derek looked small and pale as a grub. He muttered something about bent coppers and tried a flanking movement. Alasdair's large, capable hand pulled him back and delivered him to Freeman, who grasped his upper arm.

"Derek Trotter," Alasdair told Kallinikos, who dutifully wrote the name down. And to Derek himself he said, "Out and about right early, aren't we now?"

"Heard old Angus bought it last night. Just having me a look is all."

"Who told you that?"

"Dunno." The boy seemed fascinated by the mud-splashed toes of his boots.

Not just mud, Jean realized, catching a whiff of bovine manure. He'd been at Roddy's farm, hadn't he? With or without Zoe, or Roddy's knowledge, for that matter? Alasdair's nostrils flared, registering the aroma as well.

Delaney bustled forward. "Give over, lad. You didn't hear the news from a wee birdie."

Derek mumbled, "The mobile went at half past six and me mum answered. And she went, 'Oh no, he can't be dead.' And she went, 'How did it happen, then? The police have been, have they?' And she went, 'This makes no difference to . . .' And she saw me standing in the door and said 'I'll ring you later.' "

"Your mum told you that Angus was dead, is that it?" demanded Delaney.

"Yeh."

"Who was she talking with?" Alasdair asked.

"Hell if I know." Derek said, with a curl of his lip that didn't quite achieve a sneer, and at Alasdair's stern look wilted into a nauseated wrinkle.

"This is the Derek Trotter that Logan questioned about the

inscription?" asked Kallinikos.

"I don't know nothing about that," said the boy. "That's what I told Soor, erm, Logan. Why'd anyone want a bit of rock like that anyway?"

"Your friend Zoe wanted a bit of rock like that," Jean said. "You were helping her bring it back to the castle on Friday evening, remember?"

"What's all this?" demanded Delaney.

"That was Zoe," Derek insisted. "That was Friday. I was home in bed all the Friday night, wasn't I, not nicking no rocks. Ask me mum. She told Logan I was home in bed."

"And were you home in bed, then?" Alasdair asked.

"Yeh, yeh, that's what I'm saying!"

"And were you home in bed last night as well?"

"Yeh, where else would I be?" Derek's voice rose into the treble clef.

Alasdair glanced at Delaney. Delaney nodded, then turned to Kallinikos and jerked his head toward the corner of the castle. Kallinikos stowed his notebook and gestured to Freeman. "Come along then," Freeman said to Derek, and pulled him down the path.

"What's all this?" asked Derek, in an unwitting echo of Delaney.

"You don't just come walking into a crime scene, lad," Alasdair told him, "whether you've got a taste for death or no. You'll be having a wee blether with Inspector Delaney here. And it's time we were having one with your mum as well."

Yeah, Jean thought, *she keeps turning up, too.* Alasdair's "we" was neither editorial nor imperial. Delaney might have begrudged him an inch, but he was going to go ahead and take his mile.

Sputtering, Derek allowed himself to be guided around the corner of the building. Delaney and Kallinikos followed along behind, Delaney stumbling, Kallinikos's hand hovering at his elbow, but not actually touching it.

Jean and Alasdair, left in possession of the field, shared a long, contemplative look.

CHAPTER TWENTY

A tentative ray of sun brushed the hillside with color, but left Alasdair and Jean enveloped in the shadow-pall of the castle. She craned to look straight up the side of the building, past the stained stone blocks and the blank apertures of windows, some softened with molding, some harsh as knife wounds. High above, the sky was becoming silver, but the hue of the castle remained gray. "Look there," she said, and Alasdair turned to look.

Against the back wall of the castle, beneath the easternmost window of the Laigh Hall and next to a drain pipe, lay a couple of smallish boulders. Balanced against them was what looked like a rough wooden pallet for transporting goods on a truck or rail car. "That's how the kids were planning to get out of the castle after you locked up," Jean said. "They could let themselves down from the window and use the drain pipe for balance. Nothing like planning ahead."

"That wasn't there when I arrived," Alasdair said. "They might have shinned into the building that way as well, though there's no reason they didn't slip inside whilst I was selling sweeties or carrying your things into the flat."

"Well, at least you've found the postern gate. One of them, anyway. This path is another one, isn't it?" The trail zigged past a giant boulder, zagged into the trees that here pressed close to the back of the keep, and faded into shadow and tangled undergrowth. The trees grew all the way up to the perimeter wall—Jean caught a glimpse of squared stone, dank and dark, between the gnarled brown-green trunks. Back in medieval days no castellan would have let cover for enemies accumulate so close to his defenses. Tomorrow Alasdair would be out here with a chainsaw.

"I'm not so sure." He climbed several paces up the path, disappeared beneath the overhanging branches, and a moment later returned. "The track runs up to the broken corner I recorded on the Friday, where the two stretches of wall have each settled away from the other and one's caved in a bit. It'd be a good scramble to get over, but not impossible, not at all."

"Well, okay, that's fine for kids, but did Angus and the flashlight-person get in the same way?"

"On the plans, the wall's three sides of a rough rectangle and the river's the fourth. I'm guessing the wall stops short of the river nowadays, and you can walk round its end."

"Someone could always have taken a boat across the river."

"Let's have us a look at the wall before we begin searching dockyards and boathouses, eh?" Deadpan of face but nimble of foot, he walked down the path, then kept on going down the hillside. "I should have had a look at those wall-ends on the Friday. Certainly yesterday."

"You didn't have a reason to look at them until yesterday afternoon, and then you were busy." Jean fell in behind him, then against him as, sure enough, she slipped.

Alasdair took her hand and together they picked their way down the slope, treacherous with lichen, root, and concealed stone, not to mention massive black slugs like crawling chunks of licorice. The last step was the worst, down from a flattish rock at least two feet above the riverbank. Hanging onto Alasdair, Jean lowered herself to the swath of gravel edging the river, and in spite of herself gasped.

"I was joking about spraining yourself," Alasdair said.

"It's just, well, you know—I haven't, in a long time—kind of out of condition . . ." Dammit, the heat was rushing to her face, and he was the last person she needed to be blushing in front of.

But his grimace was contrite, not amused. "I'm sorry, lass. I should have taken it easy, minded my manners."

"Your manners are excellent. Practice makes perfect and everything."

His contrition leavened by a chuckle, Alasdair eased her across the gravel as though she were a soap bubble that would explode in his hands.

The river burbled along, humping up at and then spilling around rocks that in the strengthening sunlight emitted the glister of tarnished silver. The trees on the opposite bank seemed to stretch and straighten their limbs toward the warmth. Jean turned and looked up at Ferniebank, even more stern and forbidding from below, and tried to imagine the place as Ciara's healing center, serving up New Age vaporings and Minty's fine cuisine. She couldn't see the future for the past, though, which in her mind's eye gathered around the castle like ominous wreaths of shadow.

Alasdair picked his way over the rocks and pebbles toward where the end of the perimeter wall emerged from the trees. Yes, it was undercut by water and age so that its squared stones lay in disarray, making a rough and ready causeway half-overgrown by waving weeds and the sort of moss that didn't gather on rolling stones. "No one's come in that way—not a plant's been disturbed."

"Let's have a look at the opposite end. It's closer to the chapel. And to the town, for that matter."

Together they strolled toward the tumbled rocks where the chapel terrace had subsided. One of the crime-scene technicians was braced atop them like a space-suited gargoyle, scooping a teaspoon of yellowish muck into a plastic bag. "What's that?" asked Alasdair.

"Spewins. Someone was leaning over the railing there like they were spewing over the side of a boat. Last night, by the looks of it."

Well, Jean thought, sharing a glance with Alasdair, heart attack victims will vomit. The tech added that bag to a bigger one sitting beside him, one that already held bits of detritus—a cigarette butt stained with red lipstick, a soft-drink can, a . . . "There's another one of those little earring stars," Jean said. "I saw Ciara at the railing here Friday afternoon."

Alasdair peered at the bag. "Like Tinkerbelle and her fairy dust, isn't she? All right if we walk past here?"

"Around by the water, I've done that area." The tech stood aside.

"Carry on," Alasdair told him with a jaunty salute, and again he helped Jean balance across the rocks and onto the riverbank. She could have handled herself just fine, but she might as well give him the satisfaction of being the protective male—assuming he didn't step over that fine line between protecting and patronizing her.

An easy stroll along a wide, flat gravel terrace, and they reached a belt of trees less dense than the one behind the castle. Beyond them the stone of the perimeter wall gleamed in a fitful ray of sun, then faded into leafy shade. Alasdair plunged ahead, pebbles skittering. "Look at this!" Like the end of the first wall, this one had collapsed. Unlike the first, the stones had fallen so that a track as clear and dry as any garden path ran between wall and water. "The property's a Swiss cheese."

Ducking the twigs that grasped at her hair, Jean turned and looked toward the chapel. On this side the hillside was gentler, and the gravel riverbank segued into the field with the weed-choked worked stone that she had contemplated yesterday morning, pre inscription and relationship crisis. Several faint trails coiled around and through the field like preliminary sketches for an interlace pattern. At its top half a dozen constables and technicians were forming a line, preparing to leave no stone or leaf unturned.

At the bottom of the field, just where one path splayed out onto the gravel, lay a puddle. In the moist black dirt around it were impressed a mishmash of footprints, one perfectly preserved dead center. "Look here," Jean called. "That's one big foot. Angus?"

In an instant, Alasdair was crouching over the muddy patch. "I reckon so. He was wearing shoes with thick rubber soles in a waffle pattern, caked with mud. I had time to take notice."

Alasdair, waiting alone in the tremulous darkness beside Angus's body. It hadn't taken long before Logan got there. It had taken longer for the next constable to arrive. "Did you and Logan talk about anything while you were waiting?"

"He identified Angus is all. When he told me to get myself back to the castle and I refused, he didn't go on about it."

"I'm just glad you didn't leave him alone with the body, especially since he wanted you to."

"He was just claiming his territory, I reckon. But you never know, with those drawings missing and all. There're several partial prints here as well, more work for the techs." Alasdair waved at the officer in charge of the sweep and then discreetly retired along the riverbank. "Let's go back the way we came, so as not to disturb the ground."

Jean, at his heels, resisted the temptation to say, "Yes, Kemo Sabe." This was his show. This was his vocation. She was the sidekick. The helpmeet . . . Well, he kept saying "we." That was a concession of sorts.

She accepted Alasdair's solicitous if distracted hand back up the hillside to the courtyard, telling herself she couldn't worry about him being out of the loop and then feel miffed when he got back into it. Or she could, actually, being all too good at holding two opposing ideas in her mind at the same time, and quite aware that a foolish consistency was the hobgoblin of small minds.

A van stood close to the outbuilding, several people unloading equipment for the incident room. Cords and cables already curled from its door into that of the shop. Two men disappeared into the castle with Wallace's telescope and the rest of the tools and fishing gear. Derek had vanished. Either Delaney had taken him back to town, or he had Kallinikos rigging up the third degree inside. Alasdair sent a constable around the building to collect the wooden pallet, then headed toward the door of the incident room, a spring in his step and a glint in his eye, single-tasking.

No, she was not responsible for his moods, bright, grim, or indifferent. Jean peeled away from his wake and unlocked the door of the flat. Coffee. Tea was all well and good, but when the going got challenging, the challenged needed coffee.

She started the coffeepot, yawned, and unlimbered her cell phone. It was late enough to start some investigations of her own, . . . Ah. She already had a message.

Michael's voice spoke from the tiny speaker. "I'm right sorry I said that deaths come in threes. I know I didna bring poor old Angus down personally, but, well, ring us when you have the chance."

Jean had the chance. By the time she wrapped her chilled fingers around an aromatic cup of caffeinated acids, she'd already given Rebecca chapter and verse, pausing between each while Rebecca repeated them to Michael. In the background, water rushed and cutlery clanged, since it was just past breakfast time in civilized places like the Reiver's Rest.

"I don't even know who to consider as suspects," Jean

concluded. "The Ferniebank Fourteen, probably—you know, Ciara, Keith, Minty, Derek, Zoe, and their families and pets."

"Keith turned up for breakfast as usual," said Rebecca, "and inhaled the lot without even chewing, so far as I could tell."

"God knows where he puts his sausages and bacon," said Michael. "He's looking like he's not had a proper meal since the millennium."

"And then," Rebecca went on, somewhat more loudly, "he left. As usual again."

"In the Mystic Scotland van?"

"No, in that brown car he was sharing with Ciara yesterday."

"Did he know about Angus?"

"He must have, someone had turned on the TV. Not that he said anything to us. He put his cell phone down just next to his plate, waiting for a call, but he didn't get one."

"Ciara's stopping at Glebe House?" asked Michael faintly. "She'll be with Minty, then."

"Minty." Jean imagined Minty reacting to Logan's appearing with the bad news, her alabaster face immobile, her hands clasping each other because there was no other for them to clasp. Or was there? Did Angus go home at all yesterday? "I don't guess you've heard anything about the message in the clarsach. Sounds like a Nancy Drew title, doesn't it?"

"Not yet," said Rebecca. "It'll be tomorrow, Monday, a working day, before we get a full analysis. All we've heard is that the paper's authentic to the time period."

"Well, thanks anyway. If anyone drops by with a confession, or even just a coherent explanation, let me know, okay? I'm still planning to meet Ciara at the pub this afternoon, so I'll see you then."

"Good luck," said Rebecca, echoed by Michael's, "Keep your pecker up."

Not a problem, Jean told herself with a lopsided smile.

A vehicle drove into the courtyard. Cup in one hand and phone in the other, she used her forearm to shove the curtain aside. The sentry constable was closing the gate on a surge of camerapeople. A police car—it might or might not be Logan's, they all looked alike—rolled to a stop. To the accompaniment of clicking lenses, the door opened and Valerie Trotter got out, escorted by a female constable.

Thinking that it was about time the police got in touch with their feminine side, Jean turned back to the phone and punched Miranda's number, hoping her partner hadn't had such a late night that she was still asleep, whether alone or accompanied.

"Good morning to you, Jean," said Miranda, as chipper as though she'd been up and about for hours, no doubt doing good works. "I don't suppose you and Alasdair have solved the murder just yet. Or is it a murder?"

"We—the cops *et al.*—are assuming it is," Jean replied. "Alasdair's baying along the trail."

"Talked himself into the case, did he? Well done, Alasdair!"

"The D.I. in charge is crotchety, but he's no idiot. And the sergeant's a gem. You should see him, third-generation Scot, a statue by Praxiteles raised Clydeside."

"Oooh, lovely. Mind that you don't overdose on male phero-mones."

"I'm getting quite enough already, thank you. So what do you have for me?"

"You'll never guess where Ciara's—get this now—one quarter of a million dollars came from."

"Dollars, not pounds? What's she doing, cornering the international love bead market?"

"Not a bit of it. She's trafficking in the same things as you. Stories. What were you on about last night, sacred geometry? Well, as they say, there's nothing sacred. Ciara's just signed a contract with a New York publisher to write a book. *The Secret*

Code of the St Clairs, it's titled. Tied in to that *Leonardo Key* business, eh? And it's a business, an entire industry, last I looked."

The neurons in Jean's brain squealed like tires trying to keep the road. She felt her knees buckle and drop her into the desk chair. "Ciara's got a contract for a book? A novel or nonfiction?"

"My source didn't say. Not much difference between fact and fiction, these days."

"I don't think there ever was, not really." Jean looked down at Ciara's press kit, the folder innocuous as the envelope concealing a letter bomb. "She's marketing the secret history of Ferniebank. So what does she think she's got here that's worth such a healthy advance? Can the woman even write, for that matter? Maybe Wallace was going to do that while Ciara stood behind the reception desk and counted her pounds and pence."

"No pence. Pounds only, I'm thinking. And her investors are thinking as well, according to the one I spoke with."

"Money's a fine motive for murder. One of the best, Alasdair would say. *Cui bono*—who benefits? Who benefits from getting rid of Angus? And of Helen and Wallace, for that matter?" Jean found herself back at the window with no memory of standing up. There was Derek, slumped on one of the park benches, a constable hovering nearby. Valerie had disappeared into the inquisition chamber. The wooden pallet rested against the wall of the shop.

"No need to be listening in whilst your mills grind exceedingly fine," said Miranda. "I'll leave you to it, shall I?"

"You'll have to, I'm afraid. I promise I'll report in the minute I figure anything out. We figure anything out. Thanks. I think."

"You're welcome. Rear echelon, over and out."

Dazed, still clutching her phone, Jean wandered toward the bedroom. Through the Lug she could hear people moving around in the Laigh Hall, maybe searching the boxes after all. Had Delaney gotten permission from Minty? He had to have stopped by Glebe House last night—you didn't just let the widow sit and, well, chill. Although Logan would have gotten there first.

Delaney. Alasdair. *We.* She was going to have to poke Alasdair on his Ciara-sized bruise. Just when he thought he'd finally gotten a grasp of the situation, too. At least she'd have the courtesy not to start off with *I told you so.*

Although she had to start off with something. Back in the kitchen, Jean reached into the cupboard for a second cup. There were those plastic containers again. She heard Alasdair's voice saying, "Everyone dies when their heart stops. It's why the heart stops, that's the question."

Drug overdose. Poison.

Did Wallace ever cook for himself? Did anyone besides Helen bring him food? Did she get these containers from Minty? Helen couldn't have brought him what turned out to be his last meal —by then, she was dead. But then, both Wallace and Helen could have died of natural causes. So could Angus. But then again, that would put the sequence of deaths into Valerie and Zoe's curse territory.

Jean filled the second cup with coffee and headed for the door. If she had to play the helpmeet, she would do it to the hilt. Just as long as she could stand by her man, not three paces behind him.

She threw open the door to find the constable she'd come to think of as Officious Hawick mounting the steps.

CHAPTER TWENTY-ONE

Jean jerked back, but O. Hawick's hatchet face registered no startlement. With a nod toward the female constable following him by three paces, he said, "The flat needs searching."

"Feel free." Jean waved them through the doorway.

"W.P.C. Anne Blackhall. Sorry to disturb you." The woman's bright, black gaze moved from Jean to her colleague's posterior, so stiff you could bounce a coin off of it, and back again, making a clear editorial remark.

Jean grinned, acknowledging sisterhood, then balanced the coffee cup across the courtyard to the incident room. Crow-calls sounded like harsh laughter. On his bench, Derek went from a huddle of miserable resentment to a bundle of resentful misery. The constable-warden looked around at Jean. "Here, you cannot—"

"No worries," Kallinikos told him from the open doorway, and stepped aside so Jean could enter. "Mind the cables."

"Thanks. Whoa, that was fast." In little more than an hour, the room had been transformed into a nerve center, with everything from computers to charts on easels to a steaming tea kettle. The place could have been a car-rental office or widget factory, except for the unforgiving photos of Angus's body tacked to a bulletin board. Jean averted her eyes to the far corner.

Alasdair stood guard behind Delaney, who was sitting across a small table from Valerie. She was frozen in the act of inserting a cigarette between her red lips, staring over her shoulder at Jean—*I've seen you before, where was it?* Then, with a shrug, she groped around in a fanny pack lying on the chair beside her, produced a lighter, and applied flame to cigarette. Smoke billowed. Taking a deep drag, she adjusted the cardigan wrapping her narrow shoulders and concealing the Celtic tattoo. . . . Jean's visual memory clicked. That tattoo, she realized, was in the shape of a harp.

Valerie propped her elbow on the back of the chair, and held the cigarette aloft like a miniature torch of liberty. The gesture was intended to be casual, Jean assumed, but what it revealed was that Valerie's muscles were so tight they shook with an occasional tremor.

Through the acrid haze, Alasdair's gaze met Jean's. A slight tilt of his head and she remembered the crime-scene technician bagging a cigarette butt smeared with lipstick. Well, Valerie had been here yesterday, that was no secret. She'd been asking questions. So had Wallace, apparently, according to the cryptic message on the answerphone tape. If asking questions was a punishable offense, Jean herself was in for a long, long sentence.

She was still holding the cup of coffee. It had worked as a ticket of admittance, but wasn't needed—Alasdair was holding a mug dangling the tag of a tea bag, and Delaney and Valerie were equipped with the same. In the interests of conviviality, Jean took a swig of the black brew herself.

But as far as Delaney was concerned, she was invisible. Either Alasdair had given her a glowing reference, or she was simply beneath Delaney's notice. Fine. If he didn't recognize her presence, he couldn't ask her to leave. When Kallinikos pushed forward a plastic chair, she sank quietly into it, while the sergeant himself sat down on the edge of a table and turned a page in his notebook.

"Once again, from the top," Delaney said to Valerie. "Ciara

Macquarrie rang this morning, before dawn, to blether about Angus's death."

Ciara? Jean glanced at Alasdair, but he had assumed his great stone face.

"It's news, isn't it?" asked Valerie. "Dirty great news for the likes of Stanelaw. It's always been a Rutherford town."

"Where did you meet Ciara?"

Alasdair would have called her Ms. Macquarrie. Jean set her cup on the table. How could anybody drink the bitter brew without the buffering of milk? Bitter almonds—that was a poison.

"Ciara's known well enough in these parts," Valerie answered.

"But you've just returned to these parts," said Alasdair. "When?"

Delaney looked up at him, his mouth thinning just far enough to indicate that he was less than thrilled working as the first among equals.

"First of August. Moved house soon as Derek's school term ended."

"Why have you returned?" Alasdair asked.

"I've told you. Ma man gave me the elbow, didn't he? All these years, you think they'd count for something, but no. Packed his things and left with never a by-your-leave." Her voice was a whine with an edge, like a band saw. "I've got a bairn to support, and jobs are scarce as hen's teeth in Middlesbrough. Ma uncle, he said there'd be jobs here with Ciara's spa and all, and we could stop in his holiday home 'til we get our feet on the ground."

"Your husband left you," said Delaney.

Valerie's laugh sounded like Jean's coffee tasted. "Aye. Said marriage is no more than a piece of paper. Means nothing."

Jean begged to differ, but her opinion was irrelevant. So was Alasdair's, although she could tell by the quick twitch of his cheek that he had one similar to hers.

"Your uncle's name?" asked Kallinikos.

"Bill Trotter," Valerie said from the corner of her mouth.

"He's a resident of Stanelaw?"

"Aye. Owns the shop on the High Street. I'm helping him out there, for now."

"He introduced you to Ciara, did he?" Delaney queried.

She considered a moment. "Aye, he did that."

Alasdair asked, "Did you keep your maiden name when you married? Or did you go back to it after the divorce?"

"We're not divorced. Not yet. He's still ma significant other, isn't he? Significant prat."

Delaney smiled at that. Alasdair did not. Kallinikos asked, "His name?"

"Harry Spivey."

"Where did you meet him?" asked Delaney

"Here."

"Here in Stanelaw?"

"Here at Ferniebank. He was on the dig team, little more than a navvy. Thought he was a scientist, though, 'cause he had himself a term at university. Then he ran out of money, ran out of energy, found himself lumbered with a wife and child. Reverted to his true colors, then. Layabout. Chav. I paid for the flat in Middlesbrough, didn't I, whilst he and his brothers spent their giros at the betting shop and the local."

Spent their welfare checks gambling and drinking, Jean translated. Hearing stories like Valerie's made her realize that no matter how sour her job and her marriage had gone, she'd had it easy.

"Trotter," Alasdair said consideringly.

"It's ma name," said Valerie. "It's a good name. Good as Rutherford, any road."

Delaney leaned back in his chair, folded his hands across his waistcoat, and asked with ponderous nonchalance, "You have a grudge against the Rutherfords?"

Her hand dived toward the table. With a hiss the cigarette drowned in the dregs of her tea. Viciously she ground it about in the mug. "No, I've got nothing against the Rutherfords."

Again Jean met Alasdair's glance. *Right.* What had Minty said about wishing Valerie and her child well when she left the area, adding it was a shame she'd come back? No love lost, there.

"And did Ciara promise you a job at the new spa, then?" asked Delaney.

"Food service. I had me a bakery, but it went bust and closed down. Scones, buns, seed cakes, focaccia with herbs and oil—whatever you fancy."

Alasdair took a half-step forward, anything but nonchalant. "You're after working here at the castle, even though the place has a curse on it?"

"Where'd you hear that?" Valerie demanded.

"A wee birdie told me."

She rested her elbows on the table, shoulders sagging, head hanging. Her whine revved to a shriller note. "Things happen at Ferniebank. Isabel, her spirit's after revenge. When I was a kid we'd dare each other to poke about the grounds and slip into the castle, play hide and seek with Roddy when he tried turfing us out. Dead spooky it was, all overgrown and falling down. Then the Rutherfords thought to make it a paying proposition, and had the archaeologists, and me and Harry . . ." After a pause that Jean hated to think of as pregnant, Valerie went on, "Now Ferniebank's sold, for a right packet, I reckon. Polly's mum, and good old Wallace, and Angus, they're all gone. Ciara will have the place gutted and tarted up and that'll change everything."

No one replied. In the silence Jean heard the gravel outside shifting beneath various feet, voices shouting, a dog barking.

She looked again at the 8 × 10 glossies of Angus's ghastly face and wondered if it wasn't too late for Ferniebank to change.

Valerie reached for another cigarette, lit it, and exhaled so gustily that Alasdair and Delaney both coughed. "Aye, the place has a curse on it. Everyone dealing with the place is cursed. But I'd work for the devil himself if I had to, all right? I'm a single mum. I was a single mum even when Harry was about. I've got me a bairn to support. They slag you off for taking the dole, and they slag you off for working and leaving the bairn. Maybe here I can work and keep an eye on the kid both, eh? I meant to go to university myself, but no, Derek came along, and now I mean to do right by him. Though there are those who think otherwise. Am I right, Inspector Delaney?"

"Derek looks to be a bit of a problem here, Val," Delaney returned.

"He's fifteen years old. I can't stop him coming and going. I can't stop him from trying to impress Zoe or fit in with her and the local kids—they're after daring each other to come in here, same as me and ma mates, save that now there's rules, and officers about. Derek'll be away to school in Kelso tomorrow, like I was at his age. That'll keep him out of trouble."

"It may be too late for that," Delaney told her. "He's known to the police now."

Valerie flinched at that, but Jean couldn't see her face.

"Ms. Trotter," said Alasdair, "Derek's not been as forthcoming with us as we'd like. Mind you, we're not suspecting him of anything criminal. But he knows more about recent events here at Ferniebank than he's owning, and it would be in his best interests to tell us everything."

Jean waited for her to insist that Derek had nothing to do with Angus's death, that their business was their own and not the police's, but all she said was, "Ma uncle's shop needs seeing to. Can I go now?"

Delaney inhaled to speak, but Alasdair's voice sounded first. "If Trotter's your maiden name, then why's Derek Trotter as well, and not Spivey like his dad?"

Valerie went very still, like a cornered animal. "We weren't married 'til after Derek was born. Harry went on and on about him not being the real father 'til I paid good money for a DNA test just to shut him up. Now that he's walked out, I'm glad Derek's got ma name and not his. Can I go?"

"You're away into town to make a statement," said Delaney, "you and the lad both. After that, you're free to go. Don't leave the area."

"I've nowhere else to go, do I now?" With an emphatic scrape, Valerie shoved her chair back and broke for the door.

Thinking that there was a marriage made in purgatory, Jean, too, rose, and watched as Kallinikos, towering over Valerie, followed her into the courtyard. In the cheery gleam of sunshine, Derek looked even more like something that had crawled out from beneath a rock. Only a mother could love a youngling that pathetic, and she wasn't looking at him with a loving gaze, not right now.

Kallinikos gestured the hovering constable to one of the police cars and opened the door. Valerie cast a frantic gaze toward the gate, which was now covered with a tarpaulin to shut out the inquisitive cameras, and crawled into the car. Her long, lean arm dragged Derek in behind her.

Alasdair stepped up beside Jean, standing silent as the car inched onto the road and cut a swathe through the clamoring reporters. P.C. Hawick and W.P.C. Blackhall emerged from the flat. The former went to direct traffic at the gate, the latter looked in through the doorway. "Nothing of interest," she announced to Delaney, and to Jean she whispered, "Nice wee moggie."

"And he knows it, too," replied Jean.

With a half-smile, she turned back into the incident room and gazed levelly at Alasdair, who gazed levelly back . . . No, he wasn't quite focused on her face, he was just resting his eyes on a familiar scene while his brain whirred away like the finely tuned machine it was.

"Jean," called Delaney from his alpha-male table-barricade, "you didn't mention that you're a reporter."

"You didn't ask me what I did," she answered.

"Cameron's telling me you're not like that lot outwith the gate."

"I write historical pieces. Contemporary crime isn't my beat. I intended to write something about Isabel Sinclair's death back in 1569, but then, that wasn't a crime, not legally, anyway."

"And who's Isabel Sinclair when she's at home?" demanded Delaney. "The Isabel Val Trotter was rabbiting on about?"

"Does one mention make a rabbit?"

Alasdair's even gaze took on a subtle sparkle. "I'll look out one of Wallace's brochures for you," he told Delaney. "Did you take note of how Valerie called him 'good old Wallace'?"

"To cover up her animosity toward the Rutherfords, I expect."

"And her defensiveness on the topic of Derek's father?"

"That's easily enough explained," Delaney said with a hee and a haw. When Kallinikos stepped back through the doorway, Delaney went on, "Get onto Middlesbrough. Find this Spivey chap. And you, Cameron, Logan's taking statements. You and the little lady here, away to Stanelaw with you."

Jean drew herself up to her full height, such as it was, although Delaney hadn't meant physically little. "I have an interview with Ciara at the pub at two. Have you talked to her yet?"

"When we stopped by Glebe House to speak with Mrs. Rutherford," Kallinikos answered, "Ms. Macquarrie was with her."

"She's two bob short of a quid, that one is," added Delaney. "Mental."

"How did Minty take the news about Angus?" Jean persisted. "What about Ciara? Did you ask her about coming out here with Angus yesterday morning? Did you ask Minty whether she knew Angus was back—or if she knew where he went, for that matter?"

Delaney's eyes shifted from her face to Alasdair's. With a grin he asked, "You've got a taste for the gumptious girls, do you, Cameron? Maybe I should be sending over a pair of trousers."

Alasdair grasped Jean's upper arm and pulled, gently but firmly, as though trying to remove a piece of chewing gum from his shoe. "Let's be getting ourselves into town. Later, Delaney. Sergeant."

Yeah, Jean thought, *run away, live to fight again another day.* She let him pilot her into the courtyard while Kallinikos shut the door, his classic features awry with what she hoped was stifled disgust, not amusement, not with Delaney's hearty guffaw ringing out behind him.

When they reached the flat she wrenched her arm away from Alasdair's guiding hand. "And here I thought I was making points by keeping my mouth shut while y'all talked to Valerie."

"You did that. Best if in the future you keep quiet the rest of the time as well."

"So yesterday I'm supposed to report suspicious lights but today I'm supposed to keep my biscuits in the oven and my buns in the bed? I'm not going to cater to Delaney's Neanderthal sense of humor."

"He's in charge here. If he thinks you're interfering in the case, then he might cut me out of it."

"You're not responsible for my actions!" She realized her voice was rising.

Alasdair's was falling, into the soft rasp of a blade drawn

from its sheath. "This is no time for consciousness-raising, Jean. There're bigger issues at stake than your pride."

"Yeah, like your pride."

His face frosted over, his gaze going from the blue of a sunlit sky to the blue of steel. "Right. I'll be getting myself dressed. If you're coming to town with me, you'll be doing the same." He walked off down the hall.

Oh for the love of . . . Jean shook her fist at the door, hoping the gesture would filter through to Delaney's chubby chin, then with the same fist bopped herself on the forehead. What did she expect? Since when did Mars's orbit ever intersect that of Venus?

They were tired. They were hungry. They were stressed. She should heat up the leftover soup and make sandwiches—great, defaulting to the traditional female role, that was really going to make a statement. Cursing under her breath, she poured the soup into a saucepan and laid out bread and cheese, then looked around first the living room and then the bedroom.

Nothing was out of place—she'd give O. Hawick that much. Dougie, though, was no longer occupying the center of the bed. She bent over to look beneath. Aha, the fierce watch-beast was hiding, looking like a bright-eyed dust kitten. "Good idea," Jean told him, and straightened up.

Alasdair stood by the dresser, turning the inscribed flake of gravestone over and over in his hands. "I'll have Logan open the museum," he said, his voice so detached it was almost clinical. "This needs storing away with the other pieces."

"Yes, Ciara agreed with that yesterday. Even though it might be safer here, considering the break-in," Jean replied. Good, her voice was just as neutral. "Minty told me she'd taken Isabel's burning-glass home with her, for just that reason."

"The burning-glass is listed on the P and S inventory as belonging to Ferniebank."

"You want to ask her about it right after her husband's been murdered?"

"We don't yet know that it's murder."

Jean bit back some retort about big issues at stake. Speaking of which . . . "Alasdair, Miranda learned something from one of Ciara's investors."

"What's that?" He opened the wardrobe, held up a tie, then hung it back up.

"She has a deal to write a book about all the secret history stuff, you know, Ferniebank as the next three-ring occult circus. That's what got the last of the investors on board."

He continued to stare at the tie, perhaps considering making it into a hangman's noose. "Well then," he said dully, "that's right clever of her. By the by, we were standing about in the bracken whilst apprehending Derek. Check yourself for ticks."

"Ew." Jean shuddered. "Well, you got that one off me at Loch Ness."

Not looking at her, let alone indulging in any reminiscences, Alasdair collected a business-casual outfit and headed toward the bathroom.

Jean waited a minute, but didn't hear any bottles or brushes crash against the wall. Alasdair didn't throw things. He'd be better off if every now and then he did.

She took his place at the wardrobe. Her laptop and the Ancient Monuments book were still semi-concealed in the bottom—she'd get to them eventually. Right now, she had to look respectable, for both police business and the interview. . . . Damn. How many other reporters would be stalking Ciara, when it was Jean who had an appointment? At least Noel and the pub would be doing good business.

By the time she'd checked herself for blood-sucking parasites, Alasdair had left the bathroom for the kitchen, where she heard him stirring the soup. If Delaney caught him at that, would he make another crack about wearing the pants? Delaney probably couldn't boil water. As for whether there was a Mrs. Delaney to do the boiling and take the brunt—Jean shuddered again.

Dressed in her work uniform of skirt, blouse, and jacket, but no reporter's fedora, not yet, she hurried to a kitchen now fragrant with the warming soup. Alasdair was toasting sandwiches. Beside him on the counter sat one of the plastic food-keepers, now holding the inscribed stone chip nestled on a tea towel like a diamond on velvet. "If Wallace was poisoned—" she began.

"These dishes might be evidence," he finished. "Everything deserves consideration."

"Like Ciara's occult stuff," Jean told him, hoping for a wind-up and a pitch.

But he wasn't going to play. "Here, take some nourishment. You're looking a bit peelie-wallie."

He was looking sickly too, but she didn't point that out. For a few moments they simply ate. The warm food loosened the knot in her stomach. So did Alasdair's face easing from icy back to merely expressionless. She ventured, "What did Derek say? Not much, you told Valerie."

"He played the innocent again, said he was home asleep both nights, said that he was after impressing Zoe by picking up something from the crime scene. Not evidence, a polythene bag or a swab, something she'd recognize from the forensics shows on the telly. The fact that even we don't know what's evidence and what's not having escaped him."

"But you think there's more to it than that?"

"That I do. Whether he's frightened of telling or simply hanging on to that chip on his shoulder, the one lads his age develop along with whiskers, I cannot say."

Shoulder-chips were like epaulettes, symbols of status, Jean thought. And they weren't an exclusively male fashion accessory. "Did Delaney say anything about Minty and Ciara?"

"By the time Nik and Gary arrived, Minty was sitting in the kitchen, with Ciara dispensing tea and sympathy. Ciara told Gary she was working in the guest cottage when she heard a car in the drive. She looked out, saw Logan going to the front door, and hotfooted it to the main house."

"Where Minty had answered the door."

"Logan told Gary that Minty took the bad news very bravely, by which I'm guessing he means quietly, no screaming and the like. Gary's saying he's never seen a colder fish."

"She's not the expressive sort, no. But then, neither are you, not at first acquaintance."

Alasdair's shake of the head rejected any comparison. "Ciara was babbling about Angus passing over to a higher plane and surely his spirit would stay on to help with the renovations. Nik felt Minty could have done without that sort of remark, and offered to ring a relation, but Minty said there were no relations and no need to knock up her friends at that hour, she'd go on to her room and have a rest."

"You have to wonder what's going on behind that mask of a face." Jean sighed. "Delaney to the contrary, Ciara's not the gold standard of looniness. I've known students who were simply not of this Earth, but . . ."

"She'll do to be going on with," Alasdair stated, with as weary a tone as she'd ever heard him use. "And just now, we'd better be going on to Stanelaw."

CHAPTER TWENTY-TWO

Alasdair signaled the sentry constable to open the gate and release their sortie. Jean didn't try to shield her face with her reporter's notebook. She was only a member of the third estate by default, not by temperament. Rubbing her special status with the investigation in the faces of this ravening crew brought her down to their . . . But they were only doing their jobs in a competitive business. Like Delaney was doing his, in a business that had its own competitions.

At least now the cameras, the microphones, the shouting mouths and darting eyes, weren't on her case like they'd been during the academic scandal in her past. Judging by Alasdair's fissured lips, he was resisting a similar memory. He jockeyed the car through the journalistic scrum with neither curse nor comment, and accelerated toward Stanelaw, only to slow at the layby at the end of the perimeter wall.

A faint, muddy track led into the woods, now closed off with police tape that looked incongruously cheerful, like party streamers looped from tree to tree. "If you drove far down that track," Jean said, "you'd need a tow truck on stand by."

"No need to drive far, just pull into the trees and walk down to the end of the wall. In any event, Gary's folk found no car. Angus either legged it from town or from Glebe House, if he'd gone back there."

"Or flashlight-person could have driven him out here, then made his, her, its getaway."

"Aye." Just as Alasdair picked up speed past Ferniebank Farm, a tall figure leaped through the gate and raised an arm the size of a leg of lamb in the universal gesture of *Halt!*

Alasdair hit the brakes, throwing Jean forward into the seat belt. Her hand pressing her heart back into her chest, she looked around to see that the imperious figure was neither the ghost of Hamlet's father nor of Angus roaming in broad daylight.

Roddy Elliot opened the back door of the car and pleated himself into the interior. He was dressed in his Sunday best, a rusty suit and a striped tie hanging askew. "If you'd not object to driving me to the kirk, Mr. Cameron, I'd be willing to overlook the matter of the fishing tackle. I've left it a bit late to walk. Those reporters were on my doorstep like crows after carrion. Had to offer to set the dogs on them."

"Ah, well." Alasdair swallowed, probably repositioning his own heart. He accelerated again, if only a little. "Certainly, Mr. Elliot. When are services?"

"Noon." Each slow word in Roddy's deep voice sounded like the toll of a bell. "Normally I'd not hold with such foolishness as that new female minister, but I'm thinking that the word of the Lord can withstand the voice it's delivered in, no matter how dainty."

The wisest fool in Christendom, Jean thought. She extended her hand around the headrest. "Hello, Mr. Elliot. I'm Jean Fairbairn."

Doubtfully, he took her small, soft hand in his huge, calloused one and released it. "How do you do. A relation of the Fairbairns of Selkirk, by any chance?"

"Not that I know of, no, but my great-grandfather did come from Stow, near Galashiels."

"But you're a Yank, like that Keith Bell chap."

"Yes." Jean wasn't sure if that was something he expected her to apologize for, so she used it as an excuse to ask, "Have you seen Keith and Ms. Macquarrie's plans for Ferniebank?"

"My daughter was showing me a folder with drawings," Roddy answered.

One beat, two. "What did you think of them?" prodded Alasdair.

"Madness, the lot of it. The Rutherfords would have done better to tear the place down and sell the stone. Muckle good stone in those buildings, but little else save treachery and sorrow."

Treachery, Jean repeated silently. "I hear Wallace enjoyed researching the history of the area."

"Wallace was a nutter, like that Macquarrie female, spying, blaspheming—" He stopped dead, then added, "But he was a grand fisherman, for all that."

Jean didn't expect him to expand his comments to include Wallace's supposed role in Helen's death, and sure enough he didn't.

"Have you had the police as well this morning?" Alasdair's mild tone emphasized the "as well," claiming a brotherhood that didn't strictly exist.

"That I have. That dark chap with the queer name, polite enough, but I had to put him in his place when he started in with questions that were none of his business."

"Questions about Angus?" Jean asked.

"With them finding the man dead at the old romanish chapel, and me hearing someone legging it up the road, I reckon looking for clues was his business." Roddy's bemused tone indicated that a clue was some exotic species of butterfly.

No one corrected his "them." Slowing down so far an arthritic snail could have outpaced them, Alasdair said, "Your granddaughter Zoe was visiting the castle Friday. Does she stop with you often?"

"Often enough. Sleeps in her mum's room at the farm instead

of sharing with her sister. She and her granny, they . . ." He paused, then concluded, "Zoe and me, we get on well enough, even though she dresses like she's got no home and no family to watch out for her."

"Like Derek Trotter dresses," Alasdair observed.

Roddy snorted so loudly Jean almost checked the back of her neck for snot. "That young tearaway. Much better he and his mum go on back south, leave us decent folk alone. He was hanging about this morning looking for Zoe, but I'd sent her home. A crime scene's no place for a girl."

"You sent Derek on his way, then?"

"I turfed him out quick as you like. Same as I'd turf his mother out of the castle, years ago. I was caretaker there, before Wallace and Angus and that perjink Maitland wife of his tarted the place up. And now they've sold it. The love of money is the root of all evil."

"Is the castle evil?" Jean asked, not bothering to agree that Minty was finicky.

"There's aye been muckle evil in this world, Miss Fairbairn. Murder, thievery, adultery, pridefulness, drinking, and carousing on the Lord's day. Mind, I have no objection to a wee dram before dinner, but I've told Polly's Noel again and again, it's wrong to open the pub of a Sunday. But he and Polly, they're wanting money, they say. For posh clothes and posh cars and holidays. In my day we'd visit Largs and were glad of it, but no, nowdays Zoe and Shannon, they're obliged to go to Spain or Florida. This world we live in. This world."

"There's always been murder and thievery and the like," Alasdair said quietly. "There's always been folk profiting at the expense of others. In some ways, the world's a better place now than it was in, say, Isabel Sinclair's time."

Again Roddy snorted. "Isabel."

"That's a bit of inscription from her gravestone on the seat beside you," said Jean.

"Zoe was, erm, looking at it on the Friday," Alasdair added.

"She was, was she?" Roddy shifted around and, as far as Jean could tell from the corners of her eyes and the rearview mirrors, soberly considered the plastic container with its tea towel and chip of stone. Did his tangled gray brows rise and then fall? Hard to tell. "Isabel was a whore," he said at last. "Deserved what she got. Sins will out."

Alasdair hit the brakes again and swivelled, his incredulous look clicking against Jean's as it swung into the back seat. "What?"

"Begging your pardon, madam," Roddy said to Jean's stunned face. "My late wife would go on about my language, and about Isabel as well—defending her and all, like Wallace, like Gerald, but there's the truth, right there on the stone for all to see. The word 'catin.' It means—well, as I said. It's French."

"Oh!" exclaimed Jean. "You mean where that *requiescat in pace* is oddly spaced? Yeah, it looks like 'catin,' but what about that 'requies' just sort of hanging in mid-air?"

"And why a French word in the midst of the Latin?" Alasdair demanded.

"Mary Stuart, Queen of Scots, she spoke French, didn't she?" Roddy sat back, his arms folded. *Two and two make seventeen and that's that.*

He had dirt beneath his nails, Jean saw, and beard and hair both looked like they'd been combed with a pitchfork. She was reminded of an Old Testament prophet, and wondered if his ruddiness was due to alcohol after all, or to basking in the glow of his own righteousness. Turning back around, she shared yet another look with Alasdair. They'd thought Ciara was making some leaps of fancy. What was Roddy making—leaps of faith? Fancy and faith were almost two sides of the same coin, and very often involved actual physical coinage.

"So what did Isabel get, then?" asked Alasdair.

"Her death. The wages of sin."

"The fire in her room, you mean?" Jean asked. "The burning-glass and signaling her, ah, friend?"

"That's Gerald's version of events, bowdlerized for the ladies —Wallace's mother, most like, and a fine douce woman she was. My mum was her lady's maid. That's why Wallace never came forth with the truth, even in that twee bittie booklet of his. Gerald and Wallace Rutherford, they make Angus look right rational. Made. They're all gone now. All gone to their rewards."

"And what . . ." began Alasdair, just as Jean asked, "Where . . ."

"Carry on," he told her.

"Where did Gerald learn another version of events?" she asked.

"Papers, letters, the clarsach." Roddy crouched to peer through the windshield at the roofs of Glebe House and the cooking school just rising from the fields ahead. "I'm sorry to trouble you, but it's gone a quarter 'til, and it's disrespectful to come late into the church and draw attention to yourself."

Alasdair lifted his foot from the brake but didn't press the gas pedal, so that the car crept forward at idling speed. "Where are these papers and letters now?"

"Stanelaw Museum, like as not. Clarsach's been pinched, though."

"It's been recovered," Jean told him. "Did you know it has a secret compartment for messages? Is that what you mean by Gerald learning the true story from it, that he knew about the compartment and how Isabel used it? He actually wrote a poem about her, you know, based on Hogg's 'The Queen's Wake,' about a contest of harpers before Mary, Queen of Scots."

"Another whore, Mary was. And Isabel helping her with her plots—aye, you can learn a lot about folk from the company they keep and the goods they hold valuable. And what they waste their time on, poetry and all."

Reflected in the mirror, his face was as silent and secret as Glebe House with its curtains closed and its driveways vacant. *Yeah,* Jean thought, *you can learn a lot about people, poetry and all.*

So many cars were parked along the road in front of the church that Alasdair had to ease past them. More than one sightseer with a camera stood beside the fence, taking pictures of the two dark, damp holes in the ground, the yawning graves of Helen Elliot and Wallace Rutherford. Judgement Day, Jean thought, had reached Stanelaw, and the graves were giving up their dead.

"The police," Roddy said, his voice cold. "They asked permission to dig up poor Helen. Have you no respect for the dead? I replied. But the dark one with the queer name, he said 'twas all in the interests of justice. So I agreed. There's scant respect for anything anymore, not for the dead, not for justice, not for the truth."

"Sometimes," said Alasdair, "it seems not."

"I'm sorry," Jean added.

Alasdair stopped and Roddy opened the door. "Would you care to join me?"

The prospect was tempting, even though Jean's tastes in religious ritual ran more to smells and bells.

"Thank you," said Alasdair with his best courtly manner, "but we've been detailed to give statements at P.C. Logan's office."

"Oh aye, I've been directed to do the same, even though I know nothing. It's been my bad luck to live at Ferniebank is all. Thank you kindly, Mr. Cameron." Roddy shook hands with Alasdair, nodded dourly at Jean, then unfolded himself from the car and strode off up the drive toward the church. A few parishioners, for the most part about Roddy's age, stood around the open door. That straight figure like a conductor's baton draped in black, the focus of every eye, must be Minty.

Alasdair drove on, leaving Jean to look over her shoulder until the church disappeared from sight and they were on the outskirts of Stanelaw. "I guess we got him in as chatty a mood as he's ever likely to be," she said at last. "The events of the last month have to have shaken him up."

"He told us quite a bit, didn't he? What it means, I'm still processing. Like him having been the caretaker for the castle and chapel. Could be the Rutherfords paid him for keeping watch on the place, income he lost when Wallace moved in."

"That doesn't seem enough reason for the bad blood between them, though it didn't help. I think his beef with Wallace was philosophical. Religious, if that's not too strong a word."

"Too strong? He was saying that Ciara's plans are blasphemous."

"Yeah, I guess making even a 'romanish' Catholic chapel into a spa would be desecration to someone unenthused over contemporary attitudes. He's probably thrilled the way Presbyterian churches all over Scotland are being turned into bars, restaurants, offices."

"What was that about Isabel, then? A true story?"

"We saw her running into the castle, a direct contradiction of the story in Wallace's leaflet. If she was carrying secret messages for Mary Stuart and her supporters . . ."

"A staunch Protestant like Roddy could well be thinking her a traitor."

"Politics and religion," said Jean with a grimace. "There's a volatile mixture. Historically a motive for murder, over and over again. But not here and now, surely."

"Most murders are done either to avoid something or to gain something, often both at once. What would Roddy be gaining?

And how did he do it? Here, Angus, stop in for a wee dram?"

"So you've decided Angus's death was a murder?"

"Just for the sake of argument." Alasdair turned the car down a side street. The shop on the corner must be the one belonging to Valerie's uncle.

"Roddy might have a drink with Angus, but with Wallace? And would he kill his own wife?" Jean shook her head, trying to settle the careening thoughts into one pattern, any pattern, but they spun all the faster, out of control, spitting up flotsam. "Maybe Roddy chipped away the inscription—you know, preventing the whore's grave from becoming a tourist attraction."

"I was thinking that myself," said Alasdair.

"Of course you were," Jean told him. "So did Roddy really want Wallace's fishing things?"

"I expect so—waste not, want not. But there might be something in those boxes as well."

"I heard people in the Laigh Hall earlier. Did Minty give the go-ahead to search the boxes?"

"She said something to Delaney about doing whatever needed doing at Ferniebank, which he took as *carte blanche*. We'll have ourselves a squint this evening."

"In the meantime, we have another reason to get to the museum, to see what the story is with Isabel."

"Assuming it's relevant to the case." Alasdair stopped behind a nondescript brown car parked in front of a cottage that fit Rebecca's description of "vine-covered," to the point that windows and doors peered through oblong holes in the growth that had probably been achieved with industrial-strength pruning shears. Flowers of every hue rioted in the front garden. A square pebbledash addition to one side looked like the proverbial sore thumb, even with its blue sign reading "Police." It was more of a police room than a police station.

"What isn't relevant to the case? Like Valerie's tattoo—oh, you don't know about that, do you? I saw her coming out of the pub on Friday. She has a tattoo of a harp on her shoulder."

Alasdair switched off the engine, pulled the keys from the ignition, and turned to stare, eyes bright, brows at full alert. "Eh?"

"It could be coincidence, but we already have enough of those. She grew up here and was at the Ferniebank dig."

"The Ferniebank Clarsach. No coincidence, no." Alasdair jangled the keys pensively, then climbed out, locked the doors —and froze, staring at the car in front of them.

Jean walked to his side and saw what he was looking at. The brown finish of the car was splashed with dried mud, and the tires were caked with it. "Whoa," Jean said. "I recognize that car."

Alasdair used the all-purpose syllable again. "Eh?"

"Keith was driving it at Minty's house yesterday. And it wasn't muddy then, because Ciara was talking to Valerie, and her car *was* muddy."

The door of the police annex opened. Keith Bell slipped through the aperture, seeming no more solid than a tendril of smoke. Then Ciara stepped around the corner of the building like an ambulatory rose bush, despite her flowing fabrics and rainbow shades just as insubstantial.

CHAPTER TWENTY-THREE

Alasdair jolted to attention, his mental equivalent of Kallinikos's notebook and pen jotting down the particulars, his face betraying all the expression of a blank piece of paper. He opened the garden gate for Jean and she stepped through, then to the side as Ciara swept past.

Ciara's cream-puff complexion sagged just a bit, though it was hardly curdled. The tinkle of her signature earrings seemed muted and dirge-like. She was not wearing her pink pelt, but a beaded shawl that glittered as she moved. "Poor Angus, passing before his time. He'll be missed."

"How's Minty holding up?" asked Jean.

"So brave. So calm. Preparing to open the cookery school as usual this coming week. But we know that Angus's spirit will linger on, don't we?"

"Jeez." Keith was inspecting his fingertips—Logan would have taken his prints as well as Ciara's. "Most normal people —"

Ciara's voice cut through his like a flute cutting through a drone. "The pub at two, Jean? It's my shout. Is Alasdair still drinking whiskeys so dry they shrivel your tongue?"

Alasdair might be on a first-name basis with dry, but his tongue was anything but withered. "Why'd you phone Val Trotter at half past six this morning, Ciara?"

Keith looked around at Alasdair, the sunlight on his glasses hiding his expression.

Ciara stopped dead, then asked with an indulgent smile, "Aren't you the clever boots?"

"Not a bit of it," Alasdair replied. "Val told me."

"Giving her the third degree, were you?"

"By not answering the question, you're leaving me to make assumptions. And what I'm assuming is that you and Val are old mates."

Say what? Jean asked herself, but for once saw good reason not to speak.

Alasdair's supple tongue moved on. "You told the Brimberry girl to have herself the Saturday morning off just so's you could sneak about with Angus, is that it? I don't know what all this is in aid of, Ciara, but I'm advising you to come clean. Now."

"Sneaking about with Angus, when everyone knew we were doing business?" Ciara's smile broadened. "Now is no time for negativity, Alasdair. What goes round, comes round."

"Aye, that it does. Best you remember that." He made an about-face and headed for the building at a quick, businesslike clip.

Keith spun around, considerably less neatly, and plunged through the gate. "Let's go, Ciara."

But Ciara lingered, first watching Alasdair stride up the path, then turning to Jean with a sympathetic crinkle to her brow. "Over twenty years in the police force will do that to a man. Pity."

Outside the fence, Keith was climbing into the car and starting the engine. By the time Ciara reached the passenger door, he was already starting to pull away. *Was he trying to outrun the law?* Jean wondered as she hurried up the path. *Or trying to outrun Ciara?*

She caught up with Alasdair near the door of the police annex, beside a garden bench. "I'd say that was a shot in the dark about Ciara and Val, but you never scattershoot."

"No, that was no guess. Ciara's got a tattoo of a harp as well, though not on her shoulder."

Jean felt her eyes cross, visualizing where the tattoo might be, complete with the corollary of Alasdair seeing it—not that that was the issue, murder was the issue. "Yeah, Ciara and Val must not have been introduced by her uncle. At least, not as recently as Val implied. Okay, so they're good enough mates to get the same tattoo, one that refers to Ferniebank. So what? They've both got an interest in Ferniebank."

The crease between Alasdair's brows indicated that the subject was under consideration.

"What about Keith's muddy car?" Jean went on. "You didn't ask him about it."

"I'm not the investigating officer. I cannot impound the car for testing. If I'd asked him, I'd have warned him off. Logan, now, he'll get onto Delaney . . ."

Logan appeared in the doorway, arms crossed, visage grim, his five o'clock shadow more of a ten o'clock eclipse. He'd probably been up most of the night, too. "Mr. Cameron, I'll take your statement now. Miss Fairbairn, if you'd be so kind as to wait in the garden."

With a sharp sideways glance at Jean, conveying everything from *behave yourself* to *here we go again,* Alasdair stepped into the office and Logan closed the door.

Jean sat down on the bench. Keith had some explaining to do, as did Ciara, but as suspects went . . . Not that anyone was walking around with blood on their hands. No gore, as Miranda had said. Poison had once been an unusual weapon in this part of the world—stabbing, bashing, hanging, and pitching over precipices all worked just fine. Jean imagined the glee when gunpowder presented yet another way of bloodily proving your point. Poison now, poison was subtle.

Shaking her head, she focused on her surroundings. For starting in such mirk and doubt, the day had become tourist-brochure perfect, the clouds lifting and contracting into big white poufs drifting in a blue sky. Bees buzzed drowsily from flower to flower, dodging plaster gnomes half-concealed in the shrubbery. She plucked a leaf from a sage plant and inhaled the fragrance.

The "vine-covered" Mrs. Logan must be the gardener, although Logan's black temperament didn't have to extend to his thumbs. As for where the lady of the house was now, an open window behind Jean's back emitted the murmur of televised voices and eight notes of a clock chiming half past the hour. Twelve-thirty. Time flies.

Jean sat up straighter. A clock. The Westminster chimes. So Minty's house wasn't the only possible site of the anonymous phone call. Which probably wasn't anonymous to Wallace. A shame he didn't record his caller's name, but then, he hadn't expected to either drop dead or be done to death immediately thereafter.

As though echoing her musings, her phone trilled. She burrowed into her bag to find her phone had once again worked its way to the bottom. Ah, Hugh. "Good afternoon. You've heard."

"That I have," Hugh replied soberly. "Poor Angus. He could be a bit befuddled at times—so can we all, come to that—but he meant well."

"You said you met him when you were here for the museum opening in April."

"Him and his wife and a collection of local worthies, including the woman negotiating for Ferniebank dressed in what looked to be a cross between a haystack and a chandelier. Everyone was pretending not to notice."

Yeah, Jean told herself, money speaks loud enough to drown out even Ciara's overly audible clothing choices, a luxury not permitted to Zoe and Derek. Had she told Hugh about Alasdair and Ciara? She wasn't going to get into that now. "Did anyone say anything about the true story of Isabel Sinclair and the harp and . . . Well, I don't even know what to ask, it's all so vague."

"Angus was saying it was time for a true story to be coming out at last, but Madam shushed him right smartly, and I cannot say whether he was referring to Isabel or the dig at Ferniebank."

"A true story about the dig?" Jean asked, sitting up so straight her rump left the bench.

"Haven't a clue. The other Rutherford, Wallace, he was saying he'd made quite a study of Gerald's writings about Isabel and the Sinclairs and had urged the dig to begin with. But then, it was all idle chitchat whilst we stood about after the formalities, where I spoke a bit about the clarsach and played 'The Keiking Glass.' "

" 'The Looking Glass?' That's appropriate. I feel as though I've fallen through one. Any moment now, a white rabbit in a waistcoat is going to burst out of the bushes and go for my throat."

"But you're not considering coming back to Edinburgh, are you now?" Without waiting for the answer, Hugh concluded, "If I can recall anything else said at the opening, I'll phone."

"Yes, please. Any time. And thanks."

Jean tucked her phone away. Closing her eyes, she envisioned Ciara with long white ears and a pink nose. That made her smile. Now if she could just breathe deeply and relax her shoulders, which were almost embracing her own modestly extended ears.

The door of the police office flew open. Jean looked up to see Alasdair exiting the room like an iceberg aiming for the *Titanic*. "Your turn," he said, forcing the words out between his teeth.

Giving a statement was an entirely different thing from taking one, wasn't it? Especially with Logan staking out his somewhat ambivalent territory. Jean whispered, "Did you ask him about the drawings?"

"Oh aye, he took them," replied Alasdair, not whispering at all. "He's saying I meant for him to take them, that they're safe as houses here, aren't they?"

Logan stepped into the doorway and gestured Jean inside.

In the stuffy, cluttered little room, she sat where she was told to sit and accepted a cup of tea, which Logan doctored with milk from an old-fashioned glass bottle—one of Roddy's products, no doubt, evading the draconian standards of the EU. Holding the mug between her hands to quell any gesticulatory comments, she gave her name and address and detailed the events of the night before. Just the facts, no fancies—not that fancy and fact weren't getting harder and harder to distinguish. At least she didn't have to offer up her fingertips. She was already, as they said, known to the police.

Logan's thick, black eyebrows made semi-circles over his eyes, like protective arches. They didn't move while she spoke, or when she signed her statement, or as she placed the empty mug on the corner of the desk and made her escape. He made a good foil for Minty in—what? Protecting and promoting the public welfare? Keeping up community appearances?

Alasdair was pacing the garden path, fingering a strand of lavender and exchanging mistrustful looks with a ceramic fairy posing on a ceramic toadstool. When he saw Jean, he took off for the gate so fast she had to hurry to keep up, her feet crunching on the gravel path as though walking through cornflakes. "I get the feeling," she said, "that Logan is trying to signal he's not intimidated by you."

"I'm not after intimidating him." Alasdair leaped into the driver's seat and started the engine.

Jean slammed her door. "Yeah, well, it's our beliefs that make us act, not the facts, right?"

"Right." Alasdair made a deft U-turn back toward town.

"Here's a fact—a factoid, a factule—for you. Logan's got a striking clock. Wallace's phone call, remember? Maybe Logan was delivering a friendly warning. Maybe Roddy phoned in a threat while he was delivering milk."

"Circumstantial evidence," said Alasdair predictably. "Though either is possible, aye."

Jean came about on another tack. "Hugh called. He was at the museum when it opened last April. He thought Angus said something about the dig having a true story, although he could have been talking about Isabel. Either way, Minty shut him up fast. And Wallace was saying the dig was his idea. That's not what Minty told us, was it? Didn't she say she'd organized the dig to give Wallace a job after he retired and to clean up the neighborhood?"

"That she did, though her taking credit's not surprising. Neither is hearing there's something peculiar about the dig, when there's something peculiar about Ferniebank from river-bank to cap house." Alasdair stopped at the intersection with the main road and glanced into the back seat—yes, the plastic container was still there, not that they had left the car unobserved. "Logan said he'd come by presently and unlock the museum, so's we can leave the chipping."

"Good. Maybe the museum will give us the Grand Unified Theory of motivation or something."

There was the shop again, this time with Valerie herself walking off down the sidewalk. Maybe she was on her way to the pub. *Great. Let's have a convention.* "Ciara has the tattoo of a harp?" Jean couldn't help asking.

"She didn't have it when we were married. I saw it the last time I saw her, six, seven years since." The corner of his mouth tucked itself into a wry smile—Jean wasn't fooling him, but then, she never could. "It's high on her hip. She was wearing a short blouse and low-riding jeans on a warm day. When she bent over to fetch her phone from her bag, I noticed it. I thought it had something to do with Mystic Scotland, that's what she was blethering about at the time."

Oh, Jean thought. "What was she doing before Mystic Scotland? When she was with you?"

"Working for a company that published tourist brochures, postcards, those little books of ghost stories, and the like. Not so far from what you're doing, if the truth be told."

Yeah, Jean and Ciara were both story-dealers, if not necessarily truth-tellers. Jean opened her mouth, but anything else she could ask would lead to a discussion much too personal for this moment. She confined herself to, "Like those books on the shelf back at Ferniebank. I bet that's why the place attracted her attention to begin with."

The Granite Cross was impacted in cars. Alasdair coasted past the entrance to the beer garden, giving Jean the chance to ascertain that it had become media circus headquarters, heaving with people who, if they weren't waving cameras around, were hanging onto anyone who was.

By the time Alasdair found a parking spot and they strolled back, Valerie was darting into the front door of the pub so quickly you'd think she was trying to avoid meeting them. Her cardigan was now draped over her arm, revealing a tank top and the tattoo. Jean nudged Alasdair. He nodded—yes, it was the same design as Ciara's, something else that couldn't be a coincidence. The two women had not met in the last month, that's for sure, but that revelation didn't actually rise to the level of Valerie lying to Delaney. As for Ciara calling her at the crack of dawn, well, why not? Angus's death was big news.

The interior of the pub featured the usual eclectic assortment of tables and chairs, the out-of-date advertisements, the long bar fringed with beer taps on the bottom and glasses on the top.

Liquor bottles glistened in ordered ranks before a mirror that reflected Polly Brimberry as she hustled back and forth. A television sat on a shelf in one corner, tuned to a soccer—er, football match, Jean corrected herself. A door next to the bar stood open on a block of sunshine and movement.

The room was as crowded as the garden, but contained considerably less oxygen. What air there was had already cycled through several sets of lungs and was damp and musty with scents of stale beer and cooking food, plus the occasional whiff of cigarette smoke from outside. From the shortage of prostrate bodies, Jean assumed that even if there was a poisoner making the rounds of the area, he or she wasn't operating in the kitchen of the pub.

Alasdair pointed Jean toward a booth partially blocked by a pram, handed her the stone chip, and kept on going toward the bar. "Don't get me anything alcoholic, I'm spaced enough already," Jean called after him, and didn't wait to see if he snickered agreement.

"There you are." Rebecca set down her tea cup and waved Jean in to a landing on the opposite side of the booth.

Beside her, Michael drank deeply from his glass of dark ale and wiped a scrap of froth from his upper lip. "What's the latest, then?"

Jean slid onto the vinyl seat and spread her hands in an extravagant gesture encompassing several gradations of puzzlement. "The evidence is piling up, but who the heck knows where any of it fits?" She reviewed the situation, from harp to nuts of the human variety, concluding, "Here's the bit of inscription we took away from Zoe Friday night. Logan's going to let us into the museum."

Rebecca's eyes glazed over and Michael's mouth made an O, either from the amount of information or from its disorganized presentation—yeah, Jean thought, she'd barely have given herself a passing grade, a lady's C, maybe, for simply doing the assignment.

"We'll come with you to the museum," Rebecca said. "I'm not sure Linda's lungs are up to this atmosphere. And I don't mean the ambience." She looked into the pram, but the baby's eyelids, transparent as peony petals, were closed, and her tiny chest rose and fell peacefully.

Alasdair zigzagged toward them, offered little Linda a smile, and slid in next to Jean. He planted two glasses wet with condensation on the table. "Here you are, lemonade."

"Thanks," Jean told him. "Michael, Rebecca, this is the one, the only, Alasdair Cameron."

"At last." Rebecca shook Alasdair's hand across the table and passed it over to Michael, who wrung it enthusiastically.

"Pleased to meet you," said Alasdair, and to Michael, "You're the piper, then."

Michael's pipes were propped up next to him, looking like a spindly-legged creature wearing a tartan loincloth. "I'll be tuning up directly, not so you'd take notice in this crowd."

"We'll all be taking notice. Why else were the great Highland pipes instruments of war, rallying the fighters over the clamor of battle? Assuming the fighters weren't yet charging downhill, half-naked and all berserk."

"The Camerons charging with their swords," returned Michael with a grin, "into the gunfire of the Campbells?"

"That's my lot, bonny fighters but piss-poor politicians."

Rebecca's smile washed over Alasdair and splashed toward Jean. *Ah, I see the attraction.*

Alasdair lifted his glass of rich, amber fluid toward Michael, who saluted in return. *"Slainte,"* Alasdair said, and drank. For just a moment his perceptive gaze turned inward, no doubt tracing the path of the palliative into his stomach and thence to his aching nerves. Brewers, Jean thought, should be right up there with pharmacists.

Michael indicated the television. "Score's tied, though Aberdeen's having the worst of it."

"That's their *modus operandi*," returned Alasdair, and launched into a no-doubt-intelligent discussion of the fine art of football of which Jean understood nothing. So Alasdair could do sports, too. Who knew? Smiling, she sipped her sweetened citric acid and looked around.

Derek was imitating a cockroach beside a slot machine in the far corner. Valerie, braced on the bar like a sailor hanging onto a gunwale, was expounding to Noel. The publican's amiable expression hadn't exactly soured since Friday, but seemed a bit askew, caught between the rock of consternation and the deep blue sea of commerce. He was wiping glasses, his gaze flitting around the room, not really listening to whatever Valerie was saying, but nodding politely even so.

Behind a cash register stood a young woman Jean thought at first glance was Zoe, if Zoe's bottle-black hair could have gone brown overnight. But no, this girl was older, her lips pink and smiling instead of crimson and pouting, and her face was less angular, if not as full as her parents'. Shannon hurried through a swinging door and returned a moment later with two plates of food, which she deposited at a nearby table. "Your meal's just coming," she called to the booth, and sped away like a model along a catwalk, all lissome grace and swaying hair.

Rebecca pried the top off the plastic container and scrutinized the inscribed stone. "Is there a copy of the entire inscription in the museum?"

"If there isn't, we have a copy of the Ancient Monuments report." A dark wriggle in the corner of Jean's eye turned into Zoe, her appearance today part goth, part gamin. She held two plates brimming with sandwiches and salad, and stared down at the stone chip as though it were a cobra rising up from a fakir's basket.

After a moment, Michael said, "Those are our lunches, are they, Zoe?"

With a jerk, Zoe clattered the dishes onto the table. Lettuce flew.

Alasdair turned the plastic dish toward her. "Oh aye, this is the chipping you were returning to the castle. Tell me again where you found it, because I'm thinking it wasn't in the castle at all."

Her lips thinned into a red gash indented by her front teeth. She glanced over her shoulder at Valerie, who was now pushing her way toward the back door, drink in one hand, cigarette in the other.

"Was it Derek's mum telling you there's a curse on Ferniebank?" Alasdair persisted. "Is it this stone that's bad luck, or Ferniebank itself?"

"They're saying Angus is dead," Zoe replied. "Murdered, like."

"He's dead," was all Alasdair would commit to. "Who else has been telling you Ferniebank's a bad place? Your grandfather?"

Now Zoe was looking at Alasdair as though he was the cobra, her black, spiked eyelashes accentuating her dismay. "Grandad doesn't mean any harm. He's set in his ways is all."

"So set in his ways," Jean asked, "that he begrudged Wallace taking his place as caretaker?"

"Mum says Grandad and Wally, they used to fish together, but no more, not since the castle was opened up. All I've ever known is them going on at each other about the castle, the chapel, Isabel, of all things. And then the Macquarrie woman arrived, and they had rows over her as well."

"They were rowing over her and her plans for Ferniebank the

day Wallace died, were they?" Alasdair asked.

He'd asked Zoe that question before. Now, cornered, she nodded weakly. "And because my mum was taking him his meals, just like my granny did. And because me and Derek, we were hanging about there. . . . Well, Minty, she told them both to boil their heads."

Probably not in those words, Jean thought, just as Alasdair asked, "Minty was there that day?"

"Keeping an eye on her investments, I reckon. Wallace was rabbiting about Gerald's papers, but then that was something else he and my grandad were always going on about, barking bloody Gerald." Seizing a bit of her old bluster, she added, "Like anyone gives a fig for that secret wisdom rubbish."

You do, when it's filtered through Valerie and Derek, thought Jean.

"Someone does," Alasdair said. "Val Trotter, perhaps? Wallace, certainly. Maybe even your granny. Was that what she had in common with Wallace, a taste for secret wisdom rubbish?"

Zoe cast another look over her shoulder to where her mother and Shannon were replenishing a rack of snack bags. When she turned back to the table, her words spilled out in a stream of diphthongs so compressed that Jean had to strain to make them out. "Grandad says we're obliged to respect the graves, even the romanish ones, but there was that piece of rock in his dresser. After that, everything went wrong. There's Grandad going on about the wages of sin being death, and it's sinful to steal, isn't it? So I went to put the stone back."

"Last I heard," said Alasdair, "lying's a sin as well."

"You cannot blame me for helping out my grandad."

Rebecca's brown eyes and Michael's blue hadn't blinked, Jean noted. They were chewing their food very slowly and quietly, pretending to be invisible but not pretending not to listen.

"You meant to protect your grandad by returning the inscription," Alasdair said, his soft burr barely intelligible above the noise. "Protect him from supernatural agencies if not from the secular ones. What about Derek, then? Did you mean to protect him as well?"

"He's not done anything," Zoe protested. "He's thick as a board, but he means well."

There was a lot of well-meaning going around, thought Jean.

"Right." Alasdair tapped his glass on the table like a judge tapping his gavel. "Thank you. Detective Inspector Delaney will be having a word with you and your family."

Beneath her ashy makeup, Zoe went even whiter. "I don't know anything. We don't know anything. We've got sod-all to do with, with . . ."

When she didn't finish her sentence, Alasdair said, "The police will be deciding that."

An eddy in the throng was Polly, plodding along wearily, her apron stained with food, her hair matted to the sweat on her forehead. Nothing about her was sharp except her voice. "Zoe, there's work needs doing in the kitchen. The focaccia'll not be baking itself."

"The focaccia's Minty's idea, let her cook it," said Zoe, but still she retreated from the table as fast as her thick-soled, Frankenstein-design shoes could carry her.

That must be what she'd smelled the other day and interpreted as pizza, Jean thought. Focaccia was one of Valerie's specialties, wasn't it? The days when British pubs served nothing more than permutations of pork and potatoes were long gone, not that she'd found one that had a serious grasp of, say, nachos or fajitas.

"Well done," Michael told Alasdair with a nod of approval.

Rebecca leaned across the table and confided in a stage whisper, "He's good, Jean."

"I know," Jean said, but refrained from suspending herself from Alasdair's shoulder and fluttering her lashes adoringly.

He made a scoffing noise deep in his throat and washed it down with beer. "Time to have Delaney ask Roddy a few questions about the theft of the inscription."

"Roddy's definitions of desecration seeming a bit fluid," Jean summarized.

A lull in the conversational buzz signaled Logan, his uniform cutting a swathe toward their table. From across the demilitarized zone of the pram he announced, "Mr. Cameron, Miss Fairbairn, Mrs. Rutherford wants a word at the museum."

Jean almost choked on her lemonade. *Minty?*

"Minty?" asked Rebecca.

Having his priorities straight, Alasdair drained his glass before gathering up the inscribed rock and sliding out of the booth. "Well then, Jean, we've been summoned."

CHAPTER TWENTY-FOUR

Pleased that he hadn't said, "Watson, the game is afoot," Jean gathered up her bag and her notebook and scrambled to her feet.

Michael said, "We'll come across to the museum soon as we eat."

Logan was already walking away, not looking to see if anyone was following him. Jean gave her friends a thumbs-up, go-for-it sign and with Alasdair accompanied the constable out of the pub. He didn't look both ways when he crossed the street. His uniform must have magical traffic-repelling qualities.

Jean braced herself for a cascade of newspeople to burst from the beer garden—a cop, people seen at Ferniebank, something must be happening—but no one appeared. A glance through the gateway showed her why. Ciara was holding court beneath the arbor, Keith skulking in the shadow to one side, clutching a pint of beer. A wisp of smoke coiled around her, oozing from Pandora's box, perhaps, or leaking from the genie's bottle. ". . . the great secret of Ferniebank," she was saying, ". . . a press conference when construction begins on September thirteenth."

Alasdair quickened his pace, lapping Logan, and only stopped when they were on the steps of the museum and Ciara's soprano had faded into the background murmur. Logan opened the door and both men stepped aside, leaving Jean to lead the way. Misplaced chivalry, she thought. She'd get picked off first.

The cool, dim entrance hall was equipped with a reception

desk and a rack of pamphlets and books. Jean spotted several is-sues of *Great Scot* nestled next to the sort of booklets Ciara had once written. Beyond them, display cases held the ephemera of lives long gone—tools, tea cups, Granny's paisley shawl. A staircase was cordoned off by a rope dangling a sign reading "Private," and a wide doorway opened to one side.

The sunlight winked out as Logan shut the door behind them without coming inside himself. "Duties elsewhere," said Alasdair, his voice loud in the hush of the building. "Crowd control and the like."

"Minty?" Jean called, and started toward the doorway, the floor creaking. The air seemed rich as brandy or port, with old paper, stale crumbs, pressed flowers, a soupçon of mothball—the bouquet less of age than of memory.

From the room ahead came a long squeal, and light flooded out into the foyer. Jean halted, Alasdair warm and solid at her back. Minty was shoving the old wooden shutters back into the window embrasure. In a silky, black suit tailored to her slender body, black stockings, and black pumps, she looked like a styl-ish raven. The indistinct shapes of exhibits and wall-mounted boxes loomed out of the shadows behind her, their glass panes reflecting eerie smears of sunlight. "Thank you for coming." Her voice, well-modulated as always, was stretched into a higher register. "P.C. Logan tells me you found Angus's body."

"We're very sorry for your loss," said Jean.

Minty inclined her head graciously.

Alasdair asked in his most respectful but need-to-know tone, "Did Angus return home at all?"

"Of course he did. Really, reporting him missing, how un-necessary and embarrassing."

Reporting his return to the police was apparently just as un-necessary, Jean thought.

"Did he say anything that might cast light on his . . ."

Alasdair paused delicately.

"Death? He was not in good spirits, I'm afraid. Quite put out with Ciara's plans for Ferniebank. But I was able to calm him before she herself returned to Glebe House and invited us to dinner at the Granite Cross. Quite civilized of her, considering."

Considering what? Which part of Ciara's plans, Jean wondered, were she and Angus discussing in the van yesterday morning, before Minty knew he was back? Something as mundane as the local authority's consent for alteration of the property? Or something esoteric?

"Was anyone else at dinner with you?" Alasdair asked.

"Keith, Noel, and Polly, who had Valerie Trotter working in the kitchen. The woman is doing her best, I suppose. As for that lad of hers, well, he was hanging about." The light streaming through the window drew harsh shadows on Minty's deep-set eyes, hollow cheeks, and pursed lips, no longer glistening peach but colorless. She looked as though she'd been pinched in a vise, no surprise there.

Turning the sharp angle of her shoulder toward Alasdair, she reached to a bank of switches on the wall and flicked each one. First the ceiling light, and then the lights in the display cases quivered on. "This museum is Angus and Uncle Wallace's legacy. The story of Stanelaw and Ferniebank and their roles in the history not just of Scotland, but of Britain."

"The Sinclairs made the equivalent of headlines for several hundred years," Jean said. "They still are, in some circles. How else would Ciara get a book contract for something called *The Secret Code of the St. Clairs*?"

"How, indeed? Popular culture makes fools of us all these days. What a tawdry, vulgar world we live in." Minty's back, all that Jean could see of her, would have made a ramrod look slumped.

Jean shrugged her shoulders, Alasdair his brows. Okay, so

that had been a shot in the dark. And it proved that Ciara hadn't hidden her book from Minty—not that Mrs. Councillor Rutherford was happy about it. Funny how Roddy and Minty, each from his or her perspective, saw something so similar. "Roddy Elliot was saying that Ciara's plans for Ferniebank are blasphemy."

"Roddy," said Minty, "is too superstitious for his own good. Not unlike Ciara, if in a very different fashion. Helen was a saint, moderating his fits of rancor, but now she's gone."

Alasdair extended the plastic container. "Here's the bit of Isabel's grave inscription. The one we found Friday evening."

"Thank you." Minty set the container down beside her black leather handbag on the windowsill, crossed her arms over her black jacket buttons, and frowned. Maybe they should have packed the stone in something more appropriate, like a Harrod's hatbox. Not that this was a good time, Minty's summons notwithstanding. Discreetly, Jean headed right and Alasdair headed left.

The museum building might be medieval stone, walls thick and ceilings low, but its exhibits had been designed to twenty-first-century standards. Displays were sleek and minimalist, glass pane abutted to glass pane, artifacts raised on Lucite pedestals instead of nested on velvet, like tiny spaceships launching themselves into the past. They hadn't come any cheaper than the cooking school. But then, Angus and Minty probably had a grant for the museum like the one for Ferniebank.

With the feeling she was searching for something but didn't know what it was—she'd had nightmares like this—Jean eyed Roman votive figurines from St. Mary's well, pottery, metal implements, *objets d'art,* a wood and brass medieval money chest, coins from the medieval Roxburgh mint, and coins of Mary, Queen of Scots. A letter from Mary was mounted beneath a lamp attached to a motion sensor so that it was only illuminated when someone bent to read it. A shame one corner of the yellowed paper had been torn away. . . . *Hey,* Jean thought. A scrap of sixteenth-century paper had been found in the harp.

She read the label: "Letter from Mary, Queen of Scots, to William Sinclair of Ferniebank, thanking him for his hospitality after recovering from her illness in late 1566." Fine. As far as Jean was concerned, the message could be Mary's laundry list. Not only was the spidery sixteenth-century writing almost illegible, what she could read showed that the letter was in an almost impenetrable Scots, not English. Still, she had to assume the label was correct, and that this was not the sort of letter that needed to be smuggled anywhere. Rats.

To one side rose a tall glass case like Moses's column of fire, brightly illuminated, the focus of the room no less because it was empty. Jean knew what had been there before she got close enough to read the plaque: "The Ferniebank Clarsach."

Alasdair was already inspecting the blue crescents of chipped safety glass above a splintered rim of wood. "This was pried open. Why did the thief not smash, grab, and run?"

"Why did the thief dismantle the clarsach and then return the pieces?" asked Jean.

"Perhaps the thief was looking for another secret compartment. Perhaps his conscience got the best of him."

"Or her conscience." Minty strolled across the room, her arms enlacing her chest, her heels clicking and the floor groaning.

"Logan had this glass tested for fingerprints, did he?"

"Forensics found only those of tourists who couldn't keep their hands to themselves. The thief wore gloves."

Jean envisioned a black-masked burglar wearing prissy, white, artifact-handling gloves. "How did the thief get in?"

"We use a small room in the back as a kitchen. Its window

overlooks an alley. The Saturday was warm. The receptionist most unfortunately neglected to lock the window when she closed up, and the thief was able to open it. The alarm went when he opened this display case. P.C. Logan responded straightaway, but it was too late."

Alasdair's brows tightened, perhaps imagining the receptionist's head mounted on a spike outside Glebe House. "The thief happened by just when the window was left open?"

"He could well have been watching for an opportunity," said Minty.

"A right meticulous thief he was, then. But we already know that."

Minty loosened her crossed arms enough to raise a hand toward a large color photo of the harp. Its wood was dark with time and perhaps smoke, but gleaming still. The curvature of its body was repeated by its curvilinear ornamentation, artistically shadowed by the photographer's lights. Hollows that once held jewelry seemed like sad, dark eyes. The carving on the front brace was almost three-dimensional, a scaled snake or dragon curling upwards and no doubt humming along with the music.

"It's beautiful," Jean said.

"Have you heard from the museum?" asked Alasdair.

"Repairs are under way. The conservators tell me they've uncovered a secret compartment in the front brace, beneath the salmon."

So the sculpture was of the mythical salmon of inspiration. Minty could no doubt do something inspirational with salmon, probably involving butter, pepper, and herbs. "Was Isabel smuggling messages in aid of Mary, Queen of Scots?" Jean asked.

"So it seems. She intrigued for Mary during the rebellion of the northern earls in 1569, the attempt to put Mary back on the throne after her flight to England."

"Ciara said something about Gerald concealing bothersome

historical truths. Or at least spinning them into something more acceptable during his life, if not now. Is that one of them? Isabel as secret agent?"

"Yes." Minty stepped toward a TV screen set into the wall beside the photo. Her forefinger with its short but manicured nail pressed a button.

The screen lit with an image of Hugh actually dressed in a suit and tie, holding the harp as tenderly as a small child. Or, considering the slow stroke of his fingertips down its curve, as tenderly as a lover. *A musical instrument unplayed is like a woman unloved.* He raised his cherubic face and began speaking to the camera. . . .

From the entrance hall came the sound of the front door opening. Michael's voice called, "Hullo? May we come in?"

Minty spun about, keeping her balance despite the diameter of her heels. "The museum is closed just now."

Rebecca looked through the doorway. "It's my husband and I."

"Ah," said Minty. "Well then. You've been wanting a look round, haven't you, Dr. Campbell-Reid? And you as well, Dr. Campbell-Reid," she told Michael as he rolled the pram to a stop at the foot of the staircase and set its brakes.

Hugh's electronic voice was lilting about how the Lowland harp had faded from popularity when Mary's son James VI of Scotland went to London to become James I of Britain and the court became anglicized. Something similar happened to the Highland harp 150 years later, in the aftermath of Bonnie Prince Charlie's disastrous rebellion. "We have one surviving piece with a specifically Lowland title, 'The Keiking Glass.' Perhaps Isabel Sinclair played it."

His fingers plucked the harp strings and a melody filled the air, each note dropping like that rain from heaven that was the quality of mercy, not to mention beauty. Jean looked around at

Alasdair, and met his gaze coming back the other way. Yes, Isabel had played that song. She'd played it for them Friday night.

Alasdair suddenly found the floor of great interest, but Jean could still make out the reminiscent quirk on his lips. Her own shiver had a lot more to do with the flesh than the spectral.

Michael and Rebecca drifted into the room. Minty stood with her arms knotted, her face a rock scree dusted with snow, coming forth with no more of Isabel's story.

Patiently, Jean and Alasdair turned toward another display case, this one holding a miniature of Isabel, off-center, as though a second object had once sat beside it.

Isabel was depicted from the waist up, her layers of clothing and ornament, her starched collar and winged cap, making her exposed hands and face seem as vulnerable as the soft creature inside a shell. Her features were probably idealized, and yet, still, they were features Jean and Alasdair had seen before. One long, tapering hand held a jeweled cross and the other curved toward it—this, she seemed to be saying, this particular myth is my center.

The music faded into a faint resonance and died. Jean looked up to a picture hanging above the portrait, a pen and ink drawing almost overwhelmed by an ornate Victorian or Edwardian frame. . . . Her heart oozed down into her toes. While the style of the drawing, the swoop of the line and the use of shadow, evoked Gibson Girls and *Saturday Evening Post* covers, the subject was Isabel running toward the castle. Every detail repeated the ghostly image she and Alasdair had glimpsed the night before, from slippers to feathered cap to the expression that was both fearful and determined.

Beside her, Jean heard Alasdair catch his breath. He bent forward—yes, the sketch was signed "G. Rford 1910." If the miniature was from the life, then this was from the death. Gerald, too, had been allergic to ghosts. "Was this hanging in the bedroom of the flat at Ferniebank?"

"Yes, it was," said Minty. "Gerald and Wallace, they were both gentleman artists, unskilled but adequate."

"Wallace's leaflet says that Isabel's ghost walks from the castle down to the chapel, wearing a shroud."

"That there's a ghost at all is one of the fairy tales first Gerald and then Wallace created and advertised, and that now have taken on a life of their own." Minty's slight frown would in anyone else have been a scowl.

Rebecca and Michael ranged up on Jean's other side and gazed at the photo, their knowing glances catching the implication of her question.

"Why do you suppose Gerald showed her running?" Jean asked.

"Because she ran to escape her murderers," said Minty.

In the sudden, profound silence, Jean could hear every breath, the hum of the video machine, the voices from the beer garden across the street, Linda's gurgles in the front hall.

Then, with a chill teasing the back of her neck, Jean remembered the hacked bones pictured in the Ancient Monuments book. Those were Isabel's. No wonder that upstairs room was haunted. She and Alasdair should have heard screams, seen the desperate struggle, but no, all they had sensed was the aftermath. *Quiet as the grave. Still as death.* "Her enemies caught her," she said.

Minty's lips curled, but she wasn't smiling. "Wallace based his guide leaflet on the story handed down in the family, fearfully common one that it is. After he retired and moved house to the castle, however, he organized Gerald's papers and a few of his original sources such as Queen Mary's letter. Ciara was correct in one regard: Gerald did bowdlerize the true story."

Then Roddy was correct, too, Jean thought.

"The truth, however, is much less sensationalistic than Ciara will admit to, with her. . . ." A tremor of emotion crossed Minty's face, but was gone before Jean could identify it. "Mary's enemies rode up to the castle as Isabel was returning from the chapel, where she had a confederate—not a lover, a confederate. She barricaded herself in her room."

"And began burning the correspondence entrusted to her," said Alasdair, who had also seen the rosy gleam of flames in the windows of Isabel's room. "That's when her skirts caught fire."

"Very clever, Mr. Cameron. Her skirts caught fire indeed. At that instant her assailants burst through the door and stabbed her to death, then fought their way out of the castle."

Everyone seemed to be restraining their living breaths. At last Rebecca said, "I reckon her own family put the expurgated version about. It wasn't healthy to be seen taking the wrong side."

"Loyalties are often more complex than the ordinary person realizes," Minty returned.

Like truth, Jean thought. Especially when the truth is being spun like a wheel of fortune, round and round and where it stops nobody knows.

"Roddy Elliot was telling us," said Alasdair, "that the spacing of Isabel's inscription, separating out the letters that spell *catin,* proves that she was a whore."

"That tale arose to explain the mistake on the inscription," said Minty, with only the briefest wince, "not the other way round. Add in Gerald's romantic story of the monk, and there you are."

Not that there was anything wrong with romance. Jean said, "Maybe Isabel's connection to Mary suggested that interpretation, since some people questioned her morals, too."

Minty stared, what color remaining in her face draining away. Then she blinked rapidly. "Ah, yes, Mary, Queen of Scots, was quite the object of scandal."

Jean raked back through what she'd said, but couldn't explain that reaction.

Alasdair's tilt of the head hinted that Minty might be committing censorship herself. "Where are Gerald's papers now? Including that epic poem."

"Most of the originals are here at the museum, available to scholars, although I expect a few items are amongst Wallace's personal possessions yet, such as those drawings you gave P.C. Logan."

"I didn't . . ." Alasdair cleared his throat. "Ciara's been reading the originals, then?"

"I said available to scholars. She's based her work on copies made by Wallace." Minty's dark eyes glittered like obsidian in her—no, not entirely pallid face. Her cheekbones had gone crimson. A hot flash? Jean wondered. Anger? Minty's layers of ice went deeper than Alasdair's, but the woman wasn't a completely dead planet. Minty and Ciara might be sharing a bed, economically speaking, but neither was comfortable with the sleeping arrangements.

"You collected Wallace's things from the flat, did you?" Alasdair persisted. "Have you got an inventory?"

"No. Polly cleared most everything into the boxes. I pulled out a memento or two, the odd photograph and the like. There's nothing valuable left, save to a tradesman recycling old paper." Minty strode back to the window and picked up her handbag. "I asked you to stop by, Mr. Cameron, so I could give you this. Legally, it's part of the Ferniebank estate."

Everyone clustered around as she produced a small box and handed it to Alasdair. He opened it. "The burning-glass."

Inside the box, nestled on a square of cotton batting, lay a palm-sized disc. What glass wasn't covered by a flaky black crust was the color of milky tea, glowing sullenly in the light. The crust itself had peeled into what, if you looked at it slantwise and squinted, could be the map of Mexico. As relics went, this one was pretty sad . . . *Wait a minute,* Jean thought.

"May I?" Michael took the box from Alasdair's hand and held it up. "This is no lens. It's not plano-convex, it's flat. The encrustation is never soot. It's the oxidized silver backing of a mirror."

"A looking glass," said Jean. "A keiking glass."

Michael passed the box to Rebecca. "This has been buried," she said. "Where did you get it?"

"It turned up in the dig," Minty answered, "in a rubbish heap dating to Gerald's occupation of the building. It's his, I expect, no more than a shaving mirror."

"What else happened at the dig?" asked Jean.

"The usual. There was great exclamation over bits of pottery and grains of pollen. The archaeologists even excavated beneath the floor of the chapel."

"Where they opened Isabel's grave."

"A bit of grave-robbing never goes amiss, if it's in the name of science."

Alasdair reclaimed the box and replaced its lid. "This, ah, glass was in the case with Isabel's miniature, was it?"

"I'm afraid so. Angus insisted we place it here, with the genuine miniature and the genuine harp, because it illustrated Wallace's story, and the tourists make a meal of it all."

"And you removed it from the museum after the burglary," Alasdair persisted.

"I did do, yes. Stanelaw Museum has become a laughingstock after the theft of the harp. How much greater a one would it be if it were known that this, this artifact, the crux of the Ferniebank legend, is a lie. As so much to do with Ferniebank is a lie. Please give it to Ciara, Mr. Cameron, in your capacity as P and S administrator." Minty waved imperiously.

She could have given it to Ciara herself, Jean thought, but then, when she saw Ciara last night, Angus was still alive, and would have—what would Angus have done, anyway? If this was the truth about the dig that Hugh had almost overheard, surely it would have been Angus shushing Minty, not the other way around.

Minty turned back to the windowsill, pulled a set of keys from her handbag, and peeled back the lid of the plastic container. Picking up the piece of stone with its inscription, she led the way across the room—if she'd been wearing a train, she'd have expected Jean and Rebecca to carry it—and stopped beside a flat display case, which she unlocked and opened.

The bottom of the case was covered by a professionally drawn illustration of the entire inscription, the extant pieces laid forlornly in the appropriate places and drained of their reddish hue by the glare of the spotlight. Minty worked the *icj* up close to the *ac* that Wallace had been carrying in his pocket when he died, adjusted each of the other pieces a thirty-second of an inch or so, and then stepped back to contemplate her handiwork.

The display reminded Jean of the drawing that Logan had confiscated—not that she had the sketch there for comparison. Still, the five missing pieces from the top and left side of the inscription were all accounted for, while the harp was missing and presumably long gone. Not that that would stop Ciara from having a replica made, if she wanted—the upper edge of the *ic jac* pieces showed the line of the lower edge of the harp piece.

"Interesting," said Michael, "how the *er* of Sinncler is turned up at a right angle. And why's there a wee 'm' beside it?"

Alasdair said, "I inspected the inscription on the Friday, and was thinking that was a crack in the stone is all."

"Following on Gerald's fearfully imaginative opinion, Angus and Wallace felt that it was an 'm' and therefore had the artist draw it that way." Minty closed and locked the display case. "Wallace quite properly collected each of these pieces as they weathered off the inscription. And I expect Roddy Elliot had a hand in as well, Mr. Cameron. That's why Zoe had this bit."

Oh yes, Jean thought, Minty did see all, know all. Although Alasdair was way out ahead of her.

He asked, "What of Derek Trotter, then?"

"An example of the dreadful child-rearing practices endemic in our modern society." Minty retreated toward the window. "Now, if you'll excuse me, there's paperwork to be done. Birth, death, property—there's always paperwork."

"Thank you for letting us look around," Jean said.

The others chimed in with appropriate courtesies. Alasdair handed the box with the glass disc off to Jean, who tucked it into her bag. "Just one more thing," he said.

Picking up her purse, Minty looked sideways at him, making it clear the interview was at an end and he was overstaying his welcome. "Yes?"

"Did both Wallace and Angus participate in the dig at Ferniebank?"

"They stopped by from time to time to supervise." Minty walked briskly to the entrance hall, her footsteps sounding like the rat-tat of a snare drum, only to stop dead beside the pram. In her black clothing, she resembled the bad fairy leaning over Sleeping Beauty's cradle. And yet her posture wasn't malicious, but drooped like a wilted plant . . . With a snap of her spine she straightened, lunged for the staircase, ripped aside and then replaced the barrier rope. Her steps beat time up the stairs, dwindled across the ceiling, and were gone.

CHAPTER TWENTY-FIVE

Jean discovered that Minty had not monopolized all the air in the room after all, and inhaled. "It's almost two. I've got to go interview Ciara." *For my sins,* she added only to herself.

"Stopped by the dig from time to time." Alasdair repeated Minty's parting words and frowned.

"You've seen the ghost of Isabel, have you?" asked Michael. "The one in the drawing?"

"Oh yeah," Jean said. "Ironic that all three of the Rutherford men are dead but the ghost of Isabel is still walking. Running, rather."

"You're dead a wee bit longer than you're alive," said Alasdair.

Rebecca was looking at Queen Mary's letter. "Cool!"

"You're the expert," Jean said. "Does that say what that label says it says?"

"Or is it the sort of secret message smuggled about in musical instruments?" asked Alasdair.

"Can't tell you a thing, can I?" Jean whispered, and smiled at his bow of acknowledgment.

Rebecca leaned closer to the glass encasing the letter. The lamp came on, illuminating her blooming complexion, a contrast to Minty's sucked-dry-of-blood coloring. "This looks like Mary's writing. She was known for her Italian hand, as it was called." Under her breath she murmured, " '. . . it is esie to be judgeit quhat was my countenance . . . I declarit unto him my seiknes . . .' Yes, she's thanking the Sinclairs for their hospitality while visiting the sacred well, a queen not staying with the *hoi polloi* in the hospice. Here's something about a relic, but that's where the paper is torn. Maybe she handed over a relic as a bread-and-butter gift."

"Any Catholic monarch worth their sacramental oil would have a cartload of splinters from the true cross," said Jean, "enough bones to build a dinosaur, shreds of clothing . . ."

"And apparently Jesus had multiple foreskins," said Michael.

Rebecca made a face at him. "I'm sure there were relics aplenty at Ferniebank, for healing purposes and all."

"Now the faithful stop by the shop and buy refrigerator magnets." With one last quizzical look at the inscription, the drawing of Isabel, and the empty case of the harp, Alasdair led the way toward the entrance hall while Jean turned off the lights. The artifacts winked out, swallowed by shadow. The TV screen glowed silver, then faded. Leaving the shutters open, she skimmed toward the door, wondering if Isabel's painted eyes shifted to watch her go by.

Alasdair, Michael, and Rebecca were standing next to the reception desk, eyeing an array of photographs. Some were antique and others fairly recent, although the fashions of just twenty years ago looked almost as odd as bustles and dinghy-sized hats.

Jean gazed up at ranks of soldiers, a suffragists' parade, groups of barefooted children. A picture featuring a row of school-uniform-clad teenagers had their names printed at the bottom, including some familiar ones. A svelte Noel Brimberry stood between a positively willowy Polly Elliot and a rather punkish Valerie Trotter, all three posing with the adolescent self-absorption they were now decrying in their own children, such being the cycle of life.

The woman standing with them was Minty Rutherford, as unchanged as though she'd whisked through a time tunnel to the present. She'd said that teaching the local schoolchildren domestic skills became a career. As for the man beside her . . . Ah. Jean recognized him from the photo on Minty's mantelpiece. Here was Wallace in his role as headmaster.

Above the group photos, Angus's long face gazed down from a formal portrait, not smiling but looking almost startled, as though caught in some sort of act. Next to him hung a portrait of his uncle Wallace, a jowlier, gravity-ridden variation of the same face with a smile that was both knowing and mischievous. A third man was similarly equine-featured, but wore the slicked-down hair and high stiff collar of a century earlier. A thin brass plaque on the ornate frame of his photo read, "Gerald Rutherford. 1862–1919."

"Look at him," Jean said. "He's all very sober and respectable, but there's something about his eyes—you know, a sort of bulge, like the top of a can that's spoiled."

"He could see ghosts," said Alasdair. "So can we. Are we a bit off, then?"

"I'll not be answering that," Michael said.

Rebecca collected the pram. "Gerald lived in an era of mediums and spiritualists. Actually having that supernatural tickle must have given him entry to many a party."

"He was a recluse, though. Alone with his ghosts and his fancies." Alasdair opened the door.

"In a way, he's haunting Ferniebank as surely as Isabel is." Jean turned away from the photos. "First Gerald and then Wallace holed up at Ferniebank—the crazy uncles keeping themselves in the attic. Gerald had at least one son to be Wallace's father, but did Wallace have kids?"

Michael shook his head. "Noel was saying that the Stanelaw branch of the Rutherfords died out with Angus."

Footsteps clipped across the floor upstairs. A sudden screech made everyone jump. . . . Oh. They were hearing a paper shredder, its banshee shrieks starting and stopping abruptly. "What's she destroying up there?" Alasdair demanded with a frown.

"Hopefully nothing more than Angus's love letters," said Jean.

Logan came up the outside steps. "All finished here? I'll be locking up, then."

"Constable, you might consider mentioning to Mrs. Rutherford . . ." Alasdair's words bounced like popcorn off Logan's bulldog face. "Ah, never mind."

With Alasdair's help, Michael lifted Linda's magic coach down the steps to the sidewalk, Rebecca gesturing like a traffic cop alongside. Jean looked back through the open door just as darkness fell over the museum—Logan had closed the shutters in the main room.

So the burning-glass wasn't what it seemed. Instead of focusing and illuminating the story of Ferniebank, it simply reflected its viewer's own desires. As with the original story of Isabel and the squiggle on the inscription, perception was reality. And for all her professed pragmatism, even Minty was not at all immune from wishful thinking. Go figure, Jean told herself. What else was new?

Alasdair called from the sidewalk, "Jean, it's gone two."

With a sigh, she abandoned her cogitations—not unlike abandoning a mine-working, leaving an open shaft the unwary could fall down—and joined the others crossing the street. "Gerald's time, with its mediums and everything, wasn't much different from our own. People are still yearning for meaning and explanation."

"Even if they're holding their hands over their ears and humming when you give them the real thing," added Alasdair with a glance toward the garden gate, but Ciara was no longer holding forth.

"Ah," Michael said, "but what's the real thing, eh?"

In answer, Linda emitted an indignant cry. Rebecca turned the pram toward the Reiver's Rest. "Time for a change and a feed. Let me know the next installment of the breathtaking serial."

"I'm holding out for 'and they lived happily ever after,' " Jean told her. "See you later."

"I'd best be activating my pipes," said Michael, and opened the door of the pub.

The interior of the Granite Cross seemed even less ventilated than when they'd left, steam substituted for air. Michael reclaimed his bagpipes from Noel and took them outside. A moment later the wails of bag-inflating and drone-tuning echoed from the garden. Several people gathered up their provender and headed outside for the show, but not before Ciara made her entrance, swimming upstream as usual. "Ah, Jean! Bang on time—very good!"

Alasdair made a dance step sideways and back, trying to slip away into the crowd.

Too late. Ciara graced him with her sweetest smile. "Alasdair, I said it was my shout. Name your poison."

Flinching visibly at her choice of words, he returned, "Thank you just the same. I'll—" He stopped, staring at the front door. "Later, ladies."

Jean looked around to see Delaney just inside the room, peering around myopically. Alasdair wove through the crowd to his side and started speaking before Delaney could open his mouth. Delaney listened, scowled, and pulled Alasdair back through the doorway. Jean glimpsed three uniformed constables on the sidewalk outside before the door swung shut.

"Good. They'll keep each other busy whilst we have ourselves a bit of a chin-wag," Ciara said. "Beer? Lemonade? Cider?"

Oh, to be in two places at once. Resigning herself to obeying Newton's laws, Jean found her notebook and pen in her bag.

"Nothing for me, thanks. Where would you like to sit?"

"In the snug, back this way—it's a wee bit noisy in here, isn't it? Not the pipes," Ciara amended, as the bravura peal of "Blue Bonnets over the Border" burst through the back door. "They're the instrument of the country. Along with the harp, of course."

"Val's got a harp tattoo. Is she a musician?"

"I don't believe so, no," Ciara said over her shoulder. With a sigh, Jean followed her prey and nemesis into an alcove in the far corner of the pub, an intimate enough setting to merit the designation of "snug." Two young men were playing billiards, spending as much time balancing their pint glasses on the edge of the table as lining up their shots. To one side sat three small tables, one unoccupied. "Here we are." Ciara deposited her glass of white wine on the table, her woven shoulder-bag on the floor, and herself on a chair.

Jean took the seat providing a view that squeaked past the corner to the front door. "Is this where you had your dinner with Angus and Minty and everyone last night?"

"Oh aye," said Ciara, not asking how Jean knew about that. "All the usual suspects, eh?"

Jean didn't retort, "So you think murder is a joke?" Ciara simply wasn't leaping to the same conclusions a cynical journalist and an even more cynical ex-cop were leaping to.

"Minty, Angus, Noel, Polly, and Keith," Ciara counted off. "Val was working in the kitchen, behind the scenes so to speak, and Zoe and Shannon were rushing to and fro, and Derek . . . Well, Derek has a bit of a jumbled aura just now, but he's a good lad."

A good lad with a habit of sneaking around Ferniebank, Jean thought.

"Polly and Noel were popping up and down—Saturday night in the pub, mind, and the local musicians playing in the front room. Minty was getting at Noel to upgrade his catering,

281

though, just between us, Jean, I'm finding it hard to trust a cook who's that thin. Doesn't eat enough of her own food, does she?"

The issue of trust went beyond body shape. "Her luncheon was tasty enough, haggis and all."

"She had Polly cooking, just as she once had Helen cooking. Minty, she stands on the bridge and gives orders whilst the oarsmen—oarswomen—do the heavy lifting."

Jean did not disagree. "You've known everyone here in Stanelaw for a long time?"

"A few years, aye."

Tempted as Jean was to ask again about Valerie, who had not been in Stanelaw for a few years, that would come too close on the heels of Alasdair's admonition to Ciara to 'fess up. Right now she was playing good cop. "Last night, did Angus say where'd he been?"

"He tours about to get away from Minty. Brussels, London, the Yorkshire Dales. She means well, but she's treating him like a dog or a horse, not a husband."

Without commenting on Ciara's use of the present tense, Jean jotted down the particulars. "He was with you at Ferniebank Saturday morning, before Minty knew he was back."

"That's hardly the sinister plot Alasdair's making it out to be." Ciara's laugh echoed the clatter of the billiard balls. "I didn't know whether Angus meant to make his reappearance just yet is all. I should have organized myself better, so as not to put Shan on the spot, poor lass. But you mind what they say about discretion and valor—and working with Minty takes a wheen of both."

No kidding. "You and Angus, ah, must have seen eye to eye on your plans for Ferniebank."

"We got on well enough, Angus and I."

Saturday morning they weren't getting on too well. There

was another evasion, which, as Alasdair had said, left Jean to make assumptions. And what she assumed was that yes, Angus had been put out at some aspect of Ciara's schemes, but Ciara had dismissed his concerns.

"As for the plans," Ciara went on, "they've been finalized and construction's beginning next month. Keith has it all in hand, though Minty was that, well, we'll say interested, she kept after him for the details. If we all vanished the night, Ferniebank Conference and Healing Center would still be rising from the ruins."

"Angus did vanish. So did Wallace, less than two weeks ago."

Ciara looked down at her soft white hands, idly rotating a ring formed like a dragon holding its tail in its mouth. "As the prayer says, in the midst of life we are in death. Unless it's the other way round, in the midst of death we are in life. I never can remember. It's a shame folk are frightened of dying, when it's no more than translation to another plane."

Jean bit her tongue before she could ask, "Would you feel that way if your skirts were on fire and a gang of brutes was coming at you, swords raised?" Instead she tried, "How did you find Ferniebank to begin with?"

"I once worked for a company specializing in wee booklets for tourists. Several included the story of Ferniebank's 'gray lady.' Whilst I was setting the tours for Mystic Scotland, I stopped by and found that Wallace was an old soul like me. One who's aware of other dimensions."

Does that mean, Jean wondered, that Alasdair and I are antediluvian souls? She tried another leading question. "You said Friday that you and Keith would have to come back after nightfall to see Isabel's ghost. A shame you didn't make it that night. You might have caught—er—whoever chipped away the inscription. And last night you might have been able to help Angus."

Ciara toyed with her ring, her springy red curls curtaining her profile. "Well," she said at last, "you and Alasdair, you didn't need eavesdroppers and trespassers just then, did you? With him being so meticulous and all."

Jean felt her tongue cleave to the roof of her mouth and her face flush.

"Though meticulous can lead onto pernickety. See Minty." Ciara looked up, her blue eyes, a more luxuriant shade than Alasdair's, dancing. "Birds do it, bees do it, you and Alasdair do it, Keith and I do it—nothing embarrassing about it. A bit of rumpy pumpy is all to the good, isn't it? Like music and a good meal. Gather your rosebuds."

Jean thought of wispy Keith, needing his food to keep his energy up and his client happy. She thought of Valerie gathering rosebuds and coming up with the thorn that was Derek. She thought of Alasdair as meticulous, even fussy—yeah, he and Minty did have a few traits in common. She thought that Ciara maybe had gone on the offensive to deflect uncomfortable questions about coming and going surreptitiously at Ferniebank.

A drop of sweat trickled down her back beneath her blouse, drawing her follicles erect like the delicate touch of Alasdair's fingertips. Or like the ectoplasmic tickle of a ghost. She cleared her throat to recall the meeting to order, and realized too late that was Alasdair's trick. Ciara acknowledged the reference with a smile of such surpassing sweetness Jean wanted to ask for a shot of insulin on the side. She said, "Ferniebank. You've made some major discovery, it sounds like. Something about the Sinclairs? Or the Saint Clairs, rather?"

"You've heard about the book, then? Your sources are good as Minty's." Ciara's eyes went from dancing to glinting, humor sharpened into something between glee and zealotry. "That's why I asked everyone to dinner last night, to celebrate Wallace's and my grand discovery and the book deal. Although, if the truth be told . . ."

If only, Jean thought.

". . . I let the news slip to Shannon on the Friday, whilst we were planning itineraries—that girl should be sitting her exams again, she's a bit dyslexic is all. I'm sure Shan told her family and I myself told Angus and Minty earlier the Saturday, with them being investors and the like."

"The discovery and the book will make their investment pay off, right?"

"As a side effect, aye. Not that I'm turning away money—useful item, money. But the bottom line is nonmaterial. Folk are yearning for spirituality and connection. For meaning. You're writing about that yourself, aren't you now?"

"In a way, yes."

"My life's journey brought me to Ferniebank, where I met Wallace, a fellow traveler. Now his journey is ended and his part in the story is over. But he's passed on to me the responsibility of moving the story toward harmony and away from the tyranny of the religious thought-police. I've organized a press conference for the day we break ground at Ferniebank."

If Ciara wasn't perfectly sincere, Jean would eat her notebook. "You can go ahead and tell me. My magazine's a monthly. Anything I write up now won't be published until January." She didn't add that she could call Miranda's contact at *The Scotsman* and have the story in tomorrow's paper—she was in this business out of curiosity, not competitiveness. And Ciara was obviously bursting with the news. She probably couldn't keep Christmas and birthday presents under wraps, either.

"Well then." Leaning toward Jean conspiratorially, Ciara murmured, "You've read that book claiming the Holy Grail is actually Mary Magdalen and that she was buried in Rosslyn for a time."

Jean had to crane forward to hear her over the sounds of

people talking, the television announcer, billiard balls clashing like skulls, the rant of the pipes. Her nostrils filled with Ciara's perfume, which today reminded her of incense. "I've read it, yes. It's fiction. The author took stories that have been around for ages—there've been tales about the Templars for hundreds of years—and grafted them onto a modern thriller. . . ." She snapped her teeth together and wrote "listen" in the middle of her page.

"I'll be setting the record straight," stated Ciara.

Jean waited for Ciara's definition of "straight" before she handed out compliments.

"The romantic story of Isabel and the monk and the burning-glass and all, Gerald Rutherford wrote that to cover up the real story. Which is also romance, but in the larger meaning."

"Ah, yes. Isabel was actually Mary Stuart's secret courier."

"Oh, not that. That story's a cover-up as well. Gerald had a fine time weaving that with the truth in his poem about Isabel playing the harp for Mary. Not that I'd recommend reading his poem—it's like treading treacle. Still, it was right clever of Gerald and then Wallace, hiding the truth behind not one but two plausible stories."

Listen.

"You've seen Rosslyn, I reckon. You've seen Ferniebank. Same style. Same masons, like as not. No surprise, then, that at Ferniebank as well as Rosslyn the arrangement of the carvings, especially those wee boxes alongside the pillars, designate vibration frequencies. Pity they've been damaged, but by comparing the better-preserved carvings at Rosslyn, we can extrapolate."

We can, can we? Jean retorted silently. The vibration frequencies of Michael's pipes were making the dust motes dance a reel. She felt her feet tapping, and had to stop herself from getting up and tapping away. But no. The debatable shore where fantasy and reality intersected was her territory, her mandate, even if sometimes it resembled quicksand.

"If you pair the patterns with musical notes, you'll have yourself a melody," Ciara went on. "And if you play this melody with the proper medieval instrument, the resonations will dislodge stones and reveal a secret chamber. That's the significance of the clarsach."

Jean opened her mouth, shut it, and said, "Has anyone actually tried doing that?"

"Gerald did do. Well, he concealed the particulars, just as he concealed Isabel's true story. Wallace spent years working it all out, and was after completing the pattern and revealing the contents of the secret chamber when he passed on. And then the clarsach—well, we all make . . ." Ciara pressed her lush pink lips together, keeping back the rest of the sentence.

We all make mistakes? Did she take the harp to test out the hypothesis and—well, dropping it wouldn't have dismantled it. And something as cumbersome as breaking and entering hardly seemed Ciara's style. "The archaeologists took up the floor of the church and didn't find any secret chambers."

"They'd no longer be secret then, would they now? But these sorts of spiritual explorations have nothing to fear from hard science."

Hard science being just another belief system, Jean supposed. "Is this all connected with the Harp Line that was on the map in your press release?"

Ciara beamed. "Oh, very good! You've got the Rose Line extending from the south of France through Rosslyn—Rosslyn, Rose Line, right? And you've got the Harp Line defined by the arrangement of the four border abbeys. Melrose to Dryburgh to Kelso makes your upper curve, and the line extending down to Jedburgh is the back brace."

"And the arms of the harper form a line pointing from Rosslyn to Ferniebank."

"So they do. Well done, Jean!"

Sarcasm was lost on Ciara, Jean told herself. "And what's going to be exposed in this secret chamber. Hole. Thing."

"Well now. That's the secret of Isabel's grave inscription. They thought they could keep us from making our discovery by removing it, didn't they? But no."

Jean didn't bother asking who "they" were. There was always a "they" preventing the dissemination of truth, justice, and the way of the weird.

"That right angle in the *er* of Sinncler. That's the set-square of the Templars and the Master Masons. It means *et reliqua,* the remains or the relics are here. And when you add in the 'm,' well then!" Ciara spread her hands—look at me, I can pull a rabbit out of a hat!

Minty probably had recipes for *hasenpfeffer* or *lapin en croute.* Jean, though, played along. "Well, Isabel's remains were there, yes. But . . . Ah! That memorial stone to a Henry, maybe Henry the Navigator, that's got the same angled *er.*"

"And the same wee 'm' as well."

"Well, the stone's so badly damaged, I couldn't make that out."

Behind Jean's back, billiard balls clonked decisively and a player whooped. Michael's music slowed to a pibroch, a lament. Jean recognized the piece as "Lament for the Harp Tree." Or Key, depending on who you asked. The front door opened and Alasdair and Delaney walked in, this time with Kallinikos and W.P.C. Blackhall in attendance. They—there was a "they"—stood in a prickly knot just inside the door. Shannon approached them, exchanged a long, gratified look with Kallinikos, then pointed toward the snug . . . Jean dragged her attention back to Ciara.

"You've seen the burning-glass," Ciara was saying.

"It's actually a mirror."

"It was Isabel's mirror, buried in her grave with her bones. She signaled to Edward Tempest at the monastery with it, and the flashes of light attracted her murderers."

"Edward who?"

"Edward Tempest. From one of England's old Catholic families. He was helping Isabel save the relic from the iconoclasts, the ones who exiled Mary and later had her killed. Ironic, isn't it, how in the sixteenth century the relic—or the word of the relic rather, in the beginning was the Word—any road, in the sixteenth century the Catholics were saving the relic from the Protestant oppressors, but one hundred and fifty years earlier, the Templars were saving the relic from the Catholic oppressors. Soon as a religion establishes itself, it turns from the true stories, doesn't it?"

Jean felt as though her brain was shrinking away from her ears, but she kept doggedly writing.

"And the glass! The Sinclairs had it etched, very cleverly, so it looks to be no more than the oxidized backing of a mirror, with the map of North America's coastline. The Templars brought their relics to Scotland under Robert the Bruce and his Sinclair allies, and then Henry Sinclair the Navigator took Mary's relics away to safety. It's plain as the nose on your face!" Ciara grinned, but the grin wasn't expansive enough for her, and segued into a merry laugh.

Jean could only see her own nose when she crossed her eyes. "Mary's relic? You mean the one mentioned in the letter in the museum? Mary Stuart, as distinct from Mary of Guise, her mother, who had something going with the Sinclairs at Rosslyn —they might have been lending her money. Maybe they were custodians of Templar treasure or crown jewels of Scotland, who knows?"

"Oh aye, they're all named Mary. Ferniebank's well is St. Mary's well. Coincidence?"

"Sure it is. People and wells were named after popular saints . . . Oh no." Revelation swept over her like a cooler of Gatorade over a winning coach. Jean dropped her forehead onto her hand in lieu of beating her head against the table. That's why Minty had stumbled over the name "Mary." That was her and maybe Angus's problem with Ciara's plans. Which weren't only blasphemous, they were absolutely bonkers. "Mary's relic. Not a relic owned by Mary, but a relic of Mary, and you don't mean any of the sixteenth-century Marys, you mean, so help me God, Mary Magdalen."

"Very clever!" Ciara patted Jean's shoulder. "I knew we'd get on swimmingly, never mind the po-faced policeman."

Through her fingers Jean could see several po-faced policemen, Alasdair the coldest and stoniest of the lot, turning toward them.

Ciara went blithely on. "There you have it. The letter thanking the Saint Clairs for their role in hiding the relics. The burning-glass as a hint to the significance of the conspiracy. The musical notes that will reveal where the map locating the relics is hidden. The grave inscription proving that the relics were those of Mary Magdalen—she was known as the Beautiful Sinner, hence the 'catin.' The cenotaph of Henry Sinclair proving that he took those same relics to America. Taken all together, you have overwhelming evidence that Mary, Queen of Scots, and her allies meant to protect that secret knowledge. Where's your bestseller now, eh?"

There was a rhetorical question for you, Jean thought, just as Detective Inspector Delaney stopped at Ciara's shoulder.

She looked up at him with a warm smile. "Hullo, Inspector. Alasdair, Sergeant Kallinikos, please join us."

"Ciara Macquarrie," said Delaney, "I arrest you in connection with the murders of Wallace Rutherford and Angus Rutherford. You do not have to say anything, but it may harm your defense if you do not mention, when questioned, something which you later rely on in court. Anything you do say may be given in evidence."

The music stopped, the voices stopped, all motion in the room seemed to stop as Jean's already uncertain breath escaped in a whoosh.

CHAPTER TWENTY-SIX

Ciara's smile withered into bafflement. "I beg your pardon, Inspector Delaney? Alasdair, what's all this in aid of?"

Alasdair mumbled something beneath his breath that sounded like "stupid cow." His eyes, Jean saw at second glance, weren't cold as sea-ice after all, but scorched by heat.

Blackhall took Ciara's arm and pulled her unresisting from the chair. "Is this your bag? I'll just bring it along, then."

Briefly Jean saw with Ciara's eyes—her own features registering shock and awe, Alasdair smoldering, Delaney smug. And beyond, every face in the pub turned toward her, sentences hanging half-finished, glasses and forks suspended in mid-air, billiard cues held aloft. "Oh," Ciara said, her voice suddenly very small. "Here's me, thinking they simply passed over. But they died defending secret knowledge, just as Isabel did. Her romance is going on, and we're playing our own parts in it."

And that, Jean thought, her gaze glancing off Alasdair's like a water droplet off a hot iron, that was what was wrong with romance.

Kallinikos cleared a way through the crowd, people stepping back as though from a procession of lepers ringing their bells. Stuffing her notebook into her bag next to the box with the ambiguous burning-glass—yeah, fires can really get away from you—Jean followed Alasdair and Delaney. Photographers materialized and cameras clicked. Outside, in the sudden sunlight, Logan and two other constables formed a human dam.

Two patrol cars waited at the curb. Ciara went quietly, allowing herself to be placed into the first car with Blackhall as companion.

Around the corner from the beer garden came the sandy-haired detective constable and O. Hawick. Hawick was actually grasping Keith's arm, even though he gave the impression he was hauling Keith along by the scruff of his neck. Keith stumbled and his glasses slid down his nose. His gaze darted here and there like a mad mouse ride at a carnival and then crashed to a halt on Jean's face. "You gotta call my firm in Glasgow, the American ambassador, whoever. I'm in deep doo-doo here."

Jean opened her mouth, but the only sound that came out was a squeak.

"I shoulda bailed out ages ago. They're nuts, all of them—that damn Angus, face of a horse, jawbone of an ass."

"D.C. Linklater," said Delaney, "did you not caution the man?"

"That I did," Linklater replied, with a shushing gesture toward Keith.

Keith spotted Ciara's wan but very brave face in the rear window of the car. "Okay, okay, she's a lot of fun already, but I'm not going to jail for her."

Linklater seized Keith's other arm and with Hawick frog-marched him to the second car, where Kallinikos was holding the door open. "We all ate the same stuff, when Angus went green around the gills I figured he had an ulcer or something—hey!" Keith protested as the three men packed him into the car, an operation that reminded Jean of cramming Dougie into the pet carrier.

Even after Kallinikos climbed in behind Keith and shut the door, she could still hear the young man's flat but far from soft voice, "Come on, people, this is all a really big mistake."

"Away with you. I'll catch you up at Kelso." Delaney gestured and two or three more police people sorted themselves into the vehicles. "Logan, bring a car round for me."

The police cars headed out, each trailing reporters like a honeymooner's car dragging tin cans and old shoes.

Pushing aside the leftover gawkers, Logan marched toward a third patrol car down the street. His face, Jean saw, was set with satisfaction. And she also saw, across the way, Minty standing with her usual brittle dignity in the doorway of the museum. But even as Jean watched, her lips parted in an unusual, slow, and even sensual smile. *So the interloper's turned out to be the murderer. She'll get her comeuppance, then.* But if Jean couldn't see Ciara breaking and entering, she certainly couldn't see her killing.

A murmur was Alasdair and Delaney speaking fast and low, each voice overriding the other. ". . . Roddy Elliot about the inscription," said Alasdair.

"I know, I know," Delaney replied.

"Shannon, Zoe, their parents . . ."

". . . I'm on it."

". . . that answerphone tape—it's never Ciara. And the keys, have you . . ."

"We're on it."

"Valerie Trotter . . ."

Logan's car pulled up. He leaned across to open the door. Alasdair stepped toward it, but Delaney cut him off. "No."

"Gary!"

"No! Love her, hate her, makes no matter to me. You're too damn close to her. That's all." One meaty hand shoving Alasdair aside, Delaney wedged himself into the car and slammed the door.

The car sped up the street, leaving Alasdair standing on the curb. The crowd eddied around him, then dispersed. Jean tried to take a deep breath but it caught like a thistle in her throat. Delaney had just thrown Alasdair off the case because of his previous marital track. *Bloody hell.*

A movement in the corner of her eye was Michael, the bag of his pipes beneath his elbow and the drones resting on his shoulder like a soldier sloping arms. Beside him Noel was wringing both his hands and a dishtowel. "They ate here—why weren't the lot of them poisoned as well as Angus—no one will stop here ever again."

"Not a bit of it. I'm thinking you've got a right tourist attraction here." Michael indicated the people surging back into the pub, the door swinging as though it was the revolving variety.

So many others were swamping the garden gateway that Zoe was pressed up against the side of the wall. "Dad? We've got orders but Val cannot help, she's away with Derek."

"I'll play again, shall I? Music having charms, savage breasts, and so forth." Michael nudged Noel toward the influx, called over his shoulder to Jean, "I'm expecting the full account soon as possible," and was swept away with the others.

With a feeble nod, Jean looked around. Minty had vanished and the door of the museum was shut tight. Alasdair was standing as still as the statue of some historical worthy, set up in the marketplace only to be forgotten, useful to no one but roosting pigeons. Damn Delaney. Damn Ciara—there was the jawbone of an ass, not Angus.

Again pipe music sounded from the garden, this time the bittersweet melody of "Dark Island." Jean wished she could pick Alasdair up and carry him away to one of the Outer Hebrides. But then, he'd fight his way back here if he had to swim. She set her hand on his shoulder. She could have played his tendons like the strings of a harp. "Alasdair?"

His hands clenched and loosened. He shut his eyes and opened them. His jaw worked. "Jean."

"I take it the results of the toxicology tests came in?"

"Oh aye."

The police worked fast, then, their wonders to perform. "Angus and Wallace, Delaney said. What about Helen?"

"Helen died of natural causes. Heart failure. But the men . . ." Alasdair turned his back to the street. His face was a desert island composed of nothing beyond fire and ice. "Heart failure as well, but brought on by a dirty great dose of glycoside. *Scrophulariacae. Digitalis purpurea.* Foxglove."

"Foxglove," Jean repeated. "But lots of people take digitalis as a medicine. It can work differently in the elderly. Therapeutic overdoses aren't uncommon."

"Wallace was taking another medication, not digitalis. Angus was not taking anything."

"I see."

"When I was a lad in Fort William, we believed that poking a finger into a foxglove bell would kill you. It's common knowledge it's a poison. It's readily available and fast-working. Angus had his dose at the dinner here. There were bread and herbs in the vomit by the chapel wall, and Noel says he served focaccia amongst other dishes, though Angus likely got his dose in the dessert or the coffee, else he'd have dropped just there at the pub. Wallace got his dose in his dinner as well. One that someone brought to him."

Jean asked the unavoidable question. "Why arrest Ciara?"

"Those wee stars from her earrings, the chapel, the pit prison, one actually clinging to Angus's clothing. It's like she was leaving a trail of breadcrumbs."

"That doesn't even rise to the level of circumstantial evidence."

"The torch in the well. Her fingerprints were on it. Her hair was on Angus's cap. There was well-scum on that pink jacket of hers. The mud on Keith's car matches that from the layby."

"That still doesn't mean either Ciara or Keith killed him. They were having their differences, but . . ." Alasdair didn't know the full wretched excess of Ciara's plans, did he?

His hard, uncompromising eyes focused beyond Jean, beyond the pub, beyond the town. "I told Gary he was moving too fast. She'd never have thought to leave the area. But no, she had means, she had opportunity. He's thinking he can intimidate her into revealing a motive. Good luck to him. Arguing with Ciara's like punching a marshmallow. You'll just knacker yourself, and she'll never feel a thing."

And here I am, Jean thought, teaching myself to fight back. She removed her hand from his shoulder, not quite worried that he hadn't shaken her away, not quite grateful. "Did she do it?"

That he hesitated before answering told her at least part of what she wanted to know. At last he said, "No. She didn't do it. She's not got it in her. Nor has she a motive, not that I can see."

"What is the killer's motive, then?"

"Something doing with Ferniebank, has to be. There's always a reason for murder, if only in the killer's own mind." The harsh lines of his eyebrows and lips eased, if microscopically. "Delaney's left no more than a skeleton crew at Ferniebank, if you'll pardon the expression, and yet it's Ferniebank that's the point of the exercise. Let's get on with it."

Alasdair started off down the street so fast, Jean had to almost run to keep up. Get on with what? she wondered. And answered, *the job.* Free-lance knight errantry. Among all the other issues, there was now a maiden—er, a matron in distress.

He opened the car door for Jean, climbed in, and started the engine. In edgy but not uncompanionable silence, he drove up the High Street and out of town.

A few brushstrokes of purple-pink on the hills betrayed the presence of late foxglove blooms. The leaves would still be there, though, even if the flowers had passed. You could dry the leaves, you could soak them, you could add a pinch here and a dram there. . . .

The church stood deserted, no sexton digging another grave beside the two that still gaped. The Glebe lay still and silent. Behind it hunkered the cooking school, with all its dishes and implements and little bottles of spice. "It's easy enough to put poison into someone's food," Jean said. "And they're all working with food."

"Minty's school, the pub, Roddy's dairy, Valerie and her bakery," said Alasdair. "Her uncle and his shop, come to that."

"Did you hear Zoe telling Noel that Valerie took off right after the police did?"

"Aye, I did that."

"Didn't she ask you yesterday whether there was going to be any more digging at Ferniebank before Ciara took over?"

"A question that now seems a bit more than idle curiosity. I'll have one of the Ferniebank constables bring her in—like as not they're still thinking I'm *persona grata.*"

"Delaney . . ."

"Bugger Delaney." Alasdair's jaw was set in concrete, his hands gripped the wheel as though it was Delaney's throat, and yet his breathing had slowed to its normal watchful pattern. He wasn't speeding or cutting corners. The drive, Jean hypothesized, was a contemplative exercise.

She said, "Ciara's taken courses at Minty's school. She's been staying at the Glebe all month. It would be easy enough to get into the kitchens, prepare the poison, sneak it into Angus's food. Especially since she planned the dinner to begin with. Sorry."

"We're obliged to consider all the possibilities."

"Then don't you have to consider the spouse? Would Minty have a motive to kill her husband? I sure wouldn't want to get on her bad side. How many years has she been dissing Valerie, do you think?"

"I'm wondering why Val got up her nose to begin with."

"For refusing to suck up to her, maybe? Noel was saying something about those who tug their forelocks for a living, and that's him and his family and Logan—well, Roddy and Zoe aren't exactly with the program. Maybe one of the peasants got fed up and poisoned Angus, although you'd think Minty would be the target. I mean, why go for the adjutant when you can get the general?"

"Maybe Minty was the target. That's the disadvantage of poison, getting it into your intended victim. But then, the advantage of poison is that it gives you a grand alibi. Most poisoners are only caught when they do it again and then again."

"You suspected Wallace was poisoned—heavens, you suspected Helen was poisoned—but no one investigated until Angus went down."

"Exactly. Once someone solves a problem by, say, embezzling, they'll solve the next problem the same way, not stopping when they're ahead. Ciara's always overdoing, and yet . . ."

There was Ferniebank Farm, showing no signs of life, human, canine, or bovine. Roddy, too, had a date with Delaney. And there were probably detectives drying dishes in the pub kitchen, all the better to hurl questions at a passing Brimberry. "The killer was trying to solve the problem of Ferniebank. But what problem is that? Wallace wasn't trying to stop the sale or anything. He told you himself he was happy about it. And it's too late for Angus to renege on the sale or retract the planning permission. Ciara was saying they could all vanish and the conference center would go through as planned, it's all set."

"Is it now?" Alasdair stopped in front of the closed gates of the castle. The tarpaulin covering the gate twitched and P.C. Freeman peered through the iron bars. But no, the media mob hadn't hared back this way. Yet.

With its usual creak, the gate swung open. Alasdair maneuvered the car into the courtyard, brought it to a halt beneath the eaves of the trees, and slammed the door behind him so emphatically that crows squawked and a detective glanced out of the incident room.

Freeman started to push the gate shut. In two economical gestures, Alasdair stopped him and summoned a second constable from the front steps of the castle. ". . . wee house, Gillyflower Cottage . . ." That's right, he'd been there when Valerie gave her address to Delaney the first time around.

Jean waited beside the car, looking around as curiously as though she'd never seen Ferniebank before. The castle hid its secrets behind the gray precipice of its facade. The chapel hid its secrets behind the whispering leaves of the trees. Maybe Roddy was right, and the place should be torn down and sold for stone. And the grounds sown with salt, for good measure. Would Isabel's ghost still run, then, over land ruined not by nature but the passions of man?

Freeman climbed into his patrol car, drove through the gate, and headed south. The other constable took over his post at the gate. With a mini-smile of satisfaction, Alasdair returned to Jean. "All right then. What else was Ciara saying?"

Jean groaned, but steeled herself to the task. By the time he unlocked the door of the flat and waved her inside, she'd not so much led him through Ciara's maze, with its illogical branches and dead ends, as gotten him lost with her.

He stood in the doorway, less stunned, Jean estimated, than resigned. Then he ran his hand through his hair and down the back of his neck, as though wiping away cobwebs, and shut the door. "The glass, Mary's letter, the harp, Gerald's papers and all—where's your chain of custody? Where's your provenance?

And Edward Tempest sounds to be the hero of a bodice-ripper romance."

"A family of Catholics named Tempest lived in Yorkshire—they probably were involved in the 1569 rebellion, although whether there was an Edward here . . ." Jean shrugged. "Ciara's version of the occult fantasies that are going around is barely ten percent original, if that much. There are Sinclairs pontificating at this very moment about their loyalty to the Stuart cause and secret Catholicism and the Holy Grail. Even the sculptures being musical notes—I've heard something similar about Rosslyn. Religion as puzzle rather than as dogma is quite the fad these days. As for historical veracity—who cares?"

"Ciara's share is that the Scottish monarchs conspired with the Templars to send the Magdalen's relics to America, is that it?"

"I'm not even sure that's original. It's the Ferniebank angle that's new. And there's no telling how much of that is Wallace's, let alone Gerald's. Minty was right, this sort of thing takes on a life of its own."

"And Ciara's sprung this on one and all in just the last two days?"

"Apparently so," Jean said. "What I'm really wondering is why one more book on all of this stuff got such a big advance from a publisher. I mean, okay, Ciara's got writing credentials, but she'd have to have something special . . ."

Alasdair's eyes were taking on the thousand-yard stare of the combat veteran, although his version was closer to a thousand-year stare.

"Well," Jean concluded, "she's either a superb charlatan, a nut case, or a businesswoman giving the customers what they want."

"All three, I reckon, though she's not aware of the first."

"And there I was talking to Miranda just the other day about marketing belief systems. Myth as . . . Well, there's nothing wrong with myth *per se.*"

"The danger comes in hiding from the fact that they're myths." Having issued his manifesto, Alasdair strode on down the hall toward the bedroom.

Amen to that, Jean thought, and then, with a blink and a breath, noticed how dark and dreary the flat seemed after the bright sunlight and soft breezes outside. She could still smell the soup they'd reheated for lunch. And Dougie had made an aromatic deposit in his litter box, which was as good an editorial comment as any on the present situation.

She dumped her bag and started opening windows, so that the fresh air, the rustle of the trees, and the rush of the river filtered inside. She cleaned the litter box and located the culprit, who was asleep in the center of the bed with his tail draped over his nose like a furry gas mask.

Alasdair had changed into jeans and a T-shirt reading "Real Men Wear Kilts." "I'm for having a wee keek at Wallace's boxes. I reckon Ciara's got his copies of Gerald's papers, and everyone else in the area's had time to pick them over, but still, there might be something interesting there."

And it's something to do, Jean concluded. No question of stopping for a rest, even though his face was showing the strain, his mouth stretched taut as a twisted rope. "Be right with you," she told him, and didn't so much change her clothes as gird her loins with denim and a *Great Scot* T-shirt. What she told herself was that something had to give soon. Just as long as it wasn't Alasdair.

Chapter Twenty-Seven

Jean stepped out of the flat to find Alasdair standing with Freeman while the other constable pushed the gate shut yet again. ". . . no car there," the young man was saying, his freckles sliding downward in dismay. "I chapped at the door and shouted. I'm thinking the lad was playing silly beggars, going from window to window, though it could have been the breeze blowing the curtains."

"It was the lad," said Alasdair, "hiding out whilst his mum chases off to Kelso."

"Shall I go back?"

"No, we've got no warrant to flush him out. Thank you just the same. Have yourself a cuppa."

"Thank you, sir." Freeman strolled over to the incident room.

"I hope Val chased after Ciara," said Jean, "and didn't bug out permanently."

"If Val did a bunk, she'd take Derek," Alasdair said. "She left him at the cottage so he'd not go talking to any more detectives is all."

"If we could get him away from Valerie, or even Zoe . . . Maybe we can leave that window in the back of the castle open and lure him here. You know, third time's the charm."

A small, concentrated flame flared in Alasdair's eye. "That's bordering on entrapment."

"I was joking," she told him.

"I'm not joking. Not a bit of it. Here, lock the flat, please, and open the window in the Laigh Hall." Handing her the keys, Alasdair strode over to the shop, hoisted the wooden pallet, and carried it around the side of the castle whence it came.

Okay. Jean locked the flat, tucked the keys into her pocket, and marched herself into the castle.

Even with the light bulb burning in the Laigh Hall, shadows hung like bats in the vaults of the ceiling and the corners were duskily indistinct. The south-facing windows admitted some daylight but not what Jean would call illumination, and the air was dense with mildew, rot, and silence. The trap door to the pit prison was closed. Giving it a wide berth, she padded across the flagstones to the left-hand window and with a heave and a squeal raised the probably Victorian sash.

Below, Alasdair angled the pallet against the side of the building. Grasping the drain pipe, he stepped up on the wooden rack as though it was a ladder. His left hand fumbled for and found the weathered stone windowsill. Jean set her hand on his. "You could climb in yourself."

"Only if something was chasing me. Derek's no taller than me but a good deal more limber—he'll get in, I reckon. If he wants to." With a quick squeeze of her hand, he let himself drop down to the ground and headed back around the building.

Yeah, Jean repeated silently. And if he wants to, then what? Telling herself she could open a gallery at the British Museum with her collection of misgivings, she turned back to the room.

The scabrous paneling, the old door, the dark yawn of the old fireplace still held some of their derelict charm, some of their romance, the same way a cow's skull was romantic, more in symbol than in reality. She tried to imagine Gerald setting up housekeeping here, or more likely in the rooms above, with oil lamps and water basins and a woman from the village, a Brimberry or a Trotter, maybe, to "do"—to cook and clean—for him. The marble Georgian fireplace surround that was now at

Glebe House would have moderated the gloom, as would furniture and carpets.

Did Gerald sit at his desk writing about Isabel even as her ghost played the harp? Did her slippers waft over the ancient flooring, noiselessly, until her pale form leaned over his shoulder? No. Ghosts couldn't interact with the living, although at times they seemed to respond to the presence of flesh, blood, and voice.

Cautiously Jean peeled back a corner of her extra sense, but did not pick up one paranormal vibe. Forward momentum, then. She walked over to the objects in the center of the floor. Fishing rods and accessories, tools, gardening equipment, the telescope. A case holding an old electric typewriter. And six cardboard boxes ranged in a semi-circle, flaps open. She settled herself onto the floor before them, the stone so cold it sent a shudder up her spine, and adjusted her position so the door of the dungeon was in her line of sight.

Two boxes held clothing while a third held domestic odds and ends. Jean folded a well-worn wool sweater, closed an empty leather case intended for tie tacks and cufflinks, and wiped her fingers clean of the toothpaste oozing from a squashed tube. Anything valuable—or at least, conventionally valuable—had already been carried away by Minty's manicured hands.

Exhuming the cast-off shell of Wallace's body seemed less of a sacrilege than going through his intimate belongings, not just his toothpaste, but the books and papers in the other three boxes.

A waver in the light in the entrance chamber, and soft footsteps, and Alasdair walked into the room saying, "I've told Freeman and the others that we've set a trap."

"What if Derek suspects it's a trap?"

"Not everyone's as devious as we are, Jean."

She hoped Alasdair's thin smile indicated she was the grit

that provided traction in his well-oiled mental machinery. Grit, helpmeet, comic relief. She could play those as well as significant other and lover. "So Delaney didn't find anything here?"

"He's saying he found nothing. Of course, he didn't know what he was looking for. Nor do we, come to that." Alasdair knelt down beside her and helped her stack the books neatly on the floor. "Well, well, well. I'll not be fainting in amazement at those."

"Ancient mysteries, secret landscapes, hidden bloodlines, and underground history books going back to Watkins' *Old Straight Track*. The Templars. The Shroud. *The Passover Plot*."

"You've got a few of these yourself." Alasdair's forefinger nudged a book whose cover featured the word "conspiracy" in blood-red letters.

"These are the books that were on that bottom shelf in the flat, the one that's empty now. Minty was embarrassed to leave them out, bestseller or no bestseller." Jean held a dog-eared copy of the novel Miranda kept mis-naming beside her head, copying the cryptic smile of the Mona Lisa on its cover.

"Was Wallace reading this sort of thing B.C., before Ciara?"

"Oh yeah, some of these books date back to well before the nineties. See?" Jean picked up the conspiracy book and opened it to the flyleaf, which was stamped, "W. Rutherford, 12 Bruce Terrace, Kelso." "Throw Gerald's stuff into the mix, and I bet Hugh's right, it was Wallace who pressed Angus and Minty to fix up Ferniebank. And that produced Ciara, drawn like a bee to honey."

"Bees are attracted to foxgloves as well."

She glanced sharply at him, but his face was solemn, revealing nothing but interest in a spiral-bound book of drawing paper. Each page was filled with sketches of the castle and the chapel. They were amateurish, yes, labored rather than fluid, and yet they were more than Minty's "adequate."

Jean picked up a large, flat book on the history of the clarsach. "*The Harp Key.* This is straight history and musicology . . . Oh, cool." The flyleaf of the book held another sketch of the excavation, this one of a woman sitting on the edge of a narrow trench, a trowel in one hand, a small peaked chest on her lap. Jean made out Valerie's fox-like features, then studied the chest. "That's in the museum, isn't it? A medieval moneybox."

"I'm thinking the same box is in the sketch Logan pinched, only there it's Angus holding it. Perhaps. I only saw the man for a moment, and didn't know who he was."

"Coincidence?" Jean asked, but Alasdair wouldn't commit himself to an answer. Setting the book aside, she picked up an accordion folder that emitted a peculiar earthy smell. Inside was tucked a sheaf of yellowed and crinkled papers, each one, she saw as she fanned them, covered with lines of ornate but faded handwriting. She turned one toward the light and read, ". . . late, late in the gloaming, Isabel came hame."

"Is that Gerald's poem, then?"

"Ciara said reading it's like treading treacle. I'll take her word for that, if not for everything." Jean stacked the folder on top of the sketch book.

"Have a look at these." Alasdair opened another folder. "We've got star charts, road maps, maps of Roxburghshire, maps of Scotland. Here's one with your Harp Line."

"It's not my Harp Line," Jean said, taking that one from his hand. The paper was scabbed with multiple erasures, the ghosts of earlier lines still showing through. "Ciara said something about the music of the harp revealing the map to where the relics are hidden."

"Her book is fiction, is it?"

"Yeah, but she doesn't intend it to be." Jean frowned, trying to remember Ciara's exact words. "If y'all had just held off arresting her for a few more minutes I might have had it out of her, whether she's really got some sort of map or whether she's just using that 'if x is two then y is blue' logic to assume that there is one."

Still expressionless, Alasdair took back the battered page of sketch paper and tucked it into the folder with the others. "Wallace might have made up the whole thing, and convinced her there was a map. Or perhaps he was thinking Gerald had hidden a map somewhere. Inside the harp? Is that why it was stolen, because Minty would never have stood for taking it apart?"

"That must be it, it's just a matter of who . . ." A light bulb considerably brighter than the one hanging from the ceiling went off above Jean's head. She bounced to her knees and fixed Alasdair with a manic gaze and quivering finger. "Aha! That's it!"

He recoiled. "Eh?"

"Ciara got a big advance because so many of these books"—Jean's expansive gesture took in the entire pile—"are basically stuck together with moonshine and chewing gum, but she has proof! Or she convinced the publisher she has proof, because Wallace thought he had proof, because something Gerald said convinced him there was proof. Even if it's a chart of Nova Scotia and Cape Cod from Henry the Navigator's day, 1400 or so, that would be a heck of a discovery. And blazingly controversial. Not that I have a dog in that hunt, Columbus has nothing to fear from me."

She was hyperventilating. She plunked back down on the floor—whoa, a splash of cold, just not on the face—and caught her breath.

"But there's no proof, is there?" Alasdair's nod was so firm he could have driven nails with his chin. "Anyone else would be a wee bit nervy by this time, but Ciara, well, she owns the place, she can take it apart at her leisure. If it's meant to happen, it'll happen, she used to say."

"That's all well and good, but most people will start pushing toward what they want to happen. Like snatching the harp, which Ciara doesn't own and couldn't take apart at her leisure. Just think . . ." Jean was trying to think, but her thoughts were spinning around and rising and falling like carousel horses. If she could grab the gold ring—slowly, she told herself, logically. "The local people are divided into three camps. Ciara's allies, which is a list that's growing short, now that Wallace and Angus have been, er, erased. Maybe Helen was on that list too."

"It's not a safe place to be, then, though Val's still alive and well."

"In spite of the tattoo, she could actually be on the second list, the people who are gritting their teeth and going along because of the money involved. Like Minty and the Brimberrys, more or less. And then there's Roddy Elliot, hurling his verbal thunderbolts."

Alasdair wiggled one of the fishing rods so that the metal bits jangled. "Did he stop by here the Saturday morning intending to search for the map amongst Wallace's things . . . Listen to me, I'm assuming there is a map."

"It doesn't matter whether there's one or not . . ."

"So long as folk think there is," Alasdair concluded wearily. "Roddy could've had him a look at the lumber room any time since Wallace died, with no overzealous caretaker turfing him out, but he just now heard about the map. Or the book, at the least."

"Ciara herself told me she told Shannon about it Friday afternoon. Shannon told Zoe and Zoe told Roddy—she was staying with him Friday night."

"That's why Zoe herself was sneaking about. And why Roddy

scalped the inscription that same night. But what of Angus in the chapel the next night?"

"It's where he was standing when he went down, yeah, but why he was standing there? It could be something as simple as losing his cap or whatever when he was there earlier in the morning and going back to get it. Or maybe he was heading for the lumber room to look for the map, too."

"He could have looked it out at his leisure after the work began here. Or waited 'til she gave it him." Alasdair's lips thinned to a fissure of frustration.

"If Angus had been with someone when the poison took effect, he might have reached a doctor, a hospital . . ." Jean didn't need to finish her sentence. Ferniebank had claimed another life. She glanced at the trap door, half expecting to see skeletal fingers from below feeling around its edge. "So we're back for the umpteenth time to why was Wallace standing in the pit prison when he went down. Looking for the quasi-mythical map, with his telescope lens to magnify—something? Hiding the bit of inscription? Was he reacting to that phone call? Roddy could have made the call while he was dropping off a bottle of milk at Logan's house. He'd already had a fight with Wallace earlier the same day."

"Or Logan himself made the call, as a friendly warning of things getting out of hand in the community."

"How good a look did you take around the dungeon when you got the lens and the star?" Jean asked, crawling to her feet and taking a cautious step or two toward the trap door.

"I had me a look round, right enough, but what was there to look for?" Not at all cautious, Alasdair outpaced her and threw back the trap. The dank, moldy breath that wafted upwards really should have included wraiths of mist. He knelt at the edge and peered downward, Jean craning over his shoulder. She could see only the top foot or so of the ladder, plunging downward into impenetrable darkness. "Wasn't I saying on the Friday I'd not be coming in here without a flashlight? I'll fetch it from the flat."

Jean took two long paces back. If Alasdair wanted her to, she'd climb down into the dungeon. And stand there with her skin crawling while he looked for whatever there was to look for . . . Her skin was crawling now, frissons of chill trickling along her arms and down the back of her neck, dragging her skin downward so she felt as though she was clothed in lead.

Involuntarily she looked up, but she could see nothing. It was what she was hearing: light, quick steps pacing overhead, and the faintest ripple of harp strings.

CHAPTER TWENTY-EIGHT

Alasdair stood up, his hand on his stomach, grimacing. "Isabel, is it?"

"Yep," Jean told him. And, falling back on the traditional remedy for stress—no, she wasn't running away from a ghost, not at all—she said, "It's past six. Let's carry that box of papers over to the flat and fix something to eat. We can do the dungeon some other time."

He nodded, more, she thought, out of consideration for her than because he wanted to take a break. If sheer willpower could have wrenched the entire story from either stone or paper, he would have had them babbling away by now.

Alasdair collected the papers and *The Harp Key* with its sketch, lifted the box, and followed Jean past the sentry constable on the front steps, pausing only while she dragged the heavy door closed. Inside the flat, he set the box on the coffee table and sent a glance edged with envy toward Dougie, who was reposing on the windowsill like a supernally calm, if furry, little Buddha. "I've got the ingredients for a curry, if that suits your taste."

"Great, I love curry." Jean almost added *thanks for cooking,* then thought better of it. She also thought better of trying to help, and sat down to leaf through the documents in the box.

Some were typed, but most were handwritten, either in the elegant cursive of a hundred years ago or a practical if cramped modern hand. Some were originals, some were copies. Just as she emitted a gaping yawn, Alasdair placed a steaming cup of tea on the table in front of her, then walked into the bedroom.

A few moments later she heard his voice rising and falling. He returned with the Ancient Monuments book under his arm and his phone to his ear. "Thank you just the same, Sergeant Kallinikos," he said, handed her the book, then inserted his phone into his pocket.

No, there was no point in him asking Delaney for a report on the interviews with Ciara and Keith. Jean took a healthy swallow of the hot, sweet tea, clearing her throat of dust and mold and a lingering hint of bitterness, and turned back to the box.

There she found pages of notes and chronologies taken from various books, what looked like the start of a biography of Gerald, and some memos on genealogy. She did not expect to find an inventory of Wallace's papers, and was not gratified by finding one after all. Other than a few innocuous letters, Gerald's writings were confined to the musty pages of the poem. She held a couple of them up to the light, noting that the paper was crinkled and stained, as though it had gotten damp. Well, what didn't get damp, in this climate?

If either Gerald or Wallace left anything explanatory, let alone incriminating, Jean told herself, Ciara has it now.

The snick-snick of a knife and the pungent smell of sauteing onions signaled Alasdair's progress in the kitchen. Ah, she got it —cooking was something else useful he could do. As much as she'd like to collapse onto the couch pillows, she had to hold up her side. She opened the Ancient Monuments book, this time noting not only Valerie's name but also her husband Harry Spivey's, and paged through it.

The half of the book about the castle dealt with flaking stone, rotting wood, leaking slates—the renovations were little more than a desperate rearguard action against the forces of entropy. . . . Ah. There was a photo of the pit prison, layered with rubbish and dirt but far from inaccessible, if also far from the stark stone chamber of today. What had Minty said about Wallace poking about in the pit prison? Yes, Jean told herself without enthusiasm, we do need to check the place out.

There was the photo of the skeleton she now knew was Isabel's, as a quick check of the list of illustrations established. Each one of those cuts and slices had gone through living flesh into living bone. Each had been made by a living hand directed by a living mind, likely no more disturbed than by hewing wood. As Alasdair said, once you solve a problem by a certain method, it becomes easier and easier to use the same method, terrible though it might be.

There was the photo of Isabel's grave inscription, complete except for the harp, no more informative than it had been the day before. Photos of other inscribed stones included Henry Sinclair's, which was definitely a memorial rather than a stone marking a burial, no surprise there.

An inventory listed bits of pottery and other artifacts, many of which Jean had just seen in the museum. There was no mention of the mirror, whether as Gerald's shaving glass or Isabel's communications device.

A spicy aroma wafted into her nose and mouth. She inhaled, an extra brain cell ticked over, and she realized that there was no mention in the inventory of the money chest, either, the one that Wallace had drawn not once but twice, and that was now in the museum.

Frowning, she turned back to the photo of Isabel's skeleton and looked at the one beside it. It showed the area of the grave just inside the collapsed corner of the coffin. No, she hadn't imagined it—the clear imprint of something small and square lay next to the ghastly, hacked shoulder-bone. "Alasdair, that chest in Wallace's drawings. The one in the museum. It's not listed in the inventory, but there's a mark of something just that size in Isabel's grave.'"

He looked around from setting cutlery out on the table. "An oversight? Or a deliberate omission?"

"A dig sixteen years ago wouldn't have been recorded as punctiliously as one today, and the director of this one wasn't known for attention to detail—which is why he got the job at such a minor site, I bet. But losing track of a broken pot is one thing, simply not mentioning a nice little chest like that is another. There has to be some significance to Wallace drawing that chest. . . ." The thought, whatever it had been, spun through her mind and vanished.

Alasdair beckoned her to the table. "We're thinking too hard, lass. Come and eat."

Dougie leaped down off the windowsill, giving Jean a view of the lengthening shadows outside, and trotted into the kitchen, tail erect, whiskers alert. Her taut facial muscles cracked into a smile as Alasdair gravely dispensed kibble and fresh water, and indulged in a stroke of Dougie's velvet-furred head. The men in my life, she thought. They had a lot in common, not least by complicating the life she'd intended to simplify.

Sitting down, she eyed the reddish-brown curry and rice appreciatively. Alasdair had even opened a small container of plain yogurt and prepared a salad, slices of various vegetables garnished with the green commas of watercress. After one bite of tongue-searing heat, Jean reached for the yogurt and added a generous spoonful. "Delicious. You have talents I never suspected."

Alasdair mashed rice and sauce onto the back of his fork. "Cooking's no great talent. It's simply following directions."

"Brad could have burned water," Jean said, without making any comparisons that included the word "meticulous."

Dougie wandered over and sat down beside the table, looking upwards expectantly. "No way," Jean told him. With a shrug of his whiskers—*I didn't want your nasty food anyway*—he trotted over to the couch, where he began licking himself down.

After few more bites that cleared her sinuses and hopefully her brain, Jean asked, "So what did you get out of Kallinikos? Is Delaney still holding Keith and Ciara?"

"That he is, with solicitors dancing attendance. Keith's the more helpful of the two. Seems Angus was keen on getting here to Ferniebank straightaway after the dinner, so Keith drove him to the layby and even lent him Ciara's torch. Then he waited on the track, and waited, and waited, and when Angus never returned, found him lying next to the well, dead."

"That makes sense. Keith panicked, waved his flashlight around, and ran. Roddy heard his car speeding away. Poor Keith. He was probably a lot more scared of Minty than he was of Ciara, and didn't want to be the one to report Angus dead."

"Keith is saying the flashlight in the well had Ciara's prints on it because it was hers. He prodded Angus's body, so his hands were wet, and he wiped them on the pink jacket she'd left in the car. Angus's cap likely picked up some of Ciara's hair in the van that morning. Keith's not testifying against Ciara, mind, but he's not taking a bullet for her, either."

Jean said, "Ciara told me she and Keith are sleeping together."

"So he was telling Kallinikos." Alasdair shook his head. "Poor Keith, indeed, though like as not he was thinking he struck lucky."

"Where, then, was Ciara all the time Keith and Angus were here? With Val?"

"I'm guessing so, though all Val's saying is that she has information about Angus."

"She is there in Kelso, then."

"Aye, but Delaney's not interviewed her as yet." Alasdair speared a morsel of meat.

"And Ciara's not talking?"

"Oh, she's talking, she's just not telling Gary what he's wanting to hear."

And he probably wasn't asking what Alasdair would have asked, either. Outside someone crunched across the gravel and said, "Grand evening, eh?"

So it seemed—Jean saw clear burnished golden light reflected in the window glass. A car started up and the gate opened and shut. The detective must have locked up the incident room and gone on his way, either to Kelso to join in the interview-go-round or in search of sustenance more substantial than tea and biscuits.

Alasdair was forking food into his mouth as though he was stoking a furnace rather than enjoying a meal. The curry brought some color to his face—usually very fair, it had been downright pale with anger and worry for almost twenty-four hours now. Forty-eight hours, ever since Ciara had appeared, unbidden, unwanted, but irrevocably a part of the scene.

They must have married when he was very young, maybe even in his twenties. He'd been another creature entirely from the hard-bitten paladin Jean knew. . . . Well, of course. He and Ciara had to have been different creatures for them to get together. For them, Jean amended severely, to fall in love. "You and Ciara grew apart. That's obvious. But how on earth did you ever get together?"

He looked up, his startled blue glare almost knocking her back into her chair.

She screwed her face into an apologetic grimace. "I know, it's that annoying female habit of wanting to talk about things. Like the virtual pink elephant in the middle of our mutual space."

His gaze dropped back to his plate. "You're distracting me from being closed out of the case, is that it?"

"Well, ah . . ." She hadn't thought of that.

With a quick, dry laugh, he said, "We met when I pulled her

back from the street in Inverness. She was photographing the Flora MacDonald monument, and almost stepped out in front of a car. I'd gone from police constable to detective the year before, but still had the instincts."

She'd seen a photo of Alasdair as a young constable. Ah, men in uniform!

"That she was blethering on about Flora and the Bonnie Prince should have warned me off, but no, here was a bonny lass well up on her history and legend, one who wasn't scairt of seeing ghosties."

"And you were scared of seeing ghosts?"

"Of talking about them. Here's me, aged six, telling my teacher and classmates I'd seen soldiers from the old fort walking past the library and the ski shop. Not my finest hour."

"Yeah. I had moments like that, too." She chased the last morsel of sweet yellow pepper across her plate. "How long were you and Ciara together?"

"A year or so. Married for ten, mind you, but together for only the one."

"Disillusionment must have set in pretty quickly."

"Oh aye, that it did. You said once that fantasy was like alcohol, and some people alcoholics. That's Ciara. And not a mote of genuine—ESP, whatever you're calling it."

"I see now why you have that 'bah, humbug' attitude about the romance of myth and all that. She sensitized you to it."

"I've never had a taste for rubbish," he stated. "Ciara's swung a good distance to her side and I've swung a good distance to mine. If I'm shocked at what she's become, I daresay she's shocked at what I've become."

Jean had had a few moments of shock herself recently. But then, getting to know Alasdair was like excavating a complex archaeological site—no matter how many layers she pared away, there was always something else to learn. "Thanks for explaining. I'd wondered. I mean, you've never struck me as a man who could be led by his gonads."

"Well now, don't discount that aspect of it entirely." With an expression wry as a pickle, Alasdair scooted back from the table and started collecting the dishes.

Smiling, Jean headed for the sink and turned on the hot water. "It's not fair that Brad and Ciara are doing much better than we are now."

"Ah, but we're the ones seeing dead folk." Balancing their empty plates in one hand, Alasdair opened the window curtain with the other and peered out. At that instant the sunlight faded from gold to silver as the sun dropped behind the western hills.

Jean eyed the leftover curry and rice, and found a plastic container in the cabinet large enough to hold both. "Did Delaney take any of these to test for poison?"

"A few, and good luck to him, now that he knows what he's looking for." Alasdair set the plates down in the sink. "No worries, I only prepared the food we brought ourselves."

"There wasn't anything here to fix, just some salt, sugar packets, herbs. . . ." They collided reaching for the cabinet door. Jean pulled out two small glass bottles filled with desiccated greenish-brown shreds. Both were wrapped with elegant but tasteful paper labels reading, "Cookery at the Glebe," the names of the individual herbs printed below.

"Those could do with testing as well," said Alasdair.

Jean took off each cap and, very gingerly, sniffed. "That really is thyme. Or at least, if any of it's foxglove, a sprinkle of it wouldn't have been enough to kill Wallace. And this one is basil. Just like the labels say. Besides, wouldn't it have been easier to soak the leaves? A little bit of liquid poison would go a long way."

"It might have been prepared at the pub," said Alasdair, taking and examining the bottles. "Roddy, for example, he might have been hanging about the kitchens all the evening long and no one would have thought a thing of it."

"I'll admit that Roddy seems more believable as the killer than Noel, say, but . . ."

"How's he benefit from killing Angus? That brings us back 'round to the disadvantage of using poison."

"You might not kill the person you intend to kill."

"Quite right." Alasdair set the bottles on the cabinet and turned his gaze, brighter than any glass-concentrated light, on Jean. "What if Angus wasn't the target at all? What if Minty wasn't the target? What if . . ."

The tinder of her mind flared. "What if the killer was after Ciara? That's got to be it. Eliminate the troublemaker. Troublemakers, plural, first Wallace with his weird stuff and then Ciara and her even weirder stuff. The conference center and so forth would go on as planned, just on a much less embarrassing basis . . . Oh boy." She grasped Alasdair's arm.

"Your listing of the local camps. Are you thinking what I'm thinking?"

"Oh yeah . . ." Dougie sat up on the couch and peered with hard, amber eyes toward the hall closet. From which came the sound of footsteps, the light pad of slipper-like shoes on stone, echoing through the squint. "Do you hear footsteps?"

Alasdair whipped around, almost throwing her across the room, seizing her hand to keep her from falling. "You're not feeling heavy?"

"No."

"Well then," he said with a sudden grin, each tooth flashing like a tiny dagger, "we've caught us a fly."

CHAPTER TWENTY-NINE

Come into my parlor, said the spider to the fly. And there was Tolkien's giant spider Shelob, lurking in her fetid caverns. . . . But we're the good guys, Jean told herself.

Alasdair grabbed the huge flashlight, threw the door open, and balanced on the top step as Jean, designated the chatelaine of the castle, locked up.

P.C. Freeman was standing by the gate, the fluorescent yellow of his coat dulled by shadow, his usually nimble expression dulled by, perhaps, contemplation of tea times yet to come. The door of the incident room was shut, but a light in the window indicated the presence of the second constable. The noxious yard light hadn't come on yet, and the hills on the east side of the river gleamed the deep greens and golds of jewelry against a velvet-blue sky. Tonight the breeze held no trace of smoke, just the rich odors of earth, tree, and cow.

Alasdair stepped across the gravel with as much care as a tiger creeping toward its prey, so that the nagging little granules barely shifted beneath his feet. Jean tiptoed behind him up the steps of the castle. The front door was closed, just as they'd left it.

Freeman suddenly woke up and took a step forward. Alasdair gestured, palm outward, then touched his fingertip to his lips. With a nod of understanding, Freeman subsided, if standing alertly on the balls of his feet could be considered subsiding. If he tried any flanking movements, the gravel would sound an alarm.

Alasdair's voice in Jean's ear was little more than a purr. "I'll run to the right. You cut to the left, keep Derek from the window. Here, mind the torch."

Grasping the cold, hard barrel of the flashlight, she whispered, "Just as long as you don't expect me to tackle him."

"No worries. I'll do the tackling." Head down, shoulders coiled, Alasdair threw the door open and sprinted through the entrance chamber, deftly flicking the light switch as he charged by.

Derek was standing over the boxes in a classic deer-in-the-headlights pose. Or rat in the headlights. With his black clothing and long, narrow, white face beneath spikes of hair, he needed only whiskers and a tail to complete the illusion of a rodent caught sticky-pawed.

At the sight of the adults charging toward him, he emitted a squeak of dismay and leaped for the window. Jean zigged to the left, Derek zagged to the right, and Alasdair seized the boy's jacket and jerked him to a stop so abruptly that a small flashlight flew from his hand and shattered on the floor.

Echoes ran away into the upper stories and dust fell from the ceiling. From the open door of the pit prison wafted the miasma of wet dog, mingling with an aura of stale sweat from Derek's jacket. Unfazed, Alasdair transferred his grip to Derek's upper arm and spun the boy around to face him. "Turning up again, are you, lad? What's your excuse this time round?"

Jean crept closer, but not too close. Alasdair's expression was so cold and fierce it made her quail, even though she knew it was an act. A very convincing act.

Derek's knobby knees were knocking together. He stammered, "I was after seeing where the old guy—"

"Don't go wasting my time with that flannel. Why are you here?"

Derek's eyes rolled toward Jean. She folded her arms and assumed her best "why haven't you done your homework?" frown. He looked back at Alasdair.

No sympathy there. "It's well past time for telling the truth. Why are you here?"

"You're hurting me."

"Talk," said Alasdair. Perhaps the stark white of his knuckles against Derek's jacket sleeve softened a bit, perhaps not.

"Me mum and the Macquarrie woman, they've been blethering about a treasure map."

Alasdair's glance high-fived Jean's, then sprang back to Derek.

"They think I'm a baby, that I've not understood all their plots and plans, but I have done. Everything'll be all right if they find the map. So I was after finding it for them, so maybe they'd show some respect."

"And where is this map, then?"

"It was Gerald's. Has to be with Wally's stuff, don't it?"

"Why will everything be all right if you find it?"

Derek tried a scoff, but it was thin and wan. "Ciara Crackers, she'll give mum her money."

Ciara Crackers? Jean repeated silently. Not that everyone else didn't have a similar opinion of Ciara.

"How long's your mum known Ms. Macquarrie?"

"Five, six years maybe. Wally sent her to Middlesbrough, sent her to talk to mum about Ferniebank. It's always Ferniebank, isn't it, arsehole of creation."

"Your parents were here before you were born."

"Yeh."

"What happened at the dig?"

"I dunno, something about finding treasure, but then, they're still looking for the treasure map—it don't make sense anyhow."

323

"Treasure?" Alasdair asked, with another lightning-fast glance at Jean.

Treasure. Well yes, Ciara's map would bring in a lot of money, but Ciara hadn't been at the original dig, so how . . .

"It was money, that's all I know." Derek sagged and Alasdair pulled him upright. "Mum's bakery went bust. Even her posh friends couldn't stop it going bust. And Dad did a bunk and my uncles said it was all Mum's fault for not taking care of him proper. But Crackers, she's helping us."

"Posh friends?" asked Alasdair. "Other than Ms. Macquarrie?"

"Old Wally sometimes, but mostly Old Horseface, Angus. What a prat, bringing me toy trucks and the like when I'd rather have an iPod."

Well, well, well, thought Jean. Was that where Angus kept wandering off to, to see—what? A second family? But he'd never had a first family, other than Minty.

Minty. Jean tracked the thoughts moving across Alasdair's face. Oh yes, they were thinking the same thing. If she'd grabbed the gold ring in her carousel of thoughts, it was the plain gold one on Minty's left hand.

A flicker of light in the entrance chamber accompanied the sound of a car, of two cars, driving into the courtyard. Derek looked around, his expression indicating that any arriving cavalry would just cause him more trouble.

"Wallace and Angus gave your mum money?" Alasdair asked.

"It was hers, she said. She said she'd earned it. She said that Flinty Minty—oh shit, oh shit." The boy's voice rose and broke, so that Jean thought he was going to cry.

Alasdair was unimpressed. "What about Minty?"

"I can't." Derek shook his head. "She'll get me, too."

If Alasdair had been any taller his grip would have raised the boy off the floor, Darth Vader style. "What makes you think

Minty got anyone?"

Car doors slammed. Alasdair scowled. "Tell me. Now."

"I don't, I can't . . ."

"You're that interested in where Wally died, you could do with a closer look. Come along." He dragged Derek across the floor. Toward the trap door. Toward the black square opening into the depths.

An electrical charge exploded in Jean's stomach and shot sparks off her appendages. Her free hand flew up to her mouth. Was she supposed to play good cop and protest? Was she supposed to just stand there while Alasdair bluffed . . . It was a bluff, right? *Alasdair, no!*

He had the boy by both arms. At the edge of the pit. "It's not so far down. You're young, you'll bounce a wee bit, maybe no more than break your legs."

"No, please." The boy wriggled. He was going to come right out of his jacket and tip over the edge. Jean pressed her own cry of dismay back into her mouth.

But Alasdair had Derek firmly in hand. He wasn't going anywhere—unless Alasdair let go. "Talk. Now."

A heavy step reverberated from the entrance.

"I saw Minty," the boy gabbled. "Last night at the pub. A right posh bitch, me mum always called her, cold as an iron poker."

Colder than an iron poker, Alasdair said, "Go on."

"She was asking about the plans, and after dinner, the Yank, he rolled them out on the billiards table and everyone gathered round. And me mum, she set a tray with the coffees down on the table. Minty's special blend coffee, has it in from Harrod's. And Mum went back to the kitchen, and Minty, she pulled out a glass jar from that smart bag of hers, a little jar with water inside—it caught the light, I saw it, plain—she tipped it into one of the coffees and put it back in her bag."

Derek was crying now, his breath gasping, his nose running. Alasdair didn't move. "And?"

"Then the lot of them, they sat back down and she started handing round the coffees, but Noel, he took them away and handed them round himself—'Can't let you do the serving, can we?' he said. Minty didn't say a word, stirred her own coffee and watched Ciara, smiling like the woman on the cover of that book, like she knew something no one else did."

Jean could hear her own breath sieving between her fingers. What gall. What nerve. What cool. Did Minty realize the poisoned coffee had gone to the wrong person? If she had, she could hardly have leaped up with a cry of "Don't drink that!" No wonder she'd smiled to see Ciara arrested. She might have unwittingly sacrificed Angus to her cause, but she thought she'd won after all, Ciara gone and the new Ferniebank safely and tastefully under her control.

What nerve, Jean thought again, but this time she was looking at Alasdair's face. The anemic glow of the ceiling light illuminated his brow ridges and cheekbones, carved by glaciers, and cast the rest of his features into shadow.

Delaney walked into the Laigh Hall. "What's this, Cameron? Intimidating a witness?"

"I'm not a policeman," Alasdair told him. "Just how could I be intimidating a witness?" He aimed the boy away from the trap door, gave him a push, and released him.

Alasdair's eyes met Jean's. Cold as iron, hot as an anvil, expressionless and yet teeming with expression. He was an excavation, and she'd just uncovered unexploded ordnance. She shrank away.

Kallinikos emerged from the shadows behind Delaney, notebook open, pen in hand. "Come along, lad, P.C. Freeman will make you a cuppa in the incident room."

Derek wiped his nose on the back of his hand, his sniff ringing from the rafters. "Me mum, she'll not be in trouble, will she?"

"Depends on how helpful she is," answered Delaney.

"She's on her way here," Kallinikos added.

With a thoroughly cowed and yet furtively admiring look at Alasdair, Derek shambled from the room, to be intercepted by Freeman in the entrance chamber and escorted out the door.

Delaney was staring at Alasdair. "Minty Rutherford? You credit the lad's testimony?"

"It's perfectly sensible. We already knew the poison went into the coffee or dessert. Minty had everything to gain by killing Ciara, but Noel accidentally handed Angus the poisoned cup." The color was draining from Alasdair's face. He held out his hand toward Jean—oh, the flashlight. Numbly she placed the cylinder into his hand. No, he wasn't shaking. He couldn't be shaking. "Besides," he concluded, "what's Derek got to gain by lying?"

Jean realized she was shaking, too. Her stomach roiled as though she'd drunk coffee with foxglove liqueur. Turning her back on Alasdair, she walked over to the window, leaned against the chill stone of its embrasure, and gulped the evening air. Cool. Fresh. The soft, rounded hills giving up the last of the twilight into a crystalline indigo sky that faded to the east, where a full moon was rising.

"You heard the lad," Alasdair went on. "Minty Rutherford's your killer. Like as not she meant to get rid of Ciara the same way she got rid of Wallace, exterminating pests, more or less."

"That's as may be—"

"If I were you, I'd have someone making a search of the pub dustbins for that glass bottle. Likewise the bins at Glebe House. And the kitchens. She might have a store of poisons, playing the Lucrezia Borgia of Stanelaw."

"Who?" asked Delaney.

"And have a look at the rubbish bins at the museum. She was shredding documents the day."

"I'll see to it," Kallinikos said. "By the by, you were right, Mr. Cameron. When we told Ms. Macquarrie we knew about a hidden map she started talking. Or talking in specifics, rather." His footsteps receded toward the door.

"Up 'til then all we were getting was her usual twaddle," said Delaney. "But this map, hah, the woman's staked this book deal of hers on finding it, but hasn't got a clue where it is."

"Oh," Alasdair said, "I imagine she's got a clue."

"Macquarrie and Bell are in custody yet. I'm not convinced they've told the entire story."

"You've not got the evidence to hold them much longer, let alone the two streams of evidence you're needing to charge them."

"I've noticed that, thank you very much."

"So you've come back here looking out more evidence, is that it?"

"Why else come back to this godforsaken pesthole?"

A horn honked from the road. The return of the media? A flash of light in the corner of her eye made Jean glance around. Alasdair had turned on the flashlight and was inspecting the vaults of the ceiling, revealing cobwebs, dirt, chipped mortar, but no secret messages. "What of Roddy Elliot?" he asked.

With his head tucked down into his shoulders, his lower lip protruding, and his chest swelling, Delaney looked like a toad in a three-piece suit. "We charged him with vandalizing a listed monument and set him a date in court. I've sent Linklater to collect the bits of the inscription. The old codger tucked them up in his hay barn, he said, not wanting them in the house. I've never seen such a prize collection of nutters as here in Stanelaw."

"You should get yourself out more often, then," Alasdair said.

Delaney shoved his glasses up the bridge of his nose so

emphatically, Jean expected his finger to go right through his forehead. "Elliot's swearing he never phoned Wallace. He said they'd just rowed face to face. Why bother phoning?"

"Logan made that call, just as he took two of Wallace's drawings from the flat here. He missed the one in those boxes, though. If I was compromised when you suspected Ciara, then Logan's compromised now Minty's the suspect." Alasdair directed the flashlight into the dungeon.

Kallinikos walked back into the Laigh Hall, Valerie in tow. That must have been her honking outside the gates. Jean turned all the way back around, trying to read the woman's mood— anger in the glare of her eyes, determination in the set of her jaw, fear in the way she held her cardigan closed, her hands on the plackets balled into fists.

"What is it you were wanting to tell us about Angus Rutherford?" asked Delaney.

"I could've told you in Kelso," she retorted. "But no, I'm obliged to chase you back here. I'm always coming back here, seems like."

"We've got Derek in the incident room," Kallinikos told her. "Mr. Cameron and Miss Fairbairn caught him here in the castle."

"He climbed through that window," said Jean, rather surprised to hear her own voice.

Valerie's eyes kindled into a blaze. "I told him to sit tight. I told him it was none of his business."

"It is his business, though, isn't it?" asked Alasdair, and switched off the light.

"Oh for the love of . . ." Delaney exclaimed. "Cut along, cut along, let's do this properly. And you, Cameron"—his forefinger targeted Alasdair like a blunt weapon—"I expect you to behave yourself."

"Of course, Inspector Delaney." Alasdair flicked off the

flashlight and tucked it beneath his arm as though sheathing a sword.

Scenting her cub, Valerie was already halfway to the door. Kallinikos followed, her, and Delaney stumped along third in line. Alasdair stood staring after them, one moment, two. Then he looked over at Jean, his bland expression fracturing just a bit, like fine, aged porcelain. "Shall we?"

"Yeah. Let's." And she walked out of the Laigh Hall, wondering if this time she really welcomed either that *we* or that *let's*.

CHAPTER THIRTY

The courtyard was bathed in the usual sickly light. Jean made a mental note, far down below all her other mental notes, to suggest that Ciara replace the yard light with something else, an elegant gas lamp held by a brass dragon, perhaps.

Beyond the courtyard, above the eastern hills, floated a spectral full moon. Jean imagined that the whine in her ears was Dougie Pincock playing "Bad Moon Rising" on his bagpipes. But no, she was hearing a constable's radio relaying the bulletin on Minty, demoted from community booster to public enemy number one.

They'd eaten her delicious nuptial dinner, Jean thought as she hurried up the steps to the flat. A good thing the woman hadn't realized that when she offed Wallace his replacement would be Alasdair and his—determination? Sheer bloody nerve?

Jean pawed through the box, found the book with Wallace's drawing of the dig, and sped back outside and across the courtyard to the lumber room, raised above its station into an incident room. Kallinikos stepped away from the door so Freeman could exit and Jean could enter.

In the tentative light of the single bulb, the crowded faces seemed indistinct, as though they'd been swiped with Wallace's eraser. Derek huddled over a steaming mug. Valerie stood over him saying, ". . . done right, telling what you saw at the pub. Minty, was it? Aye, she was after Ciara, I reckon, not poor old Angus." Her lips, thin and wan without their red lipstick, set

---

themselves into something that wasn't quite a smile.

This time Alasdair stood to one side of Delaney and his tribunal table, neither guarding his back nor breathing down his neck. Delaney stared belligerently at Jean, maybe expecting her to whip off her bra and burn it. Staring back, she opened the book and showed the drawing to Kallinikos, who passed it on.

Delaney pondered it a moment, then angled it toward Valerie. "This is you?"

"Aye," she said. "Wally was out and about with his sketchbook that night."

"You were excavating at night?" asked Alasdair.

"Well, late of a summer's evening, after Professor McSporran went to ground at the hotel in Kelso. Set great store by his dinner, did the professor. Minty spoiled him with picnic baskets and suppers at Glebe House, but that night she was away in Edinburgh, London, I don't know. Away."

"Who was—" Alasdair began.

Delaney interrupted. "I'll handle this, Cameron. Val, you'd better send the boy outside."

"No," she said, and her claws pressed down on Derek's shoulder.

"All right then," said Delaney. "Who was here at Ferniebank that night?"

"Angus, Wallace, me."

"Not your husband?"

"He wasn't me husband, not then. He never knew the full story."

"Which is?" Delaney prodded.

Valerie inhaled deeply. "We opened Isabel's grave. That's where we went wrong. Should have let her be, but no, Wallace said Gerald opened her grave, she was already walking. Now there was a loony, Gerald. Wallace, Ciara, they're a bit off, but not mental, not like Gerald."

That, Jean thought, had also been Roddy's assessment.

"What did you find in the grave?" asked Delaney

"Her bones, mostly. They cut her down like an animal, you could see it. Dreadful. If the curse wasn't on the place already then, that's where it began. And we found Gerald's poem."

"He buried his poem with her?" Jean asked, and averted her eyes from Delaney's scowl to Alasdair's quirked lip. At least the archaeologists had science to excuse disturbing Isabel's grave. All Gerald had was a necrophiliac crush.

"That he did. Wrote this sick-making epic poem about Isabel's life and then buried it in Isabel's grave, in a wee medieval cist from the family store. Wallace said there was a poet last century—century before, now—who buried his work with his dead wife, then had second thoughts some years later and dug it up again."

"Cool," said Derek.

Valerie thumped his head as though it was a watermelon. "Leastways Isabel was already gone to bones. And Gerald never dug up the poem."

"Wallace knew it was there?" asked Alasdair.

"Aye. He was after getting Gerald's things from the grave without the professor knowing what a loony his grandfather was."

Social embarrassment runs in the family, Jean commented to herself.

"So he had me and Angus shove aside the inscribed slab, and me drop down into the grave—I'm small, mind, neither of them would fit. Then we replaced the slab. The professor came along the next day and opened it up again, and I handed over the empty chest. Wallace put it about that the poem had been amongst Gerald's papers."

Kallinikos's pen tapped his paper with the dot at the end of the sentence. Jean leaned back against the frame of the door. If she stepped outside, she'd be able to see the walls of the chapel and Isabel's uneasy resting place. If she turned around, she'd see the castle. But she didn't need to look at either to know they were there. It was like holding her hand above the burner on a stove and feeling heat, except what she felt was cold.

Alasdair stepped forward, a flicker in the depths of his eyes drawing Jean erect again. Treasure found at the dig. A chest. A treasure chest. "Was there anything else in the chest?"

Valerie's smile crimped at the edges. "A small but right choice collection of jewelry."

"Jewelry?" Delaney demanded. "Gerald's family jewels. Hah. No pun intended."

"Family, aye, or so Angus kept saying. Wallace said it was the jewelry from the harp."

Jean felt her mouth fall open, and she shut it with a pop. Kallinikos murmured, "Well now."

For once, Alasdair and Delaney wore the same expression, stunned disbelief. But Alasdair found his voice first. "Gerald stripped the jewelry from the clarsach and buried it with his poem. Angus was saying the jewelry belonged to the family, so it was all right to—"

"Steal it," Valerie said. "Wallace kept saying there were rules, some question as to whether it was treasure trove and all, it should go to a big museum. But Angus, he took it, because Minty wanted herself a cooking school, and what Minty wanted, Minty got."

"She knows all about the jewelry, then."

"She doesn't miss a thing, that woman doesn't."

And at the luncheon, Jean thought, I told Minty there was a sketch of the dig in the flat. She'd excused herself and phoned Logan, telling him to confiscate it. She knew the truth, all right. And it was a very inconvenient truth indeed.

Whether the Rutherfords had violated the laws of treasure

trove was a moot point. Even if the jewelry had been family property, selling it on the open market would have drawn the enthusiastic attentions of the National Museum, to say nothing of Inland Revenue. "Minty and Angus sold the jewelry to repay their debt," said Jean, "bit by bit, if not on the black market, at least under the counter at auction houses and to shady dealers. And Angus was seen at a pawn shop, too."

"Several pawn shops," Kallinikos said. "Peterborough, London, Dover."

"Oh, that," said Valerie. "He was shifting some of Wallace's silver cufflinks, photo frames, and such. Minty got better money than that for the jewelry."

"How much of that money came to you?" asked Delaney.

Derek looked up hopefully.

Valerie looked down at her feet. "Angus paid for me bakery in Middlesbrough and popped round with gifts for Derek is all."

"Did you think of blackmailing Minty?"

"I'm never that stupid."

"But you never thought of reporting the theft, either."

Valerie laughed humorlessly, her narrow cheeks puckering. "Aye, the likes of me, telling tales about Mr. and Mrs. Councillor Rutherford. I've had problems enough, thank you just the same."

"There's bad feeling between you and Minty even so," said Alasdair.

"She'll have none of the likes of me, that's true, but it's because of Derek here."

Delaney leaned forward, out of Alasdair's shadow. "The Middlesbrough constabulary had your husband, Harry—"

"Ex-husband. I should have quit him years ago, but inertia can be right powerful."

Jean could sympathize with that.

". . . in for an interview," Delaney went on. "He's still swearing Derek's not his son, that your 'posh friends' stitched up the results of the DNA test. He knows Angus gave you money, but he thinks it's because Angus is Derek's father, is that right?"

"Old Horse Face?" Derek made a gagging sound, but no further comments about poshery.

"Minty thought the lad was Angus's, too, did she?" asked Alasdair.

"She did that, aye, though there was never more than a cuddle between us—starved for affection, the man was, no surprise there. But Minty, what she wanted was the baby. She was after me for months to just hand him over, so she could bring him up proper, like. Even after the DNA test proved he was Harry's, she offered me money, like she could buy a human being. I deserved me share of the money from the jewelry, right enough, but not like that."

"Flinty Minty. The posh bitch." Horrified, Derek leaned up against his mother's side as though he was a marsupial aiming for the maternal pouch. Valerie put her arm around him.

Jean remembered Minty looking into Linda's pram in the hallway of the museum. She and Angus had no children. No heirs to the Rutherford name. No wonder she'd been so resentful of Valerie and Derek. Of Noel and Polly and their daughters, for that matter.

"Wallace now, he thought I deserved a share," Valerie went on. "But all he could do was send Ciara to me, so's I could answer questions about the dig and Gerald. She paid me, fair and square, for helping her with her research, her little books and tours and all. When the bakery went bust she offered me work here. We'll not long be taking charity from me uncle and from Polly and Noel."

"Why's Ciara got a tattoo of a harp like yours?" asked Alasdair, drawing a raised brow from Delaney.

Valerie's tip-tilted smile indicated she, too, knew Alasdair's role in Ciara's life. "We got to be good mates. Sisters, like. I said, let's get us tattoos, just for laughs, and Ciara, she says, let's get ones like the Ferniebank clarsach, 'cause Ferniebank's changed our lives. And now it's called me back, just as it's called her. The pair of us, we'll set the place to rights, and we'll find us our fortunes along the way."

"Does Ciara know about the jewelry?" Delaney asked.

"Aye. Very accepting person, Ciara is."

Alasdair went a bit cross-eyed at that.

"Minty doesn't know you're working with Ciara, does she?" asked Delaney.

"She was obliged to tiptoe round Minty, right enough, with her book and with me and all. Minty was right narked that I was back in town—no one's ever told her no before. Ciara's worth two of Minty, for all her daft ideas."

"Do you believe her daft ideas, then?" Delaney asked. "Is there a map?"

Valerie shrugged. "Ciara says if it's not amongst Wallace's papers, then it's here at Ferniebank. He told her the day he died he knew there was proof, though just what and where it was, he was saving for the next time he saw her. Derek here heard him hinting about it to Roddy and Minty—trying to convince them they were wrong about Ciara, I reckon."

"During the argy-bargy, like," added Derek. "Me and Zoe, we heard him saying, 'I've got the proof, and you'll be sorry when it comes out.' "

Proof? Good grief, she'd been right. Jean looked at Alasdair, but he was eyeing the massive flashlight, standing like a flagpole on the corner of Delaney's table. The pit prison. Wallace had forced himself down the ladder soon after he'd taunted Roddy and Minty. Soon after Minty had spilled the beans to Logan, who intervened. Soon after eating his fatal meal.

"Proof? And I'm Duke of Argyll." Delaney rolled his eyes heavenward. "Who stole the clarsach from the Stanelaw Museum?"

"That was poor old Angus. Ciara kept going on and on about the music and the map and all, and how Gerald must have known all about it, and what a pity the harp was locked up in the museum with the key in Minty's grasping hands, else we could have ourselves a look."

"Angus disassembled it looking for a second secret compartment with the, ah, map," said Alasdair. "Then he couldn't put it together again, so he left it in a safe place."

"We've tracked him from Brussels," Kallinikos said. "He took a train through the Chunnel, hired a car in Dover, and stopped at a pawn shop there. The dates match. And the London shop's half a mile from the auction house where the harp turned up."

"Angus was a bit timid," Valerie said, "and clumsy as an ox to boot, but a good chap overall."

"You last saw him at the dinner at the Granite Cross?" asked Delaney.

"That I did. Poor old guy. All this time he'd been going along, the way he did all his life, I reckon. Then, on the Saturday, Ciara told him of her book deal. And the balloon went up. Minty wasn't best pleased with Ciara's tales, but she carried on, seeing advantages for herself. A book, though, about Isabel and the harp as secret agents of the Templars and all . . ."

"Would attract attention to Gerald," Alasdair finished. "He wrote about the jewelry, did he? Wallace knew he put it in Isabel's grave."

"Wallace being the expert on Gerald and Gerald being the expert on Isabel." Valerie ran both her hands through her hair, so that it stood on end like Derek's.

That's what Angus and Ciara had been talking about in the van, Jean thought, when Ciara dismissed his concerns with a laugh. Angus had gone home to Minty, and—what? Had she realized something had gone wrong, and extracted the news from him like extracting a tooth? However she'd learned the truth, her response had been to once again fill her little vial of poison. Poor old Angus indeed, steamrolled by the women in his life, Minty with cool deliberation, Ciara casually, cheerfully, carelessly.

Delaney sat back in his chair, folding his hands over his waistcoat as though after a good meal. "With the book, folk would start asking questions about the jewelry. There's motive for you."

"Over and beyond eliminating the purveyors of embarrassing fancies," added Alasdair. "With Ciara and Wallace gone, Minty could run Ferniebank as she saw fit. Eat her cake and have it as well."

Yeah, but . . . Catching Alasdair's frown, Jean said, "What about Wallace?"

Kallinikos flipped through his notebook. "Polly Brimberry brought him his last meal, the leftover food from a cooking class."

"Helen and Polly took him dozens of those," Valerie said. "Easy enough to add a bit of poison. Proving it, now . . ."

Delaney's hands tightened, no doubt with heartburn. Derek shifted restlessly and dropped his mug. Valerie made a one-handed catch and gave it to Kallinikos.

Jean realized she was hearing voices and vehicles. Lights flashed. She looked over her shoulder to see headlights glaring through the gate, the media following Delaney from Kelso. Then the gate shut with a clang behind two patrol cars.

From one issued W.P.C. Blackhall, who marched toward the door of the incident room. Kallinikos brushed past Jean to intercept her, and after a muttered consultation announced to Delaney, "The dustbins at the pub are overflowing, but the crime-scene lads are having a good look. Minty's at Glebe House."

"Watch the house," Delaney replied. "If she leaves, follow her. Get on to Edinburgh for a search warrant. Don't put her wind up just yet, though. Patience, that's the ticket."

Alasdair cleared his throat, a noise that sounded suspiciously like a snicker.

Outside, D.C. Linklater was pulling a sturdy, flat box from the rear seat of the second car. P.C. Logan rushed around from the driver's side and took the opposite end. Walking crabwise, they carried the box into the incident room and set it on Delaney's table, causing a domino effect as people moved aside. Derek saw his chance and slipped out into the courtyard.

Jean found herself wedged against Alasdair, his cold, hard forearm angled across her back. She leaned away, toward the dozen or so pieces of inscription from Isabel's grave that lay jumbled together in a jigsaw puzzle. The flakes and dust knocked from their edges sprinkled the bottom of the box like pale cinnamon. The reddish sandstone had not only been easier to carve than the local gray whinstone, a volcanic rock, perhaps Isabel's family had chosen its color as a reproof to her murderers.

Jean imagined the pieces reassembled—that one against that one, and the bits from the museum fitting in along the edge. The *er* of Sinncler bent upwards because of a nodule in the sandstone, and the *requies* was separated from the *catin* for the same reason. And that really was a crack in the stone, not an "m." The inscription wasn't a secret code. It was a memorial, a souvenir of death. Perhaps Isabel's family had chosen the cross patte in honor of their Templar ancestors. Perhaps they meant it to signify that Isabel, too, had been a warrior.

X marks the spot. *Hic jacet* . . . She didn't realize she was speaking until she heard her own voice. "Here lies Isabel Sinclair who died in the year of Our Lord 1569. Pray for her soul.

Rest in peace."

"Rest in peace," said Valerie. "I'm thinking not. Not a bit of it."

Logan looked around, targeting Valerie with an antagonistic gaze.

Linklater rolled his shoulders. "Roddy Elliot, I reckon he could lift a cow. That's no light load, even piled into a gunny sack."

Jean imagined Roddy standing beside the chapel, waiting until the lights in the flat went out. Waiting until she and Alasdair were otherwise occupied and wouldn't hear the tap of chisel on stone. He had justified his act to himself. Most people could justify their acts to themselves. "Keep the dust," she said. "A skilled restorer can make a sort of glue from it and use it to put everything back together. Well, except for the harp. That's long gone."

"Roddy didn't chuck the pieces into the river," said Alasdair, "thanks for small mercies."

Valerie sidled toward the door. "I'd not be using Roddy's name and the word 'mercy' in the same sentence. He was always out and about spreading his gloom and doom, but now, going on about his dog poisoned and Helen murdered—was it from him, do you think, that she got the idea?"

"Macquarrie got the idea to poison Angus, you mean?" Logan asked.

"P.C. Logan," said Delaney, "when you took Mrs. Rutherford's statement the Saturday, did you take her fingerprints as well?"

Logan's dark features shriveled like a prune. "Why should I have done?"

"Because," Delaney told him, "it was your duty. Now look what's happened . . ."

Alasdair's arm pressed against Jean's back. Retrieving the

flashlight, he urged her on out the door behind Valerie and Derek. After the crowded little room with its lingering odors of machine oil and paint, the outside air was cold on her bare arms, raising goose pimples.

Linklater followed, and Kallinikos shut the door on Delaney's pompous voice. "You'll be obliged to make new statements," he told Derek and Valerie both. "Kelso, the morn."

"What of Ciara?" asked Valerie. "And Keith, come to that. He's a bit naff, but a decent enough sort even so."

"They'll be released as soon as may be."

Jean surveyed the courtyard, the cars, the constables, ill-met by sallow lamplight and pallid moonlight. She looked up at the castle, at the glow of reddish, orange, golden light in the window of Isabel's room. Of all the people in the courtyard, only she and Alasdair could see that. His face tilted toward that phantom light, away from Jean's gaze.

She turned to Valerie. "The burning-glass isn't listed in the Ancient Monuments report. Minty says it was Gerald's shaving mirror."

"Gerald kept it in a velvet pouch, Wallace was saying. Like a relic."

Jean felt but not did not meet Alasdair's gaze. Gerald must have taken it out of Isabel's grave—Ciara had implied as much. Maybe she was right about it being a signal device. Even a stopped clock was right twice a day.

"Good night, sir," Derek said to Alasdair as Valerie bundled him into her car. The constables cleared a way through the watchers at the gates. Kallinikos returned to the incident room, where Delaney was still bullying Logan. Not that Logan didn't deserve it.

Jean found herself standing with Alasdair in a clearing in the activity. She would have asked *now what?* except she knew now what. "Wallace. The dungeon."

"Oh aye." Slapping the flashlight across the palm of his opposite hand, Alasdair strode toward the front door of the castle.

CHAPTER THIRTY-ONE

The Laigh Hall was still shadowy, and even colder than it had been earlier. Jean shut the window. Then, squaring her shoulders, she joined Alasdair at the rim of the dungeon. "Hold the torch," he said, once again pressing its barrel into her hand.

She held the flashlight, shining it first on the ladder at his feet as he climbed down, then around the tiny chamber. Stone, dust, a small black creepie-crawlie just vanishing into a crevice. No more shiny objects. No neon signs flashing "This is it!" Or even defining "it," for that matter. When Alasdair reached up, she lay down on her stomach to hand him the light.

The stone against her breast was gritty, and not just cold but damp, centuries of dark, chill winter days filtering up into her flesh and then into her bones in a physical equivalent of her psychic reaction to the paranormal. She felt as though she was sinking into the stone, the walls closing in, the stench filling her lungs like black water. . . .

"Jean," said Alasdair, so sharply she realized he'd already said her name once. "Here."

She grabbed the flashlight and forced herself to a sitting position. "Nothing?"

"Sod-all. What Wallace was on about—well, it's easy to say he was mad, but even madness often has a logic to it." Alasdair dragged himself up the ladder, coughed and cleared his throat, and dropped the trap door with a resounding crash that echoed into the empty chambers above.

What would it have sounded like, Jean asked herself, if Derek had fallen into the pit prison? The question sat in the pit of her stomach like a bowling ball.

"Mr. Cameron?" W.P.C. Blackhall stood in the main doorway. "D.I. Delaney—"

"I'm just coming." Alasdair reached a cold, gritty hand, the same hand that had held Derek at the brink, down for Jean's hand and hauled her to her feet. She couldn't read his expression—in fact, he was doing a superb job of not having one.

"Thanks." She trudged out into the free air while Alasdair turned off the light, and mutely handed him the keys so he could lock the door. Following him to the door of the flat, she waited while he opened it for her and then strode off to the incident room, all without once meeting her gaze. Somewhere above, a dove cooed and then fell silent, as though not wanting to call attention to itself.

The flat. Home, such as it was. Sanctuary, not so much. Jean stepped into the living room. It was more like a dying room, a morgue, cold and silent, illuminated by bloodless moonlight streaming in the eastern windows and Dougie's eyes like eerie, reflective marbles. She shut the windows, sat down on the couch, and warmed her hands in the cat's soft fur, too wired to yawn, too tired to pace.

From outside came the sounds of voices and cars as the official tide ebbed yet again. "Good night, then," Alasdair said to someone. His shoes plodded up the steps. Behind Jean's back, the door opened and shut, a key turned in the lock, and the flashlight snicked back into its bracket.

After a long moment, perhaps waiting for a formal greeting, perhaps marshaling his resources, he said, "Delaney's sent Logan off with a flea in his ear—he's lucky there're no charges against him—and Freeman to collect the two drawings."

"Logan admitted to making the phone call?" Jean didn't turn around.

"As a friendly warning, he's saying, intending no threats or anything of the sort."

"Because Wallace told Minty he had proof Ciara was right, and Minty complained to Logan about things getting out of hand. And then she took matters into her own hands and doctored Wallace's dinner."

"I doubt . . ." Alasdair said, but his voice trailed away and left unresolved whether he meant "doubt" as in "suspect" or "doubt" as in, well, "doubt."

Doubt. Uncertainty. Perhaps even mistrust. Jean kept on stroking Dougie. Normally he'd have started purring, but not now. Now his ears were pricked forward, his muscles bunched, sensing her dour mood just as she could sense Alasdair standing to attention in the darkness behind her. Her gut coiled into a Gordian knot of doubt and desire.

The keys jangled onto the desk and he cleared his throat. "I'd not have hurt the lad."

"I know," she said, and she did know. "But he could've fallen in. I never thought you'd . . ."

Silence.

"Did you do it to help Ciara? To further the course of justice? Or simply so you could tell Delaney 'I told you so'? Leaving the window open might border on entrapment, but threatening that pitiful kid borders on criminal!"

Silence.

"We could've brought him in here and given him tea and cookies and made friends with him. But no, Delaney showed up, you had to make points with him."

Alasdair emitted a long, ragged breath.

"Yeah, you ended up impressing the heck out of Derek. He's male, too—you're both out there on planet Macho. I know you're having a hard time with the retirement and everything. But Alasdair, don't, please . . ." She gulped. "Don't turn into someone else."

"Who am I, then?" he asked, voice very quiet, very weary. "I'm sorry I've disappointed you. I'm thinking I've disappointed myself."

Oh. Well then. She should go to him and throw her arms around him, and yet her limbs wouldn't move.

"I'll sleep on the couch the night."

"Don't be any dafter than you already are," she retorted. Her smile died before it could form.

After another long silence, he said, "I'm away to bed, then."

She waited, ducking a gaze so keen she felt it tingling on the back of her neck, until the bathroom door closed. Then she collected her backpack, turned on the dim light above the kitchen stove, and filled the tea kettle. While the water boiled, she opened the little box and considered the glass, burning or looking, whatever, gleaming innocently on its bed of cotton. Would Ciara's psychometric friend be able to bring anything more to bear on the object than his own imagination? Jean could do that for herself.

Had Isabel been so intent on her mission for Queen Mary—it was only the nature of the mission that was in dispute, not its existence—that she'd never put together a relationship, with a monk, or a Tempest, or with some wealthy fiancé chosen by her father? Had she lived as she died, cut off from a supporting hand?

Jean put the glass back in her bag and pulled out her phone. Ah, a message from Miranda, short and sweet. "So they've arrested Ciara, have they? If that means your story's gone from heritage industry feature to front page prime crime . . . Well, do what's best. Even if it means proving she's innocent. And you, you take care."

Do what was best. Take care. *Right.* Jean poured hot water over a bag of herbal tea—chamomile and passionflower, like that was going to help her sleep. Cup in hand, she peered out the window. A solitary patrol car sat inside the gate. Light shone from the half-closed door of the incident room. O. Hawick tramped across the gravel, seeming to savor the grinding crunch of each step, like a conqueror treading the skulls of the fallen.

In the moonlight, the leafy passage leading to the chapel was as densely-shadowed as a tunnel. . . . No, a wisp of light stirred in its depths, and Isabel ran noiselessly toward the castle. She passed by Hawick so closely she'd have taken off his hat if she'd been corporeal. He kept on walking.

Shuddering, Jean clutched the mug of tea between her icy hands and turned away from the window. *Now what?* she asked herself again, but this time she had no answer. She drank her tea and went to bed, and lay beside Alasdair's back, carefully not touching him. She could tell by the way his breath caught at the ripple of harp strings from above that he was awake.

The musical notes drifted through the night, rising, falling. Maybe if she listened carefully enough, she'd hear the clink of the jewelry, given to generations of harpers or placed on the clarsach as status symbols by Isabel's own family. And perhaps she'd hear an echo from the secret chamber, the place of incriminating messages.

She dozed and woke and dozed again, and wandered through museums where fissures opened in reddish stone, and the stones rained down on display cases, smashing the glass into discs. Roddy lumbered down the high street pushing a cow in a pram. Minty upended a glass bottle, pouring a dark liquid onto the street until a black pool gathered silently around the foundations of Ferniebank. . . .

Jean opened her eyes to see the curtains illuminated by daylight. Birds sang, free of uncertainty. Alasdair was wrapped up in the duvet, as though he and it had spent the night wrestling for dominance, leaving her only the edge. That was only one reason she was chilled to the bone. At the foot of the bed Dougie curled into a tight ball, a cushion with ears, one of which twitched as she rose and dressed. In the bathroom she made the mistake of looking at herself in the mirror. Compared to the face that looked back, her passport photo was a glamor shot.

She made tea, fed the cat, and watched him play with a stray bit of kibble—bat, pounce, bat, pounce. Then she set a box of Weetabix on the table along with bowls and spoons.

Outside, the morning was brightening into another beautiful, clear, sunny day. The leaves of the trees and the hoods of the cars glistened with dew. A constable stood in the doorway of the incident room eating something out of a plastic wrapper.

Alasdair emerged from the hallway and headed straight to the teapot. Milk, tea, sugar. A long swallow and the fog lifted from his eyes. "Ah. Jean. Good morning."

"Good morning."

They sat at the table, drinking their tea and eating their cereal. Slowly she detected the beginnings of coherent thought, faint as the traces of atomic particles, both on his face and in her mind. But with the return of coherent thought came the return of doubt and confusion. Alasdair, who meant well. Wallace, who meant well. Angus, who meant well. Ciara, who meant well.

> And see ye not that braid, braid road
> That lies across the lily leven?
> That is the path of wickedness
> Though some call it the path to heaven.

The broad, broad road, she translated. The path of good intentions. Well, Minty had intended to do good for herself, that was for sure.

The phone on the desk emitted its double bleat. In one leap Alasdair had the phone off its cradle. "Ferniebank. Cameron. Ah, Gary."

Jean cleared the table, trying to guess from half of the conversation what was happening. A glass bottle. Toxicology tests. Glebe House. Ciara.

Alasdair hung up the phone. "They've found a wee spice bottle with traces of *Digitalis purpurea* in the dustbin behind the pub. Derek stopped in on his way to school and identified it. They've also found strips of rag paper with oak gall ink in the dustbin behind the museum. Gerald's account of burying the chest with the poem and the jewels, I reckon."

"Yeah, Minty would be even more eager to hide their origins than to establish the Rutherfords as models of propriety." Jean envisioned a clutch of bunny-suited crime-scene techs digging through dumpsters by flashlight, bathed in stale beer and rotten vegetables, ruing their choice of professions. "What was that about Ciara?"

"She and Keith are free to go." Alasdair started back toward the bedroom. "Gary's after interviewing Minty at half past nine. He's thinking if a cascade of sorts arrives on her doorstep before she knows she's suspected, she'll not have time to work up a response."

"I wouldn't count on it." Jean followed him, spread the duvet over the bed, and started pulling clothes from the wardrobe. "So Delaney wants enough of a show of force he's actually including you in the interview."

"You're invited as well. He's thinking you'll be there in any event, he might as well save face by pretending he wants you." Alasdair shook out his sweater. It was a blue sweater, lighter than police navy blue, darker than his eyes. His eyes that rested on dark circles like smudges of ash, rimmed by tiny creases. His eyes that were turned on her, waiting patiently as a cop on a stakeout for the suspect to emerge. He wasn't pretending anything.

All she could do was press her hands against his chest, feeling the cool cotton of his T-shirt and the firm flesh beneath grow warm to her touch. "So who's going to apologize to whom?"

"I'm apologizing to you," he returned, and his lips brushed her forehead. "We'll talk later. Just now, we've got work to do."

"Yes, we do." Jean dressed and applied makeup—what did you wear for a confrontation with a killer, anyway?—and followed Alasdair's voice to the front steps of the flat, where he was just putting away his cell phone. Crows called from the battlements. *A murder of crows,* she thought. *An unkindness of ravens. A reive of Rutherfords.*

Just as P.C. Freeman opened the gate for Alasdair's car, Jean's phone rang. Miranda, already at work on a Monday morning? No. The screen read "Michael Campbell-Reid." Neither he nor Rebecca knew anything about the latest spine-tingling episode, did they? "Hi, Michael."

Alasdair eased through the gateway and onto the road, which was free of newspeople—they were probably still staking out Ciara's wild goose in Kelso.

"Good morning, Jean," Michael said. "I'm hearing amazing things about the investigation."

"You are? Who's your mole?"

"He's closer than you think. Alasdair. He's just asked Rebecca if there's room at the inn for Ciara as well as Keith."

Jean glanced at Alasdair. "Ciara? The B&B?"

"I reckon she's still in danger at Glebe House," he said, "whether Minty's arrested or not."

Roddy Elliot paced across his farmyard, his dogs at his heels, his hands clenched at his sides, top-heavy, like a battering ram with feet. Who dares meddle with me, demanded his posture, in the immortal words of the motto of Scotland. Alasdair put the pedal to the metal.

Envisioning Minty injecting Ciara's toothpaste with foxglove, Jean turned back to the phone. "You can put Keith and Ciara in the same room, if you have to."

"That's the lay of the land, is it? And I use the word 'lay' advisedly," Michael added with a chuckle. "In the meantime, I've got news from the museum."

Stanelaw Museum? Had there been another break-in? Perhaps Angus's ghost was angry, unlike his living personality. . . . Oh! "About that scrap of paper in the secret compartment of the harp?"

"Aye," Michael said. "The documents boffins had it out over the weekend, but no joy. Or very little, in any event."

"It's not a sliver of Mary Stuart's laundry list?"

"Not so they could tell. It's not words at all, but a strip off the edge of a sketch, part of a grid, a bit of an arc, and what's likely a drip of ink. The entire drawing might have been a bairn's game."

"Or a map?" asked Jean. Alasdair looked over at her.

"If the paper and ink weren't authentic sixteenth-century, I'd say it was meant to be a power pylon. As it is, it's anyone's guess. Coming just now," Michael shouted away from the phone, and told Jean, "I'm obliged to play the good host. You and Alasdair, you're owing us a full explanation soon as may be."

"We're just hoping we'll have explanations to make. Thanks." Snapping her phone shut, she told Alasdair, "The paper inside the harp, it's the edge of a grid pattern and an ink blot. Make of it what you will."

"Angus made nothing of it, or he'd have had it out."

"Therefore, a scrap of paper wasn't what he was looking for."

The slate roofs of Glebe House rose from the trees, glistening like a freshly cleaned classroom blackboard. Minty probably sent peons up ladders with brushes and buckets of suds. Alasdair slowed and stopped behind a patrol car. Two more sat in the cooking school driveway, and a civilian, plainclothes, car was parked in front of the house. Kallinikos directed traffic, waving two officers around to the side of the Euro-barn and another to the back of the house.

"Well," said Alasdair as he set the brake, "we'll certainly be taking her by surprise."

Jean wasn't sure she'd want to take Minty by surprise, but then, everyone's options were growing more limited by the minute. She climbed out of the car and walked across the road a wary two paces behind Alasdair.

CHAPTER THIRTY-TWO

Kallinikos waved a file folder toward the cooking school in the manner of a bugler sounding the charge. "Delaney's just taken W.P.C. Blackhall inside. Mrs. Rutherford's been there for half an hour."

"I guess there's no chance of catching her with the eye of newt or toe of frog," said Jean, earning a half-snort from Alasdair and nothing from Kallinikos. Which was just what that comment deserved. If ever she was going to play the silent partner, now was the time.

The interior of the building smelled less aromatic than she remembered, as though an arctic wind had swept away any nourishing scents. Today the granite and steel work surfaces were layered with dishes and food. Everything, green peppers, yellow-white cheese, terra-cotta bowls, a bottle of ruby-red wine, shone beneath the overhead lights as though it had been waxed and polished.

Minty stood beside the sink, wiping her hands on a towel. She was clad in a "Cookery at the Glebe" apron over a simple pair of slacks and a starched blouse with the sleeves rolled up, exposing wiry forearms.

Delaney sat in a chair beside a small table, the equivalent of a student's desk. Blackhall handed a sheet of paper to Kallinikos. He drew another sheet from his file folder and compared what looked to Jean like blots but which she knew were fingerprints.

Kallinikos angled the sheet toward Alasdair. Alasdair nodded affirmatively. Kallinikos laid the papers in front of Delaney, who eyed them, nodded, and sat back. "Well now, Minty. Let's be having us a wee blether."

Jean stayed by the door, out of the line of fire. A blether, he said. A chat. Because if he charged her and hauled her in to the police station and sat her down with a solicitor, she'd have to be warned that whatever she said could be used against her—and if she didn't say anything then, she'd better not come up with a story later. But during a social visit, where she could walk away at any time, anything went. Maybe Delaney had learned his lesson about premature arrest from Ciara and Keith.

"Please be brief, Inspector," said Minty. "Polly Brimberry rang to say she couldn't assist me this morning, so I'm preparing for the one p.m. class on my own."

"You're teaching a class," Delaney asked, "when your husband's laid out in an Edinburgh morgue?"

"Holding to one's commitments is a sign of character." In the strong lights her upswept hair looked like a warrior's helmet, almost but not quite as impenetrable as her marble-lidded eyes. She had been expressionless all along, but this morning appeared to have dunked her entire face in anesthetic.

Minty started peeling and slicing a glistening purple eggplant. The blade of her knife flashed as it rose and fell, a tiny guillotine. "Have you a reason for presenting me with a search warrant in lieu of a sympathy card?"

"Angus didn't die of natural causes. He was poisoned."

"So I've been told." Her gaze downcast, Minty went on slicing and dicing.

"You were seen after the dinner on Saturday pouring liquid from a glass bottle into a cup of coffee. The bottle was found in the dustbin behind the Granite Cross. It contains traces of digit, erm, of foxglove poison. It has your fingerprints on it."

Minty waved those fingers toward a rack holding so many

small glass bottles and their multi-colored ingredients it resembled a stained-glass window without the backlight. "I've been preparing my own spices and herbs for many years, and selling them to much finer places than the Granite Cross."

Check, Jean thought. Delaney shifted uncomfortably. Alasdair stood in his knight-effigy pose, motionless. Kallinikos wrote in his notebook. Blackhall sucked contemplatively on her lower lip.

"You were seen," Delaney repeated, "pouring poison into a cup of coffee. Perhaps you intended that cup for Ciara Macquarrie."

"Sadly, there are people who are jealous of me and my accomplishments, and who would enjoy stirring up trouble for me." Minty arranged the eggplant slices on a platter and set it aside. With the flat of her knife she crushed several cloves of garlic, the sudden, pungent burst drawing a grimace from Delaney.

"Minty," he said. "Mrs. Rutherford. You are suspected of murder."

"On what grounds, Inspector?"

"On the grounds that you wanted to rid yourself of Ciara Macquarrie and her queer ideas. You wanted to cover up the origins of the jewelry that bought you this building. You wanted to have the running of Ferniebank to yourself."

Even at the supposedly off-the-wall word "jewelry," Minty didn't react. She'd probably spent the last twenty-four hours going over every possible scenario. Why else would she have tried to destroy some of Gerald's papers? "How very interesting, Inspector. How very creative of you and your colleagues." With a twist of her wrists, Minty wrenched open a jar and poured tomatoes, red and lumpy, into a saucepan.

"You were shredding documents in the museum."

"Every museum de-accessions some of its holdings."

"You were seen poisoning the coffee." Delaney's forehead

broke out in a sweat. Alasdair inspected the floor in front of his toes. Kallinikos inspected the ceiling.

"Who is this supposed witness?" asked Minty. "Have him or her face me in a court of law, and we shall see which of us the jury believes."

Checkmate, Jean thought. A mature, elegant, well-connected woman accused by a fifteen-year-old boy. Even if they cleaned Derek up, smoothed his hair, camouflaged him in a suit, and gave him elocution and deportment lessons, they couldn't keep him from being the son of a woman who had good reason to resent Minty. Even if Valerie got up and told the story of the jewelry, what proof did they . . . *Proof.* Something scuttled like a cockroach through the back of Jean's mind, but as soon as she turned the light of thought on it, it was gone.

"Mrs. Rutherford," said Delaney, heaving himself to his feet. "I expect—"

"What do you expect, Inspector Delaney? Protestations of innocence? Really, now. You and I both have better ways of occupying our time." Her stance behind the counter was neither aggressive nor defensive, just firm with a self-righteousness that made Roddy look positively profane.

Profanity was what Delaney muttered beneath his breath. "Don't leave the area," he called, and was halfway to the door before Minty replied, "Whyever should I do that?"

Jean allowed herself to be swept along in the official wake, and popped out into the open beside Blackhall's rear guard. It was still Monday morning in the real world, birds caroling, clouds sailing, flowers bobbing and weaving in the breeze. The rolling, almost feminine hills of the Borders drowsed in the gold-tinted light of oncoming autumn, all passion spent.

Delaney went on swearing, audibly this time. "Damn the woman."

Another police car pulled up in front of the house. From it

emerged Ciara, rumpled, smudged, puffy, but unbowed. She strolled over to the group gathered by the road and greeted them with a smile of transcendent tolerance. "What's this? A Lothian and Borders conference? And here's me, thinking the entire force was guarding Keith and me back in Kelso, hardened criminals that we are."

"You'll have your apology," Delaney growled.

"No worries, Inspector. You're only doing your job. Poor Angus, done to death at the very moment of our triumph. Who's your prime suspect now?"

With a firm hand on the small of her back, Kallinikos edged Ciara toward Blackhall, who in turn pointed her toward the guest cottage with a murmur of, "I'm sure you're wanting a wash and brush-up at the B&B, Ciara."

"Oh aye, Annie, a bubble bath would go down a treat. And tea, and perhaps a sausage or two, and bacon and tomato, and toast with lashings of butter and marmalade. Those nice Campbell-Reids at the Reiver's Rest, they're cooking breakfast for Keith and me even though it's going on for elevenses. Is Minty at work? She is? Then I'll just pack my tents and steal away from Glebe House." Ciara glanced around. "Very good of you, Alasdair, for arranging my transfer."

"You're welcome," he returned, his voice so dry dust swirled across his features.

In spite of herself Jean had to smile at the retreating pair, the policewoman encased in her uniform and Ciara, the strolling piñata, still chatting away. Michael and Rebecca wouldn't mind cooking an extra meal if it meant getting the news headlines and op-ed columns as well, even though neither would be completely up to date.

Which reminded her, she needed to check in with Miranda and Hugh. And she needed to—well, Ciara might be content to just let things happen, but Alasdair wasn't. And she wasn't either.

Delaney's scowl was so fierce his jowls quivered. Even Kallinikos's classic features eroded into a frown. Nothing for it, Jean told herself, and voiced the obvious. "Now what?"

"We keep on looking out evidence," said Kallinikos.

"I'll find us another stream of evidence," Delaney said, "if I have to taste everything in her kitchen myself. Nik, turn the place over. If there's one petal of foxglove in that house—or in that school, come to that . . ."

"You could find yourself a bed of foxgloves in her garden," said Alasdair, "and she'd not turn a hair. She'll not incriminate herself so easily, not that one."

Kallinikos looked from Delaney to Alasdair and back. Setting his jaw, he walked off to gather his troops. Delaney looked down at the inoffensive herbaceous border as though he'd like to deploy herbicide and flame-throwers. In grim silence, Alasdair started toward the car.

Jean looked back at the glass doors of the school, at the gleam of light beyond. A whiff of garlic sauteed in butter hung in the air, supplemented by the merest trace of rosemary. *Mary, Mary, quite contrary.* Mary, Queen of Scots, with her fine Italian hand. Was Minty cooking some sort of Italian eggplant flavored with red wine? Supposedly the alcohol in heated wine burned away, though Jean had eaten some dishes that seemed just as high a proof cooked as raw. *The proof's in the pudding.*

"Jean?" Alasdair called.

Proof. This time she stomped the cockroach of a thought before it got away. Now if she could just analyze the resulting blob of gunk, an antenna twitching here, a leg flexing there.

She climbed into the car, buckled up, and let Alasdair make a U-turn back toward Ferniebank before she spoke. "Valerie said that the day Wallace died he told Ciara something cryptic about having proof. And he told Roddy and Minty, too."

"Oh aye. Val's thinking it's proof of Ciara's fancies, the map to the relics or to America or both. I'm not sure Ciara herself knows quite what she's talking about."

"That doesn't matter. What matters is what Val and Ciara thought Wallace meant. And what matters even more is what Roddy and Minty—especially Minty—thought he meant."

"Roddy might have thought Wallace meant a map or such. It wasn't 'til he heard of Ciara's book deal, though, that he made his move, such as it was. Minty, now, Minty—"

"Got rid of Wallace that very day. But she didn't know about the book deal yet, did she? What if she put her own spin on what he said?"

Alasdair's eyebrows tightened. " 'I've got the proof, and you'll be sorry when it comes out.' Was that the word according to Derek?"

"It is, yes. Well, assuming Derek makes a good witness, but —"

"That's not the problem now. Not," Alasdair added, "that I'm seeing where all this is going to solve the problem of proving Minty's the poisoner."

"Well . . ." Jean watched the trees pass, and the farm—no Roddy now—and the wall of the castle, and didn't speak again until Freeman admitted them to the courtyard and Alasdair stopped the car.

He propped his arm on the seat and turned toward her, in full cat at mousehole mode. "Well?"

Jean took first a deep breath and then the plunge. "Minty sent Logan to pick up the drawing of the dig. She probably just told him to pick up Wallace's drawings, because he picked up both of them. He thought the one of the inscription was more important, because it had just been vandalized. The other sketch of the dig was inside that book about the history of the clarsach. No matter whether Minty packed Wallace's things or just watched Polly do it, she didn't see that one."

"Or she'd have taken it as well. And what the drawings have in common is the wee cist. The treasure chest." Alasdair's eyebrows reached for his hairline. "What if Minty's thinking—"

"That what Wallace meant was proof of them finding and taking the jewelry. His conscience bothered him. So did Angus's —that's why they helped Val. But Minty, center of her own universe, killed Wallace before he could give this proof to Ciara or to anyone else. I think Val's right. Roddy's talk about poison and murder inspired Minty to go from word to deed."

"Then when Ciara became a threat—a greater threat— because of her book, Minty did it again. At the pub this time round, ensuring the maximum number of suspects in the event this death was seen as suspicious."

"What do you want to bet Angus hied himself back out here right after the dinner because, with the book deal, Wallace's so-called 'proof' reared its ugly head again. Maybe Minty even sent Angus out here with orders to find Exhibit P."

"He meant to turn over Wallace's things again, I reckon. They were in the lumber room." Alasdair's brows knotted again. "What's this got to do with getting more evidence?"

"What if we could get Minty to commit another crime, this time in front of half the policemen in Roxburghshire? Even if she never actually confessed to the earlier murders, wouldn't that shore up Delaney's case? Wouldn't that make Derek into a lot more credible witness?" There. She'd articulated that much. Now for the rest.

Alasdair stared at her as though the mouse he was waiting for had turned out to be an orange. "Jean, you're not thinking . . ."

She climbed out of the car, almost tripping over her own feet. Her emotional paralysis of the past few years had waned too far. Her entire body felt like a numbed limb when the feeling returns, all prickles and electrical zaps. If Brad had been a dampening field, Alasdair was a live wire. What was she thinking, and why was she thinking it? But she knew the answer to both.

She led Alasdair to one of the park benches beneath the eaves of the trees and sat down. The wood felt cool and the sun, filtered through the leaves, felt warm. From here she could see both castle and chapel, one wracked, the other ruined. A hint of smoke hung on the wind.

"Jean?"

For some strange reason she was short of breath. "When Delaney asked Val if she was blackmailing Minty, she said, 'I'm never that stupid.' She's right, who'd be stupid enough to try blackmail on Minty?"

"You're not thinking that Wallace meant his remark as blackmail, are you?"

"No, I'm not. He was just trying to get Ciara, and by extension himself, some respect. He must have thought there really was some sort of proof, a map or something, in the dungeon." Jean fluttered her hand as though she could shoo the dank prison darkness away. "The point is, what if Minty took his remark as blackmail? That's why she killed him. Derek's testimony isn't much of a threat to her, but Wallace's would have been."

"Ahhh." Alasdair leaned back against the bench.

"What if I tell Minty that Gerald left a complete inventory of the jewelry and Wallace had it. That Wallace himself wrote out a full confession. Because, it doesn't make any difference whether Exhibit P actually exists or not, so long as Minty thinks it does. Perception is reality. Is it ever."

"It matters to Ciara's publisher whether there's actually a map," Alasdair pointed out. "I know, I know, that's not the problem just now. What you're suggesting is . . ."

"Leaving the window in the Laigh Hall open and seeing if Minty climbs in, metaphorically speaking. In other words, I'll blackmail her. I'll tell her we've found Exhibit P, and if she doesn't pay me, I'll publish it. In the scummiest tabloid I can find to boot." They'd come to the bottom line. Jean straightened, folded her hands in her lap, and said, "And with any luck, that will get her to come after me."

CHAPTER THIRTY-THREE

Alasdair sat up with a jolt and his face went askew, his studied expressionlessness ruptured by a tremor of emotion. "You'll do nothing of the sort. You've got—how'd you put it? You've got no dog in this hunt."

"Sure I do. I have you."

"Jean!" He bounded to his feet so abruptly that Freeman looked around from his post by the gate. "Jean, no."

She stood up and tucked her hand beneath his arm. "If you or Delaney or any of the cops mention you've got Exhibit P, Minty would probably expect a trap. Same thing with Val or Derek. She might believe Roddy, but good luck getting him to cooperate. As for Ciara—well, she already tried to kill Ciara. Let's leave Ciara out of this."

He watched her, shadows moving in the deep places of his eyes like leviathans in the sea.

"But I'm a journalist. Everyone knows journalists are unethical, right? Maybe she'd think I'm stupid enough to try blackmailing her. If she doesn't take the bait, we're no worse off than we are now. If she does—"

"You'd be putting yourself in danger. She knows you'll not be drinking a cup of tea or the like with her. She'll try something a lot less subtle."

"That's just it. She'll make an attack that isn't circumstantial, that she can't explain away." Jean saw Minty slicing the eggplant, her knife flashing, and her mouth went dry. She swallowed what felt like glue. "Let Delaney ransack Glebe House and the school. Then he and his people can walk away. I'll call Minty and tell her to meet me out here. You could hide twenty witnesses in the flat and the castle."

"She'll wonder why Delaney's giving up so easily."

"She'll figure he's giving up because she's won. She's used to winning, isn't she?"

Alasdair's arm quivered like a tuning fork. "Why, Jean? Why are you after doing this? Justice? Or are you after proving something to me—especially after my threatening Derek?"

She rested her head on his shoulder, closed her eyes, and breathed in his scent, wool, soap, an elusive salt-smoke like fine whiskey. The tickle of his sweater against her cheek was nothing compared to the friction of his personality against hers. Friction could be inspiring. It could create fire. Fire could warm you, or it could hurt. "All of the above," she replied. "None of the above. I don't know. It's just—what needs to be done."

He took her hand in his and for several minutes said nothing. Then he pulled her into a walk, down the path to the chapel. "All right then. I'll talk to Delaney. But Jean . . ."

"If I get hurt you'll kill me. Yeah, I know."

With a squeeze of her hand, Alasdair released her and pulled his cell phone from his pocket. She strolled on into the roofless nave of the chapel. There was the memorial to Henry Sinclair, ravaged by time. There was Isabel's grave, ravaged by man. The carved stone pillars stood aloof, no longer resonating to plainchant and harp.

She heard Alasdair's voice. "You've got three choices. You can go ahead with charges and see what happens. Maybe you can push through to a trial. But if the jury returns a verdict of not guilty, and likely they will, there's no trying her again. Or you can give up the case as a bad job and walk away, never mind Angus and Wallace. Or you can try Jean's daft idea."

Silence, except for the ripple of the river and whisper of the trees. The dappled shadows seemed fluid, a mingling of elements. People came and went, buildings rose and fell, but water and wind and growing green things, they were eternal.

"Oh aye, I'll be taking a black eye from Protect and Survive if the case goes unresolved—give over, Gary, you think I'd be sacrificing my . . . my own . . ."

He still didn't know what to call her, did he?

"Stage a diversion. Make your search and then call everyone away, as though after someone else. Let her think she can get herself to Ferniebank and back again with no one noticing."

Jean considered the ancient well, Mary's well, Mary the Queen of heaven, Mary the Queen of Scots, Mary the beautiful sinner, friend of God.

"All right, then." Alasdair stared at his phone, then thrust it into his pocket and turned to Jean. Clasping her shoulders, he jiggled her around, either shaking her up or settling her down. "You're on. Delaney will be here straightaway."

Oh. She had convinced Alasdair, and through him Delaney. Well, she could still change her mind. But then, nothing would change Angus's death. Or Wallace's. Still trying to catch her breath, she walked back up to the castle with Alasdair's arm around her and her arm around him. They barely had time to go into the flat, find Dougie asleep on the bed, and make a pot of coffee before Delaney pounded on the door. Alasdair waved him and his shadow, Kallinikos, inside.

"What the hell's all this?" Delaney demanded of Jean.

"The case is solved. The problem is bringing the killer to justice. I'm suggesting a way." She poured milk into her coffee and sat down, leaving the others to fend for themselves. You'd think Delaney could at least have brought elevenses, doughnuts or cream scones or something, but no. Not that pastries wouldn't have turned into paste in her throat. She took a deep drink from her mug and juggled the hot liquid around her mouth so it didn't burn her tongue.

Delaney helped himself to a cup and plopped down in the decrepit chair, which creaked beneath him. "You're telling us our business, are you? You're thinking you'll have yourself a fine behind-the-scenes story for your rag?"

"*Great Scot,*" said Kallinikos, "is no rag. Even Minty knows that."

"Minty. Queen Minty, the first and only." Delaney drank and then choked. "Is this her coffee?"

"We've been drinking it all along," Alasdair told him.

Kallinikos sat down at the table with a cup, his notebook, and several file folders. "We'll have Glebe House clear of our folk by mid-afternoon, assuming they've found nothing. If you'll ring Mrs. Rutherford, Miss Fairbairn, and set up the appointment. Use the telephone on the desk."

"In case she has caller I.D.?" asked Jean.

"Aye," Alasdair replied. "And because that phone's been tapped since early on the Sunday."

Jean wasn't in the least surprised, either about the tap or that Alasdair hadn't bothered to tell her. Why should he? She set her cup on the table and stood up.

"Minty'll not take the bait," said Delaney.

"I reckon she will," Alasdair said. "She'll be taking a chance, but she's been taking chances for years now, ever since the excavation. With the excavation itself, for that matter. Every choice she's made has brought her here. She'll keep on fighting to the bitter end."

Thanks, Jean thought toward him, even though she knew what he meant. Telling her heart to back off from her throat, she picked up the telephone on the desk.

"Her number's on the speed dial," said Alasdair. "First one."

Three pairs of eyes watched her punch the button. Three sets of breath went shallow and surreptitious. One ring, two, and she heard the clicks of a forwarded call—to the cooking school, no doubt. "Stanelaw two-four-seven," said Minty's rich, cool voice.

"Minty," Jean said, hoping her own voice clung near its usual register. "This is Jean Fairbairn. I need to talk to you privately."

"Let me guess. You've remembered that you're a journalist and not a police auxiliary."

"You could say that, yes." Jean paused, not for effect but to breathe. *Come on, you're telling a story here. One of those stories that's a lie.* "I have a business deal for you."

"My story, exclusive for *Great Scot,* is that it?"

"Not exactly, no. You see, I don't work only for *Great Scot.* I have connections with the *Sunburn* in London. And with several similar papers in the U.S. Americans, they just love scandals in the British upper classes. You'd think we never fought a revolution."

"And?"

"Alasdair's gone off with his police friends—they've taken Valerie and Derek Trotter to Hawick for questioning, maybe even charges of some sort. They've closed down the incident room. I've got the place to myself."

Minty's voice chilled even further, like vodka kept in the freezer, icy but still pourable. "Please get to the point, Jean."

"The point is, I've been looking through Wallace's personal effects. I found a sketch he did of the dig here at Ferniebank, like the one P.C. Logan took away, except it's Valerie holding the little chest like Angus was holding it in the other sketch. And that's not all. On the back is an inventory of a collection of jewelry—some very impressive pieces there. I wonder what happened to them?"

The line rang hollowly.

"Plus, I found an envelope marked, 'To be opened in case of

my death.' Since Wallace died, I opened it. It doesn't look like a will so much as a, well, confession of sorts. Answers to what happened to that jewelry."

"What are you implying?" Minty enunciated.

"I'm not implying, I'm telling you right up front. If you don't make it worth my while to keep quiet, I'll take the story about the jewelry to the *Sunburn* and the American tabloids as well. They'll love it. It'll go on their front pages, along with photos of you and your school. And then, once the story is out, Inland Revenue's going to be only one of the groups that will find it inspirational."

Jean thought she could detect a long, aggravated breath, unless it was one of the men behind her keeping himself from breaking in and telling her what to say. "And what," asked Minty, "would your paramour think of your indulging in blackmail? We are speaking blackmail here, aren't we?"

"Blackmail is an appropriate word. It comes from here in the Borders, did you know that?"

"Yes." The word came across as a sibilant, squeezed between Minty's teeth.

"What Alasdair doesn't know won't hurt him." Behind her, he smothered a scalded snicker.

"I see we'll have to have ourselves a chat," said Minty. "If you'll bring the papers here late this afternoon, after my class —"

"No way am I removing the papers from Ferniebank. You can come here. Shall we say six? I'll meet you in the Laigh Hall, where Wallace's things are now. Bring money, dollars, pounds, euros, your choice. As a down payment."

Again the line echoed. Panic spilled through Jean's chest. *Minty's not going to bite. She is going to bite. Either way . . .*

"Very well then," Minty said. "Six p.m." The line went dead.

So did Jean's knees. She dropped into the desk chair, said,

"We're on. Six p.m.," and watched the room shimmy. *What was I thinking? What have I done?*

Alasdair pressed a hand down on her shoulder, steadying the sway of the room. "Well done."

She managed to suck down a full breath. "Right."

"Her agreeing to come, that's incriminating." Delaney hauled himself to his feet. "Let's get to it, then."

Kallinikos turned to a fresh page in his notebook and started jotting notes as Delaney spoke. Alasdair interjected, "If Val can describe a few bits of jewelry, we'll genuinely have an inventory. We're needing the sketch from the harp book. Jean, can you copy Wallace's handwriting?"

"Sure. I'll rig up a confession—I bet there's paper in the desk here." She pulled open the drawer and dug through some odds and ends, including several Ferniebank pamphlets and a small paperback titled *Rocks and Minerals of the Borders*. "Here's some blank typing paper and envelopes. I could plug in his typewriter, but something as personal as a confession . . ."

Alasdair handed her a folder of papers from the cardboard box still sitting on the coffee table. "Here you are."

"And here," said Kallinikos, putting a file folder into her other hand. "The two drawings that Logan pinched. I'll have a photocopy made of the one with Valerie."

Jean pulled out the sketches. The top one was of Angus contemplating the money chest. Had it ever occurred to him to just hand the jewels over to the museum, without giving Minty the chance to decide their fate? But that would have meant revealing Gerald's follies.

And there was Wallace's drawing of the complete inscription. He had carefully cross-hatched the missing pieces, including the one that had been in his pocket when he died. All were accounted for except the one with the harp, and that was long gone . . . Another cockroach scuttled through the back of Jean's brain, only to slip into the crevice beneath *What was I thinking?* and disappear.

Somewhere beyond a thrumming in her ears, Delaney was talking. Alasdair opened the door and he and Delaney walked outside. Kallinikos followed. Feet double-timed it across the gravel.

Just keep busy. Even if it was with busy work.

All right then—what if she were an eighty-year-old scholar, what if she'd lived for years here, in this flat, alone . . . Jean went through several sheets of paper, taking her time, and finally produced a confession that she could live with. Or so she intended, anyway. Just as she folded it into an envelope and wrote in her newly acquired and suitably shaky hand, "To be opened in case of my death," Alasdair appeared with parcels of food. He stood over her until she'd forced down a cheese and pickle sandwich and a bottle of water, and then he vanished again. The clock read two.

Don't think about it.

Dougie wandered in from the bedroom and toured the room, leaping from couch to shelf to windowsill, there to settle down for a bath and a meditation. A few minutes later, Kallinikos arrived with a photocopy of the sketch from the flyleaf of the harp book, made on thick drawing paper, and a scribbled list of jewelry. Jean limbered up her old scholar's hand once again and on the back of the sketch started writing: "An enamel locket decorated with small rubies and emeralds. A diamond ring. A necklace . . ." Some of the pieces sounded Victorian, and maybe had belonged to Gerald's wife or mother. Others were very old. *Thanks, Gerald.* His hand certainly extended from beyond his grave.

The clock on the desk read three-forty-five. Jean finished the list, then got up to look outside—for what, she didn't know, perhaps to compare the angle of the westering sun with the time on the clock—and her phone warbled. Where was her bag? Oh, behind a throw pillow on the couch. *Miranda Capaldi.* "Hi Mir—"

"So Ciara's been cleared, and her architect as well! Well done Jean and Alasdair! What's happening now?"

"Ah," Jean stammered, "things are going on—I'll have to call you back."

"Oh. Sorry. Ring me when you can talk." Miranda's speedy exit, Jean only realized when she closed her phone, probably meant she'd conveyed the impression that she and Alasdair were engaged in a moment of Monday afternoon delight. Oh well, she and Miranda would have plenty of time to laugh over it all later on. So would Hugh. And Michael and Rebecca.

Don't think about it.

But she had thought about it, in outline form, with footnotes, by the time Alasdair ushered Blackhall and Kallinikos into the flat. Kallinikos hoisted the box of papers and sketches. "I'll put this with the others."

Alasdair announced, "We've got body armor for you."

Blackhall held up what looked like the bastard cousin of a straight jacket, without sleeves. "It's mine, the only female one they could turn up on short notice. I'm taller than you, though."

Jean retired to the bedroom, there to feel like a knight being girded by his squire—two squires, as Alasdair duplicated Blackhall's every tug and squeeze. The vest was stiff, heavy, smelled like chemicals, and was, as predicted, too big. "You'll be obliged to wear something over it, hiding it," Blackhall commented at last.

Alasdair pulled off his sweater and dragged it down over Jean's head, almost taking her glasses with it. She settled it around her, then looked in the mirror over the dresser. She saw a blobby blue body with spindly arms and tiny white face. "Good thing it's dark in the Laigh Hall or she'll wonder why

I've bloated up like a tick since this morning."

"You'll do fine," said Blackhall. "That's Kevlar, likely to stop a bullet."

"A bullet," Jean repeated. Despite all her cogitations, the possibility of Minty having an illegal gun hadn't occurred to her. At least the cops would have legal guns, although Alasdair had handed his back to the Northern Constabulary.

He waved Blackhall out of the room and rolled up his sleeves. "Everyone's left Glebe House save one lookout, lying in the churchyard with binoculars."

"This is going to work," Jean stated, as much to herself as to him.

"That it is," he stated, as much to himself as to her. He squeezed her arm, her shoulder now being unavailable, and bent his forehead to hers—yeah, she was buttoned up, but cheery she wasn't. Before any ruptures could occur in his carefully glaciated expression, before any fissures could break her pretense of calm, a wave of officialdom burst through the front door and down the hall.

Kallinikos and Freeman swept Dougie's litter box and assorted cleaning implements into the bedroom and started setting up recording devices in the closet. The squint, Jean thought, was actually going to be used for its original purpose. It might have been listed in the fine print on the P and S survey, but if not for Dougie, a vital part of the investigative team . . . Here came the little creature himself, whiskers smug, borne in state in Freeman's arms. "That's a grand wee moggie," Freeman told him, flirting with oxymoron, and set Dougie down on the bed.

Outside the window, the shadow of the castle was elongating over the river and toward the east. *What the bloody hell was I thinking?*

Delaney stood in the living room, holding out her backpack. "The fake documents are inside, at the top."

"Thanks." She hung the bag from her shoulder, not that she could feel it through the armor. She couldn't feel much of anything, other than a tickle of sweat. Somewhere her pulse was beating. She could hear it in her head like the flood and retreat of the sea.

Kallinikos reported, "She's left Glebe House. I've got Binns amongst the trees by the layby, if she stops there and walks in the back way."

The die was cast, the Rubicon crossed, the bridges burned. Half of Lothian and Borders seemed to be gathered in the living room. But when Jean stepped outside, not a soul was in sight. The incident room was closed tight. The gate was temptingly ajar. She caught a quick movement behind the roof parapet —what, were they going to rappel down the side of the building like marines? A crow launched itself into space and with a cawed remark flapped away.

A dog barked. A cow mooed. The sky shone, clear and peaceful. She looked behind her to see in Alasdair's eyes a storm brewing, the indigo horizon of a blue norther. Then he shut the door.

Feeling like a turtle, Jean walked down the steps of the flat, across the gravel, and into the front door of the castle. From the shadow of the entrance she heard a car approaching and slowing. Through the open doorway she saw a Range Rover turn in through the gateway. She glanced at her watch. Trust Minty to be bang on time.

Jean inhaled the musty air, exhaled her fears, and told herself, *Showtime.*

CHAPTER THIRTY-FOUR

The Range Rover rolled to a stop. Minty stepped out, gracefully, her leather boots—not quite dominatrix-style, but close—barely pressing down on the gravel. She'd removed her apron and added a tweed jacket and her leather handbag, but otherwise looked as informally formal as she had earlier.

Then a second car drove into the courtyard. A patrol car. Logan. Of course he would still trust Minty. As Jean faded back into the shadows of the Laigh Hall—the far side of the Laigh Hall, behind the boxes—she sensed rather than heard a stir of consternation from the hidden troops.

Logan followed Minty into the Hall and braced himself by the door, his expression that of an executioner testing his rope. Minty herself took several steps closer to the Wallace collection and turned her cool, composed gaze upon Jean. "Here we are, then. Like the shoemaker's children going without footwear, so the policeman's doxy creates a blackmail scheme."

"We cannot have that," Logan said.

Jean tried what she hoped was a knowing smile. "Has it occurred to you, Constable, that it's hard to create a blackmail scheme out of thin air? Minty has things to hide. That's why she's here."

"She's here as a public-spirited citizen reporting a crime," he replied. "You'd best be coming with me, quietly, now. Inspector Delaney'll be keen on hearing this story."

Minty stood draped in shadow like a Roman in a toga. Like a

375

queen in ermine. Good move, figuring out a way of getting rid of Jean long enough to destroy the threatening papers. Minty probably played nothing more than bridge, but still, she was a heck of a gambler.

Jean had to play the hand she held. She pulled her backpack around to the front and reached inside. "You'll recognize Wallace's drawing and handwriting."

A tiny burst of static caused Minty to glance behind her. Logan plucked his radio from his shoulder. Distantly, Delaney's voice said, "Valerie Trotter's done a runner. Stop her at her cottage."

"Valerie Trotter," repeated Minty, the name edged with venom.

"Sir," Logan protested, "I—"

"Now, Logan. She's got to be stopped!"

"Aye, sir." Logan hurried toward the door. "Come away, Minty, we'll deal with this later."

With a glance at Jean that was more calculated than cool, Minty walked across the Hall and into the entrance chamber. Jean stood immobile, not looking at the blank door and the bit of paneling covering the squint. *Good move, Delaney. I bet that was Alasdair's idea, bluff the bluffer.*

The sound of Logan's car roared and then died away. The front door shut, a key turned in the lock, and Minty walked back into the Hall.

Okay. Jean tried to settle the sudden shrill titter of her nerves. Minty was taking an even bigger chance now. If she intended to eliminate Jean as yet another pesky annoyance, Logan would know she'd been here. Of course, he'd cut her enough slack to wrap Edinburgh Castle. Minty's eyes burned beneath their heavily draped lids. Good, she was getting frustrated. Bad, she was getting frustrated. "Where are these no doubt fictitious documents?"

Stepping forward, Jean laid the sketch and the envelope on top of the box containing Wallace's other papers. "If you're so sure they're fictitious, why are you here?"

"I looked through Wallace's papers and saw no drawing and certainly no, ah, testament."

"The drawing was inside a book, *The Harp Key*. The confession . . ." Jean's brain lurched. "It was inside that case for cufflinks and stuff. In a false bottom."

Minty looked down at the box as though it concealed animals with sharp teeth and nervous dispositions. Then she bent toward it, right hand extended, her handbag sliding down her left arm to her left hand. After another long pause, during which she could easily have counted the thumps of Jean's heart, she stood up holding the drawing and the envelope. A whisper of movement trickled down the main staircase and she looked sharply upwards.

"Birds, bats," said Jean. "Alasdair says there are both in the rafters."

"You're not frightened, here, alone?"

The woman was a fencer as well as a gambler. Fencers, now, they used blunted swords. "Wallace lived here alone. Gerald lived here alone. They got along just fine."

"They were eccentrics. Especially Gerald, in the fine old British tradition."

"Traditional but embarrassing. A shame Wallace's enthusiasms got out of hand, and attracted Ciara. Who knows better than I do what a weirdo she is? She was the last straw, I bet. After all you'd done for the community, she barged in with plans that would have attracted the wrong element. And raised questions about the jewelry."

Minty didn't move, didn't blink.

"You didn't know about the jewelry, did you, until Angus came home with it? It bought you your cooking school, something you deserved after all your hard work. But Wallace and Ciara, they made trouble for you. A shame you got Angus instead of Ciara. That was Noel's fault, wasn't it? These people are so distressingly incompetent."

"Yes, they are." Minty's alabaster complexion was flushing an unbecoming shade of magenta. She scrutinized the drawing of Valerie holding the chest and flipped it over to consider the inventory. A tiny nod, the briefest bob of her head, told Jean that Val's listing of the jewelry had been spot-on.

"You'll go after Valerie next, won't you? You should have eliminated her years ago, but she went away. And now she's back, insulting you, humiliating you. She deserves a dose of foxglove."

"Yes." Minty wadded the drawing and threw it down. She weighed the envelope, set it on the box, then looked up at Jean. Her eyes were glowing coals. "You want your money, is that it?"

Jean stepped back. If she had learned anything from Alasdair, it was to beware drilling beneath an ice cap. Deeply buried under Minty's layers of frost and polish was, indeed, a molten core.

Jean balanced on the balls of her feet, ready to dodge. "You had the castle renovated and opened. You took the jewelry. Like James III at Roxburgh, you've been blown up by your own cannon. Is that why you didn't want Isabel's burning-glass, because it's a mirror and if you look into it you'll see who's really to blame?"

"Very clever," said Minty between clenched teeth. Her right hand inched toward the open top of her handbag.

"Or should I draw the comparison with another monarch? Did you look at Valerie Trotter, did you hear Angus and Wallace talking about her, did you see them sending her and Derek gifts?" *Breathe,* Jean told herself, and bent her knees. "Did you ever say, in the words of Elizabeth about her cousin Mary, 'she is lighter of a healthy son, but I am barren stock'?"

"Damn you to hell."

Not many people, Jean thought, could say that without plastering several exclamation points onto the end.

Minty's manicured fingers plunged into her bag. From it she whipped out a knife, a carving knife, a long pointed blade gleaming in the uncertain light as though with witchfire. Throwing the bag down, she leaped.

Jean leaped as well, not particularly anxious to see if Blackhall's vest would turn six inches of doubtless high-quality and well-honed steel. Emitting a deliberate scream—*okay! now!*—she dodged to the side and toward the door.

Instead of coming straight for her, Minty spun around to block the door. Her face, Jean noted with part of her mind, was perfectly calm except for the eruption in her eyes. The other part of Jean's mind was palpitating, looking for an escape route —footsteps thundered down the staircase and blows smashed against the front door . . .

Minty lunged toward her, knife raised.

Jean sprang for the staircase, slipped on the dusty, uneven treads, told herself that at least she was wearing athletic shoes —Minty's boots must be slowing her down. Amazing how fast she could get her muscles to flex despite the extra weight of the armor, with a deadly weapon in a conscienceless hand just behind her.

She had passed the second floor and was heading for the third before she realized she hadn't met any police heading down. Great, wonderful, glorious, they'd come down the main staircase and she was heading up the secondary one.

Shouts echoed through the building, Alasdair's voice lifted in something incomprehensible. For all she knew it was the Cameron war cry.

Not the cap house, she couldn't let herself get trapped in the cap house, with no way out but the parapet. Jean catapulted into a shadowed room on the dark side of the building, twelve panes of wavy window glass admitting only a ghostly gray light. Isabel's room.

Door. Shut the door.

She spun, seized the knob, pushed. Twine was holding the door open. Knotted twine.

Where was Minty? Had she lost track of her quarry in the upper reaches of the building, confused by echoes? No such luck. The floorboards of the hall were groaning to stealthy steps. The woman wasn't breathing heavily. She didn't seem to be breathing at all.

Jean ripped off her backpack, tore open the zipper, dumped everything onto the floor. Her phone went spinning away, its read-out bright as a candle flame. The box, glass lens, glass mirror. She rapped it against the cold, sooty hearth of the fireplace and it broke in her hand, cutting the mound at the base of her thumb with a pain that felt like searing heat. Blood welled, ran down to her wrist, caught in the fibers of Alasdair's sweater.

With the shard of glass she slashed at the twine. It gave. The door started to slide shut, as though pushed by invisible hands. She threw her weight against it and slammed it just as Minty hit the other side, first with a solid thump and then with repeated blows.

A bolt. There was a bolt. In a desperate spasm of strength, Jean freed the rusty metal rod and jammed it into the catch. She leaped backward so fast she tripped over her bag and crashed down onto her rump, jarring every bone in her body.

A knife blade worked its way between the panels of the door and moved back and forth like a metal tongue. Light. A rosy light was growing in the room, and the air was heavy, crushing her against the planks of the floor.

Footsteps. Voices. A scream of anguish, short and sharp. Jean could hear it vibrating in her ears, on and on, even after the leaden air no longer carried the sound. She heard the clump of heavy feet, blows against the door, a breath gasping in terror that wasn't her breath at all. She saw red flame spurt suddenly on the hearth and long skirts whisking past her face, and smoke rising, gray, and dense.

Male voices shouted. The door held. The flame died down. The air lifted. And the skirts, the bodice, the little cap, the oval face with its large eyes, all thinned into mist and evaporated.

Jean sat on the floor alone, but not in silence. Again she heard blows against the door, this time not mailed fists but bare hands. A familiar voice called her name, "Jean! Jean!"

She crawled to her feet, tottered to the door, and released the bolt.

CHAPTER THIRTY-FIVE

Large, cool hands seized her. Strong arms pressed her against a chest, broad and firm. "We've got her," Alasdair said into her ear, and above her head, loudly, "Bring the medical kit."

She was trembling, shudders of hot then cold then hot running from crown to toe. Still she managed to look past the crevasses in Alasdair's face to the corridor, where the darkness was now stitched with the lightning bolts of flashlight beams.

Linklater and Blackhall held Minty between them, stiff as stone. One strand of hair dangled down beside her face, its skin gone so pale it was faintly green. Her eyes stared ahead, not at Jean but past her, as though she watched the foundations of Ferniebank crack and crumble and the sheer sides collapse. Then Delaney, wheezing, holding the knife, stepped forward and intoned, "Araminta Rutherford, I arrest you . . ." And she was gone.

"Only you," said Alasdair, his breath warm against Jean's ear, "would use historical metaphors to push someone over the edge."

"I didn't," she croaked, and tried again. "Elizabeth said Mary was lighter of a *fair* son, but Derek's just not . . ." Kallinikos wrapped her hand in gauze, his touch gentle, his expression offering no comments. Her hands were red from blood and from the rusty bolt. *Caught red-handed.*

She wobbled, but Alasdair held her steady. Kallinikos collected her things and put them back in her bag, then considered the shards of sepia glass littering the floor. "Is that the burning-glass?"

"Yes. No. It was," said Jean. "That's seven years bad luck, isn't it?"

"No," Alasdair stated.

Kallinikos gingerly collected the bits into the cardboard box, tucked it, too, into her bag, then hung the bag over her shoulder. Between them, the men got Jean back down the spiral staircase, whose steps had contracted and lumpified in the last—how long had it been since she ran up them, fear lending not only wings but stabilizers to her feet?

Delaney waited in the Laigh Hall, holding the crumpled sketch and envelope. Logan stood at his side, his obsidian chips of eyes darting right and left, saying, "Minty's the killer? How . . . Well now, I'm supposing she's properly a Maitland, not a Rutherford at all."

Delaney's stubby fingers shooed Logan away. His thick glasses turned toward Jean and Alasdair. His chest swelled. "Well, now."

From far above fell a ripple of harp strings, a descending arpeggio, as though the harper was tuning his instrument—or playing a farewell. Jean and Alasdair glanced so sharply up they almost knocked heads. But the notes faded into infinity. And Jean thought, *the harp. The harp key.*

The only heaviness she felt was that of the bulletproof camisole, the only chill that of the air in the Laigh Hall. Delaney's voice, rising and falling like one of Logan's bees, rabbited on about Minty—not exactly a confession, charges, enough to be going on with.

Jean seized her scuttling thought and hung on for dear life. "The harp is the key," she said, interrupting Delaney. "Harp marks the spot."

He stopped in mid-phrase, mouth hanging open. *Poor little*

lady, his expression said, *we've asked too much of her, she needs tea and cold compresses.*

Alasdair, though . . . His brows began their roller coaster imitation.

"Get this thing off of me." Handing Delaney her bag, Jean pulled the sweater over her head and gave it to Alasdair. Kallinikos stepped forward and helped him remove the vest, leaving her standing in a slightly damp T-shirt that should by rights have been chilled but which she suspected was steaming in the cool air. Retrieving her backpack, she fished out a hairbrush and dumped the bag on the floor. "Open the door to the dungeon. Give me that torch."

Alasdair pulled open the trap. Kallinikos handed over his flashlight. Jean shone the light into the pit. Dust, dirt, stones—nothing had changed. Nothing except her own perceptions, broken into shards like the glass but more easily reassembled. "We thought the harp jewelry was long gone. We thought the piece of the inscription engraved with the harp was long gone. But Wallace noticed that the inscription is in a reddish sandstone, not the local gray whinstone."

"And so," said Alasdair, "he got himself into the dungeon with a piece of the inscription for comparison and a magnifying glass, the better to see the contrast."

"Because of something Gerald said, probably. As an amateur archaeologist, he would never neglect a dungeon."

Delaney folded his arms and with a beseeching roll of his eyes asked, "What the hell are you on about now?"

"Exhibit P," Alasdair told him. "The genuine Exhibit P, not what Minty was thinking it was. Likely not what Ciara's thinking it is. Third time's the charm."

"Here. Hold the flashlight." Jean crammed the hairbrush into her jeans pocket. Turning around, she slipped her feet over the edge, felt for and found the rungs of the ladder, and started down. Cold air prickled through her shirt. Musty, still air. The walls squatted close by, but seemed as stable and steady as Alasdair's grasp.

She strained upwards to take the flashlight from Kallinikos while Alasdair clambered down the ladder. Freeman's face appeared in the opening, then his hand helpfully directed a second beam of light into the depths. Somewhere in the background, Delaney grumbled a monolog.

"So where'd Gerald put it then?" Alasdair asked.

"The crazy uncle, archaeologist, poet, jeweler—he had an attic and he had a cellar, too." Jean crept along the walls, using her hairbrush to sweep away the dust, fine as ash. There, a small irregularly shaped reddish block was wedged between larger, if just as irregular, gray ones. She knelt down and brushed delicately at it.

Alasdair crouched beside her, shoulder to shoulder. "Aye, that's red sandstone. He must have enlarged a drainhole, or prised out a smaller stone. And what's this?" The nail of his forefinger scraped at the edge of the rock. "This looks to be plaster of paris, not mortar."

"Who's got a penknife?" Jean called toward the opening. A small opening, in a low roof. *Just few more moments,* she told the panic squirming in her gut.

Kallinikos climbed partway down the ladder to hand Jean a penknife. She opened it—the tiny blade was a miniature of Minty's, a silver fang in the narrow light—and handed it to Alasdair.

His touch meticulous, he scraped away the bits of plaster, wedged the blade into the resulting crevice, and pried. The rock moved. Jean's small fingers grasped a corner. She pulled. And the piece of stone came loose, adding rosy dust to the shades and textures of red already on her hands.

She turned the stone over and wiped it against her shirt. The hidden side was engraved with a harp. The Ferniebank Clarsach. Silently she held the piece up for Freeman and Kallinikos and, she saw, Delaney, his round face hovering behind theirs like a stray moon.

Alasdair was now using the penknife to probe inside the hole. "There we are," he said, and extracted a box about the same size as the cardboard one holding the remnants of the glass. But this box was metal and oblong, a diminutive lead-lined coffin.

Jean peered into the hole, but it was empty. The chill of the deep earth oozed up her arms, pressed against her breasts. She shrank back.

Alasdair handed up the box, the knife, the flashlight, the bit of stone. Darkness welled from the corners, the walls undulated . . . He took her arm, pulled her to her feet, thrust her onto the ladder and went back for her hairbrush. One rung, two —her back hurt. Her shoulders hurt. Her legs hurt.

Freeman and Kallinikos grasped her shoulders, then her arms, and she was reborn out of the trap door onto the flagged floor of the Laigh Hall. Why had she ever thought the room was stuffy and dark? Compared to the dungeon, it was bright and airy as the hall of mirrors in a stately home.

She regained her feet just as Alasdair emerged from the pit. If his smile wasn't smug, it was at least serene. Taking the box from Delaney's hand, he passed it over to Jean. "Open it."

For a moment she thought it was sealed, but no, the lid was merely a snug fit. She traced around it with her fingernails and eased it off. Inside lay a roll of rich crimson velvet, soft against her fingertips. Gently she unfolded it.

Light blazed. *Gold.* Amid a chorus of gasps and reverent profanity, Jean held up a gold cross embedded with diamonds and rubies. At the crossing of the two arms was embedded a crystal about the size of a watch face, holding a tiny speck of wood, cloth, bone—something sacred. The back of the cross, she noted with dazzled eyes, was engraved with the ornate M monogram of Mary, Queen of Scots.

"Is this Mary's relic, the bread-and-butter gift for William's hospitality?" she asked, her voice loud in the hush.

"Or is it a thank-you to Isabel for services rendered?" asked Alasdair.

"Either or both, it's the cross Isabel's holding in her portrait."

"Say what?" Delaney demanded.

Jean skipped the lecture on Scottish history. "There's paper, too. Old rag paper." She placed the cross into Alasdair's palm, unfurled the rolled paper, and turned it toward the light. "Another letter, like the one in the museum. I think you're right. This is the thank-you note for Isabel's secret messenger work, maybe to her family after her death . . . Whoa."

"Eh?" asked Delaney.

"There's a strip torn off the edge," Alasdair said. "The scrap found inside the harp?"

"If so, then there's a drawing on the back. Yep, there it is." She eyed the latticework, a misshapen cup, a star, a series of diamond shapes. "Although what that's all about is anyone's guess. And probably will be."

"This is all part and parcel of Ciara's fancies," said Delaney, with the satisfied air of a game-show contestant finally getting one right.

"There's more to it than that." Jean rolled the paper and tucked it back inside the small casket, then held the cloth so Alasdair could settle the cross into its embrace. She folded the velvet and replaced the lid. "There might be something in Gerald's papers explaining why he took all of these, er, family heirlooms and played his games with them. Or there might not. Whatever, it took Wallace a long time to figure it out. Although, if not for him, we'd never have figured it out."

Kallinikos held up the bit of carved stone. "Did Gerald chip the harp off the gravestone?"

"The edges look weathered to me," Jean replied, taking it from his hand. "Maybe he just picked it up while he was messing around with the grave. Maybe he hid the cross in the foundations of the castle as, well, a charm of sorts, a blessing on future generations. On Ferniebank."

"Wasted his time, then," said Delaney. "Come along, we've got Minty to deal with. I'll take that." He reached for the box.

Jean stepped back and almost fell over her bag again. Swiftly she scooped it up and tucked the box inside. "This might be treasure trove, Inspector. I'll notify the proper authorities."

"And the chipping belongs to Ciara," Alasdair said quietly. "Ferniebank belongs to Ciara."

Muttering something beneath his breath that was probably not "thanks for your help," Delaney clomped to the door and away.

"I'm not so sure the old man wasted his time," said Kallinikos. He collected Blackhall's armor and followed. With a salute, Freeman brought up the rear.

Voices echoed through the entrance. Engines roared. Then, at last, peace settled over Ferniebank. Jean and Alasdair stepped out of the castle into the clear air and a deserted courtyard. Sunset flared across the sky, gilding the edges of a few high clouds, pink, rose, gold, changeable and yet ageless.

Alasdair looked at Jean. She looked at him, noting the glitter in his eye, feeling sure her own eyes resembled kaleidoscopes. "You're looking a wee bit peelie-wallie," he said.

"That cheese and pickle sandwich must not have agreed with me."

"There're more sandwiches in the fridge. And a bottle of whiskey in the cupboard."

"And lots of hot water in the shower. I'd ask you to join me, but . . ."

Alasdair offered her his arm and escorted her to the door of the flat. "We've got enough to be going on with."

CHAPTER THIRTY-SIX

Alasdair stowed Dougie's carrier in the back seat of his car and stood aside while Jean strapped the cat in. *Again?* Dougie's disgruntled expression demanded. *We just got here.*

"Call it a strategic withdrawal," Jean told him.

"No, that's implying defeat," corrected Alasdair. "We've not been defeated."

He was wearing his kilt, a declaration of intent. His green sweater shaded his eyes with the turquoise of the western sea. When he slammed the car door, the thud echoed from the face of the castle more like the pop of a balloon than like the report of a gun. In the blush of morning sun, the dour old building looked almost cheerful, like a dowager's seamed cheeks touched by rouge.

The courtyard teemed with people and vehicles, with O. Hawick at the gate sorting the admittance-worthy sheep from the goats of the media. Police personnel were breaking down the incident room. Their supervisor, D.S. Kallinikos, leaned against the Mystic Scotland van chatting with—or chatting up—Shannon Brimberry. Her flock of tourists was wandering around the chapel all but baaing, and yet her blushes had nothing to do with her role as Little Bo Peep.

Jean grinned at Alasdair. Shaking his head in mock despair, he headed toward the emptying incident room. She stood savoring the alluring sway of the kilt above the tall socks called hose, nicely filled by the braw Cameron calves. He'd laugh if she told him he swashed a buckle with the best of them.

Her phone trilled. She hauled it out of her bag, checked the screen, flipped it open. "Hey, Miranda. About time you returned my call."

"What's this I'm hearing? Minty Rutherford? Poison, knives —well, I'm thinking I've done well to survive the odd luncheon, then."

"You never threatened her. Let me call you again in a few minutes, okay? Alasdair and I are bailing out of Ferniebank. Enough is enough."

"Oh aye, as a honeymoon cottage the place is lacking romance. As a feature article in *Great Scot,* well, I'll be standing by for the particulars."

"To say nothing of a pack of glittering generalities. Bye." There was romance, Jean thought, and there was romance. . . . The phone burst into melody again. This time it was Hugh.

Same verse, different soloist. "Up to your old tricks, I hear, courting danger as well as policemen. The lads renting your flat are right chuffed at brewing up in a daring reporter's teapot."

"The last thing I want," said Jean, casting a sharp look at her bolder brethren outside the gate, "is to be daring. Can I call you back? We're just leaving Ferniebank for healthier climates."

"No worries."

That's the idea. Stowing her phone, Jean crunched over to the door of the castle, which was just emitting Rebecca and Michael, the latter carrying Linda strapped to his chest like a wiggly breastplate. "So you're away?" Rebecca asked.

"Yep. One of Alasdair's cousins had a cancellation at a self-catering cottage overlooking Skye, so we're taking the place over. Peace, quiet, ocean views, blooming heather."

"The Gray Lady, Isabel, I think she's away as well. I didn't pick up so much as a blip."

"That's what I thought." Jean peered through the doorway to the no-longer-intimidating gloom of the interior. "Maybe when I held off an attack in the same room, that broke the pattern. Maybe my breaking the glass broke the pattern. If you can't explain where ghosts come from, you can't explain where they go."

Keith Bell shut the door of the flat, galloped down the steps, and bounded up the steps of the castle. "The sooner we get this place gutted and re-wired and everything, the better. With all the publicity, the punters are coming out of the woodwork. You gotta give them an authentic experience without giving them the *real* authentic experience, if you know what I mean."

Jean knew what he meant, but didn't have time to say so before Keith pulled a tape measure from his pocket and plunged into the building, intent on tailoring not cloth but stone. "Good luck," she called after him, and to Michael and Rebecca said, "Tourists come to see a place, but their coming changes its nature, so it's not what they came to see."

"Catch-22," concluded Michael.

"Thanks for returning my car," Jean told him. "I called the rental agency to let them know to expect you."

"No worries," he returned. "I'll hand in the car, stop by the museum with the box and all, bask in the acclamation, then catch a ride back to Stanelaw with a pair of customers."

"The letter is Mary's hand, I'm sure of it," said Rebecca. "I guess Isabel's family kept the letter in the harp as a talisman for so many years it stuck to the wood and tore when Gerald removed it. No telling where that cross has been all this time."

"Other than passed down to the Rutherfords along with the harp," Jean said. "Did you ask Ciara about letting the museum keep the artifacts until the bureaucrats decide who they belong to?"

"Oh aye," said Michael, with a quick jiggle to soothe his tiny bobble-headed parasite. "A lot depends on Gerald's will, and whether the jewels and all were abandoned, and whether Stanelaw Museum is secure . . . Well, speak of the devil herself."

Now it was Ciara who left the flat and strolled toward them. Jean could only assume her relationship—of convenience or otherwise—with Keith had survived the last few days. Perhaps getting arrested together provided the same sort of glue that solving a case together did.

"See my new earrings?" Ciara said, one plump hand lifting her curls to reveal dangling Celtic interlace. "Suits the Mystic Scotland logo, I'm thinking. Those little stars, my goodness, they turned out more trouble than they were worth."

Jean smiled, and told herself, this too shall pass, and soon.

"Michael, thank you for seeing to the artifacts. And to restoring the glass. That cross is a stunner, and no mistake, but the chart's the important item just now. I've faxed copies to London and New York. My publishers are over the moon."

"Chart?" asked Jean, with a wary glance at Rebecca, who passed the glance on to Michael.

"The drawing on the back of the letter. It's an amazing treasure, obviously the result of Henry Sinclair's voyages. Keith and I have worked it out. It's clearly a lost navigational system."

Alasdair strolled up and assumed a position at Jean's side that made a guardsman in front of Buckingham Palace look animated.

"The grid measures longitude and latitude," Ciara explained. "The diamonds are based on the shadows made at the solstices, different shapes at different degrees of latitude—the Mediterranean, Rosslyn, Orkney. The cup shape, the arc, is astronomical orbits, as relating to alchemy, as relating to the Holy Grail. The harp was the key, just as I said, the music of the spheres, eh?" Ciara's hands waved, building her castles in the air.

"Henry Sinclair's chart? That's going to be hard to prove," Jean ventured.

"You cannot prove it's not true," returned Ciara with her most brilliant smile. "This is just the sort of validation folk are searching for. Well done, Jean. And Alasdair. And how clever of you to appoint me caretaker of Ferniebank 'til I can take over as owner."

Alasdair's lean smile rejected any plaudits. "We'll be obliged to meet in Edinburgh to deal with the paperwork. Especially now that Angus is dead and Minty's in jail."

"That's true," said Michael. "Noel's called an emergency meeting in Stanelaw—there'll be repercussions from all this for years to come."

"And it's the lawyers who'll come out ahead," Rebecca concluded.

No one contradicted that. Even Ciara sobered, then recovered her smile. "Well, what happens, happens. Just as it did this weekend. I'll be getting on. Keith's working out a ghost's gallery on the top floor—poor Isabel, still walking, I sensed her there myself not two hours since."

Jean didn't contradict that, either, although Rebecca hid her face by adjusting Linda's position in the baby carrier.

"Jean, Alasdair, have a properly invigorating honeymoon." Ciara shimmered on into the castle, trailing the scent of cloves and cinnamon and a musical murmur about "home again."

Home. Ciara had found herself a home, and a community, just as she'd intended when she and Valerie got tattoos of the clarsach. Community was the goal of tales of explanation and meaning, after all. If anyone could exorcise Ferniebank, it was the unsinkable Ciara.

"What do you want to bet," Jean said, "that Ciara's chart is a sketch of the Borders mapping properties, or loyalties, or even troop movements from some past battle? Mary simply re-used a piece of paper."

"That's one bet I'll not be taking," said Michael.

Jean glanced at Alasdair, who pointedly glanced at his watch. "I'd better get on out to the Western Highlands and write something to earn my keep. Not this sort of keep," she added, with a look up at the gap-toothed parapets of Ferniebank. "This one is Ciara's, and she's welcome to it."

"You'd best get my jumper knitted before the snow flies," Alasdair told her. He shook hands with Michael, unbent far enough to give Rebecca a small, reserved hug, and even tweaked Linda's cheek.

"Bye," they replied as one. "See you back in Edinburgh—safe journey."

Jean settled herself in the car, belted herself in, and after an inventory of her body decided that trading mental aches for physical ones wasn't a bad bargain, considering. She took one long look back at the castle, the chapel, the surrounding trees, the ever-moving river. Then she turned her gaze on Alasdair. The reflection of his keen profile overlaid the facade of the castle.

Last night they'd talked, and washed, and eaten, drank, slept and woke, talked and made love and slept again—nothing like a cocktail of danger and whiskey to loosen tongues, in more ways than one. If a relationship was a do-it-yourself project, then they were doing it themselves, the hard way, one pebble, one grain of grit at a time. She smiled.

"Aye?" Of course he'd sense her smile against the side of his face.

"If I'm the grit that provides traction to your mental machinery, then you're the grain of sand beneath my shell. You know, the irritant that makes a pearl."

He turned his head toward her. A tiny flame flickered in the depths of his eyes, sunlight on the surface of a fathomless ocean, but whether that indicated affection, impatience, or both, she couldn't tell. And it didn't matter.

"Never mind," she said. "Let's go. And I do mean 'us.' "

ABOUT THE AUTHOR

Lillian Stewart Carl has published multiple novels and multiple short stories in multiple genres, with plots based on myth, history, and archaeology.

The Burning Glass is her fourteenth novel, the third book in the Jean Fairbairn/Alasdair Cameron mystery series, after *The Secret Portrait* and *The Murder Hole*. All her novels are available in print, and most of them are available in electronic form from www.fictionwise.com.

Three of her twenty-five published short stories have been reprinted in World's Finest Crime and Mystery anthologies. Most are available from Fictionwise and in two print collections, *Along the Rim of Time* and *Around the Circle of Time*.

Lillian lives in North Texas, in a book-lined cloister cleverly disguised as a tract house. Her web site is http://www.lillian stewartcarl.com.